A TIME FOR
Everything

Brona Mills

Copyright © 2017 by Brona Mills
ISBN -13: 978-1544984353
ISBN -10: 1544984359

Edited by L.S. King of Indie Solutions, www.murphyrae.net
Proofread by Emily A. Lawrence of Indie Solutions,
www.murphyrae.net
Cover design by Murphy Rae of Indie Solutions,
www.murphyrae.net
Formatted by Elaine York of Allusion Graphics, LLC,
www.allusiongraphics.com

First Published 2017

Warning: Due to some mature subject matters, such as explicit sexual situations and coarse language, this story is not suitable for anyone under the age of 18.

A TIME FOR
Everything

ACKNOWLEDGEMENTS

This book would never have been completed if it wasn't for the continued support of my family and those few friends who knew the project was being undertaken. Every nudge of encouragement and question about its progress was appreciated. As was keeping the kids out of the room while I tapped away on the keyboard!

The help and support and knowledge from my workshop buddies was, and still is, invaluable. Without them, this would still be a first draft, muddled up, pile of 26 letters. From the bottom of my heart, thank you.

To my ARCs and typo party participants! Thank you for taking a chance on a project from someone you barely knew! Hope to see you all on the next one!

CHAPTER

Thursday, March 2, 2006
07:53 (PST)
Beverly Hills, California.
I am thirty.

'It's going to kill me this time, Michael,' Audrey tells me calmly from the sun lounger.

Leaning over, I take her hand to stop her fidgeting with the blanket around her shoulders. 'I'll stop it. We have time here, David and me. We'll figure it out.'

'I don't see how I'll ever escape something like this.'

'I can change things. I know I can.' I'm clutching at straws.

'If you succeed, I won't be back. You'll lose all my visits these past years.'

'You're more important than this.' I gesture around the plush veranda suite of the Beverly Wilshire Hotel.

She gets off the lounger and navigates her way around the debris of wine glasses and plates we've collected over the last day. Hands resting on the balcony wall, staring at the skyline,

1

she asks, 'Do you have any idea what the consequences of saving me will have on your life? On all our lives? You can't risk changing something this big.'

I follow her to the balcony. 'How do we even know what we changed over time was the way it was supposed to be? Maybe we were supposed to let my life be different. What if you visiting was the thing we were to stop?'

'You don't know—'

'No, listen to me.' I clasp her hands in mine. 'We would only be changing things back to before you got here. How bad could that be?' I pull her closer to me but she gasps and seizes the side of her head.

Moaning, she cradles her head in her hands.

'I'm going to fix this.' Chills run through me and the hairs on my arms stand on end. What if she doesn't make it home safely? I guide her over to the pool and we sit on the edge. Her breathing calms to match mine. I cup water and place a cool palm to her head.

'See, I told you a private pool in a hotel would come in handy.'

She takes deep breaths to steady herself. 'Or, you wanted one last opportunity to show off.'

'Ah, there is the old "kick 'em when they're down" gal I know. I just wanted you to have enough space that you could throw your head back to the sky and breathe.'

'You're not exactly down, Michael.'

'Aren't I?' *You're leaving. What else is there?* 'It's not all about the fame and money, you know.' I wink, throwing her words back at her.

'Says the man who disappeared this afternoon for his debut Oprah appearance.' She places a hand on top of mine.

'Hey, even I know you don't say no to Oprah.' I grin.

'Yeah, but it was funny seeing you running around last minute trying to find the perfect suit to wear. You're hot enough, Michael. You don't need to worry about clothes hanging over your biceps the right way.'

I raise an eyebrow at her. '*Hot enough*? What would *Mr. Everything* say about you calling me that?'

She ignores my jibe.

'I think that's the only compliment you've ever given me.' I smile.

'There was an insult in there too.' She grins.

I chuckle. 'Seriously, though, I'm sorry for the attention and drama of yesterday. You know fine well I never schedule any work on my birthdays, it was just—'

'Oprah?' She giggles.

'Unavoidable. Time with you is precious. I'm not about to let work get in the way.'

Time is always an issue for Audrey.

'Don't worry about it. It was kind of funny seeing you try and hide from that guy with the packet of Brandy snaps.' She laughs.

'I can honestly say that was the strangest fan encounter I've ever had. I'd take people stopping me in the street for a picture any day over that.'

She gazes at the skyline. Orange rays of the sun are already breaking through the sky, creating black shadows, which stain the horizon around the Hollywood Hills. 'It's a pretty amazing view—the lights from the city, the backdrop of the hills. Surely a little English boy like you can appreciate the twinkle of the big city calling?'

'Little English boy.' I snort. 'I'll have you know I'm all man.' I nudge her.

'Seriously, though. Staying on Rodeo Drive. Looking at the Hollywood Hills in one direction. An American skyline in the other. Did you ever think you'd make it here?'

'Not without you.'

In a different time, or with any other girl, this would be a romantic setting. With Audrey, it's a poignant reminder of what I can't have.

I stare at the cluster of freckles across her cheeks and button nose. I might never get the opportunity again to share a moment of uninterrupted exploring. Her pale skin compliments her gorgeous face and her traditional Irish toasted-auburn hair. My fingers have itched to run through it for some time, and I instinctively reach towards her. She notices the move but doesn't stop me. I tuck a damp strand of hair safely behind her ear. It's not enough. I'd prefer to sit here all day with her. To relax as lovers do and innocently wind my fingers through her hair. Trail my hands down her face and body.

I wish I had more time to figure out if this relationship could ever work.

'You've managed not to kiss me for ten years, Michael. Don't ruin it now.'

I lean against the concrete railings, facing the suite and tuck my hands back in my trouser pockets, defeated.

Audrey shifts to her side to look me in the eye.

The intensity of her gaze and the butterflies she stirs in my stomach every time she does this, are surprisingly soothing. It cuts through the bullshit and makes me feel utterly exposed. Only with Audrey could this ever be a good thing.

Whatever she's thinking brings back her tears. I don't want to be the reason she looks so sad. I've made my feelings for her pretty clear, but I don't want to be the other guy.

Audrey touches her head.

'Is it getting worse?' I ask.

The tears continue and her breathing hitches.

'It's coming.' Still holding her head, Audrey bends towards me, groaning.

I pull her into my arms, wishing I could take some of the skull-crushing pain for her. I support her weight as she leans into me. She's dependent on me. I hate myself for loving this.

'What if I don't make it back?' she gasps, stumbling over the next words. 'They need me.'

The guilt of wanting to keep her to myself smashes through my conscience, making me feel like a selfish dick disguised in a designer suit and Hollywood smile.

I place my hand under her chin and tilt her fragile head up to me.

When she looks at me, I'm careful not to linger too long with my touch.

She grabs my retreating hand and holds on tight. Despite the circumstances, it makes my heart lurch. I compose myself before speaking but in that pause, Audrey beats me to it.

'Listen to me.' She swallows her tears. 'You know you're there, in the future. If this kills me, promise me you'll take care of them. Tell them I love them, I never forgot about them and I tried to get home. I really did try,' she sobs.

How could I look at her family, knowing I would have preferred to keep her for myself? 'Of course I will, Audrey. I'll always be there for you, for whatever you want me to do.'

A TIME FOR *Everything*

Audrey nods, dismissing my words. 'Don't let them forget me,' she whispers.

I rest my forehead on hers. My voice becomes unintentionally harsh. 'You know how this works, Audrey. Believe that you will make it home and it will happen. I won't stop until I find a way to make this right. You have to trust me.'

She looks at me in earnest. 'I've always trusted you.'

My heart melts.

'There's not a time or place in this whole universe that I won't be there for you. I'll fix this, I promise.' I press a kiss to her forehead and pull back. 'Say the words, Audrey. Say "I'm going to make it home safe," and most of all believe it. Close your eyes and visualise yourself home.' The spotlight, like the spark of an old gas cooker, grows at the side of her head where the pain is.

She closes her eyes, relaxes, and whispers her mantra, 'I'm home safe,' over and over.

My heart grieves as I will her safe return to someone else.

I shut my eyes against the growing light and squeeze her tight.

She mutters, 'I'm home safe. I'm home safe. I'm home safe.'

The screech that accompanies the light retreating rings in my ears. The nightmare noise seeps so far inside, I can feel my brain shake. The light changes from bright yellow to blinding white. Time is running out. 'I'll change this,' I tell her.

The light engulfs her, imploding into nothing and taking her with it.

A deafening silence left behind.

I drop my empty arms that held her a second ago. I sigh and pinch the bridge of my nose and finally let myself cry.

All the time and energy and waiting we'd done, trying to find a way to control time—or at least our perception of it—has been useless. I couldn't stop it. I couldn't control it. I couldn't keep her.

I let her go.

CHAPTER

Ten years earlier.

Thursday, 29th February, 1996

09:22 (GMT)

Cambridge, England.

I am twenty today.

'Happy birthday, Mike.' David strides into the kitchen and slaps me on the back. 'Looking forward to tonight?' He slides into the opposite chair.

'If I say *no*, will you cancel?' I already know the answer.

He chuckles. 'What time your parents getting here?'

'I'm meeting them in town at two.' I shove cereal into my mouth. 'Honestly, I could do without the family gathering. I have to work at four-thirty. I don't even know why they're bothering with such a long drive.'

'It's your first birthday away from home. At least they care enough to come down and check on you.' David leans back in his seat and slides a VHS cassette off the kitchen worktop. 'Can you return this when you get to work? It'll save me the trip.'

'I don't know why you waste your money on this shite.' I nod at the title.

'The X-Files aren't shite. There are all sorts of undiscovered things out there. Don't change the subject. You're not bringing your folks here, are you? 'Cause the guys are setting up a DJ stand.'

I sigh. 'I'll keep them away.'

'What's got into you?'

'It's the first family birthday since Grandad died.' I swallow another mouthful. 'Christmas was a nightmare. Mum served dinner between quiet sobs from the kitchen, and Dad sulked off after her in the hopes of salvaging some food and putting a swift end to the day. Today's going to be more of the same.'

'Just play the dutiful son and do lunch,' David tells me. 'You did, after all, invite them here.'

I nod into my bowl of Weetabix.

'You're lucky. My parents would never think of visiting midterm. I get a card and cash for birthdays. They don't even bother to pick out a present anymore.'

'They've taken the day off work. They gave the keys of the B&B to our overly helpful neighbour, George.'

David scoffs. 'There's no way in hell my parents would take time off work to visit.'

It takes me less than ten minutes to cross campus to where my parents wait outside the pub on the main stretch of student bars.

'Hello, Michael,' Mum says and hugs me tight.

'Why are you outside?'

'Didn't want to sit without you,' Dad answers.

I roll my eyes. Their politeness is unsettling sometimes. I hold the door open and usher them inside, giving Caitlyn a playful push as she passes me. Seven months without having the opportunity to annoy her is too long.

'Busy in here for the afternoon, isn't it?' Dad says as the four of us settle in a large booth for an early dinner.

'It's Thursday. It's the weekend for students.' I snap a beer mat in two and adjust the leg on the wobbly wooden table.

'Soup smells nice,' Dad says, looking around. 'Think it's minestrone. We should put that on the dinner menu. That would help change things up a bit.' He slaps the table in triumph.

'It doesn't fit our new theme.' Mum narrows her eyes and picks up a menu.

'What new theme?' I ask.

Mum puts down the menu. 'Well, George and I discussed it. Since our B&Bs are next door to each other, we should do similar themes, like sister hotels.'

'Sister what?' I turn to Dad.

He shrugs, puts on his reading glasses and studies the menu.

'You know, similar decor and menus and themes. So if we are overbooked, we can send customers next door,' Mum says.

'But we're never overbooked,' Caitlyn retorts.

Mum clears her throat. 'Well, no, but we might be if this new theme is a hit.'

The rest of dinner dances around pleasantries and catch-up. I avoid an in-depth conversation about handling the increased workload—the two failed modules I'm carrying over from last year.

'I thought you liked English?' Dad inquires.

'I like the literature side of things and I'm taking some elective modules on drama and playwrights, which is fun. It's the exams I'm having trouble with mostly.' Or it's my original plan of finding a safe teaching job that is scaring the shit out of me. Spending eight hours a day with teenagers who don't want to be there? I remember high school and no one wanted to be there.

'Well, it is Cambridge, Son. Nobody said it was going to be easy. Stick at it and take advantage of your fees and maintenance being taken care of with your grant. There's no way your mother and I could afford to pay for this if you decide to switch degrees halfway through.'

'I know. It's just tough to keep up with everything on top of working.' The words are out of my mouth before I realise and I dart my eyes between Mum and Dad for a reaction.

'If you're struggling with studying, you should cut down on the job. We can manage without you sending money home to us,' Mum tells me. The smile doesn't quite reach her eyes.

'It's okay. I just need to make better use of the time I do have. That's all.'

I move the attention to the quiet months of the B&B and Mum's ideas for off-season business.

After dinner, the waitress appears with a birthday cake Mum and Dad must have dropped off before my arrival. The cake, complete with twenty candles is placed in front of me. *Oh, shit.* I forgot about this. Staring at the candles, it's the first year I'm unprepared.

'If Grandad were here, he would tell you to take your time and make the wish count.' Mum rummages inside her bag, pulling out a tissue.

'Grandad would have kept us occupied for hours thinking beforehand about our birthday wish,' Caitlyn says. 'Remember how he used to make up crazy stories of adventure and achieving greatness and fortune?'

I laugh, but my mind is blank. Wishing in haste would be disrespecting Grandad's memory.

The small flames from the candles flow back and forth and glow bright yellow in the dull ambience of the pub. Think quickly. What do I want? My thoughts are overshadowed by what I hate most in life: my lack of focus, desires, and dreams and the constant battle of paying the bills, as well as worrying about the financial state of my parents.

I exhale in misery. 'I wish . . . my whole life would fall into place.' I deflate at the admission. It's not exactly a "loud and proud" wish that would make Grandad happy. Everyone turns their attention from the modest, homemade, chocolate-covered sponge cake to me. Squirming a little under their gaze, I lower my head.

I think of the life that would make Grandad proud, the one I dreamt about when I was a kid. Where anything is possible and no one put a ceiling on your dreams. The life I planned on my storyboards year after year. 'I want to be rich and successful, like Grandad was before he got married. I want to be famous. I want to make movies. And to live happily ever after.'

Caitlyn stops playing with the tape she is unwinding from her old defective Walkman and stares at me.

I nudge her arm. 'Remember what he would say every time the cake came out. "Your birthday is the time of year when the attention is on you. Ask the universe for whatever you desire when you blow out the candles."'

Dad places his hand on top of Mum's. She smiles at him but doesn't take it.

'And what are you going to be famous for?' Caitlyn squints.

I think for a moment. 'I'll be a movie star, like I always wanted to be. A big, successful movie star. I'm going to move to Hollywood, have my own production company, and make a fortune. When I'm rich, I'll let you be my housekeeper if you want. I'll need someone to clean all those rooms.'

'In your dreams,' she scoffs, shoving her headhones back in place, ready to ignore us all.

'What are you listening to anyway?' I grab the Walkman out of her hand.

'Nothing!' she screams, snatching it back.

I hold on tight, and fake a tug of war game with her.

Her eyes widen. 'Give it back, Mike. I need to listen to these.'

There's panic in her voice I wasn't expecting. 'Relax, I was only kidding.' I let go.

'Ignore her. She's been listening to her new tapes all week.' Dad waves in the air. 'What's the new singer called? Liam something. Have you heard of him?'

I shake my head. Teenage boybands aren't my thing. Movies and acting though, that could be my thing.

I could switch over to a joint honours degree next year, I realise. I have credits from the drama department already. I wonder if they would let me this far into the degree.

'Grandpa always said, "ask and you shall receive."' Mum perks up. '"Believe and it will happen."'

The candles have burned almost all the way to the bottom. Mum will be annoyed she won't be able to re-use them for the next birthday. I close my eyes and lean toward the cake. 'Make my dreams come true,' I whisper and blow the candles out in one quick go.

Mum picks up a knife and busies herself, removing spilled wax and slicing perfectly equal portions of cake. I get lost in a fantasy about living in a world of riches and fame. Mum and Dad are nattering across the table but I'm not interested enough to concentrate on what they're saying. Settling into my fantasy of travelling to exotic locations— Hawaii and Australia would be amazing to explore on a first class ticket. The seat underneath me feels a little comfier as I imagine myself relaxing on a plane. Living in Hollywood with the sun beating down on my back, makes it bearable to stroll down the street with fans chasing me for an autograph. I can finally have a job that means none of us has to worry about making ends meet. Maybe Mum and Dad could retire and enjoy some of their life. Yes, this is the career for me, Michael Knight: Hollywood A-lister.

Caitlyn removes her headphones and turns them in her hand. 'Will you really bring me with you?'

'Where?'

'When you go to America?'

'Go to college first, Caitlyn. If I get out there, your life will be first on my list to make a little bit easier.'

She smiles. 'I don't know how I'd get there on my own. I don't even have time to get a job that actually pays. I'm working before and after school in the B&B.'

She's been picking up the slack after I left. I smile at her. 'Mum and Dad need the extra help, Caitlyn. It won't be forever. I promise, when I'm rich, I'll give you a job that you actually get paid for all the hard work you do. You never know'—I nudge the Walkman in her hand—'you might meet that singer guy Liam-what's-his-face and live happily ever after.'

Her cheeks redden. 'Yeah, right. Like he's going to be interested in me. I'm not nearly as smart as he is.'

Mum passes around the cake.

'When we live in America, she better send us over her homemade birthday cakes,' I whisper to Caitlyn.

We walk to the edge of town and stop in front of the video rental shop. Mum cries softly, and I allow her the briefest of hugs. 'Come home for a visit soon. And don't forget to study more.'

God, she can be so embarrassing, in the middle of the street. Dad must feel my pain as he scoffs his disapproval at her. She composes herself with a tissue while I say goodbye to Dad.

As I turn to open the door to the store, a bright red poster in the window catches my attention. It's the upcoming release of the new Brad Pitt and Bruce Willis action movie. My heart thuds and excitement runs through me. It's a sign, two of Hollywood's most successful actors facing me. I put my arm around Caitlyn's shoulder and turn her towards the window with me. I vow, there and then. 'I'll be on a poster like that one day,' I tell her.

After the brief shift change, I restart the popcorn machine to fill the place with the sweet, salty smell before stocking the snack stand. I'm alone in the shop and wonder how to start my new career. The how-to details were never anything Grandad would talk about. For him, it was all about the end result. I should get an agent, but how? How do you even get an audition?

The bell above the door chimes as a few girls from campus come in to return a tape. I push myself off the grey carpet tiles and wipe my hands. Fumbling with the cassette when they hand it over, I nearly drop it, and the girls giggle as I catch it mid-air. *Fuck.* A movie star would not be a total loser in front of hot girls. I'll have to work on this. I make my way around the service counter to the computer and the bell chimes again. I automatically look up. It's Jessica. Shit. Any recovery I've made melts away with the heat in my cheeks.

Jessica practically flows when she walks, running a hand down the length of her long brown hair as she approaches me. 'Hi, Mike.' She smiles and nods to the girls.

She always speaks to me when we meet on campus, making me more nervous than I usually am with the female sex. Crap, I just thought the word sex and she's standing in front of me. I hope I don't blush even more. Crap, crap. I'm going to blush at the thought of blushing. The other girls leave, and I take a deep breath and practically snatch the video out of her hand. I try to act nonchalant and nod, acknowledging her. From what I've seen, David's "treat them mean and keep them keen" seems to work. If I had a quid for every girl I've seen sneaking out of his room in the morning, I wouldn't need to be a movie star. I remember when we were in halls of residence and there was campus security on the main door. I mean, how the hell did he get them in?

Jessica grins as I type the codes into the computer. 'All good?'

Is she inquiring about me or the return process? 'Sure.' I smile back and relax a little. If I do this whole fame thing, I need to get my confidence up. Being confident around Jessica is something I've never been able to do. My palms sweat as I hit a few buttons on the computer and try not to check her out. She's slender and attractive and has great boobs, especially in that tight jumper. God, what if she has some magic ability to read my mind and knows I just thought of her boobs? Oh god. I'm still thinking about them. Speak quickly.

'Did you like the movie?' I move swiftly to the stacks of videos behind me to re-shelve the tape and allow my cheeks to cool.

'Yes,' she answers a little too enthusiastically. 'Great choice. Thanks.' She leans over the counter, to keep my attention, I'm sure.

'No problem.' I turn to face her. I have no idea where to take this conversation. 'Most girls turn their noses up when I recommend independent movies.' I house the cassette back in numerical order and return to the desk. 'Some of them are a little obscure, I have to admit. I'm glad you liked this one, though. MacIntosh is a great director. He wants the audience to connect with the production and watch it again and again. When he started his career, he used to send reduced-price reels to the independent cinemas. It helped showcase his work to as many people as possible.' I rest my hand on the counter.

Jessica's smiling, but her wide eyes make her look lost. 'Really?' She forces the word out of her mouth.

This is harder and more awkward than I thought. I sink into the computer chair and move the mouse around, pretending I'm doing something.

'I didn't know that,' she continues.

At least she's trying to be kind. Most people mock me when I get carried away with cinema talk. I'm trying to impress her, goddamn it. I should change the subject. David is always telling me to relax and be myself around girls. "Only smoother," he would add.

'Sorry. I was rambling.' I hope I can salvage this. 'My grandad owned an independent movie theatre before he married my gran. He loved behind the scenes stuff. It rubbed off over the years. He talked about the production and distribution of movies rather than the content.' I snort and lean back in my chair. 'That's probably why he went out of business. Should have made sure people were enjoying what they were watching as opposed to extolling over the artwork behind movie making.'

'There was artwork in the movie? I never noticed,' she chirps. 'Like van Gogh paintings and stuff?'

I grimace inside but force a smile. 'Are you going to Dave's party tonight?'

'Isn't it your party?'

'Sort of. Well, yeah, it's my birthday, but it's just an excuse for David and my other flatmates to throw a party. I hate house parties, especially in my house.'

'It must be tough living with those three.' She grins.

I laugh. 'They usually leave me alone, but alas, it's the one day a year I have to give them.' I gulp. It's now or never. Dropping my head, I twiddle with a paperclip. 'You should come. I close up at midnight. Why don't I meet you over there?' Cold sweat runs down my back as I wait the painful five seconds of silence for her answer. Oh god, what if she says no? What if she has a boyfriend? What if she laughs at me? This could be humiliating.

'Okay,' she says, 'I'll see you there.'

I'm spared. Relief overwhelms me. I asked Jessica out and she said yes. I mentally high-five myself and check out her ass in her black jeans as she exits the shop.

That was terrifying, but she said yes. Shit, she said yes. Does she know what she just said yes to? What if she is being polite and is just going to see me there, like everyone else at the party. Fuck.

I mop the floor before closing. This is the last birthday I'm going to spend cleaning floors. Next year, and every year after, I'll be acting in the sunshine of Hollywood and making millions. What I need is someone to tell me what to do, and how to do it. A sharp light appears in the middle of the shop floor. The mop crashes to the floor when I raise a hand to my eyes. The light is small and hypnotic, but grows like headlights approaching at night. It's like witnessing a slow-motion bomb explode and ripple through the air. The 'headlights' capture my attention and draw everything together in central focal point. There's a piercing noise so loud and high-pitched I cover my ears, taking over my senses. What the hell? For a second, I think a car or truck is about to crash through the window. The noise gets louder, closer. It sounds like tyres screeching to a halt on the road but there is no disturbance around me.

The light reaches its maximum point of exploding and despite the noise, things seem calm as the light retreats, disappearing into the nothingness it came from, quieting the noise in the process. My eyes adjust to the room again.

I'm dumbstruck. The explosion of light has left behind a girl.

CHAPTER
Three

'**What the hell just** happened?' The woman flinches and gingerly touches the side of her head. She tilts her head cautiously, slowly looking around the room. I think she's as disorientated by her surroundings as I am with her arrival. She looks like a timid animal afraid of a new habitat, not sure whether to stay or flee.

'Are you real?' I reach out, unsure whether or not to touch her.

She looks down at herself and runs her hands over her stomach, skimming the top of her trousers.

I step forward and trip over the mop, crashing head-first into her chest.

She catches me and regains her own balance.

At least she's corporeal. I find my feet, pull myself out of her arms, and stand before her. She repeats the question more softly. 'What the hell happened?'

I stare completely dumbfounded, looking her over. No horns on her head or wings on her back. She looks human, normal, pretty even. She takes a step closer and squints, even though I'm right in front of her. I could touch her face, I'm so close to her. She's waiting for an answer, like I'm the one who appeared out of thin air.

The light and the noise and the imploding bomb return all at once, at the side of her head.

Her eyes widen when the light grows around her, and she drops her defensive stance. 'Michael,' she screams and grabs my arms.

The light surrounds her along with the high-pitched screech, and she's sucked inside, compressed into nothing.

Chills run up my spine, and my skin prickles with goosebumps. Bile rises in my throat. I open my mouth, forcing myself to breathe. I take a step forward that would've had us nose to nose. There is nothing out of the ordinary. No breeze, no movement, no evidence that she was ever here.

'Shit,' I say to fill the silence, spinning around to make sure she's not behind me.

I heighten my curse to a 'fuck' to check that I'm not dead, because I'm pretty sure I just saw a ghost.

This has got to be a birthday joke instigated by David. I exhale and my shoulders relax. He persuaded a beautiful woman to do the deed. Oh god, that's why Jessica agreed to go out with me; she must have helped set this up. People should be jumping out from their hiding places right about now.

I walk with trepidation behind the counter. It's safer here than exposed on the shop floor.

I wait.

Someone is probably recording it on the Art Department's video, another thing David manages to borrow on a whim.

I wait.

The clock on the wall ticks, taunting me as each second passes.

I wait.

There's no one else here. Nowhere to hide in the stacks or tiny cloakroom. I pace and run my hands through my hair. Anything to keep me moving, keep me connected to reality. This can't have happened. It's like something out of a movie.

Video. I can check the CCTV. When Tina took over management full-time, she had cameras installed at the start of the university year. She hates the petty thievery students resort to in order to avoid paying for sweets and popcorn.

I lock the snip on the front door and practically run to the computer to figure out how to play back the damn security footage. The computer monitor on the counter also displays a recording from the solo camera inside the main door. I clear the area around the keyboard, tipping empty cans and sweet wrappers into the bin. I stop the tape and rewind.

The flash of light is evident even through the distorted pull of the rewind mode. I sigh in relief. I'm not crazy. The quality of the recording isn't sharp, and it's black and white, or more like grey and white. The bright light grows. I see myself gawking like an idiot as a woman appears in the store. When I stumble into her, it looks worse than I could ever have imagined. The camera shot shows the back of her, standing a few inches shorter than me. We have our moment together and then the light comes back and swallows her up. You can't see her face. There's no sound on the tape. You can't hear her speak. How the hell did she know my name, anyway? There's not much to go on, really. My heart doubles in speed as I rewind the tape once more to see it again.

A loud rap on the front door makes me jump, yelp, and straighten all at once. My hands slide over the keyboard. Fuck, what did I press?

CHAPTER
Four

Tina scowls at me and makes a *clink clink clink* with her keys on the glass panel until I open the door.

'Mike.' She draws out my name in annoyance as she saunters in. 'Why do you have the door locked already?' She continues to chastise me for closing like a minute early and makes her way around the service desk to cash up the till. Is the screen still on CCTV or is it back to the video log?

'Sorry,' I say.

She must notice the apprehension in my voice because she turns her attention to me and her demeanour changes. 'Mike, dear, are you okay? Are you sick?'

I feel as if the blood has drained down to my toes. I'm queasy and lightheaded and I sway from side to side. 'Actually, I'm a little unwell. I was going to call and see if you would mind if I went home. I know the place is still a bit of a mess . . .' It's not as untidy as some of the guys leave it at midnight.

'Not at all.' Tina shoos me to the door. 'Best you get off to bed and rest.' She settles in front of the computer and perches her *Dame Edna* glasses on the end of her nose. Her curly hair is wild. If it were purple instead of grey-brown, you would swear it was the old Dame herself.

I fetch my jacket from the cupboard and rush out the door. I take harsh breaths to stop my head from spinning. The fresh air burns my lungs, and it's sobering. I run as fast as I can up the street and across campus, out the other side and down to the housing estate. The cold night air and dew add to the freakiness of the evening. The pale sandstone of the matching houses and bright streetlights brighten things into focus, keeping me from screaming the whole way home. Faint music and chatter from the party drifts down the street before I even turn the corner. I want to keep running, but I need to speak to David. If anyone can offer a logical explanation, it'll be him.

An overflow of intoxicated people spills out of the townhouse. They're sitting in the garden and leaning against the side of the house, laughing and talking loudly, like the alcohol has impaired their hearing. Weaving unnoticed through the crowd of smokers, I'm surprised by my disappointment that a party in my honour isn't making me the centre of attention. I trot upstairs to the kitchen and dining area and find David dutifully playing host. He's leaning against the cooker and chatting closely with a brunette, but I don't notice if it's his girlfriend or someone new. I place a hand on his arm and bend in so he can hear me over the music. 'I need to speak to you outside.' Not waiting for an answer, I turn to leave and see it's Jessica he's with.

I manage a tight smile but keep walking, picking up a bottle of beer from the bin that's now a makeshift fridge. I side-step a few people sitting on the stairs on my way back down—why they sit on the stairs, I have no idea—and move towards the picnic bench at the end of the garden. The music from upstairs leaks out the back windows. I run my hand from the neck of the bottle down to the base, wiping off the remaining cold water. Despite the breeze, the coolness in my palm is calming, so I repeat the motion with my other hand.

David makes his way towards me, handing me a bottle opener.

I open the beer and gulp until half is gone.

He eyes my unusual partake in the party spirit and tilts his head to the side. 'You okay?'

I stare at the bottle in my hand and try to formulate an answer that can describe the mind-fuck I've seen. 'I don't know.'

David sits at the edge of the bench and rests his elbows on his thighs, waiting for me to continue.

'I think I saw a ghost,' I admit.

He straightens and looks at me but says nothing.

'But she was solid, so an angel, maybe,' I mutter. The shake of fear in my voice has his attention.

'Don't be ridiculous,' he says, although he doesn't mock me.

I explain what happened. 'Shouldn't your paranormal sci-fi obsession be tingling right about now?'

'Okay then. Let's go have a look,' he says confidently.

'She's not there,' I yell. 'She vanished. That's what ghosts do. Show up and scare the crap out of you, then vanish.' I'm losing it. My sanity is slipping through my mind and out my fingertips. My hands shake, and I gaze at them, looking for answers.

'But it's on the store security cameras, right?'

A TIME FOR *Everything*

I nod.

'Mike, do you realise, you might be the first person to ever have photographic evidence of ghosts?'

Oh crap. I wonder if Tina saw it. Shit, I have no idea what I pressed when she rattled on the door. Christ, what if I deleted it? David will think I made this all up. He'll think I'm crazy.

Questioning my own sanity is put on hold as Jessica and David's girlfriend close the back door and head towards us. I jump to my feet. The solid ground kills the buzz from the beer and lets me know I'm not dreaming.

'Hey, what ya doing?' David's girlfriend asks.

What's her name? Amy? I can't be sure; I've only met this one once. I assume she's come to fetch David. She's learning fast. Don't want to leave him loose at a party too long. She wouldn't have been impressed, seeing him talking so closely with Jessica. God, why they hang around when he treats them so offhand is beyond me. David wraps an arm around Amy's shoulders. Jessica's changed into a short top and an impressive pair of tight blue jeans. Her hair is tied back. The four of us stand, facing each other, slight tension evident as no one dares to speak first.

There's no way I'm going back to the store tonight. Maybe tomorrow I'll have a perfectly rational explanation. Otherwise, I may have to deal with the fact I'm going round the twist. Jessica is the perfect excuse to stay—at least one that will be temporarily acceptable to David.

'Tomorrow,' I tell him. 'We don't open till eleven on Friday, so we can go before.' The girls exchange glances but don't say anything.

'We don't have to go if there's nothing there, Mike.' He looks at me warily, more with concern than scepticism.

'It's there. Just wait until tomorrow,' I snap.

'Okay then,' he agrees. 'See you two later.' He grins pointedly at Jessica, then at me. With Amy still caught under his arm, he returns to the house.

'Hi, Mike,' Jessica says. Her voice is high-pitched. She gives me a bottle of beer. 'Thought you might want another.'

I take it and smile sheepishly at her, not fully meeting her gaze. She pulls a small brown teddy bear from her back jeans pocket and hands it to me. The bear is wearing a party hat and holding a number five.

'Everyone should get a teddy bear for their fifth birthday,' she says proudly.

It makes me chuckle. That's the kind of smartass thing Caitlyn used to love doing.

'Happy birthday, Mike.'

It's weird hearing her say my name. It doesn't flow off her tongue comfortably. Not like the smooth familiarity I heard when the woman at the store called me Michael. Perhaps it wasn't familiarity, but desperation. She was scared when the light came back. I take a swig of beer, heart racing, realising I should have tried to keep her here. Colouring at the weirdness of the memory, I think Jessica mistakes it for something between us. She takes my hand and leads me back to the picnic bench.

I've liked Jessica for a while, ever since she helped me figure out how to reduce the resistance on the rowing machines in the student gym. God, that was an embarrassing day, needing a hot girl to rescue you in the gym.

She straddles the bench, and I do the same to face her. I don't think she's here for a nice drink with a friend; she can do that inside with anyone. She's definitely making a move.

Possibly. She opens her mouth to speak, but I lean forward before losing my nerve and kiss her. My lips move on hers a little harsher than intended. What the hell am I doing? I'm never this brave. But an evening with Jessica would certainly be a distraction from thinking about spotlight girls.

I have to stop with the mental analysis, because I'm missing what's happening. Jessica's kissing me back. Our knees touch, and the thought of our legs open is turning me on. She runs her hands along my chest and slides them down to my waist and pulls me closer. She inches forward. With one more move, she'll be on top of me. This should be happening in the privacy of my bedroom instead of outside in the freezing night. I break away and she gasps for air. It's a dramatised move for my benefit rather than an actual need.

I look towards the ground, pretending to be as affected as she is. I should apologise for pouncing on her or for stopping so abruptly.

'That's okay,' she says, sensing my discomfort.

There is an awkward silence as we sit there, not knowing what to do.

'You can kiss me again if you want.'

I don't know how long Jessica and I have been out here, but both our drinks are finished and neither of us is making a move to refill. There seems to be an unspoken acknowledgement that if we go back inside and join the party, this spell might break. The wind has picked up. Although it's been cold all evening, it was bearable because we shared body heat. But now she's shivering. Someone turns off the music in the house and the garden becomes eerily quiet.

'You're freezing. I'll get you a jumper.' *And one for myself.*

Jessica takes my hand as I stand and comes with me. My room is two floors up. The house has quietened down to chatter, the lull at the end of the evening that separates the serious drinkers from the lightweights like me. As we pass the dining room on the first floor, we see David sitting at the table with our other two housemates and a guy I've never seen before, having one of his 'serious' money-making conversations that come with too much alcohol. It's not like he needs the money, but he's hell-bent on making a fortune like his parents. David catches my eye as I walk by the door hand in hand with Jessica, but he doesn't wink or grin or shout a comment like I expect him to.

'I'll get you a jumper,' I tell Jessica at the top of the landing, giving her the option not to follow me into my room if she doesn't want to. I hope she can't hear the uncertainty in my voice. She follows me inside and leans on the door with her hands clasped behind her ass. It's pretty hot. Does she want to sleep with me or does she just want a jumper? My experience with figuring this stuff out is limited. My first and only time left me even more bewildered by the female sex and with a bruised ego, and if I am totally honest, slightly heartbroken.

Moving clothes from one side of the wardrobe to the other, I try to find something that will keep her warm while mentally checking the last time items were washed. I pull my navy blue hoodie off the hanger and resist the urge to give it a quick sniff. Do I step into her space and kiss her as I hand it over? Do I put it on her? Christ, why are there so many options? She's waiting for me by the door. Should I speak first? Make a move? Surrender the damn jumper?

She lunges towards me and kisses me faster and more aggressively before I've time to offer up the jumper. She presses against me and if she hasn't noticed my erection before, she can certainly feel it now. I take a chance and put my hands on her ass. When she doesn't object, I pull her tight against me. She unbuckles my belt and jeans. After she shoves my jeans and underwear down, she tugs the bottom of my shirt and pulls it up and over my head.

I have her top off before my shirt hits the floor. I bend down to remove my jeans and socks from my feet. I'm back at her mouth. I want to keep kissing her as I'm too embarrassed to stand here naked. What if she examines me and thinks I'm not that attractive after all?

Trying not to break the momentum, I take small steps, backing her up to the bed.

She sits, pulling me around the neck until I'm lying on top of her.

We scoot farther up the bed, so her head rests on the pillow. I still can't look her in the eye as I strip her naked, kissing down her body as I go. Who would have thought Jessica, of all people, would be naked in bed with me? Maybe I should let her get under the quilt to keep warm. She did say she was cold earlier. I search the bedside drawer for a condom and place it on the bed. Jessica shuffles underneath me and gets the blanket over us. I get the condom wrapper open and on in a decent amount of time. Perhaps this is something I should congratulate myself on *later*. As I lower myself, I slide inside her, and she gasps softly. God, I forgot how good this feels. I move in and out of her and even try flexing my hips from side to side, which she responds to by grinding her own hips against me. Things are going better than the last time I did this.

I brush her hair off her face like they do in the movies, not an easy task when I'm trying to hold my body up so as not to crush her. The sheets are loose around the top of the bed, and I move them back, but my hand gets caught on the elastic corner. Christ, this is not what I need now. What if she realises I'm distracted? I ditch the problem with the sheet and pull my hand back, but it doesn't budge farther than a couple of inches. I shift again, attempting to free my hand, but I pull too hard and fall off the side of the bed and land on the floor with a thud that shakes the mirrored wardrobes. Well, that was definitely not smooth. There's no doubt that anyone in the dining room below heard the crash.

The sound of Jessica's no-barriers laugh brings me back to the problem at hand. What the hell do I do now? I started having sex with a girl who is, let's face it, out of my league, and who for some strange reason seems to like me, and I manage to screw it up and have her laugh at me. Oh, and I'm still naked. Jessica peers over the edge of the bed, giggling, but her sweet look and humour make me realise she isn't judging me. My embarrassed smile turns into a small chuckle, and I laugh with her.

'Are you okay?' she asks as I sit up.

'At least I don't need to worry about making a fool of myself anymore.' I grin as she slides her arms around my neck and pulls me back onto the bed.

I wake with Jessica wrapped around me, her head in the crook of my arm. I stretch my arm out and alleviate some of the stiffness from sleeping in such an awkward position. Her warm body sticks to mine with our dried sweat, but I like that she didn't leave. After another two rounds of sex, she pulled the quilt up over the both of us and settled down to sleep, like it was her rightful place.

Wrapping an arm around her, I squeeze her and kiss the top of her head, knowing she'll wake. Her leg is draped over mine and brushes against my erection. She stirs and turns towards me. I smile and kiss her mouth, slowly at first, little soft kisses as she fully wakens. She responds to my invitation and moves swiftly to lie on top of me.

'Morning.' She smiles.

I push my hips up against her. She sits up to straddle my legs and rests her hands flat on my chest.

'Good morning,' I say.

Two loud, hard bangs on my bedroom door make us jump.

'I'll be out in a second,' I shout. I know it's David waking me to go to the video shop.

'We've got to go,' David yells. 'It's after ten.'

Jessica swings her legs out of bed and gathers her clothes.

'You don't have to rush off,' I assure her.

'You have plans.'

'Can I see you again?' I grab her hand and look into her eyes, determined for her to say yes. She stops dressing and answers me with a lingering kiss. I want to bring her back into bed, but for the first time since I started kissing her last night, the urge to see the video again is stronger. I stand and dress next to her, adding the jumper that led us to the bedroom in the first place.

As we descend the first set of stairs, Jessica shouts to David as she passes the kitchen, 'He's all yours.' She gives me a quick kiss on the cheek and continues down the second staircase and out the front door.

'Why are you even up? I thought you would still be in bed with Amy.' I sit at the table.

'Ah, you missed the drama last night after we left you two outside. Amy stormed off. Doesn't want to see me again. I probably should have broken up with her at the beginning of the night, left myself a free agent.' He raises an eyebrow at me. 'You certainly got lucky last night. And with Jessica. That girl's a catch. Never had much luck with her myself. I've gotta say I'm impressed. Didn't think you had it in you.'

'Shut up and let's go. This whole thing is still freaking me out. I want you to see the tape and tell me if I'm mad.' I drink the rest of David's tea and steal a slice of toast from his plate. I've eaten most of it by the time we thud down the stairs and open the front door.

'I want in and out before the store opens,' I tell David on the way. Despite our rush, it's ten-thirty by the time we get there. 'We have about twenty minutes,' I remind him as I unlock the door. Enough daylight streams through the main window that I don't need to turn the lights on. Behind the counter, I fire up the computer screen. David shuffles from foot to foot beside me. He must have thought in the cold sober light of day I would laugh it off or tell him I made it up or was mistaken. Now that I'm actually looking for the footage, I'm either about to embarrass myself or be vindicated. I don't know which one to wish for.

I hit play on the video, and David nudges me to the side to get a better view of the screen. His mouth falls open in disbelief.

My belly drops, and a choking fear rises in the back of my throat. I gulp and take a long deep breath, placing my hands on the desk to steady myself.

It was real.

'Rewind it and play it again,' David says.

'What the hell do you think she is?'

'I have no idea, but we'll find out. Make a copy of the tape and delete the original so no one else sees it.'

David follows me into my room, still talking over the plan he hatched on our way back.

'We need to start researching paranormal sightings and anything else we can find that has similarities.' He lists off the top of his head theories and categories that might apply to the *sighting*, as he calls it. He's sub-categorising different ways to research each possibility and names some physics lecturers who would be open to discussions. He keeps asking me my opinion and questions things as he runs over the possibilities. I have no idea what I can contribute. I've a headache just thinking about it all. He takes out a notepad and pen and sits at my desk.

'Run through everything as you remember it.'

'You've seen the video. You know what happened.' I try to be nonchalant.

'I need to know what you felt, both physically and emotionally as it happened. And anything else, like smells, what she looked like and what she said. It wasn't clear on the video.'

I fill him in on the brief conversation I had with the woman. But I leave out the part when she called my name right before she was taken. She called my name, like she was expecting me to be able to help her. Instead, I just let her go. Whoever she is, wherever she is, I feel like I failed her. I clear my throat before I divert the conversation onto David's other questions. 'She was a little smaller than me and a little weirdly dressed.'

'Weird how?'

'Well, it was freezing outside, but all she wore was a short blue cardigan. Her black trousers cut off halfway up her calves and she had summer shoes on. Half her feet were exposed. They were tanned, though. Her legs, I mean.'

'You got a good look at her legs?' He sounds sceptical.

'She looked like she had just returned from two weeks in the sun,' I say, ignoring his comment. 'She had long red hair, or more auburn. You know that nice shade that makes you want to touch it.'

'You wanted to touch her hair?' He puts the pen down.

'No,' I scoff. 'I just mean, well, if you met her in the pub or something, you would think she was pretty hot, is all.'

'Hot? A hot ghost? That's a first.'

'Okay, not hot but attractive.' I don't know why I'm getting defensive. 'I told you, she might not have been a ghost. She might have been an angel or something.'

David clears his throat, picks up his pen and starts writing. 'She's probably not a ghost, considering she is corporeal, but we need to officially rule it out. I can start with death certificates and see if anyone has died in the shop or the flats upstairs. We can see if anything was built there before it was a store. Find a way to bring it up in conversation with Tina. She's nosey. She'll know everything.'

'How old do you think she is?'

'Older than us. Thirtyish maybe.'

She said my name. I kick my feet around the carpet, hoping to hell I haven't turned red. She practically pleaded with me to help her. The memory pulls at my gut and my curiosity.

'We need to figure out how to get her back. We need to recreate the environment and circumstances and monitor it. We can start tonight.'

Tingles run through me. With any luck, I'll get to see her again. This time, I can help her.

Four weeks later.
Thursday, 28ᵗʰ March, 1996
18:25 (GMT)
Cambridge, England.

'I told you, I'm going out with Jessica tonight.' I carefully place another plate on top of the mound of washed dishes by the sink. My hands hover, hoping nothing crashes to the ground like a real-life game of Jenga.

'Tonight is the first complete monthly cycle.' David paces from my left side to the right, trying to capture my full attention. 'What if she shows up tonight?'

'That's what you said on the weekly anniversary and the two week and every night since. I've worked every closing shift this month, David. Tina thinks the others aren't pulling their weight. She made sure I wasn't scheduled any more nights for a while. So, I'm going out with Jessica.'

I wouldn't mind if we were making progress, but failing on such a major level is destroying my soul. When we're at home, David settles into my room to go over notes and discuss books he's read. The more he talks about it, the more I know we have nothing. He only leaves me alone when Jessica stays over.

'What the hell am I supposed to do when you're out playing happy-ever-after with Jessica? I can't show up at the video store on my own.'

'Come meet us later. You're burning yourself out too. Adding our library research time to class schedules and study time, we've been pulling seventy-five-hour weeks.' I hook the dish towel through the cupboard handle—someone else will get the hint to dry and put them away.

'I'd rather not,' he snorts.

'You avoid her. Does it annoy you that the longest relationship you've had with a girl is through me?'

'I've got more important things to do,' he scoffs. 'It'll be worth it when your little light-girl comes back. Don't you want it to be you?'

'Want what to be me?'

'It's possible this girl, your little spotlight or whatever the hell you call her, has appeared somewhere else, to someone else.'

My gut churns.

'There is every possibility she is going to appear again. Don't you want to make sure we follow up every real chance of her coming back to us?'

'We can't even agree on what she is.'

'It's the elimination process that takes up most of the time. I've told you that.'

'I'm so tired of all of this.' I'm starting to think he's full of shit. 'We aren't even sure she is a ghost. You can't find anything to back up the theory that people come back from the dead in a bomb of light and corporeal form. Mostly we have a whole load of things we know the *light-girl* isn't. She is not a green alien.' I tick off on my fingers. 'She's not

37

a warrior princess from another universe sent to steal our power source.' We're almost sure about that one. 'She's not a reincarnated dinosaur ghost intent on forcing the planet back to its origins. Seriously, where did you even find that possibility?'

David remains impassive.

'She's not a whole host of weird and wonderful things listed in your *Paranormal Sightings and Conspiracy Theories* or whatever encyclopaedia you're accessing on the campus computers.'

'This is our most solid idea.' David clasps his hands together and brings them to his face like he is begging me.

'To wait for her to come back? That's not an idea. It's a last resort.'

'Just keep your questions on you,' he says.

I tap dramatically on my back pocket and grin. 'Your wish is my command.' David has compiled a list of questions and prepped me on what to do if and when she returns; don't freak out, don't fall on her again, ask her name and what she is.

'She was there for three minutes, so we need to be specific with what we want to ask. It's going to save time if we have a lot of things ruled out.'

Three minutes, how the hell did he time that?

'Michael?'

'What?' I ask.

He looks at me quizzically. 'Did she say something, right before she disappeared?'

I swallow. 'No. Why would you think that?'

'Never mind.' His jaw sets tight. 'I need to go to the library and check my e-mails.'

The crushing disappointment in my inability to help someone in need, takes over every inch of my body as I drag myself with desolation out of the kitchen.

I invite Jessica round to my place before we meet up with her friends. I give her a long, deep kiss before she sits on my bed, but it does nothing to shift my heavy-heartedness.

'Hi,' I say eventually.

'Thought you were avoiding me this week.'

'What? No. I've just been busy these past few days.' Crap, what if she doesn't believe me? 'Seriously, I'm exhausted. I could do with an early night, but I wanted to go out with you. I know I haven't seen you much lately.'

'We could stay in, watch a movie?' she suggests, getting up. She flicks through a couple of videos on my desk. 'What's this?' She holds up a copy of a VHS labelled *Grandad's Magaluf 18-70s Holiday*.

I lunge across the room and take it out of her hand. 'It's not. Well, I mean, it is. It's just . . .'

'What?'

David labelled the security footage of the light-girl thinking he was funny. The last thing we wanted was one of the guys to find a hidden tape, assume it was porn, and watch it.

My bedroom door is flung open and David storms in. His yelling starts before he crosses the threshold. 'She said your god damn name!'

Jessica folds her arms, mouth open, ready to start her own yelling. They both stare me down.

'Who?' Jessica has a look of thunder on her face, daring me to answer. 'Who said your name?'

Shit, this looks bad.

I rub my eyes, hoping the answers will come to me. 'Can you please give us a minute to talk?' I drag my hands down my face.

'Who?' David says. 'Who do you want to talk to?'

'Jessica, can you give us a minute?'

'This will take more than a minute.' David's arms are at his side and his entire body is still with tension.

I slip my hand into Jessica's and kiss her cheek. 'I'll come round to your flat when we're done.'

'Fine.' Like a defiant teenager, pissed at her parents, Jessica huffs out, not bothering to close the door.

David waits until we hear her descend the two flights of stairs and let herself out the front door before he speaks. 'I don't know why you put up with that.'

'What, a girlfriend? We can't all go around dumping girls off the back of a stupid four-week rule.'

'Why didn't you tell me she said your name?' He sounds a little hurt. 'She knows you.'

My head snaps up. She wasn't looking at me funny; it was recognition. That's why I felt the need to protect her.

'You're connected.'

I stutter, 'H-how?'

CHAPTER

Eleven months later.
Friday, 28th February, 1997
09:53 (GMT)
Cambridge, England.
I am twenty-one today.

Moisture covers the square mirror on the wall, and I lean on the bathroom sink to steady myself. I try to breathe through the leftover shower steam. Why the hell did I drink so much? My tongue feels permanently stuck to the roof of my mouth. I gag on my toothbrush. The paste is too minty and gritty. Someone should invent hangover toothpaste. Perhaps I'll mention it to David. It could be his next science project.

I think about tomorrow with trepidation, the one-year anniversary from when my *spotlight-girl* came. It's my last attempt with David at recreating the environment and waiting around for her to show up. Or not show up. I can't wait for it to be over. It's consumed our lives for too long. My grades are getting worse. My life plan of becoming miraculously famous and out of this financial hole has faded into the background.

I tighten the towel around my waist and drag my feet to my room. It's going to be a long day. My first class is at eleven, and I'm planning on a five-mile speed-training run before that. Although this seems like a reasonable time to be out in the world, I would rather crawl back into bed and sleep. Jessica's gone. She must have left while I was in the shower. She sneaks off like that, no longer waiting to say goodbye. My bed looks inviting. I miss having it all to myself. Two people in a double bed, fighting for control of the duvet does not make for a good night's sleep. Sober or drunk, it's becoming a task.

I toss my wash bag on top of the desk. The air behind me trembles, the vibrations tickling the back of my neck. I turn slowly. The air is rippling, like when you skim a stone over water. The familiarity is overwhelming. The spotlight, suspended in mid-air, expands. The light-girl is coming. I'm not terrified, like I thought I would be. Circling the light, I admire it as it grows. Shielding my eyes with my hand, I take a brave step forward. How does it work? We ruled out ghosts, but what the hell do we know anyway?

With a piercing screech, the light vanishes, leaving the woman again. Standing behind her this time, my voice croaks as I speak, 'Helloooo?'

She startles and spins around.

Christ, why did I have to sound like an old lady popping into a neighbour's house to say hi?

Looking as weary as she did a year ago, she gives the room a quick scan. Seeing through her eyes, I'm suddenly aware of the pulled curtains, unmade bed, clothes thrown around the place, and the stale smell of alcohol.

She even checks out the ceiling and frowns.

This whole thing must be weird for her too. Maybe she has no idea what's happening either. We assumed she was going to have all the answers.

'Michael,' she says.

It feels more like a confirmation this time.

'Yes, I'm Michael, Michael Knight. How do you know my name? Who *are* you?' Now I've found my voice, I don't want to stop talking. 'Wait a second.' I take two quick strides to my desk and rummage through the drawers. 'I have it here somewhere. Just hang on.'

I toss sheets of paper aside and dig deep until I find the list I once carried everywhere with me. Starting at the top, I fire them at her all at once.

'What are you? Where are you from? If you're dead, how did you die and how did she, sorry, how did *you* get here? Where did you go last year and why are you back? Can anyone come through, and why have *you* come through twice but no one else has yet? Is anyone else coming? Can you control the light, and how does it work?' I take a deep breath. The paper shakes in my hands.

She stares at me.

I haven't given her any time to answer. Christ, I can't even remember the first question at this stage. Blood pulses in my ears.

She opens her mouth but doesn't speak. She looks around the room again. 'What?' she finally asks.

I drop the piece of paper on the desk. 'Who are you?' I say slowly, trying to calm my heart rate. There's pressure in my chest, in my breathing.

'Audrey,' she replies with an air of caution.

She has a name. Well, that makes her human, sort of. 'How did you get here, Audrey? How did you come back from the dead?'

'What are you talking about, coming back from the dead? I'm not dead!' Her auburn hair falls around her face as she almost screams the last words.

Her accent distracts me from what she's saying. I can't place it. Growing up in the tourist industry, I usually catch accents pretty quickly.

'You're not?' I was holding onto that theory. 'Are you sure?' I edge towards her, letting her know I'm not scared. 'Sometimes they say ghosts don't even know they're dead.'

She furrows her brow like she's getting angry. Not crazy ghost angry, just regular pissed-off chick angry. 'Like the sixth fucking sense? I'm not fucking dead. Stop saying that.'

I sit on the bed. 'What sixth sense?' I'm wearing nothing but a towel, so I sit a little straighter than I normally would and try to position myself modestly. Thank god David convinced me to start cross-training with weights. My body is finally morphing into something I'm not totally embarrassed about. But my cheeks heat under her steady gaze.

Clearing my throat to break the silence, I rise to get dressed, holding on to the towel. She doesn't move out of the way, and my arm brushes hers as I cross the room. Goosebumps cover me—nice ones, not the scary axe murderer ones. I pick up my jeans and T-shirt from the desk chair as her gaze follows me. I wait for her to turn her back. Oh god, I never grabbed any underwear. I'm going to have to hunt for clean underwear, in a towel, in front of her.

'Sorry,' she says and faces the wall.

I dress quickly while Audrey strolls around the room, keeping her back turned. She takes a zip-up hoodie from the back of my chair and shivers as she shrugs into it. She has on a thin top and a small cardigan that only covers half of her back. I wonder what happened to the bottom half. 'You must be cold wearing that.'

She glances down at her clothes and nods once.

I'm embarrassed she knows that I have paid that much attention to her body.

Leaving the zipper open, she crosses the ends around her torso. 'This is all yours?' she asks, indicating the pile of notes and books on my desk. She moves my university crest hoodie and a dirty football out of the way and aimlessly flicks through the pile of notes from my last assessment.

I clench my teeth, causing a vibration to run through my jaw. They're in order. Sort of. 'It's my work. I'm a student here.' I place a hand on top of the notes, putting an end to her disarray.

'A student? How studious of you.' She laughs at her joke.

It's not funny, but I laugh at her attempt to make light of this whole freaky situation. I can't believe how normal she is, like when you're at a party and get left alone on the couch with one other random person and have no idea what to say but then realise you both love Red Dwarf.

Without hesitation, she closes the distance between us. Standing in my personal space, she places an open hand on my cheek. I hold my breath and resist the urge to lean into her touch.

'You're real,' she whispers.

Irish. Her accent is Irish. It's so cadent.

'Yes. So are you.' The tension in me dissolves, despite her being in my space.

'You're so young.'

Not really. 'I'm twenty-one. Well, tomorrow I will be.'

Her face is right next to mine. I can't help but feel she is giving me permission to stare at her. I did her no justice in my description to David. She is utterly beautiful. Her face is perfect, smooth and pale, like that of an angel. A guardian angel? I step back before I do anything monumentally stupid. It's not just her legs that are perfect and tanned. She looks like she just stepped off a movie set. She is totally out of my league and . . . married. She's wearing the biggest diamond ring I've ever seen. If she's not dead, then someone is certainly looking for her. My confidence crumbles as I awkwardly shift my weight from one foot to the other. Just be cool.

A smile tugs at her lips. I think she enjoys seeing me uncomfortable.

'You came to me in work last year, too.'

'That was a year ago? I thought it was . . . now.'

'Wow, so you're like, travelling at the speed of light then. I read about it when we were researching what happened.'

'You *researched* this?' Her voice is laced with acid.

Why would she be mad? 'After you disappeared last year, yes. Shit.' I pick up my watch from the floor beside the bed. 'How long have you been here?'

'What do you mean?'

'Last year, you were only with me for three minutes before you disappeared. Where did you go?'

'I didn't go anywhere. I told you, I'm just here.'

'There is a theory on people travelling through time and space exceptionally fast, and it means they experience time

46

differently from everyone else. So what was a second, or instantaneous, for you was a whole year for the rest of us. Well, it's all theory, but now we can figure out for sure.'

'There was light. I remember bright lights.'

'I've seen them too,' I tell her. 'And the noise. Do you remember that?'

'Yes.' Her voice cracks.

'What did it feel like? Why haven't you disappeared yet? Can you control it?'

'I don't know,' she yells. 'I have no idea how this is happening.' Her eyes fill with tears.

'Well, you're kind of the expert in this. We were hoping you would have some answers.'

'David's the expert,' Audrey corrects me. 'Maybe he knows. And he needs to figure out how the hell to get me home.' She hesitates. 'I have a family waiting for me. I need to get back to them. They'll be scared not knowing what's happened to me.'

'David?' How the hell does she know David?

Audrey points to the floor, where David's room is two floors below. 'David,' she confirms.

CHAPTER

Six

'David's no expert,' I insist.

'I am too,' David shouts from the door.

The daylight shines in through the hall window, backlighting him in the doorway and casting an ominous shadow over his figure. Squinting, we stare at each other in a silent standoff.

David breaks first. 'Sorry,' he says. 'Just heard Mike here slagging me off so thought I would at least stick up for myself.' He glances towards Audrey and then back at me. 'You just out the shower?' He nods at my wet hair.

He's really asking if this girl was here while I showered. If she was here all night. I grab the towel off the bed and finish drying my hair. He's probably in mental heaven thinking I've cheated on Jessica and with a total hottie. His patience for Jessica has worn thin over the past few months, and at every opportunity he tries to convince me to break up with her.

'You looking for help with something?' he asks Audrey, fishing for incriminating evidence.

'Physics, actually,' she replies. 'We were just having a conversation about—'

'Wait, let me stop you there,' David says. 'I'm in the middle of switching subjects. I can point you in the direction of a few guys who would be happy to help *you* out.'

The emphasis on the word *you* is small, but it's still there. I dart a look of warning at him to back off, but his attention is still on Audrey.

Audrey jumps to her feet, yelling, 'Why the hell would you switch out of physics? You need to un-switch.' Her eyes are wide and anxious.

'Excuse me?' David seems as perplexed as I am.

I ask, 'What has David studying physics got to do with anything?'

'You can figure out what happened to me,' she tells David. 'You can get me home. You're the one who is always talking about this.' She mimics a deep English accent, '"It's my life's work, my whole career." Everything you ever achieve is from physics.'

David cocks his head and eyes her, head to toe. 'Is this her?' he asks me in a clipped tone, not taking his eyes off her.

'Yes,' I say as I stand next to him. Both of us face her.

'The girl you met last year at work?'

'Yes, this is the woman who appeared out of a ball of light and vanished—until today. Her name is Audrey.'

'And she's real.' He sounds relieved.

'Of course I'm real.' Audrey scowls.

David asks her the same questions I asked but allows her the time to answer. She gives each one serious consideration and tells him what she told me. He fills her in on his research over the past year, how it has taken him so *long*, how *smart* he is, and that he has a couple of theories he would love to talk out with her. He's is trying to impress her, and she's hanging on every word.

'The noise is the worst,' Audrey says. 'I think I heard it before I saw the light, but I'm not sure. It all happened so fast. The light was blinding. I felt like I was pulled and jolted and falling, all at the same time. I don't know.' She rubs her forehead.

'You've not disappeared yet, and we need to figure out why, how long you might be here and where you're going after,' David tells her.

'I need to go home. You need to make sure when I leave that I go home.'

David stretches past me, takes my bag off the desk and empties the contents. 'Let's go.' He puts the empty bag over his shoulder and leaves.

Audrey looks at me and shrugs and we follow him downstairs. We hurry out the front door and down the street before we fall in line with him.

'Where are we going?' I hiss. We're out in the open where anyone can see her.

'The physics lab. I still have a load of notes in my locker, and if we need to double-check anything, there's a library in the basement.'

She wraps her arms around herself. Shit, I should have given her a coat. She's still not dressed well for February. 'You're wearing the same clothes as last year.'

She looks at me from the corner of her eye.

It takes a couple minutes of speed-walking to get to campus. The science building is tucked at the back of a quiet courtyard, and a few straggling students are still walking to class. I watch the other students carefully. I hope that the light doesn't come back and claim her in front of them. We enter the old sandstone building and our footsteps echo in the high-ceilinged hallway as we head for the grand stairwell.

'Meet me in the basement. Get one of the tables at the back and make sure it's out of the way where we won't be overheard.' David lunges up the stairs two at a time and is out of sight.

In the basement library, Audrey and I find a large table and spread out, claiming the space as our own. She sits down opposite me and fidgets with the zipper on her jumper.

'Try not to worry, Audrey.'

'I have to get home to my kids, Michael.'

'How old are they?'

She studies me for a beat. 'Two, four, five, and seven.'

'Wow, four kids? Boys or girls?'

'I don't think you need to know this. Let's stick to what's happening.'

'I'm just making conversation.'

She leans forward. 'When I get back, will they know I was gone? Do I go back to the time I left, or is time passing there too?' She wipes a tear from her cheek and whispers, 'I don't want them to think I've left them.'

I grab her hand across the table. 'We'll figure it out, promise.'

David approaches us, his arms full of document wallets and piles of paper. He places them on the table with a thud, forcing our hands to part.

'Can't we do this at home?' I suggest.

'There's not enough room, and there are resources here I need to use. We need to spread this shit out and see what's relevant now. I also don't want the guys at home seeing this.' He opens the backpack he filled from his locker and takes out more stuff.

51

The files are the polar opposite of the study notes on my desk. Everything here actually does have an order, although its neatness is masked by its sheer volume. There are notes and drawings, photocopies of pages from textbooks with highlighted passages and handwriting in the margins. David's been busy.

I whisper, despite no one being in the vicinity to overhear us, 'Where the hell did you get all this?' There hadn't been this much information when we were working on this together.

David lines up pens on the table as he answers. 'When we started our research last year—'

'We didn't find anything,' I cut him off, irritated.

'And that pissed me off, so I kept looking.' David places his hands on the notes. 'It's why I was going to switch subjects.' He glances at Audrey, to include her in the conversation. 'This was getting in the way of my assignments. I dropped down to an easier course so I would have more free time for this. Kind of ironic. I find something worth researching, and I have to quit the subject to continue with it.' He cuts to the chase. 'What are you?' he asks her.

'A woman. You?'

'I'm sorry. I just mean if you're not a ghost or an . . . alien . . . ?'

She looks at him through narrowed eyes.

'Then, you're a person, right?' he asks.

'No shit, Sherlock, I'm a person.' She hesitates with her next sentence. 'I'm from the future.'

'How do you know you're from the future?' he asks.

''Cause when I woke up this morning, it was 2016, and you two were in your forties, not your twenties. I was . . . home, then I was . . . out somewhere, talking to a friend, or I might have been on the phone. I'm not sure. The light was so strong . . . and the noise. Then I saw Michael. It's a little disorienting. I was at his workplace first, but he said it was last year.' She looks down at the table. 'Then I was in Michael's room and he was all naked and twenty-one.'

'You were naked?' David asks, eyeing me in shock.

'I was just out of the shower,' I squeak a little. 'I had a towel on.'

She smirks and tries to hide a laugh.

'If you're travelling from one year to the next instantaneously, you must be travelling at the speed of light,' David mutters as he flicks through his folders, looking for something in particular.

'That's what I thought.' My excitement at being right has me nearly bouncing in my seat.

'How am I doing that?' she asks.

'I'm not sure.'

She drops her head and her lip trembles.

'I can make an educated guess, though,' he reassures her.

She lifts her head up, relief on her face. He launches into an explanation, rattling off theories and referring to articles he's read. 'Most of the paranormal apparitions and disappearances have been rationalised by the medical profession over the years categorised as delusions or dreams. Even drug-induced hallucinations, schizophrenia and somnambulism, were all to blame for most sightings. But there are theories about mental possessions, where someone time travels and flirts from one body to another.'

Her face falls. 'I don't think that's what it is. I've spent a lot of time with people who specialise in physics and . . . stuff. There's a theory I've heard, and it sounds like it could be real. I mean, I believed it was possible when I heard it. I just never thought it would be proven or seen in my lifetime, or that I would experience it first-hand. Just a theory, right?' She chuckles softly.

He moves to the edge of his seat, waiting for her to explain.

'You told me,' she says.

'What do you mean, I told you?'

'I know you in the future.' She looks at each of us.

'Stop,' he commands. 'We can't go down this road. We shouldn't know about our future lives. It can cause all sorts of cosmic paradoxes. What if we change something? What if we change the *wrong* thing?'

'I know,' she says quickly. 'You told me that. Some people should only know certain things about their future. But you need to know this. You need to get me home to my family.'

'Go back,' I tell her. 'You can tell us some things about our future, without causing a cosmic what'sitabox?'

'Paradox,' David says.

Audrey takes a deep breath. 'Too much information in the hands of the wrong person can have a devastating effect on their future and the future of people around them. That's why global things can never be changed. If people try and stop terrorist attacks, the information they have and actions they take to stop it could create an even more devastating past. Or if the person in question is of importance to the universe, like a leader or someone of significance, changing their path can have cataclysmic effects on the world. According to David, that is, so . . . could be a load of bull and all.' She smiles.

'Then why are you here with *us*?'

'Everyone is important. Some people can have the whole world handed to them on a plate so to speak, and they never make a difference. Others are always going to be pre-destined to create change, good or bad, in the world. It's those people who need to be careful not to stray too far from the path they are supposed to be on. One slip, and it could have an impact on a lot of people's lives. It's exhausting if you think about the whole chicken and egg theory too much. And the theory has a lot of holes in it. Even Liam thinks so.' She directs her attention to David.

'Hey, it's not my theory. You're the one who brought it up,' he tells her while he scribbles the name Liam, in his notes with a question mark after it.

'It is your theory. You told me. I don't care whether it's right or not. I have a life in the future. I have . . . people who depend on me. Figure this out and get me back to them. Understand?'

David nods. 'You're already having an influence on what's happening,' David says. 'We should stick to safe territory. Figure out why and how you're here. Just the basics until we know what we're doing.' He picks up two books and hands one to each of us. 'See if you can find any quotes or pieces that reference Ethan Bennett.'

I open the book and keep my eyes on Audrey.

'Happy Birthday, Michael.'

'I told you it's not until tomorrow.'

'You don't do the two-day thing?'

'Pha, hell no. I'm not that high maintenance.' Realisation hits me. 'You came last year on my birthday. Although it was my actual birthday then. Leap year and all. We don't celebrate my birthday until the first of March on the other years.'

'Some people born on a leap year celebrate on the 28th of February,' David says. 'It depends on the time of birth. I'll look into it.'

'It was Michael's birthday in the future when I left. What's so important about his birthday?' Audrey asks.

I shrug. Like I know. 'Maybe you're like my guardian angel?' I test my theory.

She emits a full belly laugh. 'Is that the best line you've got?'

I dismiss her teasing. 'I asked for one last year. It was my birthday and when I blew out the candles on my cake I wished for . . . for my life to fall into place. Later that night you appeared.'

'Why didn't you tell me this?' David asks.

'I didn't think it was related,' I hiss.

'What? You wished to be famous?' She finishes the thoughts I didn't have the guts to confess to.

'How do you know that part?'

'You want to be famous?' David asks.

'I wanted to be an actor when I was younger. They have these amazing lives. I decided to hell with it. My family could do with a bit of luck. Let's chase the grandest dream I can think of. My granddad always said if you want something, ask for it, believe it will happen, and it will. And you came.'

'This can't be real.' She closes her eyes and inhales a deep breath.

I take her hand. It's cool, so I rub my fingers over the top, trying to give her a bit of heat. She catches my gaze and holds it. It's intense, staring deep inside me, where we normally try to hide from people. She's not afraid to openly stare at me, even with David seated next to her. And I let her. It relaxes me. It's like she can see everything I am, but still wants to look.

David moves his gaze from me to Audrey and back again.

'You get to be the actor you wished to be, with fourteen-hour days, the never-ending schedule and the paparazzi following you everywhere. But your life isn't your own. People depend on you. You sure you're up to it?' She asks.

I gulp. 'Yes.' Anything has to be better than this. 'Actors are important people in the world too,' I tease. 'People always turn to entertainment when everything else in their lives is crappy. It's a form of escapism.' I shrug. 'Obviously for those of us who can't travel through time to escape.'

'I didn't escape.' She looks hurt.

David tosses the book he is holding onto the table with a purposeful thud. He moves his head with exaggeration from Audrey to me. 'Oh, for Christ's sake,' he says as he leans back in his chair. 'Do you think Mike is important enough in the future for the universe to send you here and guide him?'

She thinks for a moment. 'He's the ambassador of Feed US. It's part of the Charity Starts at Home initiative. It's a big deal. You help out, David. Call in now and then for a chat, gives us money, flirt with the office girl. You know how he is.'

'Hey, I'm sitting here,' David says, pretending to be affronted.

'Just saying.' She smirks at him. 'We've helped millions of Americans put dinner on the table, and breakfast and lunch too.

'We?' I ask.

She gulps. 'I help run the office and organise the fundraising side of things. Get the press involved. You drum up publicity, investors, and donations. If it wasn't for your involvement, we couldn't accomplish half of what we do. Like I said, you're important in a lot of people's lives.'

I sink into my chair. 'Wow. That's, well, a lot to take in. How do I get something like that started?'

'I thought you don't worry about the how?'

I exhale slowly as reassurance comes over me. Apparently, I can make life a little easier for other people. 'Is that how we meet?' I wonder out loud.

She shifts in her seat. 'I knew you before. Well, everyone knows you, being famous and all.'

I sit there, waiting for more of an explanation, and cock my head to the side, willing her to answer.

'My husband knows you,' she blurts too loudly.

'Shh,' David whispers, looking around.

Audrey lowers her voice, and we move closer. 'You started the charity with my husband. Once I met him and got married, I sort of fell into the job. Bored housewife and all.' Despite the joke, tears glisten in her eyes.

'Is he rich too?' I ask.

'Excuse me?'

'I only mean, you look like you have money. And if you work for a charity, your husband must be rich to keep you and four kids.'

'To *keep* me?' Her voice is high-pitched.

'Shh,' David nearly shouts it this time.

'No, no. Not keep you as in stop you from leaving. I mean keep you, so you can afford not to work.' Shit, this is coming out all wrong. She glares at me, her mouth pressed into a thin line.

'Let's move on, shall we?' David saves me. 'Audrey, you've physically travelled through time.'

'Opposed to what, *not* being physically here?'

'Exactly.'

Audrey and I sigh and pinch the bridge of our noses. I chuckle. Is this something she always did or did she pick this habit up from me in the future?

58

'There are documents about possession, people who claim to have travelled through time, taking over a person's body and mind temporarily.' He flicks through his notes as he speaks, searching for a specific page. 'It was classed as a mental breakdown, schizophrenia, or multiple personality disorder. I read it briefly and dismissed it. Your body is here. You're not possessing someone else's body. Are you?'

'No. I'm me.'

'Just checking.' David grins. 'What about yourself? Could you be possessing your younger self in this time?'

'I'm thirty-five, so do I look thirty-five to you in this body?'

'Sure,' I pipe up too quickly, then backpedal. 'Well, you could be younger.'

'Am I sixteen? Are we in Ireland? 'Cause in 1997, I was sixteen years old, living in Ireland with my parents, and probably still grounded for sneaking out to that damn Valentine's Day dance.' She chuckles.

David smiles his big, I-want-to-impress-you grin. 'Did ye get lucky?' he asks in an awful Irish accent.

'What is that? Welsh? Canadian?'

I laugh hard, delighted she's quick enough to make fun of him. Typically girls laugh at his ridiculous jokes, trying to impress him. David darts a look in my direction; he's not used to being shot down.

'And no, you don't look sixteen,' I mumble, staring at the table.

David flips through books, pretending his flirting went unnoticed.

'What's your surname?' I ask her.

She looks at me from the corner of her eye. 'Why?'

'Just thought it might be worth while looking you up.'

'I'm not giving you my surname. You're not going to look me up. We're not going to meet in this timeline until we're ready. Let's put all our focus on getting me home.'

'How did you know she said my name?' I ask David. 'Her back was to the camera, and there is no audio on that equipment.'

It's David's turn to squirm in his seat.

'What? You get a little obsessed, watching the tape over and over again?'

'Fuck off, Mike.' He turns to Audrey. 'I was observing it for research.'

She shrugs and looks like she couldn't care less.

'It was the shock on your face when she reached out for you. I figured something else happened and couldn't work out what. I sent the tape to this guy I know in California. He found me online last year. He's a physics lab assistant and does all sorts of modules and work for extra credit. He's starting a forensic science course, and I asked him for help.'

'You sent the tape to someone?'

'Relax. I edited it so there was nothing out of the ordinary. Told him I thought my girlfriend was cheating on me, and I wanted to know what she was saying, but her back was to the camera. He enhanced it and got a reflection of her lips moving from the main window. He sent it back so I could figure out what she was saying.'

'What about the disruption of physical time caused by the outdated atomic clock time-recording mechanisms?' Audrey asks.

'Hm,' David says.

'Hm? Is that your answer? What the hell does it mean?' I scrutinise them both.

'It's the missing time caused by leap second changes in atomic clocks. Right now, our clocks only measure time. But some people think an element of that recording has a certain control over our perception on the control of time. Something that could, in theory, facilitate time control. Or parallel universes and time travel, if you will. And our perception of things in the universe, after a long time, can become the reality,' Audrey explains. 'There is research being done on the theory that each leap second creates unmeasurable worm holes and universal changes as our reality tries to keep up with the changes. It's David's research.' She glances over at him. 'Proving unbalanced time.'

How the hell didn't she realise, she's been sitting there with a chunk of the answers?

'The world of science is trying their hardest to uncover it,' she tells David. 'You specialise in time and the implications of our inaccurate recording of it.'

'How is time science?' I ask.

Audrey rolls her eyes. 'Our recording of time based on the Earth's rotation has always been slightly off, by the smallest of a decimal,' she tells me. 'Our clocks can't properly record the smallest of changes needed to the exact accuracy. Every so often the atomic clock will create a leap second adjustment.' She turns to David for confirmation, and he nods.

'But the shortcomings of the atomic clocks are creating more inaccuracies. Technically there's all this extra time. Like on a leap year, when we get an extra day. But where does that day go on the years we don't have it? It never should have been there in the first place, and the universe needs to find a place, for this extra time. They used to record leap seconds once a year, and now we're up to twice. Soon, it'll be four times a year, and it's predicted over the next few hundred years, we will need to add leap seconds a few times every month. The seasons are shifting ever so slightly, and everything is getting messed up along with it. Our need to record and categorise everything is causing major problems in our own perception of the universe.'

'And you know what they say about time travel.' David tosses his pencil on the table.

'"It doesn't matter when we figure it out".' Audrey chuckles.

'Why is that funny?' I ask.

'Because,' David says, 'It doesn't matter that there are only a few added seconds so far. In a hundred years, there might be enough to facilitate time travel. Just 'cause we don't have the means of understanding it yet, doesn't mean it's not already happened in the future. And once it's happened, it's all in the past, so to speak.'

'There is something else. David started the research on lost time,' Audrey tells me.

'I thought it was added time.' I'm annoyed they seem to be best buds on this in the future.

'Yes,' Audrey says. 'But it's the theory on where the leap year day goes on the non-leap years. Did I not mention this?' She laughs. 'I remember the first time you explained it to me, David. It was over my head. But it was the time travel and alternate realities that got my interest. I mean, a well-respected scientist talking about how it was all theoretically possible. The more you spoke about it, the more I realised that science was serious about this. That they, too, don't know the capabilities of the Earth.'

'I'm a well-respected scientist?' David's eyes widen.

'There are others involved too. You always get loads of funding for your research. I think it's because of the exposure you bring. TV scientists have taken off, like celebrity chefs.'

'So he's like the Ainsley Harriott of the science world?' I chuckle.

Neither of them laughs. I thought it was funny.

'Ethan Bennett and Stephen Hawking back a lot of your theories, and no one really disagrees with them,' Audrey finishes.

Okay, now I feel like an idiot.

'Professor Stephen Hawking?' David asks.

'I thought we weren't supposed to know stuff about our own futures,' I squeak.

Audrey ignores me. 'A lot of your early stuff was with Ethan. He's your main go-to guy.'

David drops his gaze to the books on the table. It's as if he's struggling to decide whether or not to ask her more.

'Kinda gets you hooked, doesn't it?' I tease David. 'You find out some stuff, and all of a sudden, you want more . . . but wait. Didn't you stipulate a stupid rule about talking too much to the time travelling guardian angel?'

'David,' Audrey says, cutting over me. 'You need to know this. You need to get this right.' Her voice cracks. 'I have no idea what's happening to me, and I need to get home safely.'

David looks lost, staring at the pile of notes on the table. 'Maybe this is why you are here, to help me discover this. I mean, if I told you in the future, maybe it was to make sure you tell me here, in the now.'

'I don't want to be your little guinea pig,' she whispers. 'I didn't want any of this.'

'Audrey, you're a time traveller. You must be here for a reason, something worthy,' David says.

'I thought we established her reason for being here,' I jump in.

David continues as if I haven't spoken. 'The fact that you have come to Michael twice,'—he glares at me—'makes me think you are connected to him somehow.'

My heart beats faster. At least what I feel for her isn't a weird obsession in my head.

David runs his hands through his hair. His frustration leaks out as hostility. 'Come on, think,' he hisses, trying to control his volume in the library. 'The cosmic forces of the fricking planet chose you for a reason and sent you to us twice. There has to be a bigger reason. Are aliens going to take over the planet unless we stop it?'

He's being sarcastic, but Audrey answers him seriously.

'I've never heard you speak about aliens before. You're always so concentrated on time. I just need you to send me home.'

'Home?' He sounds a little mad. 'If it's all right with you, I'd rather keep you here since you're the most amazing discovery science has ever encountered in the history of FOR-EV-ER.'

Audrey's eyes fill, but the tears don't spill. If I stick up for her, maybe he will redirect some of his anger to me instead.

'Hey.' It's all I can think of saying. Fuck.

Audrey scrapes her chair across the floor as she stands. Resting her hands on top of the table, as if she is preparing to take him on in a fight, she leans over. 'I'm a PER-SON and I have somewhere to be.' She turns on her heel and leaves.

'She's not your latest science project,' I snap when she's out of earshot. I get out my seat less dramatically than Audrey.

'Hey, wait, man,' David says. 'She's not going anywhere. Just give her a minute. She'll be back.'

'How can you be so callous with her?'

'How much of this do you think was my discovery?'

'What do you mean?'

'What came first? Did I discover all this the first time round and tell her what I know, or do you think she came here with the information and told me for the first time? Do I owe her a huge favour?'

'I have no idea, but I'm pretty sure you're a selfish prick.'

Audrey is halfway up the basement steps that lead outside when I catch up to her.

'Don't go,' I call after her. 'Don't listen to him either. He's a geek at heart, really. Once he gets his claws into something academic, he finds it hard to concentrate on anything else.' Out on the grass, the cool breeze is calming and helps clear my head. I glance around. 'Where *are* you going?'

Audrey rubs her forearms and shivers. 'I have no idea. Do you ever get that anxious feeling deep inside your throat, like you're about to choke because you should be somewhere important but can't remember where? I feel like. . . I'm missing something.' She chuckles. 'I normally have my kids swinging out of me. My arms feel so light being on my own.'

David appears at the top of the stairs and looks from me to Audrey.

'I can't go back in there,' Audrey tells him. 'I feel like my head is going to explode with all the information.' She places a hand over her left temple. 'I get stress headaches, and it feels like my skull is crushing in, right here. I need to go lie down. Maybe if I fall asleep, I'll realise this is all one big dream.'

'It's okay.' I place a hand on her forearm. 'I'll bring you back to mine for the night.'

'Now there's an offer no one ever refused,' David quips, but Audrey doesn't bite.

She nods and I lead her down the path.

David and I exchange worried looks. 'I'll take her,' he says. 'You go pack up our stuff. I can go over a couple of more questions I have on the way, just in case.'

Panic sets in. What if she disappears in the middle of the street? What if I don't get to say goodbye? I jog down the steps to get back inside the library, before the anxious feeling in your throat Audrey described, seizes hold of me. I stop in the middle of the steps. I'm not sure where my important place is right now. The fear runs all the way to my stomach, flipping it upside down. Audrey is looking over her shoulder at me as she walks away with David.

'Don't go anywhere.' I smile, hoping she can hear my concern rather than David's earlier threat.

She looks like she might cry.

Shit. I wait until she walks around a curve in the winding path before I continue inside.

As I jog through the library, I repeat a mantra in my head. Please don't go.

CHAPTER
Seven

I catch up with Audrey and David as they open the townhouse door.

'That was fast,' David says.

'Didn't want to waste any time,' I say, catching my breath.

'Get some food,' David tells me as we pass the kitchen. He takes the bag filled with our library notes out of my hand and keeps walking.

I swallow my irritation and watch David and Audrey ascend to the second floor. David has much better culinary skills than me. What the hell is quick? In the kitchen, I find a loaf of bread and make sandwiches. I tuck a bottle of juice under my arm and take three glasses from the cupboard and go upstairs.

Audrey has already lain down on my bed. Her eyelids keep fluttering open as she fights exhaustion.

David opens my bag on my floor and silently spreads out his notes again. David quizzes me this time, jotting on a pad as I reply.

'We have a lot of work to do here. It might take a while, but with the three of us, we'll be able to get through it a lot quicker than I did last year. Plus, we have a new source of primary information.' David tosses a pencil at Audrey.

'That's a good idea, but I have nothing left in me right now,' Audrey says, closing her eyes.

'You can't go to sleep,' David whispers.

'We don't all get excited over science, David,' I tell him. 'She probably needs the rest.'

Audrey keeps her eyes closed, but I see the hint of a smile on her lips.

David whispers instructions to me on what books and journals to search in and how to categorise our findings and cross-check with him.

It's only a few minutes before Audrey's breathing is deep, and her arm relaxes beside her face.

'God, she must have been exhausted,' I say, staring at her.

'Hm,' David mutters into his book.

I catch sight of the clock next to my bed. 'Shit. I'm meeting my parents for dinner tonight. I have to go.'

David's mouth drops open ever so slightly before he speaks. 'You're joking, right?'

'Sorry,' l say as I back away. 'I need to go. It's a four-hour drive for them and I can't ask them to waste the petrol money. If I say I'm sick, my mum will want to hang around. It'll be quicker this way.'

'Don't do anything stupid.'

'Like what?'

'Like ask for another guardian angel.'

I scurry down the stairs. Did I cause Audrey to travel through time? I can't tell David everything. He'll think I'm crazy. I close the front door quietly behind me. Hopefully, by the time I get back, David will have sorted out the science side of things. Walking down the street, I breathe deeply into the mist. It's bloody freezing. I hope Audrey doesn't disappear while I've . . . disappeared on her. I'll have the quickest dinner ever and go straight back to studying with David. Wow, there's a sentence I never thought I would have the conviction for.

'**Sorry we couldn't come** tomorrow on your actual birthday but some leap year babies celebrate on the twenty-eighth as well,' Mum says as we settle at the table in the pub.

'Just as well I'm no longer a baby.' I try to block out the drone of loud chatter from the tables around us.

Dad hands me a menu, and I realise I'm starving. My hangover is back. The thought of food makes me think of the charity. What the hell must it feel like to be so hungry, you need to depend on someone else's handouts?

'What you having?' Dad asks.

I scan the choices for the cheapest option. 'The burgers look good and they already come with chips. That'll do me nicely.'

'Anyone want to share a starter?' Caitlyn asks.

'No,' I tell her. 'Just order dinner.'

If the life Audrey has told me about plays out, then my parents would never need to worry about bills or petrol money, or where the most economical place to have a family gathering would be. 'So tell me, what's this great idea George is using to increase advertising reach in the off-season?'

Mum tells me all about our neighbour's ideas. I'm nodding in the right places, trying to hide my frustration. They're working fifteen-hour days for basic wage and to pay the bank and the tax man. Their eyes are baggy and their skin is blotchy, and they look exhausted. I hope what Audrey said is true. Maybe in the future, we can make a difference in people's lives.

'Sounds like a good plan,' I assure Mum when she stops talking.

It's while catching up with nonsensical conversation that a stab of loneliness comes over me, and I realise how much I miss my family. After dinner, a chocolate fudge birthday cake arrives at the table, and Dad sings Happy Birthday.

Here it is. I gulp.

'Are you making a wish?' he asks.

Despite David not taking me seriously, I should have asked him exactly what to say. Fuck. 'I want, enough time to work my life out.'

My parents look at each other. It is a cryptic wish. Mum worries about everything; our health, our grades, but mostly about being the perfect parent and having the perfect kids. They'll probably talk about what I wished for when they get home tonight. They'll be concerned about whether I'm coping well at university. If I was crying for help, or if I was suicidal or on drugs, even if they should visit more or see me less.

'*And* to be a rich and famous actor,' Caitlyn says.

Everyone laughs.

'You've not given up on that one, right?' she asks. ''Cause I'm counting on you too, remember.'

'Let's have cake and then we can walk down by the river,' I suggest. I don't want to chase them off. After we're finished, I claim the leftover cake to take home for Audrey and David.

David is sitting at the desk in my room when I get back.

'Did she wake up?' I ask, relieved to see Audrey's still with us.

'She hasn't moved.' He hands me a book.

Sitting on the floor, I lean against my bedroom door, every so often glancing at Audrey to make sure she's okay. Just after midnight, exhaustion takes over. I toss the last book down and rub my eyes. I don't bother to mark off the book, as per David's instructions. It's going to piss him off. 'We need to call it a day.'

David eyes me over the top of his notepad.

'We're only going to get sloppy.' My thoughts return to something Mum said earlier about leap year babies celebrating their birthday the day before. 'Where do you think the twenty-ninth of February goes on the non-leap years?'

'I don't know.' He closes his notepad.

'It's a lot of time just to vanish.'

'Technically it doesn't vanish, it's categorised differently. We'll put it at the top of the list for tomorrow.' David stares at Audrey. 'You better sleep on my floor. If you take the couch, the guys will know someone is in your room.'

I never thought of what I might have to explain to the guys or Jessica, if someone tells her I have a girl here.

David's radio alarm turns on at 9:00 a.m. We both jump. Fuck, we should have set it earlier. Is Audrey still here? We run up the two floors to my room and sneak inside to avoid waking our flatmates who share my floor. Audrey's still asleep in my bed, and I relax.

'I'll make breakfast,' David whispers.

The sound of the door shutting stirs Audrey awake. 'Hey.' She sits up and takes in her surroundings. 'Oh,' she says with disappointment. 'So, not a bad dream after all?'

'No. You hungry? David's an amazing cook. It's the main reason I keep him around,' I joke. 'He's getting started on breakfast. I have a feeling we're going to have another busy day.' I perch on the end of the desk, as Audrey stretches.

'Where are you from, anyway?' I ask.

'Dublin.' She clasps her hands together, pushes them out, and cracks her fingers.

'I've never been to Ireland.'

'You should go.'

I nod. I'm not sure if she's telling me to go, or making conversation.

'What's it like in the future? Do you have cars that fly?' I'm mocking a little, but in all seriousness, I want to know.

She shakes her head.

'Am I really famous in the future?'

She does her slow exhale frustration thing, and I smile. We have this other little connection.

'Yes, you are. Maybe I'm the reason you're famous. I could be the one who shapes you and gets you ready for stardom. You used to tell me so much about your life and career, how you saw your future rolled out in front of you like a road. That you had help and guidance. Do you think you were in some way trying to prepare me for this?'

'Of course.' I shoot off the desk. 'I'm going to make sure I tell you everything about my life, so you can tell me now. It's so perfect. When we meet in the future, you won't know this has happened, but I will, and by god, I'll make sure we stay friends, so you know everything about me.'

Audrey stares at me. 'So that's the only reason you would be friends with me in the future? So you can benefit from it in this time?'

'Of course not. I'm sure we're good friends. We'd have to be.'

'You know, in the future, you're a lot less caught up in yourself. Even being so desirable and all.' The sarcasm is clear.

I don't want Audrey to think I'm an asshole. 'I want to make sure I can make a difference for my parents. You have no idea how much they struggle and not having me around to work for them is taking its toll.'

'You have to live your life too, Michael. You can't stay at home forever.'

'Tell me more about the charity. It must be pretty good to tear you away from your family every day.'

'I'm lucky. I only work one day a week, and I can do everything else from home. It's the best part about the technology explosion. Access to the Internet, emails, syncing calendars. A lot of people work from home in my time. Even in the middle of changing nappies, or at the park with the kids, I can check for updates or notifications.'

'Sounds busy.'

Audrey laughs. 'It is, but I prefer it that way, and at least I get to be at home.' She drops her gaze. 'My husband works every day, and although we travel with him if he's on location, he's still gone most of the time.'

'Location?'

'He's mostly a producer now, but he has done some directing too. And the charity takes up some of his evenings.'

'How did I get involved with him?'

'I'm not sure. Through work, I think. I told you, by the time I got on board, he had most of it up and running. I just took over the scheduling and things.'

'So, what are the specifics I'm going to have to do?'

'You set up a fund to provide American families with necessities. You started in California, because that's where you were based at the time and able to approach local donors. Those in need receive an allocation of food based on their income. We own warehouses in easy-to-reach locations, where people can purchase groceries at cost price. After a few years, the charity grew.'

'Wow, that's impressive. And it's all happened from donations?'

'Yup. You use your position to get large cash donations from people who can afford it. Businesses donate goods and services, and some people donate their time to help with logistics, or advertising and fundraising.'

'Why doesn't the government help if people can't even afford to eat?'

'There's state welfare, but many people fall between the cracks. It takes weeks, in some cases months, before families receive any help. It's fucking ridiculous, Michael. Two months with no money to feed your kids, and all the government does is blame it on paperwork and promise that all payments will be backdated. The utility companies won't wait. They're cutting people off. And what the hell do you tell your kid? "Don't worry, honey. I know you're hungry, but in three weeks, we can eat again." Fuck that. It got worse after the recession. Something more is needed.'

'There's going to be a recession?' Chills run through me. Grandad lost his business in a recession. That, and the fact that he split his time with Gran. Eventually he was forced to take a crappy job for crappy wages.

'It's going to be tough. You lose a little in comparison to a lot of people, but you get through it.'

'But there are so many people relying on me. If I do this and I succeed, my family is going to need me to keep them afloat. What if it all comes crumbling down one day? I couldn't deal with letting them down. With letting you down.'

'You've never let me down, Michael.' She smiles.

'I remember one year, business was slow in the B&B. I heard my parents arguing over money once,' I confess. 'It was something silly. I think my dad bought an expensive brand of milk, or he'd gone to the more expensive shop. Things got so tight they were screaming over milk. I mean, who wants to worry about the price of milk? Mum cried for ages that night. I understand now, it was the pressure of trying to keep a business, a house and family afloat, but still, she was devastated. A few bad weeks, a quiet season, and we were broke. It happened so easily. Throw in a recession, and the whole country is going to be fucked.'

'That's why we're trying to help,' Audrey says. 'We use your profile to highlight the issues, encourage donations, and hold fundraisers.'

'And your husband? He must have made a name for himself in Hollywood too.'

'He did. You attend all sorts of events and even run three marathons. The best part is it's still growing. We're moving across states and hopefully we can cover the whole of the USA in the next couple of years. Maybe even the UK, too.' She winks.

David nudges the door open with his foot, balancing three cups of tea in his hands.

'Ah, just in time.' I take two cups from him and pass one to Audrey.

She hands it back to me. 'Can you make me coffee?'

'Sure. Could do with a stretch.'

It takes no time to re-boil the kettle and make the coffee. I return along with last night's leftover birthday cake and hear whispering through the crack in the door. Audrey's glorious accent is rushed and anxious.

'You shouldn't be doing this,' David says.

'I told you, David. I don't know much about these things.'

'Me neither. The stock market isn't my thing.'

'That's exactly my point. In the future, you own a lot of stock in commercial products and tech companies everyone knows is successful. Even me.'

David snatches a sheet of paper from Audrey's hand. 'Just give me the list.'

'You need the cash to keep your research going. You've already done it, so just grow a pair and do it again.'

David storms out of the room, nearly knocking into me as he goes.

'Ooh, cake.' Audrey takes the tinfoil wrapper out of my hand.

'What was that all about?'

'Nothing. Just some things he needs to do to get me home.' Audrey settles back on my bed and crosses her legs. 'Where were we?'

'Me. Famous. Rich. Charity. All is good, forever and forever.'

Audrey smirks. 'Very funny.'

'How quickly can you make this happen?'

'I don't think I just wave a magic wand, Michael.'

'Try it.'

She laughs. 'Abracadabra!'

'I don't feel any different.'

She scoffs and bites into a slice of cake. 'Your mum's cake is the best, you know.' She takes her coffee and heats her hands around the cup. 'You don't become famous until you're twenty-five. You're in a few movies before then, which you always said taught you a lot, but no one was screaming your name in the street until, what, 2001? Let's start at the beginning. You're twenty-one, right?'

'So, what did you learn from *The Cat's Hat*?'

'I have no idea what that is. Is it my first movie?' Trying to quell a burst of adrenaline, I hop up on the desk.

'It was your first movie. I've never seen it but you filmed it when you were twenty.' There's panic in her voice as if I should already know this. 'You said David's friend in university got you the job. You met him at your birthday party, and he was looking for extras for some minor roles. Didn't you meet him? God, what was his name?'

Oh, crap. 'My birthday party last year?'

'Probably.' Her face falls. 'Why, what happened?'

'I kind of didn't go to the party. Well, I did, but I was so freaked out after you showed up, I went straight outside. Then Jessica arrived, and I stayed with her the whole time.' I slide off the desk and stand. I'm too embarrassed to say I spent the night with a girl. I blew the start of my career because of a girl.

Audrey panics. 'Don't you see? Even me being here only a few minutes has changed your future. What else did I change?'

'We need to get organised,' I tell her. 'You need to give me as much information as you can.' I won't screw up again. There's too much at stake. 'I want the career. Nothing else.' Grandpa couldn't get the balance right either when it came to relationships. I'm going to make sure that never happens to me. 'No wife or kids getting in the way.'

'Excuse me.' Audrey sounds mad but at least she isn't panicking anymore. 'I'm a wife and I don't think I *get in the way*. Actually, those who succeed in life often do so because they're not alone. Have you ever thought of that? Besides, what makes you think I have any control over how any of this plays out? It's your life. You're the one who is going to have to make those decisions.'

'I know this whole time travel thing must be hard on you.'

She darts her eyes at me. 'Really, you think?' She gets up from the bed and sits on the desk chair. She twirls the chair to face me, as if she's ready for an interview.

'So . . .' I hesitate, trying to find the right words. 'On the personal side of things, I don't want to be tied down. I have to work hard, do what I need to do and go anywhere I need to go, without worrying about a girlfriend or answering to anyone.'

She smiles tightly. 'It must have been lonely for you.'

'That's the first mistake my Grandad made,' I explain to Audrey. 'He met my gran and spent all of his time on her. Eventually his business dissolved right in front of him. He had to take his old job back at the warehouse, and it killed him to walk in there every day.'

'How do you know it killed him?' she accuses. 'Maybe he loved going home to his family every night.'

'It must have killed him. To have your dream career and lose it because you dropped the ball when some girl came along?'

'She wasn't some girl. She was your grandmother. Your mother wouldn't be here if they'd never spent time falling in love. Neither would you.' Her eyes fill with tears. 'A whole lifeline dissolved. Now that's a butterfly effect.'

'I don't want to have any distractions. To be a successful actor in Hollywood, I'm going to have to work hard and—'

78

'Don't forget writer, producer, director.' Audrey throws her head back and spins on the chair.

My heart stops. When it beats again, blood pounds in my ears. 'What?' The word gets stuck in my throat.

'Sorry.' She stops spinning. 'You have your own production company. I did mention that.'

'No, you didn't.'

Audrey comes to sit at the side of the desk with me, placing her hand on my arm like she has done before when I'm freaking out.

'You said you wanted it all, right? Why would we have stopped at *actor*?'

'I don't know where to begin.' I look down at my feet.

'Twenty-one was a big year for you. You dropped out of university for no reason, your mother said, got on a plane, and moved to LA. I used to be so in awe of your courage to just pack up, not knowing what might happen. You never said you had a time travelling guide helping out.' Audrey nudges me teasingly.

'Well, sorry to burst your bubble.'

'I'm still in awe, Michael. To give up your safety net, and break your parents' hearts and their bank account a little. To leave your friends behind and move to another country, all because some strange woman appeared out of thin air and told you to. How do you know I'm not trying to destroy your life?'

'I just know.' I can feel how important she is and is going to be in my life. 'You're too nice to be that mean to someone.'

'Thank you.'

The smell of bacon and sausages cooking downstairs stirs my stomach awake. I hope David will bring it up. It's not like we can take Audrey downstairs for a communal breakfast. 'There must be hundreds of people moving to LA looking for the next big break.'

'*Hmmp*, thousands more like. When I met you, you were already famous. People send you scripts and offers. Sometimes they beg. You used to talk about the auditions you did in the beginning and how awful you were.'

I stare at her wide-eyed. 'Gee, thanks again.'

Audrey laughs. 'You get better. Thank god. But I'm not sure how it all started, or how you get an audition. Stella organises that for you.' Audrey lets out a long breath. 'Maybe you should have asked her to be your time travel buddy.'

'Who's Stella?'

'She's your agent. Simon Lewis's daughter?' Audrey waits a beat. 'She's a big deal in the agent world. Only has a few clients, but she always makes a success out of those she represents. She's picky about who she takes on. Maybe she was with you in the beginning too. Maybe that's why I'm still here. My first time travelling challenge. Once you have Stella, things will get easier.'

'Do you have her number or how to get it here, in 1997?'

'We can't call her. She won't take you seriously if you ring her up and say, "Hi, I'm still in England, but can you be my agent?"'

'How do I get in touch with her then?'

'I think she lived out in Lakewood when her son, Max, was younger. She worked in Cici's store on Rodeo Drive. It's this fabulous independent clothing boutique. I shop there sometimes. She mentioned the commute taking up so much of her day and earning crap wages. A lot of employees rely on commission in the US, but Cici helped her through a tough time. She always has us go in and buy something when we're out that way.'

'I can't afford to pop over to America to meet her.'

'I know . . .' She drops her gaze and nudges me. 'But you need to get over there. It's where they have Hollywood, you know. I know you're worried about your parents going bankrupt without your help but it isn't for long. You pull them all out of it. You always do.'

I snap my head up. I want to argue with her, tell her she is wrong, but I can't. If I speak, I'll choke.

Her face whitens at my reaction. 'I'm sorry. I shouldn't have landed that on you. Honestly, I'm still trying to figure this out in my head. What's happened already for you, what you know and what you don't. What and how to tell you.' She moves to the bed, avoiding my gaze when she crosses the room.

'Do they lose the B&B? It's not just a business, it's our home.' I follow her to the bed pleading like she's the person taking it away from us.

Audrey nods and places a hand on my cheek. 'But you get it back,' she says firmly. 'You need to be brave, Michael. You can do this.'

I gulp the lump in my throat and try to be the man she knows in the future. I need to do this. I'm ready to do this. 'What do I ask Stella?'

'*Tell* her you want to be an actor. No, tell her you *are* an actor. Fake it till you make it, right?'

'Fake what?'

'Everything.' Determination takes over Audrey's voice. 'If anyone asks if you can do something, like horseback riding or snowboarding, you either say *yes* or *I'm taking lessons*. Got it?'

'I can't do either of those things. If I tell them I can, what if they ask me to show them? They'll expect me to be good.' I'll make a fool of myself.

'Calm down. God, it's strange seeing you so full of self-doubt. Whatever they ask just do it. In the future you get lessons and help if you need to, but generally, you just go along with everything. It's all acting, really. Pretend that you can. Everyone else does it, so don't panic.'

I tut. 'Easy for you to say.'

'Most importantly, don't take *no* for an answer, from anyone. If you want something, you have to make sure you get it. And you need to start working on those people skills. Kissing ass is the key to success in this business. And hard work. And talent too, I suppose.'

'That's not a tall order at all.'

'You get pretty good at it.' Audrey chuckles. 'You always get what you want,' she says more seriously. 'Usually, when you meet someone, you ask them about themselves. In fact, I think most people do that. It's polite. But you do it more in-depth than other people. It's what makes you so desirable—your ability to make others feel important.' She shifts on the bed, twisting around to face me, and takes my hand. 'When people are around you, you make them feel like they are the most interesting person in the room. It's a psychology skill. Obviously something you're gonna learn over time.' She squints at me. 'Try it. See what you can get from me.' She looks at her hand in mine and lets go, allowing me to focus on the first lesson on my new life.

I clear my throat. Find out more about people. Make them feel special. Got it. 'What kind of stuff do you like?'

'That's no good,' she scolds. 'That's something a twelve-year-old boy asks a girl when he's trying to get his first date.'

'Well, what the hell do you mean?' I'm appalled at her comparison.

'First off, you compliment someone. Not about how they look or that they're attractive. People don't have much control over that. Not true beauty anyway. It starts small. You make them feel like their decision to buy and wear a particular outfit was a good one, and you build it up over the conversation or over time if you have it. Making bigger compliments on the bigger decisions they've made in their life. Their choice in car, partner, kids' names, the house they bought in the neighbourhood they live in. You link it to yourself and how you would love to live there, or you thought about calling your kid that name.'

I raise my eyebrows at her. She can't be serious.

'People look up to you, and they respect you. Basically, you're telling them you're envious of them and then they feel like they've made good choices. They know they can make more good decisions, like invest in your company or make donations to your charity.' Her pace speeds up at the end. 'You manipulate people into doing the things you want them to do, but in a nice way.'

'That's a little freaky.'

'I think this whole thing is a little freaky,' Audrey says.

I laugh at the ridiculousness of the situation. My heart skips a beat when she joins in. Her entire personality flows out of her truly beautiful face when she laughs.

'Go on, compliment me.' She nudges me with her elbow. 'Subtly and not corny, like that guardian angel crap.'

'Em . . .'

'Nothing?' she mocks.

Nothing but the fact that your beauty is completely and utterly striking. I hope you're my guardian angel, that you're

83

mine. 'I don't know. You have lovely eyes.' She does. She doesn't try to hide any bullshit behind them either.

'Oh my god, don't ever use the "you have lovely eyes" line.' She rolls those beautiful brown eyes at me. She doesn't flinch or look away.

I'm not brave enough to tell her it wasn't a line. 'I know nothing about you.' I shrug, not wanting her to make fun of the things I like about her.

'Yes, you do. You need to pay attention straight away when you meet someone. I've travelled here from the future and told you this morning that I'm from Dublin, yet you've asked me nothing else. You've not even asked how I am, how I'm feeling, or what it's like to travel through time.' She's practically shouting now. 'You could tell me that I was brave. You could tell me not to worry, not to panic, because you would make sure I was okay. That you would look after me and get me home to my kids. That you'd make sure I'd be okay here. Hell, you've not even asked me what Ireland's like.'

I nod, ashamed. How can I tell her I do think about those things? I just didn't want to lie to her, tell her it would be okay in case it wasn't. I wondered if she was scared or how much she missed her family, but I didn't know how to get her back to them. Would we still be friends in the future, like she said, or would she have to deal with this on her own? What if she returns and time has passed without her? What if days, weeks, months have gone by? If she tries to tell her family what happened, would they think she was crazy? What if we can't get her home at all?

'You're risking so much. What if I'm no good? If I fail, this will all be for nothing.' My face falls as I try to hold my entire family's future together.

84

She smiles. 'It's not all raw talent. I mean, part of it is, but you're also going to have to learn. No one expects you to know everything. One thing I do know, Michael Knight, is you're very good at your job.'

I look up to see if I can read those eyes. She's still smiling at me, and I automatically smile back.

'You look good when you smile,' Audrey says. 'You should always smile. In the future, you're dealing with pressure from work and the charity too, I guess. You don't smile as much as you used to.'

'So I'm a miserable bastard then?' I'm annoyed she might think this of me.

'No. Just busy and tired. You still have your looks, though, and to be a totally hot forty-year-old man in Hollywood is pretty impressive. The girls who used to follow you around have grown up and are now women who follow you around.' She smirks. 'All you need is confidence. You have everything else. You're hard-working. The talent is there, the looks and personality are there. And believe me, it's a rare thing to be a nice person in Hollywood. People remember you for that. Hollywood's a tough place. You're gonna need as many allies as you can find.'

'I'll remember that.' I rub my head in frustration.

Audrey massages the side of her head. 'There must be some force out there that needs you to turn into the man you are in the future. You make a difference in people's lives and you need to be the Hollywood superstar to make that happen. You said so many things over the years, that now, it makes more sense. Like you were trying to tell me that I was there with you in the past. I might not be here to change something. What if I'm here because I was always the one who helped you in life? Think about it. Would you have had the guts, all on your own, to take that chance and move to America? Leaving your family broke without your aid?'

I shake my head.

'So between the two of us, we need to make sure you do everything the way you always did.'

'Piece of cake, you're from the future, you know everything.'

'Not exactly. I know a lot about you, but there are details I don't necessarily know. There may have been some stories or information over the years that I sort of never listened to.'

'You never listened?'

'It's not like I knew how important it was going to be. We'd be at a dinner party with David and other people in the industry who are always talking about their struggles and how they got their careers started. After a while, you sort of tune out.'

'So you're telling me, we might screw up or make a wrong decision, and my whole career, and the charity depending on that, might not happen?'

'Without the exposure you bring to FEED US, thousands of families might suffer from that butterfly effect. As much as you were an ambassador, you had a lot of input in the concept and start of it. It might never get off the ground without you. And don't forget your personal life. Imagine not moving to America and your family life being diverted in the wrong direction. This is the path we need to lead you down, to make the world a little bit of a better place. Because believe me, there are some people out there who are alive because of you.' Audrey takes my hands, a show of our union. 'If I get to be the one responsible for turning you into the man you're going to be, then I'm gonna take that opportunity and make damn sure we don't screw it up.'

'So we'll concentrate on my life. We'll let David concentrate on the physics side of the time travel. Maybe the theories on the why and the how to you being here will meet in the middle and we will figure this whole thing out.'

The light bursts from the side of her head, hard and fast, and I drop her hands to shield my eyes. It swallows her up, half blinding me in the process. The screeching noise pierces my ears as the light retreats.

She's gone.

I touch the air where her face was only a few seconds ago. Everything is still. No swishing and swooshing as everything settles into its rightful place. No warmth, no glow. I collapse face down on the bed, passing through the space where she vanished. I smell her on my sheets, the one piece of evidence that she's a part of my life.

Directly below me, David bangs around the kitchen as he pulls out plates and cutlery. What will he make of Audrey leaving so suddenly? I can't believe he didn't hear the noise of her departure. In fact, none of the guys heard it yesterday morning, either. Maybe it's only loud because I'm always so close to her.

Will she come back next year?

David comes up the stairs, running two at a time. Something's wrong. I leap off the bed, and as I pull my bedroom door open, I hear the source of his concern. Jessica's here.

'I can find my own way to his room,' she tells him.

It's our anniversary. I forgot.

David rushes past me and into the room. He thinks Audrey is still here, and I don't know if he is trying to hide our supernatural finding from Jessica or help save me from an argument. I meet her at the top of the stairs and kiss her on the cheek.

'What's with him?' she asks.

'He needs some notes and stuff. You want breakfast? I was cooking up a storm downstairs.'

'Smells great,' she says.

I take her hand and tug her down the stairs.

David makes up a plate of food while I get two mugs from the cupboard.

'I need to speak to you when you're finished here,' he tells me as he leaves the kitchen.

Jessica puts bread in the toaster, and I decide this is as good an opportunity as any to take the first step of my new life.

'I'm moving to America,' I say, impressed with my newfound confidence.

'What? ' She looks confused, and I don't blame her. 'For how long?'

'Forever, hopefully. I'm dropping out of uni. I want to be an actor.'

'Since when?'

'I've always been interested in movies. You know that.'

'Everyone loves movies, Mike. It doesn't mean you drop out of a great university and move halfway around the world.'

'I'm doing this. I wanted to tell you so we can say goodbye.'

'Goodbye? You're not even going to ask me to come with you?'

'You should stay here and finish your degree, stay with your family.'

Maybe I was never supposed to hook up with her in the first place. I was supposed to meet that movie guy at my birthday party. Audrey said we'd already changed parts of my life. Maybe we have interfered with Jessica's destiny too. Maybe she was meant to be with someone else.

'Oh.' She clears her throat and pushes her cup across the worktop.

'I mean, let's face it, it's not like we were in love.'

Her arm rears back and delivers sharp, piercing stings all over my face. Christ, she slapped me. I never thought I would be the guy who got bitch-slapped. She storms out of the kitchen and down the stairs as I touch my face to assess the damage. Shit, that didn't go well.

At least when I tell my parents I'm leaving, I know my mum won't slap me.

I bring David fresh tea as a peace offering for making him wait.

'What the hell happened?' he asks as soon as I open his bedroom door.

I set the tea down on his desk and tell him about Audrey's discussion and disappearing. David takes notes as usual, and makes me go over it again and again.

'What were you working on?' I ask.

'I wanted to see if there was a way to harness her time travel ability. Work out if it is something we or Audrey could control. And more specifically, bring her back.'

'Made much progress?' I ask, pointing to the pile of rubbish on the floor.

'I realised it was mostly all crap, so in a sense, yes. Some things sound right from what Audrey described, or theoretically sound right. There are a couple of people I want to speak to. They have theories that might take us in the right direction. Jessica gone?'

'Yeah,' I say, feeling gutted. 'I told her I was moving to America. Audrey told me to go.'

'America? Whereabouts?'

'LA, where all wannabe actors go,' I quip.

David closes the book he was reading and flips the back cover open to show me the bright white spotlight on the cover. He turns the jacket of the book towards me so I can read the bottom.

Professor Ethan Bennett
is currently the Chair of the Physics Board
at the University of California, Los Angeles,
where he conducts research
with his son and University Fellowship, Liam Bennett.
The family live in Los Angeles.

'I'm coming with you.'

CHAPTER

Eight

Four weeks later.
Sunday, 30th March, 1997
18:00 (GMT)
Blackpool, England.

The bus driver turns off the motorway for Blackpool and slows at the bend taking David and me through the city. An unexpected twinge of excitement runs through me when we stop at the traffic light. Round this corner is the beach, and the view gives me an incredible sense of freedom. David's sleeping head bangs on the window as the bus moves, and we go over a bump.

'Aww,' he grunts. 'This is exactly why I avoid public transport.'

I chuckle. 'You've avoided public transport because you've never needed to use it. We're nearly there.'

'After five hours, I would like to think so.' He sighs. 'We should have taken the train.'

'Yes, but we're saving our money, right?'

'Right,' he says determinedly. 'Five weeks on a student budget, no dates, no new trainers. It sucks.' He kicks his not-so-old trainer off the chair in front of him.

I stretch my legs into the aisle, and they crack in relief. 'It's exhausting,' I agree, 'sitting here for hours doing nothing.'

'I'm not doing nothing,' David says. 'I've been evaluating things in my head.'

'Of course you have,' I scoff.

The road to the bus station takes in the entire stretch of the Pleasure Beach. David's like a puppy on the way to the beach. He's practically bouncing in his seat, taking in the fairground lights and market stalls spilling onto the street. The sun has almost set, and the dull evening background makes the scene picturesque. The pier is lit up by the golden sun, and the coloured lights from the attractions announce the start of the nightlife.

'I still can't believe you've never been to Blackpool. Seriously, every kid in the world has spent a weekend here.' It's the reason so many B&Bs like ours manage to survive.

'My parents insisted on educational, cultural experiences on holiday.'

'There's culture here,' I say, without pausing to think.

'Can we go to the beach tomorrow?'

'Sure, although it will be freezing. And if we go too early it will stink of donkey shit from the animals' beach runs. Don't think you're ready for that experience. Better to go later in the day.'

The bus pulls into the terminal. We grab our backpacks and dash down the aisle. I'm dying to get off this bus, even if it means confronting my parents sooner about leaving the country. Once outside, I take a deep breath, inhaling through my nose. The smell of cool, sea-salt air is homely.

'Ready to face the inquisition?' David asks.

'I'm hoping, with you here, they won't go too crazy when I tell them I'm dropping out.'

'You should have just called them like I did.'

'Yes, but your parents were pleased about the offer of a full scholarship in America. My parents are probably going to kill me.' The realisation turns my stomach, but my feet are itching thinking about moving somewhere new. 'Come on, let's get this over and done with. It's only a half hour walk home.'

We stroll the short distance from the bus station to the B&B, with David reiterating the latest theory he wants to discuss with his new lab team in the States. 'I know a couple of people over there, but I'm going to have to wait until funding kicks in to bring them on-board.'

I'm nodding as he speaks. It does sound interesting, but why he asks for my opinion is beyond me. It's *all* a little beyond me.

The walk home brings back memories. Growing up here, riding my bike home from school, running around the street markets and stealing bags of candy floss. The smell of mini doughnuts frying at a stall makes me miss this place.

We turn off the main strip and jog down a long road of large detached B&B houses, each with its own unique and inviting signage out front. All neighbours, competing for business and trying to stay afloat. The dark green sign with gold trim reading **Knight's B&B**, sways back and forth in the strong sea air from the west. The sign matches George's **Hodge's B&B** notice next door in size and colour and calligraphy. This must be the first step in their sister hotel idea. Nothing else looks like it's been worked on yet.

Caitlyn spots us from the living room window. She wails like a lunatic before disappearing from view and opening the front door to greet us. 'Oh my god, what are you doing here?' she screeches, giving me a tight hug.

'Just visiting. Why are you so happy to see me?' Caitlyn's been behaving, like, well, a teenager these past couple of years. It's nice to see she still likes me.

'Of course I'm happy to see you. Only this time I didn't need to sit in the car for an eight-hour round trip, listening to Mum and Dad bickering the whole way.' She shudders in mock horror. 'Hi, David. You hungry? Dinner service is just finished, but I'm sure Mum will cook you something.'

Sitting around the dinner table, my parents and Caitlyn sip tea as David and I polish off a plate of cheese-topped lasagne and homemade brown bread. I'm soaking up the remainder of the Bolognese sauce with the crust, clearing pathways on the plate with each sweep, when David drops the bomb.

'Mike wants to let you know about our plans to move to America.'

The last mouthful of dinner gets stuck in my throat, and I have to force the bread down with water before I can talk.

Mum is the first to speak. 'America? George's daughter went off on one of those student summer job things one year.'

'Bit pricey, though, for those airfares,' Dad cuts in over Mum's story. 'You'd need to get a better paying job before buying plane tickets and sauntering off for the summer.'

'Not for the summer, Dad. A few years maybe. David's been transferred to the Physics Department, and I'm going with him.' My nerves have made us sound like a couple. 'We're leaving next week.'

'Next week? You'll fail the year and lose your funding, and won't be able to finish your degree.' Mum slams a hand down on the table. 'Why don't you wait until the end of the academic year and arrange a gap year? It's only a couple more months.'

'David has a thesis he wants to pursue and there are professors he knows who are willing to supervise his studies. He has a place to stay, and I'm going with him.' If we don't move mid-term, David won't be able to start at his new university until September. That's five months away, and Audrey told me to go now.

'Why on earth would you do that?' Dad clunks his mug on the table.

'You know I always wanted to be an actor, and what better place than America to start?'

'When did you want to be an actor?' Mum asks, narrowing her brow.

'Does no one ever listen to me? I've told you my last two birthdays that's what I want to do.' I push my empty plate away in frustration. 'Why the hell did you think I used to do those stupid shows on the pier? I like acting. It's pretty cool. The summer shows never paid well enough for me to give up working and do it full-time.'

'Well, if the boy wants to move to America and be an actor, I say let him,' Dad says, dunking a biscuit.

Dad's so nonchalant he probably thinks I don't have the guts to go—or the money.

'Don't be ridiculous, John.' Mum's voice rises in pitch. 'How can he move to America at the drop of a hat? If he gets in trouble, we can't help him.'

'We can't even help him out here. No point in worrying about him in America,' Dad argues.

David interjects. 'I'm going to be funded for my research. Plus, my parents are happy to send extra money over. I already told Mike he can sleep on my floor until he gets started. It'll be nice to have a friend there with me.'

'We don't need any handouts,' Dad states.

'It's not charity,' I cut in. 'I've been saving for a while,' I lie. 'David's offer is only if I need it.' I catch David's eye. If they find out he cashed in the business-class ticket his parents bought for two in economy, they would be mortified they're not in a position to help me.

'We went to London yesterday and picked up our visas.' We were pre-approved but still had to stand in line for six hours. 'I have to stay enrolled in university for the following year, so it's not like I'm totally dropping out. It's like a student gap year. I've made arrangements to put my module credits on hold, and I can pick them up if I come back.' I smile at Mum, then at Dad, trying to reassure them. Returning home is something I have no plans to do.

'Michael.' Mum turns to me. 'The only reason we are managing is because your rent is covered by your student grant. How can you afford to pay rent on your own, with other bills too?'

'Don't,' Dad bellows. 'Don't ask him to stay here and help us with our bills. We got ourselves in this mess. It's up to us to pull through. He's a grown man now, Jean. We can't stop him.'

'He's not a grown man. He's a boy. He's our boy.'

'I bloody well know who he is, Jean. You don't need to remind me, like I'm some idiot.'

'I didn't say you were an idiot.'

'You just said—'

Caitlyn rolls her eyes at me and leaves the table. David and I swiftly follow her to the family room. We can hear Mum and Dad still bickering through the wall.

'What's that about?' I ask Caitlyn. 'I thought I'd be in for more of a lecture, rather than them going at each other.'

'Ugh, they're always like that these days. I swear, I was cleaning room four the other weekend, and I heard them arguing over free-range eggs. They're crazy.' She shakes her head and shudders dramatically.

I chuckle. Caitlyn will fit right in when she comes and works for me.

Five days later.
Friday, April 4, 1997
07:45 (PDT)
Los Angeles, California.

The first step outside the airport terminal makes me feel like I'm slowly going to suffocate. Warm, dry air hits my face and runs through my nostrils as I take a deep breath meant to calm me. The sun is already bright, and David slips on his sunglasses with a grin. I should have brought a pair from home. I wasn't here to relax and sunbathe, but I never expected to need them just walking around.

'Let's get started on the rest of our lives.' He slaps me on the back and strides towards our free designated transport.

Our hostel for the next month has sent their bright yellow coach for airport pickups. Stepping inside, my heart sinks a little. The bus is like an old tin can, with '60s-style seats; plastic and not one bit comfortable. The interior looks like it was ripped out and someone forgot to replace it. It's a shell of a vehicle, with seats screwed into the floor.

'This is not exactly setting expectations of the accommodation high,' I say. We sit near the back and drop our bags on the floor. The bus fills up fast with young backpackers chatting excitedly. The busier and louder the bus gets, the more ominous the feeling in my gut grows. David twists in his seat to chat with the girls behind us about their recent experiences in Fiji. I'm only half listening, trying to convince myself that something amazing and life-changing is going to come from this trip.

Someone's bag bangs into my shoulder as they squeeze past, forcing me to lean all the way into David. Everyone has one or two pieces of luggage, which have to be placed on the floor or on their owners' laps, making the bus more uncomfortable and overcrowded. There's no air-conditioning, and once the doors close and the bus pulls out, the various smells, from stinky feet to stinky people, are overwhelming.

David turns back to face me. 'Feeling the harsh realities of making it on your own?'

I sink into the seat, overcome with failure already. 'I didn't even make it into the country on my own. I'd still be stuck in England if it wasn't for you and Audrey.' I pull the backpack on my lap closer to my chest to protect myself from prying eyes. The last thing I need is for people to see my fear. I'll be finished before I even start.

With the bus on the motorway, I get a feeling for the size of things over here. I release my grip on the bag, and David and I gawk out the window. The chatter on the bus dies down as I expect most people are admiring the new landscape, like us. The buildings must be twenty stories high and clustered together, letting strips of the early morning sunrise slip through. The cars are bigger, and the lanes of the motorway are ready to swallow up anyone not strong enough to hold their own. It's overwhelming but thrilling. There're no limits here. Everything and everyone can be as big as they want to be. Nervousness disappears and I relax. I imagine living here and realise for the first time, I can do this.

The bus pulls into the sweeping driveway of the hostel, which has a view of the motorway exit. Crappy location but huge impressive building. It must be at least ten times the size of the B&B. It looks like an old American-style motel, which would have been high-class in its time. The peach paint is crumbling around the edges, but I'm excited. If this is cheap for LA, I'm dying to see what money can get you.

'Let's go check out our new home.' I follow the line of backpackers off the bus and through the doors.

'The girls on the bus told me to pay for a week at a time. You still get a discount, but then you're not committed for a month,' David whispers as we stand in line at the reception desk.

'Good idea.' My gut churns. I've no idea when I'll be able to afford to send money home to my parents again. This move has already added to their financial difficulty. I have enough to cover rent for the first month and an extra seventy-five dollars in my wallet. I'm praying it goes far.

'We can move into UCLA campus next week when I matriculate. Fuck it, there's no point spending money we don't need to.'

'You sure you don't have a roommate?'

'Yeah. It was more expensive, but my parents didn't mind. We'll pool our money together and see how long it lasts,' David suggests.

I nod. That means he will be helping me out considerably more. We'll be financing ourselves like a newly married couple, struggling to make ends meet.

The reception area is a vast empty space that stretches the entire length of the building, with doors at the back wall leading outside to the bedrooms.

'Our room is on the second floor,' David says as we climb the stairs. He stops at the top of the first floor as I continue up the second flight of stairs.

'Mike, in America the first floor is called the second floor.'

I trudge down the few steps and join him outside the room. 'It's too early to even explain that one to me.'

'The ground floor is called the first floor.'

'Seriously, dude. Too early.'

'Lift/elevator. Pavement/sidewalk.' He chuckles. 'I could go on all day.'

I glance over the railings, to the pool, which is unexpectedly clean. Next to it is a fully stocked bar and lots of plastic loungers.

Despite the early hour, people are already lying out sunbathing. I don't think I've ever seen so many student-types up this early in England. The weather really does make a difference. I didn't notice David open the bedroom door and go inside until I'm facing the dark and dingy room.

'Okay, this is why it's cheap,' I say.

'You pay per bed per night. What did you expect?'

'You pay by the night in the B&B, and this is not what we give people.' I cough as stale air gets caught in my throat. 'How hot does it get here?'

'Just wait until noon, when the sun is high. You'll appreciate the cool breeze of the morning.'

'Breeze?' The curtains are still drawn to keep the light out. The room is packed to the edge with five sets of bunk beds. If you opened the door the whole way, it would hit one of the beds and probably the feet of whoever was sleeping in it. Aw, crap. That person is going to be one of us. Some people are still sleeping in their beds, while other bunks are already claimed with people's belongings.

David throws his bag on the top bunk. 'Mine,' he shouts.

I glance at the lower bunk, but I'm distracted by the old, stained carpet under our feet. I dump my bags on the floor. 'I don't even want to sit on that bed, let alone sleep on it.'

There is a crooked picture on the wall that looks as old as the carpet. I nudge the frame to straighten it and get a glimpse of much cleaner wall. 'How the hell can we sleep somewhere so dingy?' I whisper, trying not to wake anyone. The picture slips back in place, still crooked.

'Let's go downstairs and figure out how to find Stella,' he suggests. 'At least by the pool, we can fool ourselves that we are on a Spanish holiday with an apartment all to ourselves.'

'Fine. It will distract me from thinking about what the hell the showers will probably look like. My sanity can't handle that experience yet.'

David gets two cans of Coke from the vending machine, and we sit at an empty table by the plastic loungers. He leans back and stretches his arms, checking out the girls by the pool. 'What do we know about Stella?'

'Not much. The Arts section in the library only vaguely covered her father's career. The rise, fall, and rise again. He spent a few years at the top, directing real box-office successes.'

'Like what?'

'*Twenty-Three Two*, *Blue Sky* and a couple others I haven't seen. I tried to get Tina to order them before I left, but it never happened. Then in the early '80s, the media reports stopped. I can only assume his career crashed, or he stopped working for a while. He showed up again in the early '90s with his own production company. A much smaller one with a lower budget, but his own all the same. It's pretty impressive, even though the tabloid report made it sound like failure.' I take a swig of Coke.

'I suppose the size of your success is what matters in Hollywood, rather than success itself.'

'Check this out. The report focused on Stella running the office for him and hinted he didn't have enough cash to hire more employees. But that's going to help us. If Stella used to practically run the place back then, by now she's going to be a fantastic agent. I think I can forge a connection with her. I know what it's like to help your parents with their business. You get to know the ins and outs quickly. How to juggle three people's work and get paid a little some weeks and not at all on others. Stella's hardworking and loyal to her family. She's like me.'

'But where are they now?'

'I don't know. The information dried up after that. The only solid lead we have is from Audrey, about the woman who owns the store on Rodeo Drive. She's still Stella's friend in the future.'

'At least we have an address.' David rises from his seat.

'Is this it? One street? What the hell is all the fuss about?' I say. Rodeo Drive is nowhere near as big as I expected. It looks like any other high street, albeit a little wider and well-groomed. The pavements are cleaner and the stores have security guards dressed in suits. The cars parked on the street look like they cost more than some houses, but even Blackpool strip is longer than this.

'Look on the bright side. We'll find the shop much quicker.'

Most of the stores are still closed, and we take our time perusing the street and crossing at the junction of a huge, expensive hotel. I'm in awe at the contrast between it and our motorway hostel. *This* is an impressive building. The pristine and polished hotel doesn't have a speck of paint or fabric out of place. The steps leading up to the main doors are trimmed in gold, and the doorman's uniform is classic and flawless. I want to go inside to see what it looks like. 'Do you think we'll ever get to stay in places like that? Bet they have clean showers and carpets.'

'Maybe.' David smiles. 'All depends on you from here on out, doesn't it?'

'After I get a job, maybe we could go in for a drink. Lunch even.' I should call home, tell Mum to paint the outside of the B&B. First impressions do make a difference.

'There it is.' David points across the road.

The pink-and-white sign on Cici's Boutique sways in the breeze, and my heart beats faster as we cross the street and approach the door.

David steps aside and lets me take the lead. I curl my hand over the glass door handle and push. The door doesn't budge. 'It's locked,' I groan. The white engraved opening hours on the glass panel attached to the wall says they open at ten. My watch says nine-thirty. I yank the handle a couple more times in frustration. 'I can't believe we flew all the way from England, and the bloody store isn't even open yet.'

'Relax. There's a bench behind us. We can sit and wait.'

The sun's getting stronger, and sweat forms on my brow. 'We've travelled for twenty-one hours, waited around three airports, took two buses to get here, and they can't even open the bloody store at nine.' I flop onto the bench and cross my arms. It makes me even warmer, so I unfold them, place my elbows on my knees and hold my head, trying to calm down. To sit in the sunshine and wait would normally be pleasant, but frustration makes me irritable.

'It's no big deal,' David says as he settles next to me.

The bench is surrounded by flower beds overflowing with colour. Christ, even the streets are better here.

David nudges me and points to the red convertible driving past with two young women in it. 'Not an awful place to wait, eh?'

I look up at the sky, expecting the answer to hit me, but all I see are palm trees lining the roads, emphasising the vastness of American streets. After about ten seconds, I jump up and pace. 'What should I even say to her?'

'Just be yourself, Mike, only a little smoother.'

'Gee, that helps.'

'Looks like you don't have any time left to be thinking.' David nods towards a young woman walking down the street.

She slows down in front of Cici's and is searching through an expensive-looking handbag while balancing a coffee cup in the other hand. I've learned in my one short morning that a lot of people are beautiful here. She's not much older than us. Her hair is the right shade of blonde, without that cheap dyed look a lot of girls seem to think guys like.

Taking a set of keys from her bag, she smiles courteously at us before unlocking the door.

Shit, that was my opening. I step forward, trying to make eye contact. 'We're looking for Cici. We were told we could find a friend through her. Stella Lewis.'

She pauses with her hand on the door handle before she turns to speak. 'We don't hand out employee information. Who sent you?'

Oh, come on. Don't start this confidentiality crap now. I'm so close. 'I'm Michael, and this is David. We know Stella, sort of,' I mutter.

'Huh. Look, I don't know what he promised you, but I never got any money. Why else would he leave? You should go too, or I'll call the cops.'

Shit, she thinks we're here for money? To steal from her, or rough her up?

David steps out from behind me and puts his hand out to introduce himself. 'Sorry for the confusion. I'm David Wembridge. This is Mike Knight. I think there's been a misunderstanding. We're not here for anything untoward.'

She stares at his hand but doesn't shake it.

David continues to smile and drops his hand, not taking offence or losing his confidence. 'We've just flown in from England, and a friend of ours told us to meet up with Stella. We have business to discuss with her, and we weren't sure how else to contact her. If we could give you our contact information, maybe you could pass it along to Cici when she gets here.'

Why the hell didn't I just say that?

'What do you want to talk to Stella about?' Her tone has softened a little.

'It's sort of private.' I say.

'I'm Stella,' she says. 'Tell me what you want, and don't waste my time. I have to get inside and start work.'

'*You're* Stella?' I squeak.

David sighs.

'We're here about your acting agency. I know you're the best. I'm an actor, and I just moved here. I need you to represent me.'

She relaxes. 'I'm not an agent.' She smiles like this is enough to send us on our way. 'I'm a sales assistant.' She pushes the door open, and once inside, she locks it while avoiding our eyes.

'She's not an agent?' I ask David.

David puts his hands on his hips and tries to say something but comes up short.

'She's not a fuckin' agent,' I yell. 'Audrey said Stella was my agent.' I stalk back to the bus stop. 'We never even considered she might not be an agent yet. I can't believe we came out here with only half a plan.'

'We're going to figure this out, Mike. It's only day one. Things aren't going to fall into place hours after we stepped off the plane.'

David manages to calm me down before we board the bus and head back. The stop is a ten-minute walk from the hostel. When we turn the corner, I see the peeled peach-painted building, and the stark difference from the hotel on Rodeo Drive slaps me in the face. 'I can't even afford to live in shared accommodation for long. How did I think I could support my entire family for the rest of their lives?'

'It's going to take time,' David says. 'Remember how long it took for the idea of a career change to sink in? And we had Audrey to help us. We'll go back tomorrow and talk to Stella again. She might meet us for coffee, like an interview or something. She's pretty damn hot, don't ya think?'

'Don't,' I warn. 'I'll go by myself tomorrow. She's going to be my agent. I need to start making things happen for myself. Besides'—I playfully jab him on his shoulder—'don't need you charming the pants off the one person who can help us here.' I need to prove to myself and to Stella I'm a take-charge kind of guy.

The next day.
Saturday, April 5, 1997
09:30 (PDT)
Los Angeles, California.

I'm ready to leave the hostel as David slides on his sunglasses and follows me out the door. 'I told you I want to do this myself.'

'I want to take you somewhere first.' He digs in his backpack and hands me a leather sunglass box with some sort of logo emblazoned on it. 'You're gonna need those. We're going to be here for a long time.'

Standing on Hollywood Boulevard outside Grauman's Chinese Theatre, I'm speechless. It's surrounded by tourists taking pictures of actors' hand and footprints in the cement. Why didn't I bring a camera?

'I figured you needed reminding what this is all about,' David says. 'You think yours will ever be here?'

'I have no idea,' I whisper. I don't know what I should be thinking anymore. I don't know if I can handle any more pressure.

'We're not finished yet,' David says.

We cross the road and follow the stars' names along the Walk of Fame, dodging other tourists doing the same. I smile when I see fellow Englishman Patrick Stewart's name alongside American actors like Eddie Murphy and Jack Nicholson. How much work did these actors have to do to make it here?

David approaches a handful of people waiting by the side of the road and pulls out his wallet.

'Two, under the name of Wembridge.'

A man wearing a blue cap embroidered with *Star Tours* consults his clipboard. 'Ah good, we've been waiting for you. Right, folks, everyone on board,' he shouts.

We climb into the white minivan. The leather seats are comfortable, and the air conditioning is blasting. David and I move to the back, allowing the family and an older couple to take seats closer to the front.

'Tour of the stars' homes.' David laughs. 'Can't come all the way out here and not go for a drive around our future residence, can we?'

I glare, hoping the others didn't hear him.

'First stop is the Hollywood Hills and the famous Hollywood sign,' our tour driver says enthusiastically.

'Well, if that's not a sign, I don't know what is,' David jokes.

'I'm sure every would-be-actor has thought the same thing.'

An hour later, we have driven as close to the Hollywood sign as we can get, and Bill, our tour guide, has given us info on hiking trails if we want to get closer. We have driven around Beverly Hills and into Bel-Air to view the outside of the even more expensive homes. We slow down near the gates of a property on a hill. Bill takes over the speaker phone. 'Now, folks, you might recognise this particular home from the TV show *The Fresh Prince of Bel-Air*.'

The family up front pull out cameras to take pictures.

A car horn honks loudly right outside my window and a white convertible overtakes us.

'Some of the locals don't like the tour buses coming up here, so we're going to keep moving along,' Bill says, pulling back onto the road.

'I don't know why they call it a tour. All we can see are the gates outside the houses,' David says.

Sometimes we get lucky and get a glimpse through the gates. The homes are beyond huge. They must have at least ten or twelve bedrooms. The gardens are impressive. I used to cut the grass and deadhead the flower beds at the B&B during the summer months and it could take the best part of the day. These grounds are easily twenty times the size and in much better condition.

'Hey, Bill,' I call. 'How many people would work in a home this size?'

'That depends on how much the owners are willing to do themselves,' Bill answers through the microphone. 'Here, they wouldn't be seen doing much. They would probably have a pool guy, a maintenance man, a gardening team, someone to detail their cars, a housekeeper, and a lot of folks have a full-time chef. You've got to remember, a lot of houses out here double as party and entertainment venues, so there are standards to maintain.'

My stomach falls as I think of the need to employ staff. Imagine having to make sure I earn enough to keep paying people's wages.

The minivan takes a detour around Rodeo Drive, and everyone else departs for photographs at the street sign. I get up, and my shorts stick to the back of my legs. Ugh. Outside it's hotter, but the sense of freedom to stretch my arms and legs is worth it.

'You go talk to Stella,' David tells me. 'I'll get back on the bus and see you at the hostel later. Good luck, man.' He pats me on the shoulder.

'Thanks. I'm going to need it. And thanks for this.' I point to the tour bus. 'It was great.'

He grins. 'See any houses you like?'

'Shut up, dude. No need to jinx us.' I glance at my watch; it's nearly twelve. 'At least I won't ambush Stella when she's opening up again.'

As I continue my walk down Rodeo Drive, two girls raise an eyebrow at my clothes and trainers. I need to borrow some of David's jeans and shirts if I'm going to be around here a lot. I touch the sunglasses he loaned me earlier. Who knew that expensive sunglasses could be comfier? I wonder if you automatically feel at ease decked head to toe in designer gear.

What the hell can I say to Stella? How can I compliment her without it coming across as a pickup line? I need to say the right thing so she will talk to me. A guy brushes past me and his shopping bag slams into my side.

'Hey, watch it,' he yells, striding past.

God, why is everyone so rude on this side of town? The street is busy this time of day, and everyone I pass is either carrying huge designer shopping bags or dressed like they can afford to. There are a few tourists, who look as out of place as I must. I pass a family, and they nod a polite acknowledgement. We both know we are only visiting here.

I pause outside the door to Cici's and take a deep breath, bracing myself. Before I can push the door open, someone pulls from the inside and greets me enthusiastically.

'Hello there,' she says, inviting me in. Her impeccably clean cream skirt and top fits right in on Rodeo Drive. Her welcoming smile seems genuine. I suppose if you want to sell designer clothes to the rich, you need to look the part.

'Hi,' I manage. I don't step inside. 'I'm here to speak to Stella?' It was supposed to be a statement, but it didn't come out that way. I feel like I'm hovering on the threshold of a girl's house, asking her parents' permission for a date.

'Come in, come in. She's out back.'

I enter the store and am cooled by the air conditioning. This has recently become my all-time favourite invention. The store is spacious. A group of women are examining dresses on sleek black clothes rails. There doesn't seem to be a men's section. Thank god. I don't need to pretend I'm interested in buying something.

'Mike.' I offer my hand, and she shakes it firmly.

Cici leads me to the black polished counter at the back of the store. 'Are you here to take Stella out? She's not dated since, well, a while. And such a handsome boy you are.'

My cheeks burn with embarrassment, and I'm not sure if it's because a lady my mother's age has called me handsome or that she thinks it's okay to call me a *boy*.

'No, no, I'm not here to take her out. Well, I was going to ask her to go for lunch. Not like a date or anything. I have some things I need to talk to her about.'

'Well, if you're not interested in a beautiful young woman, other people are going to get there first.' She waves her hands around theatrically as she talks.

The mention of a beautiful woman makes me think of Audrey. I wonder where she is right now. 'It's a business proposal. I'm an actor, and I know she has experience in the industry. I need an agent.'

Cici's eyes widen.

'Part-time, of course. Nothing that will interfere with her job here.' The last thing I need is to piss off her boss by trying to poach her services.

'No need to panic, dear. I would be delighted for Stella to return to a better paying job. It's no secret she needs the money, but you know her and the movie business,' she says light-heartedly.

She assumes I know Stella better than I actually do. I decide not to lie but smile politely.

Cici calls Stella in the back room. While waiting for her, Cici tells me how great an employee Stella is, and I am trying my best to think what else Audrey mentioned about Cici's boutique.

'. . . and you're British, Michael. How very exotic.' She swoons.

Not if you're British. 'Just Mike,' I tell her.

'How long has Stella been working here?'

'Not long after her dad, you know?'

No, I don't. I smile tightly, knowing by her hushed tone that Stella will be mad if she overhears this.

Stella appears through thick black curtains hanging behind the cash register, slightly out of breath and straightening her hair. She stops when she sees me. 'I told you yesterday I'm not interested in anything you have to say.'

'I just want to have a chat, see what I can offer you.'

'Stella,' Cici scorns. 'Don't speak to such a nice young man in that manner. It's your break now anyway, so go on out with him and don't be so rude. He's British! They don't stand for any of that impoliteness.'

Stella looks at her watch. 'It's not even twelve-thirty. I don't go on lunch till two.'

'Take half an hour now and take the rest later.' Cici points to the door. 'I won't have any arguments in front of the customers. It's unprofessional.' She saunters off to assist her customers.

'There's a Starbucks down the street. Let's make this quick,' Stella says as she marches out the door.

I order a coffee, and Stella asks for something with lots of words in it. All I catch is *non-fat*. It's my first opportunity to charm her the way Audrey taught me. 'Nice choice,' I say as I hand over brand-new, crisp, American dollars.

The only time I'd seen American money before was when George's daughter was heading to Wyoming on a summer visa a few years ago. She took all her savings to the travel agents and ordered her money in advance. When she got it, George stopped by to show us. "Feels like monopoly money, and they're all the same size," he said as he passed them round. Dad wasn't impressed.

The cashier hands me less change than I was expecting for two drinks. Shit, this place is expensive. Mental note, don't come here often. I stand next to Stella, waiting on our order. A few minutes of awkward silence pass, and I alternate staring at the floor and out the window. Our drinks are placed in front of us, and I sigh in relief. Stella's looks incredible. It's coffee of some sort, that part I manage to decipher. It must be cold, as it is in a clear plastic cup filled with ice and topped with cream, toffee sauce, and a long, thick green straw. It reminds me of ice-cream sundaes at the pier.

I carry the drinks to a leather couch next to the window. I'm disappointed as I place my regular hot coffee on the table. I thought I would fit in drinking coffee. The complexity and fast-paced ordering makes me feel inferior in the everyday setting of a cafe. Instead of sinking in and relaxing, we perch on the edge of the couch opposite each other.

Stella gets straight to the point. 'What do you want with me?'

'I'm an actor. I have a friend in England who told me about you. You're going to be the best agent in Hollywood.'

'I'm not an agent. Not even close.'

'Not yet, but believe me, you will be, and you'll be great at it.'

She shrugs and doesn't make eye contact with me.

Where is her resistance coming from? 'Did your dad's company fail again?'

Stella stays silent.

'It wasn't your fault. I know what it's like to work for your parents. I know what it's like to feel guilty when it all comes crumbling down. But in the end, it wasn't your responsibility.'

Her eyes dart to me, but she doesn't raise her head fully. 'Then why does it feel like it was?' she asks.

I smile. 'Because you're a good person, and good people feel like crap when bad things happen to those they love.'

'She wound it up after he died. Sold it off to the highest bidder and kept every last cent for herself.'

'I'm sorry.' I've intruded on a family tragedy. I don't want to ask what happened. I don't want to ask who *she* is. I've been insinuating I know her family, and I don't want her to realise that all I know is her name.

'Thank you. It's getting easier each year. It's Max I feel for. My dad would have been a great father figure for him. I know people judge him about his decisions in the end, but he was a good man.'

She turns her attention to her drink. 'I've already lived the Hollywood life. It's not as sparkly on the inside.' She twiddles her straw.

'Just think how you can take that experience and turn it around for both of us. You're in a unique position. You were exposed to the inside workings of Hollywood, and I bet you met loads of contacts when you worked for your dad. Plus, you've already seen success and failure, and you know the things that make it happen. Imagine having it all again. I mean, look at your life. Is this what you always dreamt it would be?' I rest my arms on my knees and play with my coffee.

She thrusts the straw into her cup. 'There are plenty of agents in LA. Find one who will represent you and be on your way.'

'I don't want *any* agent. I want you.'

'Why?' she grumbles.

'Because you're going to help make my future. It has to be you.' Audrey's assertiveness is infectious.

'No,' she says flatly.

'I'll pay you more than the going rate,' I tell her because I'm desperate.

'Can you even act?' She raises an eyebrow.

I don't miss a beat. 'Yes.' *I think*. Fake it till you make it.

Stella looks like she is thinking things over. 'I can't just decide to be an agent. You need an office, which I don't have, and you need clients, which I don't have. And you need experience.'

'Which you do have,' I interrupt. 'You don't realise it, but you do. You know more than you think. I can be your first client. Can't you work from home till we get going?'

'We?' she asks.

'If we're going to take a chance on each other, it's only fair we both work at it. Look, I can help with the setup. Neither of us is going to make any money till I start working. We need to move as fast as we can. Believe me, I'm going to be Hollywood's next big thing. I'm going to make millions, and as my agent, so will you.'

'I don't have the time. I have Max, and I work full-time. Add the commute, and I'm exhausted.'

Audrey told me not to take *no* for an answer.

'After work and weekends then.'

'I have a child. When I get home, I don't just sit around. I'm lucky if I get a chance to shower by myself.'

'What about asking for a day off from the store? Or get a childminder.'

'I can't take time off. I'm a single parent living in a home I can't afford, with my mother, who's also broke. I'm sorry, but I don't think I can do this.'

'I'll get a part-time job and cover the day's wage you'll miss. That will help with the bills, right? Give you time off work to be my agent. I can make up the difference.' I need a job anyway. I don't have much money left. 'We'll make sure we have the same day off. You can let me know what else needs to be done, like assistant work and I'll do it in the evenings.'

'Why are you so desperate to have me work for you?'

'Just say yes. What do you have to lose?'

Stella stares at her coffee.

'I know your dad was hot stuff or whatever in the movie business. This could work out.'

Her head snaps back up. 'My dad was "hot stuff" until he lost it all. I mean everything. He divorced my mom, and we lived on state welfare while he tried to rebuild his life. I was pregnant and scared. You know what he did then? Gave it all away to his fucking mail-order bride. When he died, she got everything. The only good thing was that everyone who was in my life for the money went away too.'

She bends over the table and whispers with an evil tone, 'You really want people to screw you over for your money? 'Cause this is the right place and the right career path to go down. Friends are rare in life, and when you're young and rich and vulnerable, everyone wants a piece of you.'

I clear my throat. 'Look, if this is going to work out, let's be straight with each other. I'm going to be a success, and everyone will know who I am. My movies are going to be box-office successes, and Oprah is going to have me on her show many times. Guys are going to want to be my friends, and girls are going to want to get in my bed, and I might even acquire a stalker or two, so I need an agent who can handle it all.

'I need to know who to audition for. I need to be told what to do and how to improve. Proper guidance, not someone who shows up once a year to see how I'm doing. I need to know whose ass to kiss and where I can find that ass.'

'Well, look who just turned into a diva.' She laughs. 'I gotta love the confidence. If you can do half of what you say, we'll be home free.'

'So you're in?' After a moment's silence, I push her again. 'I can do this, Stella. I just can't do it on my own.'

'Maybe,' she whispers.

'Maybe?' My heart beats faster with excitement.

The door swings open, and Cici rushes in.

Stella jumps from the couch. 'What's wrong?'

Cici is pale. 'Max was in an accident. He's at St. Mary's Medical Centre.'

Stella grabs her bag.

'Your mom rang the store. He fell in the park and split his head open. I have a cab outside.'

Stella is already near the door as Cici follows her out.

'I billed it to the store, just get to the hospital.'

The door chimes as it closes behind them.

I sink into the couch and stare at our empty cups. Max will be fine. Audrey spoke about him in the future. Well, in her past. I wonder how old he is in Audrey's time. How long can I stay here before they kick me out? There isn't one comfy seat at the hostel.

A newspaper left at the table next to me catches my eye. I look for the job section. 'Excuse me.' I beckon the passing waitress. 'Is this the best paper to look for jobs?'

The waitress smiles at me. 'Hi.'

'Hi.' I grin. 'Employment section?'

She places her tray on the table and perches on the arm of the sofa, keeping my gaze. 'What do you do?'

'Actually, I'm an actor,' I tell her. 'That girl was my agent. She's setting stuff up for me, but I need a job in the meantime to cover the bills.'

She's still smiling at me.

I should say something else. I give her a discreet once-over, trying to find something other than her good looks and supermodel height to compliment. 'I like your . . . trousers.' Shit, it's out of my mouth before I can stop myself. What the hell kind of compliment was that? Audrey wouldn't be impressed.

'Oh, trousers.' She laughs, tossing her head back. 'You British are so cute with your words. Let me talk to the boss. We could use an extra person on the first shift. I'll make sure he puts you on with me so I can train you.'

Being a young English boy might work well for me here. 'That'll be great. I knew LA would be full of friendly people.' I drop the newspaper on the table. 'I'm Mike Knight.'

'I'm Sophie. You know, this could be good for you. Lots of people from the movie industry come in here. You might get to know a few.' She winks and takes off.

Wow, did I just manage to convince her I was an actor and successfully flirt at the same time? This is turning out to be a wonderful day. The waitress returns with a huge smile on her lips. 'We can test you now. Give us two hours to see what you're like. If the boss likes you, we can get you on the schedule this week.'

'Great.' I can check in on Stella and Max after. If the accident and emergency departments are anything like England, they will be there for hours. They might need some help. It will let her know I'm serious about taking on running the business and splitting the work between us.

Sophie gives me a brand-new, spanking-clean uniform to start my training as the newest Rodeo Drive barista. Only in

America could they give such an exotic sounding job title to someone who works in a cafe. Coffee shop, I correct myself. Critiquing my new look in the full-length mirror on the back of the door, I try to straighten the wrinkles in the apron from being folded in the wrapper. I hate uniforms. They're so rigid.

Tina let us wear our own clothes in the video store. The last uniform I wore was in my after-school job at Harry's Fish and Chip Shop on Blackpool Pier before I left for Cambridge. It was a second-hand, brown-and-red striped, slightly too big shirt. It came with a smell and permanent grease feel. Uniforms were expensive, and you couldn't expect a new shirt when you started work. You had to earn the privilege of a new shirt. Three years and no new shirt. The thing was wearing thin when I was asked to return it for the next guy.

Here I am, after two days in the land of opportunity, and I'm the owner of crisp new trousers, or pants as I have been told, a white shirt, and a long green apron.

Staring in the mirror, I don't know how I should feel. I've segued from one low-paying job to another.

Sophie pushes the door open and nearly bangs into me. 'You're already dressed. Thought I might get a sneak peek at the fresh blood.'

Fresh what?

'Follow my ass out here.'

Christ, I'm going to have to learn a whole new lingo. I hope the customers don't speak like that.

Twenty-five minutes later, and I wish I had a notepad. Thirteen different blends of coffee, and I'm expected to know them all. I thought coffee was black or white, sugar or none. Why did people even put cream in there? What's wrong with milk? You could get low-fat, half-fat, no-fat. Every customer knew exactly what they wanted, and there seemed to be some personal satisfaction in ordering super fast to see the barista fumble with keeping up.

I manage not to screw up too much, thanks to Sophie. She's stuck so close we keep bumping hips.

'You're doing great there, newbie.'

Sophie bumps me again, and I spill coffee all over the counter.

'Ready for some advertising?' she asks as I mop up the mess.

When your manager asks you to do something, they're not actually asking. Sophie hands me a massive brown, fluffy pile of clothes. I hold it up to get a better look at it. It's a jumper. Oh god, it's a suit. One of those mad, dressing-up suits.

'There's a tray of cinnamon buns next to the grinders. Hand them out as samples as people come through the door. Be nice. Ask them if they want one with their coffee, and let me know when you're running low. They're going to love your gorgeous face, and that accent will seal the deal.' She winks. 'You can change in the break room.'

I carry an outfit of what looks like a dead brown animal through the back. I find leg holes, which sink into brown trousers, leaving the middle section around my ass and belly overly large and brown and fluffy all the way up to my neck. I struggle with the arm holes but manage to dig my hands through brown sleeves. Staring down at myself, there are dark brown lines running rings around the midsection. How the hell do I know if this looks right? Shuffling out front, I find the tray Sophie has waiting for me and it hits me. Yes, I am a giant cinnamon bun. Great.

'Good day, Mike. If you're new in town, I can show you around tonight if you want.'

'Thanks. I'm with a friend, and we're getting to know the place on our own.'

'Girlfriend?' she asks sweetly.

'Just a friend.' I smile but don't look at her. Sophie is cute and not much older than me. If she had asked me out in England, I would have dropped dead. 'I don't have time for any relationships just now. I came here to work on my career, and I'm going to be busy. I don't want to let anything get in the way.' *Phew*, that sounds all right, doesn't it?

'Well, if you ever change your mind, let me know. You're on the schedule for 6:00 a.m. tomorrow.'

I go to the emergency room at St. Mary's Hospital. I take a seat near the door and wait, wondering how to find Stella. Resting my arms on my legs, I scope out the area where patients and family members are coming and going. As long as Max hasn't been admitted to a ward, they should be leaving from here. Assuming they haven't left already. I should call Cici's store and get some information from them.

My patience is rewarded, and Cici comes out to use the coffee machine. I practically jump out of my seat.

'Mike, what are you doing here, dear?' she asks with a tired smile.

'I wanted to check on Stella and Max. Can I do anything? Get you something?'

'You truly are a nice young man, aren't you? Max is okay,' she says as she sits, sipping her coffee. 'Has some stitches and a bandage around his head. We're taking him home. It's Stella I'm worried about. She can't take another blow like this.'

'I don't know too much about her dad's death,' I admit. I stretch my arms back, opening up my body, urging Cici to do the same.

'Oh, she doesn't talk about it much. Suicide has a nasty reputation, doesn't it?'

I gulp. The grief placed on our family when Grandad died was unbearable, but I can only imagine how tough this situation is.

'When he lost his money the first time, everyone was devastated. Stella was only a tot then, and after the divorce, he changed. Eventually, her mom, Pamela, was evicted from their home. He had taken out a second mortgage without telling her and wasn't making payments. She was mortified.'

I nod in agreement and move my hand closer to Cici's in commiseration.

'Things picked up over the years and then crumbled again. We all thought Simon would pull through, but it must have been too much for him. God knows what was going on at home with that new one. Trophy wife or whatever you call them these days. Gold diggers was what you called them when I was young. Don't know what she did to the will, but Stella and Pamela were out of it.

'Stella got nothing. Best thing that could have happened to her, though. Sure made that asshole of a boyfriend disappear. He was a strange one. Stella was used to handling people sniffing around her dad's money, but as soon as she got pregnant, he had hold over her. I've seen it before, that look of fear when your boyfriend comes into the room. That's not right. Not right at all. As soon as he realised Stella wasn't getting any money, he up and left. Horrible, mean son of a bitch. Poor girl has a constant reminder of him every day. She's stronger without him.'

'I'm sure she doesn't look at Max and blame him for who his father is.'

'Not Max.' Cici pats me on the leg. 'The scar on her forehead. I'm sure you've seen it. Every time she looks in the mirror, she must be reminded of the night he almost killed her. She hides it well most days with her make-up and bangs.'

I gulp. And here I was, trying to convince her to re-enter that world.

'She said it was just one slap, and she smacked her head on the bathroom counter. A punch, more like it. But ten stitches down the front of her head must have scared the life out of her. I don't think he was even sorry.

'Here they are,' Cici says, placing her Styrofoam cup under the seat. She walks over to meet Stella, and I follow.

The receptionist slides a sheet of paper over the desk, and Stella holds her breath. Cici takes the bill and hands over her credit card. Stella's bottom lip trembles. 'I'll pay you back,' she whispers as she lifts Max in her arms.

'Don't worry about that now.'

'What are you doing here?' Stella asks me.

'Wanted to see if I could help. We're partners now, right? I'll help you get home.'

'You need to leave,' Stella hisses. 'I don't even know you and being here is completely inappropriate.'

She's right. I don't know her, and she doesn't know we'll be friends in the future. She shouldn't trust me or let me into her life. Not this fast. 'I-I'm sorry,' I stutter. 'I'll go.'

Three days later.
Tuesday, April 8, 1997
07:32 (PDT)
Los Angeles, California.

God, how is it possible to sweat this much when you're sleeping? I roll over in the single bunk and shake my sheet to create some fresh air. All I have on is my boxers, and I'm contemplating shaving every hair on my body off just to be a little cooler. The door opens, and I pull my foot back into the safety of the bed. I learned that one quick. The door bangs off the frame of the bunk, and a blinding light fills the dingy room. I try not to groan.

'Get up,' the figure tells me. 'Come on, dude, you need to get up. Stella called.'

'What?' I sit up and bang my head on the metal rails under the top bunk. I groan. Rubbing my forehead, I twist out of bed and face an already dressed David. 'What do you mean, she called?'

'I went to visit her at the store yesterday and gave her our number.'

'What number?'

David holds up a mobile phone. 'Our new cell.' He grins.

'Where the hell did you get that?'

'Relax. It's a pay-as-you-go phone, so it didn't break the bank. Besides, you have to be reachable.'

'What did she say?'

'She asked if you can go over to the store before it opens.'

I knock on the glass doors to Cici's Boutique at 8:45 a.m. Stella unlocks the door for me.

'Thanks for seeing me,' I tell her.

She locks the door behind us.

'I'm sorry about showing up at the hospital the other night. I was just trying to help.'

'I know.' She straightens her grey dress, worthy of any high-flying career job. 'Cici totally chewed me out the next day about throwing you out.'

'She seems nice. She's good to you.'

'She is. That's why I need to do this. I owe her far too much money at this stage. I'll never be able to pay her back.'

'So you're still in?'

'I need to properly discuss things with you.' Stella pulls out a stack of papers and a pen from her bag. She leaves most of them on the counter. 'Another bill to add to the pile,' she says as she tosses the hospital receipt and her keys back into the bag. 'When you make it big, Mike, you can buy good health insurance for your kids.'

I'm unsure how much sarcasm is intended.

She clicks her pen and flips a notebook open. 'The terms you discussed. I want to go through them. Sort out the logistics. Who is going to be responsible for what. What you're willing to do and not do. If you are willing to pay for childcare, I found a place I like that can take Max one day a week—'

'Yes. Absolutely. Whatever you want, I'm in. Can I ask—not that I want you to change your mind or anything—but what changed? The other day you were so unsure, and now, you're different. You're in charge. You're what I expected you to be all along.'

'This is what I used to do. It's a lot of work in the beginning, but it can be worth it. I want to change my life. I don't want to worry about paying hospital bills and cab fares home,' she says more forcefully. 'You and Cici are right. I can do this. I have a lot of contacts. I spent my whole life watching my dad work. If you're as good as you say you are, we can make a career out of this.'

Stella is relying on me now too, and she needs this to work more than I do.

'All you need is one big break,' she continues. 'A great movie, an opportunity, a good client, and the rest will fall into place. You might just be the one for me.'

'Good, 'cause I know you're the one for me.'

'What's the catch?' Stella asks cautiously.

'No catch, promise.' I give her my biggest no-bullshit smile. This is going to work.

CHAPTER
Nine

Two weeks later.
Monday April 21, 1997
09:05 (PDT)
Los Angeles, California.

'You can't act.' Stella glares at me.

I was afraid of this.

'We've spent two weeks getting set up and organising ourselves, and I never even checked to see if you could fucking act.' She runs her hands through her hair. 'I can't believe I did this.'

I lean against the wall in the storeroom at the boutique. Cici is letting us use the store when it's closed to rehearse, and the office upstairs during the day for making calls and getting me auditions.

'It's not that bad,' I tell her. Honestly, it wasn't. I picked a scene from a tatty old book I found my first year at Cambridge. I thought it was okay. Good even. The book itself was worthy enough to claim space in my backpack when I moved here.

Exasperated, she tugs my arms down to my sides. 'It wasn't great either. You have to loosen up. All you did was read a scene from the book. There were no feelings, no acting.'

My legs shake. I've given David and Stella and maybe even Audrey false hope of a better life. I've even quickened my parents' journey to bankruptcy by no longer supporting them. I try to keep my face impassive as the guilt runs through me, seeps down my throat, and tightens my heart.

'I know there isn't much space, but pretend these boxes aren't here. Use them as props if you need to.'

'Do you want me to do it again?'

'Not yet. You said you haven't acted in anything professionally but how about indie or rep?'

'Eh no, I don't think so.' I'm not entirely sure what she is talking about, but I've already made enough of a fool of myself. 'I did local theatre when I was young, but that was mostly for drunk tourists over the summer. It'd be a stretch to call it acting.'

'It is now. We should put that on your résumé and label it theatre work. Everything you have done we need to make sound as fabulous as we can. So get rid of that self-doubt. There hasn't been a trace of that any other time we spoke.' She grabs the book from my hands and scans the pages on the short walk to the couch. 'What about classes?'

'I was an English student before I left England.'

'Why would anyone in England study English?'

I chuckle. 'Not as a foreign language. Books, literature, grammar, and stuff.'

'English Lit then? Why no acting classes? No drama groups or anything?'

I shake my head and try to stay confident. 'A couple of modules, and I joined the drama group, but it was only emerging. We didn't do any productions before I left.'

'Here is my first favour to you. Go to Roberto Leone at the university. He runs an evening acting class. He was a friend of my dad, so consider yourself already enrolled. He won't do you any favours other than that. You've got something basic here, but you have to work hard. If he says you can improve, then we have something. If not . . .' She crosses her legs. 'You're probably gonna just suck forever.'

I nod my appreciation.

'Hey,' Stella says, uncrossing her legs and closing the book. 'There's something about you we can build on, but you need to be in this if you're going to achieve all you promised me you would. It's not going to happen overnight.'

I cross the room to sit with her on the couch. 'My friend told me that too. Guess I'm just scared that it won't happen at all. I have a lot at stake here.'

'I think we've done all we can for today.' Stella holds up the book. 'Can I borrow this?'

'Sure. I haven't read it in a while anyway.'

She laughs hard and slaps me playfully on the arm with the book. 'Don't ever go to an audition unprepared again.'

I laugh at her unexpected playfulness. 'No problem,' I say as I rub my arm. 'Consider that a permanent reminder.'

Stella nudges me with the book again. 'Come on.' With newfound energy, she jumps off the couch. 'There's something I want to show you.' She grabs her bag and leaves through the front of the store. I stuff my hands into my jeans and follow her out.

We pull up at the side of a deserted road. On the horizon large black iron gates glimmer in the sunlight. Even though no houses line the street, like everything in Beverly Hills, the pathways and flower beds are hoed and deadheaded. Stella hands the driver a pile of money, and my stomach churns. She can't afford this, wherever she's taking me.

'We're going to be about half an hour if you can wait and take us back,' she tells the driver.

He counts the money and nods.

'We're going to have to walk from here,' she tells me.

Climb is more like it. The gates in the distance lead to a gated community, offering those who are willing to pay for it, extra privacy, so that the everyday folks like us couldn't drive by and gawk at the sheer size of their homes.

Stella runs up a steep grass hill and scales the side of the wall, dropping unnoticed on the other side. I join her, thudding on the concrete when I land on the back street of one of the houses.

It's like I'm no longer in LA. The street is quiet and calming, and birds twitter in the palm trees. Only two houses are visible from here, the one next to us and a neighbouring home far away on the right. I follow Stella along the edge of the property we landed on. The sandstone wall surrounding it goes on for what feels like a mile before we reach the brown wooden gates that close off the property to prying eyes.

Stella peeks through the centre gap of the gates, then presses the intercom buzzer, ducking out of sight of the security camera. After a couple minutes of silence, she whispers, 'I don't think anyone is here.'

'Then why are you whispering?'

She giggles and places her foot on top of the lower hinge and holds the top of the adjacent wall. 'Habit, I guess.'

'You do this often?' I huff as I squeeze my foot onto the same hinge she gracefully used.

She pulls herself up and sits on top of the wall facing the property. 'Come on up. You have to see this.' She scoots over to let me sit next to her.

'What are we looking at?' I ask.

'My home. This is where I grew up.' She smiles sadly.

I gawk at the house. 'Wow.' The front doors are wide and arched like the entrance to a castle. Each window on the ground floor is unique. Some are bay-style and some are large and unobstructed, offering wonderful views to the inside of the house. It's like looking at framed pictures of what the owner wants you to see; a grand piano in one room, a collection of art in another. Each room upstairs has a balcony, one of which wraps around the entire left-hand side of the property. Who knew the front of a house could have so many edges?

'How big is this?' I ask.

'About fifteen thousand square feet. Six bedrooms, eight bathrooms, a game room, media room, cinema room, gym, gourmet kitchen, eight-car garage, yadda yadda . . . you get the drift. Oooh, secret kids' room right there off that corner bedroom.' She points. 'And a pool house out back that is bigger than where we live right now. I have a child, and there is a good chance I could be homeless one day. I used to worry about manicures and hairstyles and having designer toilet paper in the guest bath.' She wiggles her fingers in the air. 'I have to apply my own nail polish for work.'

'Imagine.' I gasp in mock horror.

Stella smirks. 'It used to be the kind of thing I thought should be illegal. Now I think it's disgusting that a house this size has one gold-digging whore living in it.' She gulps.

'Why did they build it with more bathrooms than bedrooms?' I ask.

She laughs at the ridiculousness of it, or maybe at me. 'I don't know. It's what they do out here. Despite everything that's gone wrong in my life, my mom's alarm goes off at six and she looks after Max while I work. At least we have one wage coming in, right?'

Stella leans on the palms of her hands and swings her legs against the wall. 'I wish the evenings weren't so strained. I get home around eight at night, then the real work begins. She frustrates me sometimes, with everything that we've been through. I wish she could hold it together better.

'Everyone said it would be hard to raise a kid on my own, but I never realised how endless it is. It's tiring. And expensive. Everything a kid needs is so damn expensive, and that's before we even get to do any of the fun stuff.

'I've reached my limit of struggling. I've gotten to the stage right before a little bit of sanity leaks out of your brain. I'm tired of living paycheck to paycheck, of telling Max we can't afford some things in the grocery store.' A sob escapes. 'I'm twenty-four, and I'm just exhausted, Mike.'

I place my arm around her shoulders, but she straightens and wipes the tears from her face.

'Why did you bring me here?' I ask.

'To show you what you could have if you're willing to do what I tell you. Because I can do this. I can get us to the stage where we don't need to worry about the price of milk.'

'Excuse me?' My heart hammers.

'I said, I can do this.'

'No, the milk.'

'It's something my dad used to say. Some people worry about the price of milk. Now I know exactly what he means. I can be a damn good agent.' She takes a deep breath, steadying herself. 'And I'm going to own this house again. No matter what, I want it back.'

We sit in silence in the taxi most of the trip back. The cab drops us at a bus stop one block over from Rodeo Drive. One line switch, and an hour and a half later, we near Stella's home. Christ, is that what she has to do to get to and from work every day? It's surprising everyone on the bus is so solemn. If I had to do that commute, I would be banging my head off the window in frustration at every set of traffic lights.

In the walk up the pathway, she slows her pace and her shoulders drop. 'Brace yourself for a three-year-old ball of energy.' She pushes her keys in the lock. 'I bet you a thousand dollars, the moment I walk in, my mom will go upstairs and clock off for the day.'

'If I had a thousand dollars, I'd give it to you.'

'Mommy's hoooome,' Max screams as he runs and throws his arms around Stella's legs.

Stella's home is tiny in comparison to the mansion she grew up in. The front door opens straight into the sitting room with a small kitchen at the back. A staircase at the side of the room leads upstairs. I wonder how Stella felt the day she realised this was where she had to live. Did she cry, or was she just grateful to have a roof over her head?

'Hi, baby boy, how's the head?' Stella sweeps Max up in her arms.

'I'm not a baby,' he screams in annoyance and kicks free.

'Did you eat?' Stella asks as he runs back to his toys on the couch.

'He had a sandwich,' Stella's mom answers from the kitchen doorway.

Stella nods. 'This is Mike. Mike, this is my mom, Pamela.'

'It's nice to meet you.' I cross the small room and extend my hand. She shakes it weakly and smiles in acknowledgement. Pamela squeezes past me and heads upstairs.

This place is duller than you would expect from two female occupants. It's clean and tidy and presentable, and is filled with decent furniture slightly too big for the room. But it's not a vibrant home. Decor costs money, and Stella certainly can't afford to waste hers on paint. It's like the life has been sucked out of the home and the occupants too.

A door closes quietly upstairs. Stella sits next to Max on the couch in front of the TV.

'We won't see her till tomorrow,' Stella says, flicking through a pile of unopened mail she picked up from the hall table.

'It's not even dinner time yet. Won't she be hungry?'

'This is how she lives. She can function when she needs to, but the moment she can escape, she does.' Stella tosses the mail on the coffee table. 'Sometimes we exchange pleasantries about the day. She might even tell me what picture Max drew or a game they played. She's a great babysitter, but that's as far as it goes. The grandmotherly element of her is missing. No hugs or kisses or telling him stories. If I think about it, the motherly element to her was always missing.'

Stella scoops Max into her arms and carries him into the kitchen, and I follow. She sits him on the worktop while she makes sandwiches for us, and Max asks her a hundred questions about where we went today and how the bread gets inside the plastic sleeve.

The two of us sit at the table while Max settles under Stella's feet, playing with the dinosaur toy that had apparently tried to eat him earlier.

I ask Stella about the boutique.

'We've only been open four years, which is pretty new for Rodeo. I thought it would be a great job, returning to my old surroundings. I loved shopping when I was doing it on my dad's credit card. I have one designer handbag left, and it kills me to know it could pay my rent for a couple of months. It's the one thing I kept. I hate showing up for work looking like I can't afford the things I'm trying to sell.'

I wonder if anyone who works in those shops can afford the things they sell.

'Cici let me help with the rebranding of the store and ordering. We had to do some remodelling and interior design. It's not CEO stuff, but it's nice that Cici values my opinion, and it makes me feel like I'm helping her. She didn't have to hire me. I just hope she is doing as well as she expected. There is so much competition, it's crazy.'

'She seems like a nice woman to work for,' I say, swallowing my chicken sandwich. 'I bet she'll have a few loyal customers over the years.'

Three months later.

Wednesday, July 16, 1997

09:02 (PDT)

Los Angeles, California.

'I think we should move in together,' Stella says outside the crèche door.

'Excuse me?'

'As roommates, you idiot.' She waves at Max through the window as he runs to the standing sandpit at the back of the room.

I put my wallet back in my jeans pocket. Paying for one-day childcare was more expensive than I ever thought possible. Stella and I stroll to her house and back to our *office* for the day.

'If we bring David in on this too, we might be able to afford it. Living together, we could get a lot more work done in the evenings when Max is asleep, and you and David could help out keeping him occupied. It's the little things I need help with, like making a phone call here and there. It's not professional when a kid is yelling in the background. I'm drowning. I think this could help us all out. And aren't you sick of crashing on David's dorm floor?'

'It will be worth it in the end, Stella, oh ye have little faith.'

'You are spending a shitload of money you don't have.'

'So you can work for me.'

'Yes, but so far that's all that's happened. I'm working, but you're not.'

I knew this would come up. The last four auditions Stella managed to get me into, I never even got a call back.

'So far, I've only invested time in this,' Stella says. 'And quite frankly, the day off from being a mommy has been a welcome break. I can keep going, but I'm not sure you can.'

'I can.'

'Good, 'cause you're getting better. The classes are paying off. I can see how much you've improved. You take direction and critique, and that's something that will work well for you in the future. Let's make this a little easier financially on both of us. We'll speak to David, see what he thinks.'

'David already suggested cashing in his prepaid accommodation and looking for a cheap place for us. I'm sure he would be up for sharing with you.'

Stella smiles. 'He's a good friend to have, Mike. I'm going to make some repeat calls. Let people know we're still around. I have to go to lunch with Julie. She suggested a meeting a couple of weeks ago, and she's a good source for a first job. And I've decided we can no longer take *no* for an answer. I need to think and work like my dad.'

Thinking of Audrey, I smile. 'Good advice. I swear your dad sounds exactly like my friend.'

We reach her place, and Stella stops on her front step. 'Mike, I need money to pay for lunch. I can't be taken seriously if I don't act the part. Fifty bucks should cover it for drinks, too.'

'Oh.'

'You don't have it?'

'No.' I'm totally wiped out this week. 'I'll ask David.'

We step inside her house. 'This is what I'm talking about. If we all lived together, we wouldn't be paying two rents and two sets of utility bills. We would have the extra cash for these things.' Stella drops her keys on the hall table on top of a pile of unopened mail and reaches for the phone.

A red final notice on the envelopes catches my attention. I need to talk to David and make sure we can find somewhere that will house the five of us. I perch on the arm of the couch and flip through a script from the coffee table while I wait for Stella to finish her call.

She hangs up and jumps into the room. 'Lunch is at two.'

'I'll get the money from David before then. And we should start looking for a place big enough for all of us. It'll kind of be a relief for me, too. Hiding from campus security is stressful.'

She flops down on the couch. 'Things are going to work out, Mike. I honestly didn't know how much longer we could keep living here. The rent is so high, and with the rates and utilities. I was stupid to think I could ever earn enough money on my own to keep the place going.'

'One day, we'll be living in the Hills, reminiscing about the days we used to share a bathroom.'

'Deal.' She smiles.

Ten weeks later.
Friday, September 26, 1997
14:45 (PDT)
Los Angeles, California.

The door to Starbucks opens, and Stella bounces in.

'You've got it,' Stella chirps across the room. 'Your first official paid acting job. I just got the call, and I couldn't wait till tonight to tell you.'

I knock the cup I am filling and nearly spill steamed milk all over the counter.

'They need to replace the guy they originally cast, so production has already begun. They want you on Monday morning. I'm going over to pick up the script then we can rehearse tonight. It's going to be a tough few days, but it's here, Mike. The start of the rest of your life has arrived.'

Stella swoops out of the cafe as quickly as she came in, and I haven't said a word. I should be relieved and excited, but a bag of nerves churns around inside me. Should I tell Sophie and book the time off work, or should I quit? Is this it? Is this the big break I've been waiting for?

'Hey, dude, is that mine?' The guy waiting for his extra-hot chai-latte becomes impatient. I finish the drink order and start the next.

I meet Stella in our new apartment. The coffee table is covered in script pages and notes. It reminds me of the last time Audrey showed up and the amount of studying we did. A few boxes Stella still hasn't unpacked yet are pushed against the back wall, along with the rest of the furniture.

She springs into the living room. God, she is energetic when she's excited. 'Sorry about the lack of space. My dad always had an empty room designated for rehearsal. But alas, we don't live in a mansion yet. Max is in bed, and we have the rest of the night to rehearse. And no one has to worry about getting home. I told you this would work out for the best. If I think of anything during the night, we can go over it first thing in the morning.'

I drop my jacket on top of the boxes. 'Let's get started then.'

David thuds down the hall into the living room. 'Where do you want me, boss?'

'Just stand there until we need someone to read the other characters,' Stella says, handing him sheets of paper.

David salutes her. Stella grins. 'You can work the camera. We need to record this and then go over what we have.'

I glance at David. It's not like him to take an evening off. Since we got here, he's been spending his days and most evenings studying and working on his research for Audrey. The one and only date he's been on, I came back to the dorm early and interrupted him. He didn't even kill me the next day. I just figured he didn't have the time to be dating. He hasn't made a move on Stella since I told him to leave her alone. I thought he was respecting the fact that she was going to be a major part of our future, but I wonder if it's because he actually likes her.

CHAPTER

Four months later.
Friday, January 9, 1998
18:37 (PST)
Los Angeles, California.
I'll be twenty-two in seven weeks.

'Told you my suit would fit you,' David says from the couch.

Stella gets up from next to him, adjusts my tie, and yanks down the arms of the jacket. 'How do you feel?'

'Like I want to throw up.' I take a deep breath. 'I still can't believe neither of you will come with me. Stella?' I raise an eyebrow. 'You've worked just as hard for this as I did. Your help with this role was like gold dust. I owe you a night out.'

'This is the part I want to leave behind.' Stella smiles. 'Besides, you've already invited Sophie.'

'Only because you didn't want to go.' *And because Audrey's not here yet.* David's confident she'll arrive on my birthday or the day before, like last year. That is if she's coming back. He doesn't have a specific time locked down yet, but apparently he doesn't have as much raw data to go with, whatever the hell that means.

Stella goes to the kitchen and turns on the radio. The sound is drowned out by the opening and closing of cupboards and moving of pans and utensils. Stella and David have become the default chefs of our house.

'Audrey's probably seen the movie already, in the future,' David tells me.

'What?'

'Audrey. You always look a little lost when you're thinking of her.'

I shrug. To me, she is lost. 'I'd love to show her what we've managed in such a short space of time.' If Audrey was here now, she would be able to calm me down. I'm sure of it. 'I'd rather be going with her than some random date.'

'Sophie's not random,' David says. 'She's your boss. The boss that held your job open during six weeks of filming.'

'I didn't expect to have to go back straight away.'

'Well, you know Stella. She wants you to invest your earnings into more classes.' He turns towards the kitchen, despite her being unable to see him. 'It's a good idea. And we're managing.'

'I just don't think it's a great idea to date the boss.'

'It's not a date. It's a movie premier.'

'She might think it's a date. She keeps looking at me like she wants me to ask her out.' The words tumble out of my mouth without a breath to slow them down. 'She switched to the weekend shifts, so we've been seeing a lot of each other again. That's how I ended up inviting her when I was bitching that you two wouldn't come with me, and I would be going alone.'

Sophie listened eagerly when I told her about being cast in the male supporting role, and how I'd made a point of showing up early to learn as much as I could. I even made a joke about how I thought I was pissing people off with all my questions and hanging around on days I wasn't scheduled to be there, but I think she thought I was fishing for compliments.

'You couldn't piss people off if you tried,' she said.

'Hm, I think there are about fifty people on that set who could argue with that,' I said, and she laughed and shook the hair off her shoulders.

I didn't tell her much more. I didn't feel comfortable having her awe at things I told her.

'I'm surprised you asked her.' David drops back on the couch. 'Didn't you say she was a sexual predator?'

'That's not what I said,' I squeak. 'I said she was a little too obvious about her intentions. Besides, she's never short of attention at work. I'm sure she'll move on soon.'

'She must think you're playing hard to get. Just don't sleep with her. She doesn't sound like the kind of person you want hanging around.'

'Since when do you care what people are like before you sleep with them?' I scoff.

David glances at the kitchen.

Stella has her back to us, leaning over the counter, chopping vegetables.

'Shut up, man,' he says, annoyed.

I laugh. I think I've just found David Wembridge's soft spot: he cares what Stella thinks of him.

I walk the red carpet with Sophie on my arm and am directed to a group photo call in front of the movie poster.

Sophie is ushered to the lobby to wait. She steps into my space and gives me a peck on the cheek as she leaves, and I automatically slip an arm around her backless dress. Camera lights flash, and dread runs through me at the thought of a photograph of me on a date is going to be out there for eternity.

I have a three-minute interview and then I'm ushered inside to wait for the main cast. Sophie hands me a bottle of beer, and I sigh, relaxing. Not bad for my first time. I take a gulp of my drink and scan the people outside. The crowd is bigger than I had initially thought, and they scream when three limos pull up, one after the other, bringing the lead cast.

With everyone in place in the theatre, the movie begins. I've never been in a cinema this grand before. The seats are cream leather and almost double the width expected. There's no sticky floor or stale popcorn smell. A trip to a regular cinema is expensive in America compared to back home. I wonder how much this theatre charges. The other half really do have it all.

It's forty-five minutes before I appear on screen. I shift nervously in my seat when I see myself. God, this is awful. I had no idea I looked that awkward. I should have stood straighter. I'm slouching, and it makes me look shorter. My accent is stronger when it's surrounded by Americans and tainted with new words I've picked up since I moved here. This is torture. I've died and gone to hell if I have to watch anymore of this. I don't have much dialogue left and then I'll merely be present in the background of a few more scenes. I can handle this. Only one more hour to go.

And there it is.

145

The one scene the director kept reshooting, take after take, and it looks like he finally gave up.

The one word that will be the bane of my life.

At the time I had no idea what was wrong with my pronunciation. Why the hell didn't he play it back for me? I could have changed it.

Now it's out there on film forever.

I pinch the bridge of my nose and sink into the seat.

A few snickers resonate around the movie theatre, and it takes all my strength to pretend all is fine.

I have made a dick of myself in my first movie. I mean, christ it's not even a hard word to say. Resting my elbow on the armrest, I support my head, while I'm really trying to cover my face.

'You were great,' Sophie says as the lights come back on. We stand, and she gives me a peck on the cheek. 'Congratulations.'

'Thanks.' I force a smile, still blushing from embarrassment.

'Let's get drunk,' she suggests a little too eagerly.

'I'll meet you there. I have to mix with a few people first.' I walk her through the lobby and sulk off for the bathrooms.

Networking a room is hard. I approach some people, and after polite introductions, I can't think of anything else to say that doesn't come off like I'm giving them my résumé. After an hour of not making any contacts or getting offered business cards, like Stella had prepped me for, I join Sophie at the bar. She has a drink waiting for me and orders another two as I face her.

'Tough crowd, Sugar?'

'You have no idea.' I slam down the first mouthful of what I predict will be many beers.

I planned on dropping Sophie at home, but when we get in the taxi, she gives the driver my address. I lean back against the headrest and close my eyes. How the hell does she know where I live? I hope it's from work records and not some crazy stalking thing.

She slides her hand up the inside of my thigh. My head spins when I open my eyes. She kisses me hard and deep on the lips, a mixture of her sweet perfume and wine overloading my senses. I kiss her back without thinking. This has been a crappy night, and I want to end it on some sort of positive.

Inside the apartment, I lead Sophie to my room and leave her by the door as I prepare to wake David and tell him to sleep on the couch. I crack the door open, but he isn't home. I take Sophie's hand and pull her inside.

The light from the hallway wakes me as it spills through the crack in the door. I lean up on my elbows. Sophie is whispering in the living room. I creep to the doorway and lean out.

She's dressed, clutching her heels in her hand and making a call to a taxi company.

David is lying on the couch, pretending to sleep. His eyes catch mine and I smile, trying to reassure myself I'm okay with the fact that she is sneaking out on me.

I close the door quietly and lie back in my bed. My heart beats faster with disappointment, not because of Sophie herself, but she has illustrated what this life could be like.

Beautiful women throwing themselves at me in front of the paparazzi for the faintest possibility of fame or a free drink. How will I be able to tell who is actually interested in me? Especially once the real fame comes, like Audrey said it would. How can I ever have a regular relationship again?

I told Audrey I didn't want a relationship to get in the way, but never? I'm not sure. I never asked her about my future relationship status. Am I forty and alone?

I sigh and roll over.

At least I'll see her soon.

Stella is waiting for me in the kitchen. She taps her fingernails on the granite with impatience, rather than engaging in her usual morning routine of fussing over Max. 'Do you have any idea how much of a dick you looked like last night?' she hisses so Max doesn't hear.

I switch the kettle on. 'I had no idea I was so terrible.'

'Not the movie. I've seen worse, believe me. Everyone has one that totally blows. I think the director's having a breakdown. You were the second actor hired for that role. I don't think he even knew what he wanted. Don't take not being able to pronounce some words personally. Call it a character trait,' Stella says, dismissing my entire night of embarrassment.

I exhale. 'It was one word, and I know how to say it. Usually.'

'Whatever. I'm more concerned about the bloody press beforehand,' she groans. 'God, Michael, this is what makes or breaks you, whether people like you and are willing to spend a chunk of their paycheck on seeing your movie on a Saturday night. The studios are interested in actors who can make them money. We need to do damage limitation and get press training done.'

'What are you talking about? I only answered their questions.' I bang two mugs on the worktop.

'What you have failed to notice is that the people you have seen interviewed have already established themselves as credible actors. They have reputations and fan bases. When they voice their opinions on controversial issues or their personal struggles, it's welcomed as something humbling.' She wags her finger at me. 'But when the new kid on the block complains about how he is still sharing a room "'cause he can't afford the rent in LA," it comes off as entitlement.'

'Oh.'

'Oh, indeed.' She taps her nails on the counter again and picks up the phone. 'I have a lot to do today.'

I scamper from the kitchen before the kettle has finished boiling.

Five weeks later.
Saturday, February 14, 1998
21:17 (PST)
Los Angeles, California.

'I have to go home.' I empty my drawers and organise things into piles on top of the bed.

David either doesn't think I'm serious or doesn't care, as he continues to lie on his bed, flipping through pages of a textbook. 'Is this about the premier sucking? 'Cause if it is, you've got to man up. It was weeks ago and Stella said it's normal to screw up now and then.'

'I've not been offered any jobs since. I'm sponging off you, and it's not fair.'

'Dude, we knew this before we got here. We know the tables will turn soon. After everything we've done so far, it would be insulting if you packed up and left now. Audrey is due next week. At least wait for her.'

'You said she should show up wherever I am, so what does it matter?'

'You know what I mean, Mike.'

I sit on the bed on top of a pile of shorts and pick up a stray sock. 'Caitlyn called. My parents are filing for bankruptcy.'

David whistles, closes his book, and sits up on his bed opposite mine.

'It's my fault. They were getting by when I could afford to help them. Coming here tipped all of us over the edge.' I ball up two socks and throw them on the bed. 'The one acting job I did get paid crap. I'll always be living week to week. If I had stayed in university, I'd be nearly graduating now and going into a permanent teaching position with the council. Pension and everything. I can't stand this, not knowing when the next job is coming.'

'But we do know,' David says. 'Audrey knows, and she told you to do this. We have more of an insight than anyone does. Do you really want to go back to Blackpool? Be the English teacher who could have been something spectacular, living the rest of your days wishing you'd stuck it out a bit longer? Think how pissed Audrey is going to be if she shows up on your birthday and you're living at your mum and dad's, waiting on a job offer from Newbridge High. If she comes back—'

'What do you mean, if?'

'Well, so far, we have been doing the things she tells us to do. What if you go back on her advice and she doesn't return? Is that a risk you're willing to take?'

David's being sly. He has no idea what keeps Audrey coming back, but he knows I won't do anything to jeopardise seeing her.

'It's all down to you, mate. All our futures depend on you and Audrey. She's not just helping you, it's me and Stella and Max too. Don't ruin Stella's chance at making a career for herself, and a real income and life for that boy. To enable someone to do that is a gift. She deserves it. You know she does.'

'I feel like Audrey doesn't tell us everything.'

'I'm not going to deny she is cautious with some things. I suppose she has to be. But Audrey gave me information, scientific information that wouldn't stand up in tests. And people to interact with. The only reason I have managed to pursue it this far is I know it's real. And the other things, general information about the future, has already given me an edge in the Science Department. I know things that are being developed right now. I know how things are going to progress. We can trust her. Why would you doubt that?'

I shrug.

'Audrey doesn't have the slightest clue how much she knows,' David tells me. 'She talks about stuff all the time. You've just got to know what to listen for. Don't question her on every little detail. She opens up more when she thinks you're not really listening, and she's not scared about what she might be saying. You brought us into this, Mike. Gave us some hope for something incredible. And the people Audrey spoke of using your charity, those are real people. They have names and wives and husbands and kids. They're people who are struggling, who don't have anyone else to help them through the tough times. Don't back out now.'

I nod my agreement.

He leans over and slaps me on the shoulder. 'So don't get down in the dumps when you don't have enough money to pitch in for the heating bill this month or the groceries next month. We're a team, and by god, you're going to make up for it in the future.'

Two weeks later.
Sunday, March 1, 1998
05:50 (PST)
Los Angeles, California.
I am twenty-two today.

We expected Audrey yesterday. Last year, on a non-leap year, Audrey showed up on the 28th of February.

She didn't show.

I can't swallow this lump of worry in the back of my throat.

All night was spent tossing and turning, and I haven't slept at all. What if I fucked up so badly, she won't come back? I rub my eyes and shake my pillow out.

David and I waited around the house for her all day. We sent Stella and Pamela and Max off to the beach with a picnic and bought them movie tickets, trying to keep them out of the house for as long as possible. We even went through the ritual of making a cake and blowing out the candles after dinner. Nothing happened. Not even a glimmer of light.

I need her more than ever. I don't know why, but I feel cheated. The movie was awful. The whole thing just didn't work. The quality of the picture was poor, the script was dreadful. And let's face it, we were all amateurs, scrambling around, trying to take the lead. I'm still avoiding looking in people's eyes, terrified they might recognise me, especially at work—that's Starbucks work, 'cause I'm still there.

Now I know why celebrities wear dark glasses and hats. They aren't trying to look cool or start new trends. They want to go out and not have people shout things at them in the street.

From what Audrey said, I thought it would be good things people shouted. So far it wasn't. I bought my first baseball cap and wear it pretty much everywhere I go. With my head down, it partially covers my face.

'That's the problem with movies, Mike,' Stella told me. 'You never know how it's going to be. If it sucks, everyone looks at the actors in dismay. If it's great, the director gets an award.'

People at work had been quick to slag me off for a few days but swiftly moved on. Sophie switched shifts again so we rarely see each other anymore. That part suits me fine. I've decided I won't take a date to these things again. I'll take Stella or David. At least they were honest with me. They helped me see the places that needed improvement and talked about different ways I could have approached the scene and what to do if it happens again.

''Cause it will happen again,' Stella said.

'I'm still new. Surely the movie industry will give me time to learn?' I'd asked her.

She only raised an eyebrow in response. Apparently the studios and the public wanted their stars perfect.

Lying on the bed, I gulp. Why am I putting myself through this kind of ridicule? I can't live my life with everyone judging me and telling me I'm not good enough. If Audrey doesn't show up again, I'm going to take that as the sign I need to go home. Maybe she wasn't my guardian angel after all.

If Audrey knew I was behaving like this, she would roll her pretty eyes and tell me to get over it.

I glance at the bright red digits on the bedside alarm: six in the morning. I've been awake for hours. David is sound asleep in the bed opposite mine. Why the hell isn't he as worried as me?

I go down the hall to put the filter pot on.

I have taken some more of Stella's advice and switched to coffee to keep me awake when I've loads to do.

Stella tiptoes down the hall behind me, trying not to wake Max. It's rare when he sleeps in, and we all benefit from a quiet cup of caffeine first thing in the morning.

I hand her my mug and get another from the shelf. We wait for the drip pot in silence. She's been my rock through all this, a surprise really, since she never wanted the job in the first place. 'Everyone has a crappy day at work, Mike. This is just one of ours, immortalised forever on video,' she had told me.

'What classes are you going to enrol in this semester?' she asks after her first mouthful of coffee.

'A little too late for lessons, don't you think? I've already proven I suck at it. I'd be ashamed to walk into a room full of aspiring actors and say, "Guess what? I had a shot and fucked it up, so teach me how to act."'

'Everyone keeps taking lessons. Well, the good actors do. Your job relies on knowing what to do when the camera is on.

Sign up for other subjects too. Look at writing and directing, cinematography, maybe even producing. Once you have a feel for what other people's jobs entail, it will make you more aware of why your part has to be so precise.'

'If I look into it, will you stop pestering me first thing in the morning?' I snap.

'Enrol in them, and I will leave you alone. I have to cover the morning shift at work anyway. Use the rest of your paycheck for the classes. David and I have you covered this month.'

I try to hide my awkwardness at the mention of money.

David comes into the kitchen and takes my cup of coffee from the counter. 'You going to work?' he asks Stella.

She nods. 'I'm leaving in twenty minutes if you want to catch the bus with me.'

Stella goes to get dressed, and I have the freedom to scamper back to my room. I lie on the bed and close my eyes, wishing I could wake up in the future. In Audrey's future, where all this is a distant memory.

The familiar high-pitched screech *that once frightened the life out of me runs through my brain and leaks out of my ears. My arms feel like they're floating through air despite my legs being crushed downwards. The light is strong behind my eyelids. I try to shout to Audrey as I'm thrown backwards and I jerk in the bed, finding the space between* dream *and reality.*

My heart beats fast, and I keep my eyes closed, trying to bring some cohesion to the déjà vu feeling of the dream. I can hear someone moving across the room. Audrey. I jerk awake.

'You're here.' She's sitting on David's bed. My heart is thumping at double speed and goose bumps run all over me.

I hold my breath, hoping it will help me appear more laid back about seeing her.

'Where are we?' Audrey asks, looking around the new bedroom.

'You disappeared.'

'Well, as I was saying,' Audrey continues. 'You need to find Stella. She's your agent in the future. You should—'

'Let me stop you there. You've been gone for a year again. We found Stella, and she's helping us—'

The front door slams. 'Michael? David? Are you here?' Stella screams and she runs down the hall.

God, how long was I asleep? I never even heard her leave.

She bangs hard on my bedroom door, calling our names again. I open the door enough to slip outside and yet keep Audrey out of view.

Stella is pale, and her hair has come loose from its clip.

'What happened?' I ask, holding her arms.

'Max's dad is back.'

CHAPTER
Eleven

Stella looks past me into the room, straining her neck to get a better look. She must have seen Audrey.

A moment of panic sets my heart racing. Audrey shouldn't meet people who might recognise her in the future. I step fully outside and pull the door closed. 'What's going on? Where is he?'

'He came to the store this morning when I was opening up. Cici let me leave once she got there.' Stella speaks fast, and her breathing is laboured with fear.

She had the same look on her face when David and I practically accosted her outside the store when we first got to America.

'The last time he was here, he wanted to take Max and me to Mexico with him. He said we were his family, and we should be together.' Stella wrings her hands. 'Michael, he's bad news. I don't want Max growing up around him. I don't want Max turning into him.'

'It's okay.' I walk towards the living room, knowing she'll follow.

'He uses people. He's not going to leave without getting what he came for.'

'We're going to sort this out,' I tell her.

She looks me in the eye. She's terrified. 'We're not going with him. I don't care what happens. I'd rather die.'

'Stella, listen to me.' I clasp both her hands in mine. 'We're a team, remember? Trust me that we'll sort this out for you. We'll get him to leave.'

Stella slides her hands out from under mine and leans back on the couch. 'He left the first time when he realised I wasn't getting any inheritance. He must have heard I was working in the industry again. I've been spreading my name around, trying to get you work.'

'He assumed you had money because you're working as my agent?'

Tears run down her face, and she nods.

Fuck, this is my fault.

'I need to pack. I need to be ready to leave.'

'Leave?'

'My mom will come with me. We'll be okay, Mike. But if we stay, we won't be.'

'Stella. You can't run. Let us help you.'

'Do you have any idea what happens to boys who grow up around violence? They go from hiding in the corner of the room, crying, to the one who hits their mother, their girlfriend, their wife. I won't let that happen to Max.' She trails off, and tears roll down her cheeks.

'You're safe here. David and I are here, and we're not going to let him hustle his way back into your life. In case you haven't noticed, I kind of owe you one.'

'But he'll expect to be able to drag me, kicking and screaming somewhere else.'

'We won't let him.'

'If he gets his hands on Max, I'll go with him. Of course I'll go.'

'He won't get Max, I promise you. Let's wait for David to come home. We'll talk it through. But Stella, I think it's time you're honest with us and tell us everything about him.'

'I'm going to start packing.' I try to interrupt her but she keeps talking. 'I'll wait for David. He said he'd be back before lunch. But if I have to leave, I want to be ready.'

I nod once and give her what I hope is my serious face.

Stella wipes her hands across her face and takes a deep breath. 'Who's the chick?' She nods to my bedroom.

I hesitate. 'She's a friend. She just got here. Actually, I think she might be able to help us.' I get up and scurry off to my room before Stella responds. I pause at the door and call back down the hall, 'Stella?'

'Yeah?'

'Don't ever think you're alone.'

Audrey's staring out the window when I get back.

'My friend, she's having some trouble,' I explain. 'She's the girl you sent me here to meet. Stella.'

'I know who she is,' Audrey says, turning to face me. She perches on the windowsill. 'How's it going, you all here living in one tiny apartment? Did Pamela set the kitchen on fire yet?'

'No.' My eyes widen. 'Was it bad?'

'I'm not sure.' Audrey chuckles. 'I think you always exaggerated. You were always dramatic. Do you love her?'

'Who, Pamela?'

'Stella. Do you?'

'No.' I'm falling in love with you instead. 'Why?'

'You two were always so close, and I was never in the right position to ask, I guess. Have you slept with her?'

'No. Will I?' Christ, what a ridiculous question. I wouldn't sleep with Stella, and I don't think she would ever sleep with me.

'I'm not here to tell you who to fall in love with,' she snaps. 'I always wondered, that's all.'

I roll my eyes and cross the room to sit on the windowsill with her.

'He doesn't hang around long.' She straightens up like she is happy to pass this piece of information along. 'Max's dad. I heard you talking on the other side of the door.'

'What do you know about him?'

'Not much. I remember you all talking about how he showed up right after Stella started working for you. He was sniffing around for some money and you got rid of him. Real deal too. You even paid Luca to make it legit.'

'Paid Luca to do what, kill him?' My voice is higher pitched than I like.

Audrey raises an eyebrow. 'Luca Vargas is your lawyer. You set up a no-contact order and paid him off to make sure he couldn't return for any more money. You know, in the future when you and Stella and David are all *mega rich*.' She jabs me playfully.

'How much do we pay him?

'I don't know, but it was enough that it worked. And honestly, it sounded like you couldn't afford it at the time, so however much you have now, it's more.'

'Where do we get it from?'

'Don't know,' she says.

'God, you're just full of useful news, aren't you?' I don't mean to snap at her, but this is important.

'Do you have any idea what I'm risking by being here? I have a family I should be looking after. I should be with him right now.' She pulls her sleeve up and rubs the inside of her arm. 'He needs me more than you do.'

I glance at her arm and see the name Andrew written in faded biro on her arm. 'Your husband? You getting the outline of a tattoo done?'

'I'm not really the tattoo kind of person.' She pinches the bridge of her nose.

I chuckle at Audrey's trait. I wonder if she really did get that from me.

She narrows her eyes at me, laughing. 'How are you getting on with the whole acting thing anyway?'

'Maybe if you'd told me the movie was going to suck and pointed me in the direction of a good one, things would be going a lot better.' I gesture at the tiny room, furnished with two single beds and a shared dresser.

She laughs, and I join in. It's the most relaxing laugh at myself I've had in a long time.

'Oh, don't be such a baby. Everyone makes bad movies. The difference between those who have long, successful careers and those who vanish into obscurity is they don't give up at the hurdles.' She softens her tone. 'Don't beat yourself up. You're still miles ahead of those who aren't even trying. Take what you can from this as a learning experience and move on.'

And there she is. My guardian angel, with all the right words to pull me out of my self-pity and bullshit despair.

She exhales loudly and groans as she places her hand on her forehead and bends over. 'I think I'm going to throw up.'

Grabbing my waste paper bin, I empty it on the floor and pass it over, putting my other arm around her shoulders. I guide her over to my bed to sit down.

Audrey rests her head in her hands, elbows balanced on her knees.

'I think I was in a car crash,' she says after a few moments. 'A truck came at me from the side.' She touches the side of her head as if she can see it in her mind's eye. 'I remember the lights. It's strong. It's the bright lights making me want to throw up. And my head is pounding. Oh god, you were right. I'm dead.'

'You're not dead. You're here, remember?'

'Is this how I got here, the disturbance in time?'

'I'm afraid that is a question for David. I'll call him. He'll be at the lab. Why don't you rest until he gets back?' I pull the blanket off my bed and pick up her feet when she leans back. 'I'll get you something to eat for when you wake up.'

Audrey winces as she lays her head down.

I gently slide the blanket over her. 'I'll be back soon.' I back away from the bed to stop myself from placing a kiss on her forehead.

'Thanks, boyo,' Audrey whispers as I close the door.

My heart thuds. Off-limits, I remind myself.

I stop at the convenience store at the end of the street and pick up a pre-packed sandwich and Twinkies for Audrey. I don't even know what she likes, so I get a bottle of juice, a Diet Coke, and three different flavours of crisps, just in case. The phone box is outside the store and I dig in my pocket for change.

The call connects to the UCLA physics lab. 'Liam speaking.'

I see David across the street walking home. I shouldn't hang up without explanation, but I need to get him before he is too far away. I shove the phone back on the hook and yell. I manage to get his attention and wave him over. 'Audrey's back. And I think something is wrong this time. With Stella too.'

'Is she still here?'

'I think so, but she's going to leave if we don't help her.'

'Are you saying she can control it now?'

'Not Audrey, Stella. Look, let's get home. I'll explain on the way.'

David glances at my bag as we head up the street. 'Since when do you buy such luxuries?'

'It's for Audrey.'

Getting David caught up on the morning's events takes us the whole way back to the apartment.

'Are you making much progress on how to control the travelling? I think she's scared, David.'

'I'm not sure. But I have a few theories.'

We step inside and find things strewn all over the place. Furniture has been pushed out of the way like Stella's rushed through the room and had no time to step around it. Clothes and toys are scattered around the room, discarded as if they were a hindrance. The kitchen cupboards are wide-open, items thrown around the shelves like they have been scavenged.

'Looks like Audrey's not the only one who's scared,' David says, eyeing me. 'What the hell do you know about Max's dad anyway? Are we dealing with a total-psycho-who-might-kill-us-if-we-get-in-the-way kind of ex? Or plain old green-eyed monster jealous?'

'Are either of those a good option?' I look around the apartment, taking in the upturned chaos that materialised in the half hour I was gone. By the door are two backpacks. She isn't wasting any time.

Stella marches out of the utility room, her arms full of clothes and a pair of Max's shoes.

'Stella, what the fuck?' David says. 'Is there a room you haven't turned upside down? You have to tell me what's going on. Right now.'

I take the grocery bag down the hall to Audrey, pausing at the door, hoping not to wake her. I crack the door open. She hasn't moved since I left. When I see the rise and fall of her chest, I relax. She looks peaceful. Maybe one day I can take all her troubles away.

When I tuck a strand of auburn hair behind her ear, I get a good look at five tiny freckles scattered over the left side of her nose. I can't believe I never noticed them before. They're the cutest freckles I've ever seen. I sneak back down the hall and join David and Stella in the middle of their conversation.

On the couch, David is holding Stella's hand. His thumb runs over a red bruise forming on her wrist. 'Where's Max?'

'My mom brought him home. They're watching TV in our room. I think I need to go, David.'

When Stella lifts her face, she's in David's personal space. Neither of them moves away. I notice a small white scar running from her bottom lip to the middle of her chin. Normally her make-up is perfect and must hide it. I wonder if Max's dad did that to her. Was it the same night he smashed her head? Or maybe the violence went on longer than she let Cici know.

'I don't think he knows we live with you. I got a cab home and doubled round a few streets to make sure no one was following me.'

'Stella, at least here you have people to help if things get worse. Where are you going to run to?'

'He's here for money,' Stella snaps. 'And if he doesn't get it, he's going to take Max from me until I get him some. He'll keep us for as long as he wants. I'm not going to sit around and wait for that to happen. My son has to be safe.'

Stella sobs and bends over, throwing her head in her hands, unable to stop the tears.

Pamela comes out of her room, closely followed by Max, who is clutching his Spiderman doll. 'Mommy, why are you crying? Do you have a sore belly?'

Stella puts her arms out and he climbs into her lap.

Pamela joins them on the couch. 'We don't have anything to give him this time.'

'What did you give him before?' I ask.

Pamela explains, 'We didn't have much, but after he realised neither of us was getting any inheritance from Simon's estate . . .' Stella winces slightly at the sound of her father's name. 'His *behaviour* got worse. He made sure we knew how serious he was about getting something before he moved on.'

'Why didn't you go to the police if he was violent?' David asks.

'I did.' Stella gulps. 'They didn't do much, and it only made things worse.'

David flinches.

'I sold my house,' Pamela says. 'There wasn't much equity left on it, but I gave him the cash, and we thought we would never see him again.'

'Prayed we would never see him again,' Stella corrects. 'I was so stupid to get involved with him in the first place.' She strokes Max's hair. 'I should wish I never met him, but I got something remarkable from it, and I could never wish that away.' Stella dries her tears with her other hand.

Realisation hits me. 'We pay him again.' I meet David's eye and nod in the direction of our room.

'It's no good,' Stella says. 'He came back and he'll keep coming back. He'll take Max from me eventually, I know he will.'

'We pay him a lot and get a lawyer to help us. We draw up a contract, and he can't come back into the country,' I tell them.

'How the hell does a contract keep a man like that from coming back?' David spits.

'I don't know.' I turn to Stella. 'You must have something on him. Something we can use as a bargaining tool to keep him away. Audrey said he can't come back into the US, and with the money we give him, he stays away for good.'

'Who's Audrey? How can you be sure he won't come back?' Stella asks.

Fuck, I didn't mean to say her name. 'I don't know. What I do know is it works. Stella, you need to stay here, talk to David, and work out what you can use on Max's dad. I have to find us a lawyer.'

Leaving the apartment, I go to the phone booth to get information on Luca Vargas. I look over my shoulder, hoping to hell Stella was right and she wasn't followed home.

There's a listing for Luca in Sherman Oaks and hope that he too is at the start of his career . . . and cheap.

I was wrong. The building is only four stories high but wide, and I'm impressed by the sleek glass exterior. The small parking lot out front houses some expensive looking cars. Despite it being a Sunday afternoon, the lot is busy. I push the heavy revolving door and step inside a crisp grey lobby.

The concierge instantly approaches me. 'Can I help you?'

Confidence will get you there. 'No, thank you,' I reply firmly, sidestepping him to the information board. Don't make eye contact, I repeat over and over. Vargas and Smith's office is on the fourth floor. I proceed to the elevator and don't look back.

The elevator opens into the reception area of the law firm. It smells luxurious—fresh air and flowers and crisp clean. Expensive. The carpet is springy under my feet as I walk over to the polished mahogany reception desk.

A forty-something, extra-tanned, teeth-so-white-they're-blue guy sits behind reception and greets me. Apparently, everyone in this city, at some stage, has tried or is still trying to be an actor. I hope in ten years' time, someone won't be walking into Starbucks, thinking the same thing about me.

I return the smile. 'Luca Vargas, please.'

'Of course, Mr . . . ?'

'Knight.'

The receptionist checks his book. 'I'm so sorry, Mr. Knight. I don't seem to have you here. Mr. Vargas never schedules meetings on a Sunday. With whom did you make your appointment?'

Lie. Lie. 'Helen.'

'Helen? Sorry, there is no Helen here. Are you sure you have the right offices?'

Two ways for this to go. Be a dick—shout and blame *Helen* for the fuck up and hope to god Luca isn't mad I yelled at his receptionist, or flirt and manipulate.

I fold my arms on the counter and lean in. 'I'm sorry . . .'

'Cerdic,' the receptionist finishes.

'Cerdic,' I say and bring my hands to my mouth as if I am contemplating something. 'I don't know who took the appointment. All I know is I've been waiting three weeks to meet with Luca, and I have a pressing contractual obligation that needs to be pushed through by the end of the day. My appointment is for noon and it's now'—I look at my watch and take a moment for the theatrics—'Five after. If I don't get in there, we're all going to lose a shitload of money.

'I know you're working overtime on the weekend and I bet you Luca doesn't even know half the things you do for him.' I wait, hoping he realises I'm paying him a compliment. 'But do me a favour. Show me in, and I won't tell Luca the appointment got lost.'

'Okay.' He smiles as he gets off his seat and heads down the hallway.

All the internal walls are glass, allowing me to peer into the empty offices as I go by. Luca's working at his desk. There's no one else in the office. Thank fuck for that. I would have lost my nerve if I had to wait around.

Cerdic introduces me, and Luca politely apologises and says he wasn't expecting me while glaring at Cerdic, who backs out of the office.

Luca gestures to the leather couches in the middle of the room. 'Sit down.' Perched on the end of the sofa opposite, sitting in the position of power, Luca clasps his hands together. His cufflinks glint in the light, and his Latino skin is prominent against his white shirt. 'What can I help you with?'

Straight down to business. Luca is letting me know he doesn't have time for pleasantries.

I explain Stella's situation and her fear for her son's safety. I add in my concerns to hers. 'What I want to know is, if we have information on him, a bargaining tool, if you may, can we use that and some bribe money to sweeten the deal? We want to make this as legitimate as it can be. We want him gone for good, and we don't want him to come back in the future with his own lawyer and start shouting about contractual loopholes. We don't ever want to see him again. I heard you are the best and the only one who can make this happen.'

'It's possible,' Luca says without hesitation. 'Depends on how much will satisfy him and what your leverage is.'

I bluff. 'It's the right amount, believe me. I'll fill you in on the specifics once I have you on board.'

'Play it that way if you want. You should know for this kind of thing I bill eight hundred an hour.'

Of course he does. 'How many hours is this going to take?' I ask too quickly. Christ, now he knows we can't afford him.

'It depends on how much you're willing to pay this man to stay out of the country and what you have on him. This is a complex matter. I can fix it for you, but you're talking maybe thirty-five to forty.'

'Hours?'

'Thousand. Thirty-five to forty thousand dollars. This isn't exactly a run of the mill situation. You in?'

'Okay,' I say, despite my mouth going dry. 'Get started.' I rise from the couch, desperate to be out of here.

'Michael.' Luca leans back in his seat. 'No offence, but I'm going to need half upfront.'

He's unsure of me. I don't blame him. You don't get to be successful in life without calling people's bluffs and going with your instincts.

'When?'

'Close of business tomorrow. Means I can have it ready to present before the week is out. I take it time is of the essence?'

'You have no idea,' I say.

When I arrive home, the place has been tidied, and Stella and Max are in their room. In my room Audrey is awake. She's sitting up on my bed, still under the covers, and David is with her. Seeing him sitting on my bed like it's his place with her ignites some caveman claim in me.

'I've been telling David what I remember about the crash,' Audrey says.

The bag of junk food is still sitting where I left it. I guess waking up to the realisation you might be dead or dying kind of kills the appetite.

'I was upset. I remember crying. Maybe I couldn't see something on the road. I'm not sure. I heard a screeching noise and then my car was hit from the side. It was so loud, the crash. My hands were on the steering wheel, and I grabbed on tight, trying to hold on to something. I was thrown sideways. My legs hurt'—she rubs the tops of her thighs—'where the seatbelt pinned me down. I think I banged my head on the window.'

'I think it's the catalyst that brought her here,' David murmurs.

'I think so too,' she tells me. 'I remember David talking about it over dinner years ago. He was making this whole big deal about his new theories, how all the laws need to come into existence at once.'

'What laws?' I ask.

'Physics, time, attraction—all of them. Once they are all aligned, it is easier for them to work. I never thought he was serious, about time travel and moving through different versions of reality and universe. It's a little quirky, you know. Unless it's actually happening to you.'

I drop onto David's bed. I rest my elbows on my knees and hang my head, thinking about the first night she appeared. 'My birthday. I know we dismissed it before, but I made a wish on my birthday. You keep appearing on my birthday. The law of attraction is the connection, like you said. They must have all been aligned at the right time.'

David smacks his hand gently on his thigh. 'Why would you, out of all the people in the whole world, get exactly what you wish for when you blow your candles out? Everyone does it every year and their wishes never come true.'

'Because it was specific. And I truly believed it was real. I didn't just wish it, I saw it. And that is how you get what you want in life. My grandad told me. He would get us to clip pictures from magazines and make storyboards of how we wanted our lives to be. His instructions were the same every birthday when we blew out the candles. "See it for real, shout it loud and proud and believe it's already yours."'

'And it worked?' Audrey asked.

'On my seventh birthday, I wished for a new bike. I got upset waiting for weeks for it to miraculously appear in the living room. Grandad told me, "you don't have it because you keep waiting for it, you don't believe it is yours yet."'

'That sounds like some fucked up shit to be placing our faith in, Mike,' David says.

'You think I don't know that? But, it did kind of work in the end. It's stronger for leap year babies on our leap birthday, or so he told me. I blew out the candles the next year, a leap year and low and behold, my dad wheeled a brand-new shiny black and yellow bike into the living room. Dad was just as excited as I was.' I grin. 'He kept ringing the bell and moving it around making engine noises, pretending it was a motorbike.'

'But your parents bought it. They saw you were upset the previous year,' David says.

'That's what I said, but Grandad still insisted it was the universe at work. Caitlyn got a bike later that year too, not from Mum and Dad but from a wish. She wanted a bike like me and had seen one advertised on TV with a pink basket and yellow flowers on the front. We got a call to say that Caitlyn had won it in a raffle she hadn't even entered.'

Audrey leans forward.

'Our neighbour, George, had been in London for the week visiting his sister when *Harrod's* toy department had the exact bike in a raffle. George put Caitlyn's name on his receipt for the entry. He knew how much she wanted a bike. Grandad was ecstatic. He insisted it was down to Caitlyn's precise wishing that did it. Mum was just grateful to George.'

'So you think your birthday wish miraculously made a girl jump back in time to help out your career?' David asks.

'That's the thing, you don't worry about the specifics, or how it works. You just focus on the outcome. I think Audrey might be the catalyst to make the desire materialise. I believed this was mine. I sat there and lived through my life, and I felt like it was already mine.'

'Do you think Michael's right?' David asks her.

'He has a point. The "ask and you shall receive" law of attraction is pretty big right now. Or it will be in *my* right now.' She clears her throat. 'Those who claim they know how to use it have high achievements. And you're all about the positive mental attitude thing. Personally, I thought it sounded a bit wacky, but for some people, practising the philosophy is the difference in being able to live a peaceful and prosperous life.'

'Wacky?' I remark. 'This could be the answer to everything—to why you're here, to how you're here, and you thought it was wacky?'

'Well, Mr. Knight, why don't you make sure you explain the significance to me in the future, and I'll make sure I know everything there is to know. There are loads of books and websites teaching the principles of the law of attraction. Make sure I read it in the future if you're so sure it's important.' She sighs. 'Besides, I don't think the philosophy of it has all the answers for us. There's nothing about time travel or parallel universes. It's more positive thinking and living. You know, like a self-help book.'

'You travelled through time using a self-help book?' David drops his notebook. 'Remind me to invest in that one.'

Audrey picks up a pencil from the bedside table and throws it at him playfully.

Irritation churns in my chest. I really don't need to see them flirting. 'Stop it.' I enunciate every letter.

'Ooooohhhh, check out Mr. Bad Mood in the corner.' Audrey laughs.

David chuckles along with her.

'I can't believe you did this, Michael,' Audrey says.

I gawk at her. 'It's not like I knew this would be the outcome.'

'But you knew. In 2016, where I'm from, this is your past. You let this happen to me.'

'I'm sure I didn't *let* this happen. Maybe there is a reason, maybe we get you back, safe and sound.'

'If there was a way for me to get home, you would have made sure I knew.'

'Then why did I let you come here without a way home?'

'I have this feeling, right here'—she presses on her breast bone—'that I have to change something.'

'I wonder if the trauma of coming here is making you forget what happens in between. That's why you have the feeling that you should be somewhere else, or forgetting something. Your subconscious knows this isn't where you should be,' David says.

'Even my conscious knows this isn't where I should be.'

'I didn't mean to put you in danger by bringing you here,' I tell her.

Audrey purses her lips. 'Where do I go each year? Do you think when this is over, I'll go back in the car?' She looks at David for the answers. 'What if I die there? What if this whole time travel thing is what's keeping me alive for now? When this stops, what will happen to me?'

I wait for David to answer but after a second of silence I realise he has no idea.

I lean forward and take Audrey's hand in mine. 'I'm going to fix this for you.'

'It might not be that easy, Mike.' David holds his hands up in defence. 'There might be a bigger picture here. Something we're not seeing. Things like this don't happen for no reason. We shouldn't put all our energy into trying to stop it. The ripple effects alone could be catastrophic. Maybe we should

174

figure out how to get you home safely with minimal impact on the universe.'

'Or me?' Audrey asks. 'Maybe you should try to get me home with minimal impact on me.'

CHAPTER
Twelve

'**Where are we going** to get that kind of money?' David has been pacing the bedroom the entire time I've relayed my meeting with Luca to him and Audrey. 'We'll also need bribe money to pay off what's-his-name.'

'We shouldn't tell Stella yet,' I say. 'She's scared, and we have no idea how this is going to play out.'

'Doesn't Stella have the money from the studio?' Audrey asks. 'It must be from somewhere big, because it was like half a million you paid him—'

'How much?' I squeak.

'You said you got an advance from someone who was helping you. You must have got it from the studio.' She looks from me to David and back. 'Who the hell do you know that has half a million dollars to lend?'

David cocks his head. 'Plus Luca's forty grand.'

'I can't get a loan from the studio. I've been in one movie; they don't even know my name.' I flop on the bed next to Audrey. 'I wouldn't know who to go to. I can't even get through the gates without a pass. I'm an unemployed actor in LA, working at Starbucks. The last acting job I got paid seven hundred and fifty dollars. How can I convince anyone I'm good for half a million?'

'We'll find the money somewhere,' David says. 'We need to stick to the original timeline as much as we can. If we change something this big, there's no telling what will happen to Stella and Max. And you too, Audrey.'

'Me?'

'If we change something important, we might end up sending you back to a different reality.'

'I already considered that possibility,' she says. 'What about the companies I told you to invest in?' she asks David.

My stomach flips. I knew they were having their own talks about the future. I lie back on the bed and rub my eyes.

'Nothing has come of those yet,' David replies. 'So far there's been a few hundred here and there—nothing big. You said yourself you only knew of the things that were hugely successful in your present. That's another fifteen years for us. It's gonna be a long-term investment.'

'Are you sure Stella doesn't have it? What about her mom?' Audrey asks.

I turn to Audrey. 'If Stella had it, she wouldn't be killing herself working two jobs, and Pamela certainly wouldn't be sharing a three-bedroom apartment with four other people. They don't have it.' I look at the ceiling. 'None of us do.'

'No. But I do,' Audrey whispers. She's staring at her hands, twisting her fingers.

'You don't even have a coat. How do you have half a million dollars?' I ask.

Audrey stops fidgeting and holds her left hand in front of her, stretching her fingers. 'My engagement and wedding rings. They're a million dollars, or they will be when I first get them. I never wanted something so expensive, but he insisted I get the best.' She laughs, for some reason finding this funny. 'Values change over the years, but it's still going to be pretty damn close to a million dollars for them both.' She slips the rings off and holds them up.

I sit up. 'You're going to give us your rings?' This woman has come through time and time again for us. 'Why?'

'This must be what happened. How else are you going to get the money this quickly?'

I clear my throat. 'We can pawn them.' I stand and put my palm out. 'There are some high-end places in Beverly Hills. Such is the life here. One day you're buying diamond rings, the next you're pawning them to pay someone off.'

Her hand shakes as she drops the rings into my palm.

'We can buy them back for you when we have our own money,' I assure her.

'Jesus, Mike, a little tact would be nice,' David says. 'They are the only connection she has to her family right now, and it's gotta hurt.'

Audrey hasn't taken her eyes off me. 'Make sure you give them back to me one day.' She closes my hand over, securing the rings inside.

'Thank you, Audrey. You have no idea what you've just done for Stella,' David says.

'Actually, I do.' Audrey smiles tightly. 'I'm glad I can finally be the one to help out financially.'

'I should go before they close.' I have to get out. It's unbearable to see her heart break when I take a little piece of her husband away from her.

As I close the bedroom door, I catch a glimpse of Audrey turning to David. 'We need to talk about something,' she tells him.

'**Seven hundred and fifty** thousand dollars is going to be wired into my account tomorrow after the ring is authenticated,' I tell Audrey and David. My heart is still racing. I panicked on the way home. Audrey is only ever here for a short time, and I left her. 'I asked the guy to call me if anyone is interested in buying them. We can keep track of where they end up.'

'All we need now is for Stella to come up with something to use against fuck-face,' David says.

Audrey tells David, 'You need to be the one who goes to Max's dad. He has to think the money is coming from you and Stella, and not Michael.'

'Why does it matter?' he asks.

'Because she's your wife.'

Jesus fuckin Christ, what?

David and I look at Audrey. She's not joking.

'Stella is your wife in the future, and I honestly think that's the only reason Max's dad has stayed away. He'll finally see he has lost the control he had over her. When he sees you're fighting her corner with her, he'll know he doesn't have a choice but to back off. The information you get on him is just security and the money you give him is enough that he can walk away feeling like he won. You don't want him ever to feel that she got the better of him; otherwise he'll be back and it won't be for money.'

'Stella's my wife?' David whispers. 'But how, when?'

'I don't know. You two started dating pretty soon after you moved in together. I thought you were already engaged when Max's dad came back, but obviously not. Maybe it's my interference that's slowed things down.'

'She's a pretty good catch, you know.' David nods. 'She really married me?'

'So it would appear,' Audrey says.

David marches out of the room and leaves the door open for me to follow, but I close it and turn to Audrey.

I'm a little jealous. Looks like David is going to get his dream career and the family life balance all sorted.

'I think I'll let David speak to Stella on his own. I haven't spent much time with you today.' I smile, but inside I'm dying, knowing she'll probably leave soon.

'It's been a busy day.' She grins. 'We've got a lot accomplished.' Audrey pushes off the bed and opens the wardrobe on the opposite side of the room.

'What you doing?' I ask as she pulls open boxes on the floor.

Irritation builds at the back of my throat. The last thing I expected was her to riffle through my stuff.

'I'm looking for something.' She discards books and folders of notes on the ground like it's her own possessions she's going through. 'It's finally dawned on me why I'm here this time.' She pauses to read the title of a book, tosses it, and keeps looking. 'I know I was all cryptic before, but I wasn't sure how much to tell you. I realise now that by not telling you what you did, you didn't do it. It strengthens the theory I was here all along.'

I settle on the floor next to her. 'So you're going to tell me the specifics of everything, because now you're worried that you were always supposed to be here to tell me?'

'You always said you had great advice on what to do. Like you had everything handed to you on a plate.' She shrugs. 'Maybe you did.'

'Hey, I'm working here. I'm working *hard*.'

'Everyone works hard, but not everyone makes millions of dollars. They have two jobs, three jobs, to keep the money coming in and still don't cover all the bills. Some, like you, get a dig-out in life—from parents who could help pay the rent, a friend who nudged them in the right direction or paid for their ticket to America, an opportunity . . .' She pulls out the book I used to audition for Stella with: Rita Castillo's 1969 novel *Break the Piece*.

'Tell me about this,' she says.

I stare at her. 'Why?'

'Humour me.'

'The main character is a young boy, Pietro. The product of a teenage single mother. He was devastated after starting the search for his father. His mother told him he was conceived through rape. She knew her attacker, a boy from school. Through acquaintances, she heard that this so-called man had grown up and moved to the city where he defended criminals like himself.

'Years later, the boy graduated from law school and was determined to put his father in jail, where he belonged.'

She smiles. 'I don't need a plot summary. I've read it. Tell me what it means to you.'

'What does it mean to me? I don't know. It's a good book.'

'So good that you read it in a day?'

'How the hell do you know that?'

'Guardian angel, remember? I know everything,' she teases.

'I found it in the discard section of the public library my first year of university. It was the tattiest book left on the shelf, and I felt kind of sad looking at it.' I cringe. She's going to think I'm crazy. 'So I picked it up and promised myself to read a chapter. I flipped through a couple of pages while standing there and got hooked. I took a seat and read until closing time, then finished it at home that night.'

'Why?'

I look her in the eye. 'I was feeling miserable, and the story stirred something in me. The drive for a better life and a successful career. To stop at nothing, to make things for your family that little bit easier.

'The book was fraught with conflict between the son and his mother over his career choices and his reasons for them. He thought she would be proud of her son, taking the opportunity to put the monster who changed her life behind bars. He never realised that she had put the experience behind her. He ended up sacrificing his relationship with his mother for the greater good.'

How much of my family life am I sacrificing, chasing this career? I don't want my story to finish the same way.

'Why did you keep it?' she asks.

'Because I wanted to be reminded of what anyone could achieve. Why do you want to know this?' I stare at the floor.

'This is your first big break.'

'It's a book.'

'You and Stella are about to write the screenplay for it and get your first taste of what's to come.'

'You've got to be kidding.' Excitement tickles my stomach. I take the book from her, brushing her fingers in the process. 'How the hell do I do that?'

'Stella knows what to do and where to go for help. But you need one big difference from the book. You gotta add in a girl.' Audrey smirks.

I laugh and lean forward to hug her but falter when Stella and David start shouting at each other in the living room.

'What the hell is going on?' I scramble to my feet and run out the door.

'What do you mean you got money to pay him off?' Stella asks. 'How did you get that kind of money, David?' She sounds nervous, and I don't blame her.

'What's all the yelling about?' I ask.

David, practically bouncing on the spot, points to Stella. 'She has something we can use on him but won't tell us.'

Stella looks like she is about to tear us all apart. Her face is red and blotchy from crying and fighting with David, and it looks like she has a whole lot of energy left to burn off. 'Where did you get the money, Mike?'

'I got it from a friend. It's a loan.'

'And is your *friend* going to come looking for their money with a baseball bat?'

'I have a contact at the studio,' I lie.

Stella collapses on the couch, brings her feet up to the edge, and buries her face against her knees.

'You've already done so much work for me, and we've not even made any money yet. Consider this your retainer. But we need to know what you have on him.'

'Can't we just leave it alone?' she asks. 'If we have the money we don't need anything else.'

'He'll come back, Stella, just like this time. We have to fix this properly,' David tells her.

Stella rolls in a ball and cries. 'He killed someone,' she whispers.

Holy fuck.

David sits next to Stella and wraps an arm around her, encouraging her to go on.

'There was a bar fight.' She sighs and sits straighter.

'They were playing cards, and the new guy cheated him, or so he said. He had been losing all night. He always got angry and out of control when he was losing. We left and got in the car. He wouldn't drive home. He said he needed to cool off. But the other guy came out, and we followed him for a few miles until we were in the hills. He kept saying the man screwed him and had kept looking at me across the bar like he wanted to screw me too, so he was going to teach him a lesson. He flashed him over, stabbed him in the stomach, and threw him in the dirt.' Stella's chin quivers as she remembers what happened. 'When he got back in the car, he told me he punched him but there was blood all over his hands and his clothes and I knew what he did.' Her voice is hoarse when she continues.

'Part of me was relieved that he took his anger out on the guy and not me this time.'

David runs a hand through his hair, bringing it to rest on his chin.

'It was on the news the next day that a body was found,' Stella says. 'A whole night lying on the side of the road dead. I'm a horrible person. The guy was dead, and all I could think was—thank god it wasn't me. He said he had a friend in the police department and that's why they never took my reports of his violence against me seriously. He said if I went to the cops, he would make sure I was named an accomplice and I would end up giving birth in jail. That the baby would be taken away from me.' She wipes her nose on her sleeve. 'He said he would find a way to get out and take the baby and make sure he raised him to hate me forever. And then . . . the body went missing from the morgue. Tampering of evidence, they said on the news. He was so deliriously happy, said no one would ever find out it was him.

'My mom knew I was scared and I couldn't leave. It was the same with her. When she married my dad, they signed a pre-nup, and when the marriage started to go downhill, she was scared to leave. She had no money of her own, no job, and a kid to support, so she stayed. I always wondered, what if she'd never felt trapped? Would they have managed to sort out their differences? Was it the feeling of suffocation that made everything worse? Every day I watched her get a little more miserable, until it consumed her. He was a good person, my dad, but he never thought about the hold he had on her.

'Are you sure your lawyer can keep him away from us?' she asks me.

'I'm sure.'

CHAPTER
Thirteen

The next morning.
Monday, March 2, 1998
07:50 (PST)
Los Angeles, California.

David paces the open space between the living room couch and kitchen, while Stella makes Max's new favourite breakfast of eggs and soldiers.

'We need to have an offensive approach.' The information about David and Stella's future relationship seems to have heightened David's already obvious protectiveness towards her.

'What if we piss him off and he holds a grudge?' I ask.

Stella places an egg into the boiling water. 'He won't be happy I'm choosing to stay away. He's not going to listen if we go in all nice and ask him to leave us alone.'

'Bullies respond to bullies,' David says. 'They only respect people they fear. We need to be someone he fears.'

'You're right,' Audrey says from the doorway. 'You need to be forceful, and it needs to be David.'

Stella drops a plastic spatula on the counter to get a full view of Audrey.

'Why David?' I ask, ignoring Stella.

'Because David is going to adopt Max. It's part of the contract Luca works out. Max's dad will sign away his rights, and after you two get married, he doesn't come back.'

'What the hell is going on?' Stella shouts.

'Stella, listen,' David says, stopping her in her tracks.

'I'm not going to let the first guy who comes along adopt my child, David,' she yells.

'Luca fixes it,' Audrey says. 'He sets up Max's adoption and puts in clauses that take any legal and medical rights away from David as well. Basically you use David's name to take him away from his father, but you don't pass on any legal or parental rights to him. You can sort it out that—'

'Who the hell is this girl?' Stella surveys us one at a time.

Audrey crosses the room. 'You need to do whatever it takes to protect your son.' She blinks a couple of times and swallows hard before continuing. 'So take the damn help.'

'Okay, enough of the bullshit,' Stella says. 'What I don't understand is, if you have someone who can lend you that much money, what the hell do you need me for? Why don't you just get a real agent? Why the hell are you living here?' She throws her arm in the air in disgust.

'Hey, I like our new place.' The insult is, well, a little insulting.

Audrey sinks to the floor, kneeling next to the coffee table.

'You've got yourself in some serious shit. People who lend that kind of money want it back with interest and they will kill you for it,' Stella says.

'It was me,' Audrey says, picking at the remainder of the crisps I bought her yesterday morning. 'I gave them the money. I told them to find you. You're going to be important in all of this but don't think you're getting a free ride. You're going to have to work your ass off to pay them back and get Michael to where he needs to be.'

'Who the hell are you anyway?' Stella practically stomps her feet.

Audrey pauses with a piece of food mid-air. 'I'm from the future.'

I sigh and pinch the bridge of my nose. It's ridiculous, hearing her say that out loud.

Stella laughs. It's a slow, broken exhale of a laugh to start with. The hysterical giggle turns to sobs, and she crumples, falling on the chair. David sits on the arm of the chair and wraps his arm over the back.

Audrey ignores Stella's tears. 'You need to get working. You're all behind schedule, and I think I might have something to do with that.' She turns to David. 'I was trying not to interfere, but maybe I am supposed to. Otherwise you won't actually do what you are supposed to do.'

'Finally,' I say, exasperated. 'Let's get cracking on this.'

'Slow down,' David says cautiously. 'I still don't know how much detail we should be going into here.'

'David, the butterfly effect has already started. You and Stella were already engaged by this time, and me being here has slowed this down.'

David flashes a look at Stella, who is still curled up on the chair.

'Mike already had a few movies in the pipeline by now, and you get the screenplay signed for pre-production soon. You need to get on that now, and I mean 24/7.'

Stella stops crying, staring at us.

A shrieking noise snaps my attention back to Audrey. The light is growing around her head, and it's about to claim her. I grab her, clinging to her. 'Audrey.' It's a desperate plea, trying to keep her.

'It's okay, Michael.' She takes my hand. 'Get the screenplay to Sunshine Studios. Use the leftover money from the sale of the rings to secure production and then get involved yourself. You have to do things to get noticed. Don't panic. Stella knows how to do most of the production work already, and she can get additional investors. She knows what she's doing. Just get your asses in gear. Learn about casting and time management. I'm coming back, and next time, be ready.'

The screeching sound and blinding light explodes, and Audrey disappears.

Stella stands, her face blank and her arms by her side like a statue, staring at the empty space where Audrey was.

I remember seeing that for the first time: the fear, the wonder, the rise of vomit in your throat. I'm still getting used to the how and the why. I forget about the sheer void of thoughts that happened the first time.

'Stella?' David says cautiously.

'I know this is confusing,' I tell her.

Stella runs to her room, and we follow.

Sitting on the edge of Max's bed, Stella strokes his hair while he continues to watch TV, oblivious to what unfolded in the next room.

'He's okay, Stella. You don't need to worry about him,' David says. 'Audrey has come to us a few times. She's here to help us.'

189

'Who is she?'

'A friend,' I tell her. 'She sent us to you. You help us all get out of this mundane life, and she says we did it. In the future, you are this remarkable agent, and you make a fortune. So do I, and David, too. She has told us how to do it. Now, we just need to make sure we do.'

'I don't ever want another day like this.' Stella strokes Max's cheek.

'I know it's scary, but you get used to seeing her come and go,' I say.

'Not that.' Stella walks back to us in the doorway. 'Max's dad. I don't ever want to feel that . . . helpless again. If I didn't have you two, he would have taken us. We would be dead soon.'

David takes her hand. 'Audrey told us to find Luca and make the deal with Max's dad. She even gave us her wedding rings to pawn and pay him off.'

'Why?' Stella croaks as she meets my eyes.

'Because you're our friend and I didn't want to lose you, too,' I say. 'In the future, you're never helpless again.'

'Who else did you lose?' Stella asks.

Audrey, every year. 'No one,' I say.

'Do you think her plan is going to work?' she asks.

'It'll work,' David tells her.

'What do we need to do?' she whispers.

'You two get working on your careers. Let me deal with the rest,' David tells us.

'How are you at writing?' I ask Stella with an arched eyebrow.

CHAPTER
Fourteen

One year later.
Sunday, February 28, 1999
16:53 (PST)
Los Angeles, California.
I am twenty-three tomorrow.

I'm standing on a raised platform on a lot outside the studio, and despite the safety reassurances, it's windy up here. With twenty-five people looking up at me, I can't freak out. It's my first onscreen stunt, and I need to prove I can do this.

'Stay up there, Mike,' the B-Unit director calls. 'We need to double-check this sequence.'

'Okay.' It's not that high. It was a job to get me up here, and we're running behind schedule.

Twenty minutes later, my legs are getting numb. There isn't enough room for me to move around or sit down. The original idea was that I make the small jump from windowsill to windowsill, and it would be over in two minutes. Stunt was available for the wide shot, but I volunteered to do it. How hard could it be? Obviously, it was the waiting around that was going to kill me. I'm shifting my weight from one foot to the other to keep the blood flowing when I spot her.

Her perfect red hair under the headset is unmistakable. What the hell is Audrey doing working here? Unless it really is *her*, the younger version. Leaning left, I crane my neck to get a better look. If she would turn ever so slightly, I'd be able to see her face. She's ushering a group of extras into place. Maybe this is why she keeps her secrets. Our paths are going to cross sooner than she told me.

A quick glance down, and I see there is no one near who could overhear me. 'Audrey,' I yell.

She doesn't turn around. Her long hair bounces around her hair tie and the headset.

I lean out farther. 'Audrey,' I yell again.

If she would just turn around, even a little, I could see her face properly. I lean farther to the left and twist around. I can almost see her.

The crew returns, re-assembles, and organises their equipment, and I lean back against the fake wall.

'We're ready now, Mike,' the director says.

Thank god. The sooner this is over, the sooner I can go find her.

'Whenever you're ready, turn around, look down at the camera and then jump left, got it?'

'Got it.' Spinning around to face the window, my foot slips. I clasp at the top of the sill but there's nothing to hold on to. Ironically, time slows down like it does in the movies, and I see every inch of the building as I fall. I panic. I'm going to miss Audrey tomorrow. All thoughts are knocked out of me when I hit the ground on my back, knocking the wind out of me. I gasp and try to cough.

It feels like an eternity before I breathe again. People hover above me, calling my name. How can I answer when my lungs have no air?

A flash of red hair appears above me as the girl clutching a walkie-talkie tells the director, 'The set medics are here.'

I close my eyes in disappointment. It isn't even her.

Coughing, I finally manage to clear the void and inhale.

When the paramedics snap a collar brace on my neck and strap me to a gurney, I smile. I'll probably get tomorrow off and I can spend it with Audrey. I'm the only twenty-three-year-old actor in Hollywood wishing my years away. I need to tell Stella to book my birthdays off every year. I don't want to waste what little time I have with her. She consumes my thoughts the rest of the year. I saw a pair of warm, fluffy socks on sale over the Christmas holidays and immediately thought of her bare feet and how I'd love to wrap my hands around them.

The paramedics tighten a strap over me, securing me to the gurney, and load me into the back of an ambulance. It's the most excited I've been all year. A weird masochistic thought pops into my head: maybe my subconscious helped me lose my balance? People have been known to do worse in order to spend time with a beautiful woman.

I've been dozing since I was brought in, but this time when I wake in the dark, I feel more coherent despite the pain when I breathe. The only sounds I hear are loud and regular beeps coming from machinery and fluorescent lights humming in the hall. I glance around for water, and pain darts through my back. Everything hurts. My bones feel like they've vibrated inside my skin and I feel darts of pain from the shuddering after effects. Muscles ache I didn't even know existed. My body is as traumatised as I am. I feel like I've been hit by a bus despite only being hit by the floor. I'm in a private room in a private hospital. The studio must be picking up the bill because my basic health insurance policy, covered by the Screen Actors Guild membership, doesn't stretch this far.

Tension and stiffness are in every movement as my muscles try to adjust into a relaxed state from the brace of impact. It's been hours since the accident. Why the hell is the pain getting worse? I fist my hands into the sheets and attempt to get into a sitting position. I fall back. I'm better off staying where I am. A quick check of myself, and I'm not in plaster, so no broken bones. No bandages on my upper body. Lifting the sheet, I moan in pain. My arms are sore and heavy, like someone filled them with cement while I was sleeping.

A nurse strolls in and runs through some vital checks. 'You're one lucky fella. No serious injuries, but we need to keep you for forty-eight hours under observation.'

'You said I was fine?'

'Yes, but we were informed by the studio that you landed on your head.' She clicks her pen and scribbles notes on my chart.

Great. I'm sure that will be the butt of all jokes the next few years. *Michael landed on his head and has never been right since.* I touch my temple and think of Audrey and the headache she complained of from time travelling. I bet mine is nothing in comparison to hers.

'I'll get you some meds.' The nurse places the chart on the foot of the bed and leaves me alone.

Stay still and it won't hurt, I repeat over and over in my head.

The nurse returns and hands me two tablets and water.

I throw them down the hatch as she announces, 'Just a little something to help you sleep.'

Wait, what? I can't sleep. Audrey's coming. 'I need to stay awake.'

The next day.
Monday, March 1, 1999
05:45 (PST)
Los Angeles, California.
I am twenty-three today.

The birds chirping near the window wake me, and the sunlight shines through my eyelids. My heart races. Did Audrey come while I was unconscious? Did anyone see her arrive? What if she was caught and whisked off for experiments?

I brace myself to get out of bed. I open my eyes, and Audrey is there, asleep on the couch against the back wall. I lean up to get a better view of her and check the time. Quarter to six. Slowly, I shimmy off the bed, and my feet touch the cold linoleum floor. I sigh and relax. The dull ache all over my body is still there, but it's not as bad as it was last night.

I check I've underwear on under the hospital gown, thank god. I sit on the bed and stare at Audrey. She looks so peaceful when she sleeps. Her red hair has fallen over her face. I'd love to tuck it neatly behind her ear and caress her, to reassure her that being awake can be peaceful too.

I wonder why she didn't call David to come collect her. She's clutching one hand in the other, tucked by her head, and my attention is drawn to her missing rings. I hope her heart isn't hurting without them.

Looking around for my clothes, I find a miracle. My backpack is on the chair by the bed. I slide off the edge of the bed and open the bag. It's full of fresh clothes, my wash bag, some cash, and a bottle of soda. David must have been here. I catch sight of a black bin bag on the floor and bend over like a ninety-year-old man, my body creaking. It's full of the clothes I was wearing on set, cut to shreds. Jesus, I hope the Costume Department has spares. I tie the bin bag up and pick up my backpack. I shut the door to the private bathroom and thank the world for the perks of expensive insurance policies.

Showering is harder and slower than I thought it would be. It's awkward manipulating my arms as I wash. The hot water bounces off my shoulders, causing more pain than it should. I dry myself with a fluffy towel worthy of any hotel.

I ease my legs into clean underwear and stretch my arms out as far as the tension will allow to slide on my T-shirt. I get one leg into my tracksuit and lose my balance when I attempt the other. I grab a hold of the sink to stop from toppling over and let out a girly scream.

The door is flung open. Audrey rushes towards me and holds my arm as I lean against the sink. My bare arms tingle under her touch. I steal a glance at my underwear to make sure nothing is on show. Her eyes follow my gaze. Fuck, why the hell did I look?

'Come on, let's get you back in bed,' she says.

God, I've missed her voice. It's so soft and lyrical as the words tumble out of her mouth.

She helps carry me back to the bed. I drop my head on her shoulders with defeat and catch the scent of marshmallows from her hair. I inhale and hate myself for loving it.

Audrey eases me back in the bed.

'I never saw you get here,' I say.

'You were out for the count.'

As she tucks the sheets around me, a stab of jealousy for her husband punches through my stomach. If he were ever injured, Audrey would be there for him night and day to look after him. All I ever get is one day a year.

'I've been thinking. Maybe I need a girlfriend.' She has someone else in her life. Why shouldn't I?

'I thought you wanted to concentrate on your career? No distractions.' She sits on the chair by the bed and crosses her legs.

'Yeah, but you know . . .'

'Are you getting lonely?' She chuckles lightly.

'A little,' I say, when all I want to say is I miss you when you're not here.

'Huh. I didn't know you felt like that. You're always so focused and confident in the future.'

'Seeing David and Stella together this past year got me thinking. If they can have great careers and still be together, why can't I? Maybe I jumped the gun, assuming my grandad was wrong to give it all up for love. He was happy with my gran, I think. She died when I was young, so all I ever knew of her was from stories. He was lonely without her, so he must have been happy when they were together. Does that even make sense? My head is all jumbled.'

'It does.'

'What I mean is I think he might have happily given up his career to be with her. I always saw it is a negative thing.

Maybe it's the people who have a little bit of everything I should be jealous of.'

'Michael Knight, you sound like a man in love,' she teases.

I am. 'Not yet, but hopefully one day.'

'Ouch, how does Jessica feel about that?'

'I haven't heard from Jessica since I left England.'

'You aren't back together yet?'

'Back together?' I sit up. 'When do we get back together?'

She avoids looking me in the eye. 'All I know is she was with you at the premier, and everyone made a big deal out of how you added in a love interest to the screenplay and named her after your girlfriend.'

'I named the new character after her because she's been my only real girlfriend. It sort of popped into my head, and Stella ran with it.' And it would have been too obvious if I named her after you.

'Forget I said anything. They also made a big deal out of you being so young, doing it all: writing, co-producing, acting.'

'Who did?'

'The press, your fans, everyone. I think it's how they fell in love with you.'

'People fell in love with me? Why?'

'Michael, in this industry, when they love you, you've made it.'

I lie back on the pillow and stare at the grey panelled ceiling. 'The girl in the screenplay—I don't think we've written her well enough. I mean, the only relationship I've had didn't end on good terms, and I don't want to focus on that.'

'There's still time to change things. There were good times, right? Or think of how you would have liked things to go and make it up. Create the perfect girl.'

198

Like you?

'Do me a favour. I know I said to forget I said anything, but consider changing her name.'

'Why?'

'Because you wrote your ex-girlfriend into your movie and immortalised your relationship for everyone to see again and again.'

'My ex-girlfriend. You just said we were getting back together. Unless we split up again?'

Audrey doesn't speak.

I try to fill the silence with small talk about the last year. 'We already sold the screenplay. We're wrapping filming soon. It's given us enough money to move into a four-bedroom townhouse. David and Stella got married like you said they would, and they claimed the master bedroom in the house. Pamela, Max, and I have our own rooms finally.'

She nods and agrees like she's interested in what I am saying.

'I'm managing to save some money, even after paying Stella her percentage. We all want to be in a better position before we move out on our own. Despite the extra room for David and Stella, tensions are flying in small quarters. Starting a marriage in shared accommodation can't be ideal.'

Audrey shivers and wraps her arms around herself.

'You should put my jacket on. It must be here somewhere.' I look around. I need to get a few things for her when she's here.

'I didn't realise you were all fighting at the end. You made it sound like so much fun. Like college, where you all live in each other's pockets.'

'We're not fighting, but David and Stella are bickering about the lack of space. How do you make it work?'

'Make what work?'

'Your marriage? Your husband has the busy Hollywood career, and you still make it work.'

'That's the difference. For us it's not hard work. We want to be together. Don't get me wrong, we fight. We argue, nag, and annoy each other, but you do that with your best friend, don't you? Live with someone long enough, and you settle into a comfortable way to find your own space. Tell each other when you're pissing each other off but also grow closer and want to spend every day with each other.'

She knocks off her shoes and tucks her bare feet under her legs.

'It's like . . . imagine being a kid and getting to hang out at your best friend's house every day. You would wake up, excited and ready to spend your day with them. And when you grow up and that person is your spouse, well, that's pretty damn special.

'If David and Stella want to get along better, they need to realise it's the little things that matter.'

'Like?'

Audrey nods to the pile of sheets on the couch she slept on last night. 'Like getting them a blanket when it's cold in the middle of the night.' She chuckles.

'Ah, well then. I guess the nurse who made up the couch for you while I was unconscious is totally into you then.'

'Or, you know, calling them after a bad day at work and asking if they need anything. Hugging them when they feel sad. Being their backup, their best friend when they think the whole world is out to get them. Saying the right thing at the right time. Or sometimes it can be saying nothing at all, just sitting right there next to them.'

The smile on Audrey's face drops, and she stares at the foot of the bed. She always looks sad when she's thinking of him.

'How did you know your husband was the one?'

''Cause there was never any bullshit from him,' she answers quickly. 'I always thought actors would be players. Using their skills to lie to women. But from our first date, I could feel it.'

'Feel what?'

'That this man was going to be around forever. He was going to be the best friend I wanted to rush over and see every day.'

There is silence for a few minutes. All I can hear is the beeping of machines and someone pushing a trolley in the hall.

'You fell from a window,' she says.

'Yeah.' I giggle hesitantly. 'Told you about that, did I?'

'No.' Her jaw is tight for a moment. 'I read your chart when I got here.'

'I was doing this low-key stunt, and I fell. That's all.'

Why wouldn't I tell Audrey this in the future? Maybe there are things that I, too, have been filtering. If I knew I was going to be injured, there is no way I would have been up there. I needed the confidence to do the stunt and get the scene shot.

'Why did you fall?'

'What do you mean, why? I fell. I'm not exactly an expert.'

'Yes, you are. You normally are an expert at stuff before you go ahead and do it for real. Haven't you been training?'

'Training at falling off of a windowsill? The studio didn't exactly assign any pre-training for me.'

'It doesn't matter what the studio does or doesn't do. You have to look after yourself. Usually you spend weeks or months, researching and training, both physically and mentally. You manipulate your body to the way the role needs you to be. You lose weight, you gain weight. You learn foreign languages, train with experts in driving and martial arts. You shave your head, you grow a moustache, for god's sake. You educate yourself on certain aspects of the characters' lifestyle, background, and culture.

'Even if some of the things aren't featured in the film, you still do it to make sure you can move and perform like the character. If scripts change or plots get driven in other directions, there are no major setbacks due to your lack of preparation.

'And by god, you figure out how to fall from a damn window safely,' she yells. 'That's what separates you from the rest. Your dedication, your willingness to do whatever the role needs.' She lets out one of her long, exaggerated breaths. 'It's an annoying situation. When you make it to the top of your game, the studio will give you pretty much anything you ask for. But when you're starting out and need it the most, you need to pay for it yourself.' She smiles.

I'm annoyed at myself. I've done nothing like that for this role. If I had been prepared with basic stunt training, maybe this could have been avoided. The production has lost time, and it's my fault. I pull at the sheets, anxious to change the subject. 'Do I really grow a moustache?'

'Yes.' She laughs, like I wanted her to. 'And sooooon.' My playful, happy, and relaxed Audrey is back.

'Tell me what happened.' This time it's a friendly question rather than an accusation.

I relay my memory of the accident and fill her in on the details of how the movie is progressing.

Breakfast is wheeled in, and my stomach rumbles.

'Come on,' I tell Audrey. 'You want to get up here and take what you can before I devour it all.'

Audrey jumps onto the bed and grabs the blueberry muffin. 'Mine,' she yells, falling on the bed, laughing.

I'm tired when we finish our food and push the empty tray away.

'You should lie down and sleep.'

'I'm fine,' I lie. I've missed her so much, the last thing I want to do is sleep while she's here.

'What about you? You couldn't have got a good sleep on that couch last night.'

'I feel like I spend all my time in hospitals now.'

'Do you?'

Audrey blinks. 'I don't know. I don't think so. I have an uneasy familiar feeling about them. I suppose between four kids and now you, I must have had a few trips to the ER.'

'Maybe you were brought to the hospital after your crash. We should ask David.'

'Maybe.'

'Tell me some things about the future.'

She reassures me that I'm on the right track so far with the movie and fills me in on things that we change mid-production. She spends the next hour filling my head with movie ideas and work that I do after this, along with pitfalls that I avoided. My eyelids get heavy and flutter closed. 'Keep talking, your voice is soothing,' I tell her.

'You're not going to remember anything if you fall asleep.'

'Don't talk about work then.'

'What else do you want to know?'

'Hm, tell me about the best vacation you've ever had.' I rest my head on the pillow and stretch out my sore limbs.

'That's easy.' Audrey shuffles in her seat. 'Paris, after we were married . . .'

It's 4:00 p.m. and a nurse moving around my room wakes me. I jump with a start, searching for Audrey. She is still there, dozing on the couch.

'Friend of yours?' the nurse asks. 'She's pretty stubborn. She snuck in last night and wouldn't leave.'

'Yeah.' I sigh and stare at Audrey. 'She's my friend.' I hope I'll have her friendship forever. I can't begin to imagine a future where we don't even know each other.

I should write down all the info she gave me today and list any questions I have when she wakes. Something I rarely get the chance to do.

I have about half a sheet of paper filled when David thunders into the room. 'Mike, you're awake.' He sits roughly down on the side of my bed, dropping a pile of papers on the cabinet next to us.

Audrey jerks awake on the couch from his voice. I frown at him as Audrey's face lights up. She gets up to hug him. She never hugs me hello.

'It felt like you were never coming back,' he tells her. 'We missed you.'

Audrey rolls her eyes.

'For you, maybe. I saw you only a few hours ago. I've kind of liked the break.' She hits him on the arm.

The two of them sit on the couch, facing each other. 'I need to know everything you remember from when the light

204

started to take you last year, to the point you returned last night,' David says.

They run through it all three times until her eyes grow heavy. She needs a break, so I move the conversation to something less draining. 'Audrey, is there anything you miss that we can get you while you're here?'

'You mean like my family, my husband and kids, my life, the knowledge I'll get through this and see them again?'

'N-no,' I stutter in a mild defence of my stupid question. 'I just mean, is there anything we can do for you or get you?'

'D'ya know,' David interrupts, 'we don't know anything about you.' He gets off the couch and joins me on the bed. 'Friendship is a two-way thing. How do we know if we even like you?' he asks, grinning.

Audrey giggles. 'You don't think you like me?'

'You show up and say we're friends, but you haven't given us much to work with. You might be one of Mike's weirdo fans.'

Audrey laughs softly. 'Yes, sometimes I think I must be. What do you want to know?'

'What do you like?' I jump in.

'In general, or do you want to narrow it down?'

'Start with general, then I'll know,' I tell her.

'Know what?'

'Just answer the question, Audrey. What do you like?'

'I like . . . family days out. Especially when we leave work and phones at home. It's even better if we manage to get a day when no one is giving us shit. California sunshine and beaches and quiet and alone time, but it makes me nervous after a while. My house is so busy and loud, silence is usually a bad sign.'

'Who gives you shit?' Adrenaline pumps through me, ready to take on her fight for her.

A machine next to my bed beeps, and Audrey gets up and presses a button, silencing it. David and I exchange looks as Audrey sits back down, not noticing what she's just done.

'Paparazzi, fans, Internet trolls,' she continues.

'Internet what?' David asks.

'People who take up more room in the future than they should.'

I smile. 'Now I know your priorities. You went straight to the things that are important in your life.'

'Ah, so you're not just a pretty face then,' she teases.

'Pretty? Hell no. What's the male equivalent of pretty? I'd rather be called that.'

'Ha-ha, I don't know. Handsome?'

'Hell no,' David says. 'Our man Mike here is sexy as hell, don't you think, Audrey?'

Audrey glares at him and doesn't answer.

My cheeks flush, and I quickly change the subject. 'Do you miss home?'

'You know I do,' she says with a croak in her voice.

Shit. 'I meant Ireland. How long have you lived in America?'

'I moved to America on a student visa. Met my husband and never looked back.'

'It was that easy?'

'God no. It was only supposed to be a gap year. But once I met him, I wanted to be with him forever. There was no need to go home.' She smiles as she relives the memory. 'I miss my family when I think about it. It's not until I emigrated, I realised what I had left behind.'

'What's your family like?'

'Mental.' She chuckles and sits on her legs again. 'I have five brothers and one sister, and we all grew up in a three-bedroom house. I was the youngest, so it never seemed crowded to me.'

'That *is* mental. Makes me think I was blessed only having to put up with one of Caitlyn.' I cock my head at David. 'Imagine another five of them.'

'Do you go home much?' he asks her.

'No.' She smiles tightly. 'You know how it is, busy career and all. He doesn't take much time off, and I wouldn't want to go without him. I couldn't make it through the airport with four kids and a trolley load of luggage on my own.'

'You have four kids? Jeez, how old are you, again?' David asks.

'Older than I look, obviously.' She mock scowls.

'Well, this little get to know each other was great,' David announces as he stands. 'But I've got stuff to look over, and I need to pick up Stella and Max on the way home.' He raises his notes in the air. 'What time did you get here?' he asks Audrey.

'Em, about 2:00 a.m., I think.' Audrey shifts in her seat. 'You and Stella got married? That was quick.'

'No need to wait around when some time travelling ball of light shows up and tells you who your future wife is, right?'

Audrey holds her breath. She recovers quickly, but I notice the look of fear on her.

'I said spotlight, not ball of light,' I say, embarrassed by my lame nickname for her.

'I have the theory worked out on the different times you arrive and leave.' He waves his notes in the air. 'And it's pretty accurate.'

'What is it?' Audrey asks.

David unrolls his notes and lays them out on the bed.

'It's a spreadsheet.' I look at him.

'It's a time travel spreadsheet. So far Audrey's time of arrival and departure each year coincides with Mike's annual birthday.'

'Not always. Sometimes it's the day before or after. And it's always a different time,' I tell him.

'It's the exact time of your annual birthday, which coincides with the atomic clock.'

'How is that different from his actual birthday?' Audrey asks.

'Everyone's actual scientific birthday is not always the one year anniversary from when you were born.'

'How the hell do you figure that?'

'It's actually a pretty well known fact, Mike. There are 365.242 days in a year, which means your birthday is 365 days, five hours and forty-eight minutes and forty-six seconds after your time of birth. And that means every year, the time and sometimes the day, shift ever so slightly. Plus, the atomic clock leaps change our data. So I should be able to estimate the time of Audrey's arrivals within a few seconds. However, the time of birth on your birth certificate is subjective.'

'Subjective?'

'There are a lot of discrepancies at play when recording a time of birth. It doesn't matter in everyday life if it is thirty seconds or a minute off, or even if the clock on the wall in the delivery room is wrong by twenty seconds or so. Some people might write down a 16:44 birth as 16:45 if they glanced at the clock. My lab assistant, Liam, thinks the head birth versus the body birth may be a factor in it too.'

'Okay, that's more detail than I needed.'

'Just saying. He has a medical background, so his observations are a little different than mine. I'll be back before your twenty-four hours is up.' David waves as he heads out the door.

Audrey smiles at me when he is gone. 'Spotlight?'

'Hey, you told me to cut the guardian angel crap. It was the best I had.' I try to be funny. 'So, Ireland? I've never been.'

'You'd like it. It's similar to England in many ways, only the streets and the houses and the buildings feel older. The land isn't as built up. I love flying home and looking out the window as the plane comes in for landing. There is so much green for miles. The farms and fields and there are some pretty amazing beaches and islands. It's a shame it's cold, otherwise we would have it all. I've travelled around the world and the most breathtaking sight is coming home. It's beautiful. The people are friendlier too than most places. Everyone finds it weird when I tell them we even say hello to strangers on the street.'

I glare. 'Why the hell would you talk to strangers?'

She giggles and her face lights up. Not the blinding spotlight that claims her when she travels, but the glimpse of a no-worries, happy Audrey. It's obvious how much she loves the memories of the place. I can't believe her husband doesn't take her home more often.

'We have the best tea in the world. Just don't tell the Chinese. And we have white pudding for breakfast.'

'White? What about the black pudding?'

'We have that too. And there is this supermarket chain that does incredible sausages. Honestly'—she leans forward— 'the next Irish-born and bred person you meet, ask them about the sausages. We've all smuggled them into the US to make an awesome Sunday breakfast.'

'I'll do that.'

'Every child is scared of wooden spoons, and boiled 7-up cures every ailment.'

'Boiled 7-up?' I ask, totally disgusted.

'Every mother will tell you so. I should call for the nurse and tell her,' she says, reaching over the bed and pulling on the cord that calls the nurse. She fumbles under the sheets, looking for the button. 'Get her to boil some up, and you'll be out of here in no time.'

I fight against her hand as she searches in vain.

'We should patent it. Pharmaceutical companies would pay a fortune.' She lightly scrapes her nails across my side as she searches, and it makes me jump with laughter. She's still laughing as we fight each other for the button.

This is too close for comfort. I'm painfully aware I'm lying here, wrestling with a woman I would gladly drag into my bed in a second. Knowing she would reject me if I tried, I scold her more forcefully than I mean to. 'Stop it.'

Her smile fades. 'Sorry,' she says and slips back into her seat, tucking her legs under.

I pinch the bridge of my nose and hope the blush on my face and bulge under the sheets subsides.

'You said you miss the cold?' I ask, trying to get back to the easy flow we've had.

'California is so hot all the time. Don't get me wrong, I love it. That's why I stay.'

'I thought you stayed for your husband and his amazing career. The one I want,' I mutter at the end.

She smiles brightly. 'I do. That's why we're here and not away from the mayhem. But if I asked, he would move.'

'How would he work away from LA?'

'We always said we would only do this as long as it worked for us as a family. Don't get me wrong, the house is paid for, and the kids' college fund is waiting on them. We have our pension and vacation funds. It's not like we would be walking away with nothing.'

'I'm sure he said that.' I wonder if a man with the career he always wanted would walk away if his wife didn't want to live in the city anymore.

'He did it,' she says. 'After we had our first child, I had a hard time adjusting to motherhood on top of our already crazy lives. I felt like I was failing, and he was so busy with work. I felt alone.' She tries to hide the hurt in her eyes behind a smile, but I can see right through her.

I hate him for making her feel that way.

'My family was on the other side of the world. I had, literally two friends in LA at the time. Everyone else in my life was acquaintances and work colleagues. Real friends are truly worth their weight in gold, right?' She gathers her hair in one hand and twirls it around her hand. 'I felt myself snapping. I told him I wanted to leave. Not him, just our lives.'

She stops playing with her hair and twists her hand around her left finger where her rings used to be. 'I thought I could take a break, a long break back home in Ireland—and come back fully charged and ready to take on the world. He agreed.' She shrugs. 'I thought it was a little weird. He always had a packed calendar of work for like a year in advance. Here I was in the middle of a meltdown, and he had all this time off. He re-arranged other things he was working on and told Stella to conference call everything else.'

'Stella?'

She shifts in her seat. 'Stella's his agent too. I told you, she only takes on the best.' She looks at me in dismay. 'Don't tell Stella. You need to let that happen on its own. The last thing you need is Stella picking up clients, hoping to find him. It will split her focus. Trust me, this one will work out.' She lowers her gaze. 'He packed our bags, and our little family of three got on a plane and moved back to Dublin.'

'He gave up his career for you? Why?'

She side-eyes me. 'Because his family is more important to him than his job, Michael,' she snaps. 'Just like your grandad gave up his career for love.'

'But you still live in LA.'

'We were in Ireland about three weeks when I realised the grass was not any greener. Knowing I wasn't trapped was so freeing. Knowing that this man I loved and adored also loved me back and was willing to do anything to make sure I was happy. I could live anywhere, and he would go with me.'

Her words remind me of Stella's confessions of Pamela and her torture of being trapped within the financial burden of a pre-nup. Audrey got one of the good ones. It hurts like hell, but I'm happy for her. I like that she isn't miserable in life.

'We ended up staying a few months and used it as a vacation. He still worked, albeit less. He needs to work. I understand that now. I think everyone does, or they will stop and die. Ireland was where he worked on his writing career. He started his production company and finished a screenplay he had been too busy to work through. By the time we got back to LA, he was in pre-production. It was a great move for him, too. Out of the limelight, the mayhem calmed down from the paparazzi and fans, but he still got to work on movies, which is what he loves.'

'That does sound pretty amazing.' I want her to keep talking but would rather she didn't talk about him. 'Tell me more about Ireland.'

'I miss winter especially, and Christmas.' A smile back on her face. 'In Ireland, it's so cold, you would come home from work and the fire would be lit. Then it was a quick change into the PJs and spend the rest of the evening indoors. The lights would be twinkling on the Christmas tree and it would give the smell of the outdoors, inside. I miss being freezing cold and wrapping up in a warm blanket, to warm up next to the fire, like you're thawing out. It's not the same here. There's never even a threat of snow.'

I should have bought her the socks. They had a picture of a damn Christmas bauble on them. 'Is that why you're wearing summer shoes in February?' I can't fathom why she would have bare feet this time of year. I get that it's cool in California and being from the UK this is like a good summer month for us, but surely she must have acclimatised by now.

'Maybe.' She grins. 'Or maybe I just like being defiant.'

'Defiant against what?'

She takes a moment to answer. 'Fashion. Social acceptance. I hate to fall in line,' she answers a little too proudly. Maybe she's trying to convince herself rather than me.

'Audrey, can I ask you something?'

'Of course, but I can't promise to answer.'

'It's not about me, it's David. Why didn't you tell him sooner about him and Stella?'

'Honestly, I'm worried I told him at all. I didn't mean to. It just came out and then I had to keep going.'

'Why are you so worried about changing things? You said you thought you always showed up and told us everything.'

'Love is different. You're supposed to fall in love all by yourself. What if they were never meant to be together? Maybe because of me, they went down that path. What if there was someone else out there for both of them, but I redirected them? It's scary to think I could change someone's life so much.'

'You came here to change our lives.'

'Once the heart's been changed or damaged, it takes a lot to heal again.'

'David and Stella are great together, though,' I assure her.

'Yes, they are. They're friends, and David is a great dad to Max. I know they needed to be together. I'm just scared, that's all.'

'About what?'

'Who else I might be changing.'

The next day.
Tuesday, March 2, 1999
18:33 (PST)
Los Angeles, California.

Forty-eight hours after being admitted, David carries my bags out of the hospital as I shuffle tenderly next to him. The sun shines low in the sky, and I have to squint to make it across the street. I recognise her straight away, walking towards the hospital. From how I'm feeling right now, and how things ended, I would have probably kept my head down and let her pass by, but I shout her name, knowing from what Audrey said yesterday, she'll turn around, and we'll be reunited.

'Jessica,' I yell.

'Mike, oh my god. What are you doing here?' she says and wraps her arms around my neck to give me a hug.

My body is battered and bruised and hurts like hell. I involuntarily let out a gasp, and she lets go.

'Jesus, what happened?' she asks as she assesses me.

'Filming accident,' I tell her. 'Do you work here?' I glance at her scrubs.

'Yeah, I got an international placement here after graduation.' She smiles. 'Hi, David. Twice in one week. This is kind of freaky.'

'Twice in one week?'

'I bumped into David the other day in a bar in Santa Monica.'

CHAPTER

One year later.

Tuesday, February 29, 2000

08:28 (MST)

Jasper, Alberta.

I am twenty-four today.

'She's half an hour late,' I tell David on the phone. 'You said you had the exact times worked out. What if she isn't coming back?' I run a hand through my hair and rest it on my chin. 'I should have stayed in LA,' I mutter.

'Dude, you're in a different time zone. She's due just before nine.'

The sweat that had collected around the middle of my back cools as I relax. She'll be here soon.

'Give me an hour on the phone with her at some point today. I have some questions for her. And chill out, Mike. She's going to love it.'

'Okay, talk later.' I sit on the ottoman at the edge of the leather couch and spin my cell phone around in my hand.

Waiting. Nine comes and goes, but Audrey doesn't. The seconds tick over on my new Omega watch: 09:01, 09:02. The spotlight starts to form mid-air. My heart beats faster. The light gets bigger and brighter, and the shriek of the noise is deafening. There she is, my little spotlight.

I sigh in relief, and my tension lessens but doesn't disappear completely.

Audrey stiffens, sensing it too. She strides towards me, not breaking eye contact. She kneels on the floor at my feet and takes my hand as I hang my head. I must look worse than I thought.

'What happened?' she asks.

'Nothing.' I lie, not wanting to ruin her surprise. 'Everything is fine,' I say, looking at her hand resting on top of mine. I run my fingers over hers, cherishing the fact she's not wearing her rings. 'I was worried about you. You were late.' I straighten.

Small red and green flashing lights beam on the mantelpiece and grab her attention.

She takes in the room. Her mouth forms an *O*. She stands, smiling at everything I have spent the last two days setting up in fine detail. Hands at her mouth, she laughs, and her eyes fill with tears.

I've never been so glad of a plan coming together. To hell with my troubles. Audrey is here, and she's happy.

'Oh, Michael. What did you do?' she finally asks in awe.

'Well, you said you missed the cold. This is the best I could do,' I say with a hint of smugness.

Audrey glides over to the fireplace and picks up a pinecone from the mantel. Holding it close to her face, she inhales.

We can see the snow on the ski slopes through the back windows. A fire crackles in one corner. Mulled wine simmers on the stove and fills the whole cabin with a warm fruity scent.

'You gave me Christmas,' she whispers. 'Jasper?'

'You've been here before?' I'm a little disappointed.

'No, but I wanted to. You talk about the Canadian Rockies with such fondness, it always made me want to visit.'

The two-story, four-bedroom cabin Stella found for me twinkles like Christmas day. Fairy lights sparkle around the fireplace, and red and gold Christmas decorations brighten every room. The lavishly decorated blue spruce cost a fortune out of season, but I insisted on a real one for her. The smell of outside inside. A thick red ribbon tied around the inside of the front door wraps the whole place up like one giant Christmas present.

'Thank you,' she whispers. She clears her throat and goes to the couch where fleece pyjamas and fluffy socks await her. She runs her fingers over them and smiles.

I want to ask what she is thinking, to be part of her happiness, but I'd rather pretend that smile is all for me. 'Since you looked after me so well in the hospital, I thought this year I could do something for you. We'll take the day off from time travel research and information swapping. Just chill and do nothing. Like a regular Christmas.'

'I'll go change,' she announces as she hugs the pyjamas to her chest.

I pour warm mulled wine into two Christmas novelty mugs and return to the couch, where Audrey has settled under a blanket.

'I put your clothes in the wash. Just remind me to throw them in the dryer when they're done.' I flick through the TV channels. 'Anything you want to watch?'

'Don't care, as long as it's not reality TV.'

'What's that?'

'Nothing.' She yawns. 'Ask David. He owns his own reality TV station.'

David was right. Sometimes she divulges information without realising it.

We're on our fourth mug of wine and have abandoned watching telly. I'm accidently getting Audrey drunk.

'All I am saying is, you must be like a millionaire by now, and I am drinking hot wine. You couldn't spring for some champers? It is Christmas, after all.'

'It's not Christmas. It's February. And if I knew you got this hostile when you drank, I would have gotten the kiddie-crap no-alcohol stuff.' I laugh as I steal the bowl of popcorn from her.

'What does Jessica think of you always spending your birthdays with me?' She nibbles on a piece of popcorn.

'I told her I'm working. I tell everyone that. No one's ever questioned me about it.'

Audrey nudges me. 'You must be happy with how things have turned around for you. We're in a very expensive looking cabin and you look, well, better dressed.'

'What? I looked shabby before?'

'Not shabby, just—'

'Poor?'

She laughs in a drunken, delighted way but recovers her serious tone. 'That shirt probably cost you more than what you used to pay for rent.' She runs her hand from the top of my bicep down to my elbow. 'Feels pretty expensive. And the pants—'

Holy fuck. If Audrey strokes my leg, I'm done for. I jump off the couch.

'Michael.' Audrey sits up on her knees. 'I was just messing around. I wasn't doing anything . . .' She purses her lips, looking concerned rather than embarrassed.

I wave in dismissal and pretend I was getting up anyway. 'Want some food?'

Despite it being mid afternoon, we tuck into a traditional English breakfast, with Audrey's taste of Ireland added in.

Audrey smirks. 'The sausages are good, aren't they?'

'Yes, they were totally worth the hassle of getting them here.'

'You're so funny, Michael.'

'Funny?'

'Yeah, it's just . . . I can't believe you did all this. Why would you do this for me?'

I shrug. 'Because I wanted to.' *I wanted to impress you.* 'I bought the B&B back.' I want her to know there is a reason I don't have her rings back yet. My money's not all getting spent on designer shirts and watches.

'That's wonderful.' She drops her fork. 'You must be so relieved.'

'I am. Things went well last year. I'm on my third movie and big stuff is coming up. Lead roles, some more complex stuff. I'm busy, but I love it. I've so many people to make it up to, I'm taking advantage of work while it's being offered.' I smile. 'When people like Steven Spielberg ask you to take the supporting role in their movie, you don't say you're too busy. This is the first few days off I've had for a while. I've still not found my own place yet. I'm on location a lot of the time, but Stella and David are storing most of my stuff in their basement—in Calabasas, of all places.'

'Nice. Still a step down from what Stella's used to, right?'

'We have our eyes set on Beverly Hills, but Calabasas is a major leap from where we were before. The money being offered to me for movies is unreal. I pay Stella twelve percent, and I hired a publicist, too. Caitlyn graduated and is working as my assistant. I'm relieved she said yes. It's nice to know I can employ someone who isn't going to screw me over.'

Audrey smiles. 'She likes it here. I know that's important for you. Although don't be surprised if she takes off for a few years in one of her tantrums.'

'*Ugh.* As long as she doesn't go hitch hiking around the country. I could do with not worrying about her wellbeing on top of everything else.'

'How is everyone else? Do you see your parents much?'

I sigh at the thought of them. 'I haven't been home since I moved here. At first I couldn't afford it, and now I don't have time. I flew them here when Caitlyn got her sponsorship visa, but I only managed to spend two evenings with them before they had to go home.'

'That's a shame.'

I pour us more tea, glad we both seem to be sobering up.

Audrey pushes her empty plate aside. 'Are you going to tell me what's wrong?'

'What do you mean?' I shove a piece of sausage in my mouth.

'When I got here, something was wrong, and you never got the chance to tell me.'

I stare at my plate, pretending to chew while attempting to swallow the huge lump in the back of my throat.

'I know something's wrong, Michael. You can't hide anything from me.'

'My parents have split up.' I place the toast back on the plate and tilt my head at her, waiting for the divine answer you would expect from your personal guardian angel.

'I'm sorry.' She doesn't sound shocked.

'Did you know it was going to happen?' Of course she knew. This is old news to her. Anger prickles my insides. How could she not sound a little more upset for me? I want her to explain herself, to have some catastrophic future-altering reason not to have warned me.

'I did.'

'Is that it? That's all you're going to say? Why the hell didn't you tell me? I thought once I got the house back for them, all the bickering and worrying would be over. You're supposed to be my fucking angel.'

'I'm not an angel,' she says calmly. 'I'm anything but perfect, so get rid of that assumption right now or you and I will never work.' She takes my hand. 'I didn't tell you 'cause you've been hell-bent on this career. No baggage, you said. No personal stuff.'

I jeer at her. 'You could have given me some sort of warning. I could have fixed it.'

'You can't fix people falling out of love, Michael.'

'I could have tried,' I yell, getting up from the table.

'They grew apart a long time ago. It just took them this long to realise. In the future, you're okay about this. It never crossed my mind to tell you, and you said they lived separate lives even before the affair.'

'Affair?' The blood drains from my face.

'Oh god, Michael, I thought you knew.'

My anger dies, but my heart breaks for my mum to have endured this. How could Dad do this to all of us? I feel sick, dizzy. I sit back down and sink my head in my hands. How can someone continue a relationship with someone if they don't love them? If they want someone else?

Jessica's face comes barrelling into my mind. I don't love her, but I'm still in a long-distance relationship with her. I don't feel as bad as I should. Honestly, I think her feelings are as luke warm towards me as mine are towards her. It's like we're both playing the game of a grown-up relationship while waiting on the real deal to come along. Is this what my life is going to be? Spending it with someone between work commitments, while all the time fantasising about the one who keeps disappearing on me?

'Does she know yet?' I ask.

Audrey narrows her eyes, like she doesn't understand my question.

'Does my mum know about the affair?' I clarify.

She shakes her head. 'It was your mum who cheated, Michael. And your dad found out. That's when they split up.'

I push my chair back and stand up. The mixture of shock and nausea and too much wine earlier knocks me off balance, and I stumble into the doorframe on the way out. I crawl into bed and give in to grief. My family has fallen apart. My life is one hotel room after another. I wished myself into this life, and we're all in too deep to change it. Even if I did find a real relationship, I don't have the time to be the devoted husband someone like Audrey deserves. I'm only alone for a few minutes before Audrey comes quietly into the room.

She shuts the door behind her and lifts the sheets, sliding in behind me. She hooks her arm around my chest and squeezes me tight. 'It's okay, Michael,' she whispers.

I grab her hand and pull it to my chest, clinging to her.

Please don't let go.

CHAPTER

One year later.
Wednesday, 1ˢᵗ March, 2001
10:59 (CEST)
Paris, France.
I am twenty-five today.

When you book a trip to Paris, everyone tells you what an incredible time you'll have. The sights, culture, architecture, food, and romance are all things you'll never forget. Your expectations are high, and the city has to work hard at getting a reaction from you. But when you're not expecting it, it's completely and utterly breathtaking. I hope.

The shrieking noise and blinding ball of light have become things of comfort. I stand near the window, so when the light retreats, leaving my spotlight girl behind, she'll see the view and know exactly where she is without me having to say, "Hey, I'm trying to impress you, so I brought you to Paris this year."

Caitlyn found me a hotel suite that has an unobstructed view of the Eiffel Tower, without having to go out on the bitter cold balcony.

'Well, that's certainly an entrance,' Audrey says, staring out the window.

'I do believe you are the one making the entrances.' I grin.

'Yes, but you are making the locations more and more extravagant. It's like you're trying to outdo me.' She gestures at the vintage-decorated, five-star suite. 'I see things are still going well?'

'Better than expected, thanks to you.'

Audrey smiles softly.

'I wanted to give you something for helping me. For going through what you're going through. For giving me your advice, your time, your rings, your shoulder to cry on. I need you to know I appreciate it all.'

'One night here can run the food bank for a week.' She's not giving me hell, simply letting me know.

'How do you know that?'

'Because I've stayed here before.'

My heart falls, but I try to hide it by rubbing a hand over my face like I'm tired.

'I know exactly what this cost. That's why I know you are trying to upstage my entrances.' She raises her eyebrows.

'I'm here for work.' The words tumble out of my mouth.

'Liar,' she jokes as she opens the balcony doors and breathes deep when the cool air hits her face. As she passes outside she touches the heavy red velvet curtains that are held open with gold tie-backs. She leaves the doors open. The crisp, clean freshness sneaks inside the room. It reminds me of Christmas last year in Jasper.

'You're going to freeze out there.' I follow her out and wrap a blanket around her shoulders.

She ignores me and moves to the edge of the balcony, leaning on the wall and staring at the famous tower.

I want to wrap my arms around her and keep her warm. Enjoy the view with her, rather than next to her. Instead, I lean back against the balcony facing her.

'What's with the suit?' she asks.

'I told you I was working,' I lie again. When I was fitted for this suit, the first thing I thought was, I think Audrey would like me in this.

'You're definitely getting better with age, Michael.'

'Better looking?'

'Better at acting.' She snickers.

I undo the jacket and put my hands in my pockets to stop myself from touching her. 'It's a nice view.' I look into her eyes.

'It really is,' she says, meeting my gaze.

Fuck. My heart rate doubles. I didn't bring her here to kiss her, but she looks so damn perfect. Why couldn't I get a mysterious time travelling guardian angel who was less angelic?

'So Paris. What's really the occasion?' she asks abruptly.

'Holiday.'

'You needed a break?'

'You did. You deserve more than one day off, and this year called for an extra special setting. Come back inside and have some coffee. We've got a long day ahead of us.' I briefly rest my hand on her lower back, ushering her back inside.

'No David? I thought since my headaches were getting worse, he would make a point of being here.'

'The headaches are getting worse?'

Audrey nods. 'I told him last year.'

Her one-hour phone call had turned into a three-and-a-half-hour marathon. I got bored, took off to put the kettle on, and Audrey closed the bedroom door. When I came back, she was whispering, and I felt like I owed her a bit of privacy.

'David never told me.' I close the balcony doors behind us. 'If he did, I would have made sure he was here for you.'

'We should make a list of questions for him,' Audrey suggests as she sits on the couch. 'Make sure he works on a few things before I come back next year.' She lays her head on the arm of the chair and closes her eyes.

'He's been working hard on this, Audrey. Just because he's not here doesn't mean he's given up on you.'

'I know he's busy. I've given him a lot to work with, and with Stella and Max now, he doesn't have a lot of free time. Believe me, I get it. All I'm saying is things are getting more intense. Whatever's happening to me when I travel, it's getting more . . . violent.'

'What the hell do you mean, violent?' I sit on the coffee table in front of her and take her hand.

Audrey opens her eyes. 'In the beginning, the shifts were instant, and I didn't notice them. Now I go somewhere.'

'Where?'

She hesitates. 'Back in the crash maybe? I don't know, but I feel like I linger there for a second or two. It hurts.'

I need to make sure David is with us from now on.

'Do you think David will ever have answers for me?'

'You have a lot of answers too, remember?'

Audrey chuckles. 'I guess I do. In this reality, I'm pretty damn desirable too, with all of my scientific knowledge, eh?'

I look away.

'I'm exhausted,' Audrey says. 'My eyes are so sore.'

I bend over the side of the chair. 'Don't go to sleep. I have plans for us today.' I tap her feet as I walk past her into the kitchen area. 'There are things going on with David and Stella. That's why he isn't here.'

'What happened?' She straightens.

'Nothing.' I fill the coffee pot and wait in silence. My annoyance with the whole situation boils along with the brewing of the coffee. David's been through hell these past few months, and he still managed to keep his head in the game and work. He couldn't face Audrey this year, and I don't blame him. 'To anyone else, I would say that it's personal, but I guess you've embedded yourself in our lives so much it kind of is your business.'

'I don't know why you're so upset. I'm trying to help you. I'm trying to give you the information you need.'

'You're keeping more from us than you ever share. I mean that was a pretty shitty thing to do to David.'

She sighs. 'They broke up.'

'No.' At least they hadn't when I left two days ago. 'Do they break up?'

Her face falls. 'This is the reason I don't want to talk about these things.'

'Christ, do any of us get to be happy?'

'Don't tell him,' she pleads. 'If this is going to happen, let them be the ones who make the decision.'

'If you hadn't interfered in the first place, it might not have happened at all.'

'You said they hadn't broken up yet. What are you talking about?'

I stare at her for a minute. She genuinely has no idea. It's not my news to share.

'Fine, don't tell me. Just don't get pissed at me the next time you think I'm holding back. And FYI, David asked for this. He says he still loves Stella, and he doesn't regret the time they had together. I thought it was weird, him talking about his ex-wife so fondly, but that was obviously his way of passing the information along.'

'He said that?'

'They're still good friends, despite the messy split. He's going to need you. Things will be rough in the beginning, but after a while, they're okay apart. He's a wonderful dad to Max even after all these years.'

'That's the problem. I know he loves her, despite your possible interference in pushing them together, or their time schedule ahead or whatever. They always were good friends. I think that's what David was looking for, someone to settle down with. Have kids with . . .'

'It's a shame he never had any of his own.'

'He doesn't?' I gulp. God, I can't tell him that. It would break his heart.

The coffee pot stops dripping. I fill two mugs, adding a heaped spoonful of chocolate powder to Audrey's.

'Michael, if something is on your mind, perhaps you should just tell me what it is.'

'You're a mother. Maybe you can explain why she did it?'

'Did what?'

'If you don't know, that means none of us told you about it in the future. There are some things you don't go around telling everybody. There are some things that still hurt, fifteen years in the future.'

'What is it?'

I turn my back and stir the mocha. I don't want to see the look on her face when I tell her. No matter what, Stella's my friend too, and I don't want to see anyone judge her. 'Stella had an abortion.'

'Are you sure?' she finally asks.

'She told David.' I return to the couch and hand her the mug. 'They were both excited about the pregnancy in the beginning. She went away for the night for work and told him what she had done when she got back. He had no idea she was even thinking about doing something like that. She said she changed her mind and didn't want any more kids. That she didn't want to feel like she had to rely on anyone anymore.'

'God, he must have been devastated.'

'He was. Mostly he's angry she could do something like this before even discussing it with him. I understand where he's coming from. How can a girl just decide to abort your baby? I mean, they're fuckin married. They have Max already. They wanted to start a family of their own.'

'Trust me, whatever her reasons, it wouldn't have been an easy decision to make, Michael,' she scolds. 'She already has a child. She understood what she was doing.'

'I don't think they're going to get through this,' I confess.

'You said they were still together. Maybe this time will be different?'

'I could tell them you told me they are still together in the future, that they get through this. They survive.' I sound desperate, but I feel like I'm in this relationship with them.

'You can't do that. You can't force two people to be together.'

'Maybe you fucked up. Maybe they never should have been together in the first place. Maybe, leading them down that path, they missed that one person they were supposed to spend the rest of their lives with and be happy. Maybe each other is all they have left.'

'Don't say that. I don't believe I can change things that big. I *can't* believe that,' she chokes. Her head falls and her shoulders drop. She looks defeated. 'He didn't re-marry. It's like he's waiting on *the one* to come back into his life,' she says. 'He'd turned into a total player by the time I met him. He's not as bad now.' She looks like she is contemplating something but keeps it to herself. She takes a deep breath and pinches the bridge of her nose.

Despite the circumstances, I smile at the gesture.

'So what work do you need help with?' The emotional Audrey is gone. She settles on the couch and crosses her feet on the coffee table, ready for business.

The next day.
Thursday, 2nd March, 2001
06:00 (CEST)

At 6:00 a.m., the alarm on my phone wakes me, and I sneak into Audrey's room. I gently shake her awake. 'Come on. It's getting light.'

Once she joins me in the living room, I pull a black winter coat out of a bag behind the couch and hand it to her.

'Where did you get this?'

'Cici's Boutique.'

We stroll out of the hotel and a few miles up the street to a small bakery. The smell of fresh pastries and ground coffee is tantalising.

'You have to get in early if you want the good stuff,' I tell her as the assistant hands me two brown bags with the things I've pre-ordered.

Audrey turns towards the tables, but I take her hand and lead her outside. 'We're not staying here.'

Once outside, she drops my hand, and my heart lands with a thud on the ground. I pass her a steaming mocha and carry the breakfast bag.

'Where are we going?' she asks.

I can't resist the urge to keep her in the dark and sip my coffee to keep from smirking. 'You'll see in a few minutes.'

We turn the corner to Notre Dame Cathedral. The grounds are deserted.

'Oh my god.' She laughs. 'It's all ours.'

It's 6:45 and the sun isn't fully up. The sky is dark blue. The mixture of darkness and isolation, and the size of the cathedral makes me feel insignificant in the grand scheme of things. I step up onto the small wall to get to the grass area and hold my hand out for Audrey. I open my loot bag and take out a large picnic blanket. Shaking it out theatrically, I lay it on the ground and bow to Audrey, indicating for her to sit. 'My lady.'

'Why, thank you, Mr. Knight.'

I kneel on the blanket and lay out napkins, paper plates, and the selection of pastries.

'I have to say, this is impressive.' She moves closer.

The smell of melted butter from the croissants is tantalising. 'I slaved all morning,' I joke, handing a golden brown one to her.

'Have you ever been here before?' She crosses her legs, rips a piece of croissant off, and dips it in her mocha.

'Paris? No. I remember you talking about it, so I thought you could show me around.'

'You seem to know your way around pretty well already,' she says.

'Got here two days ago. Wanted to find my feet, make sure we could see the sights and not get noticed. I thought if we came here early morning, we might be lucky and get some solace.'

'People starting to follow you around?'

'Yep. Spent the first day in the hotel, Googling the best pastry shops.'

'Is it as good as you thought?'

'Google? We have it in America. No need to come to Paris for the Internet.'

She snorts. 'The fans following you around, smartass.'

'It was in the beginning. The first time it happened, I was jogging along Venice Beach and this guy ran out of a cafe and chased after me. I never heard what he was shouting because I had earphones in, but when I stopped, he was happy I had acknowledged him. He was a big *RedMen* fan and asked me to wait while he went to buy a disposable camera.'

'That was nice of you.'

'It was a big deal for both of us, I think.'

'It was a good movie.'

'It opened so many doors for me. Well, apart from the ones you were opening.' I grin. 'It's pretty hard to go to the shops without someone wanting to speak to me.'

'You're going to have to get used to it. Otherwise, you'll turn into a hermit.'

I already prefer time alone inside now, rather than risk getting hassled by people.

'It's a figure of speech, Michael. You're going to have to stop taking everything I say so damn literal. Remember that man on the beach and how you both felt. Because through the years, for people who meet you on the street, it's going to be their first time. They're going to have that same feeling. It's only going to get old for you.'

I take a swig of coffee.

'Know how important it is for them. Your career will last if people like the person behind the actor.' Audrey nods at the landscape. 'Build a cathedral. It's like life, or a career. One brick at a time and look what you can achieve. It's beautiful, isn't it?'

'It sure is,' I agree without lifting my head.

'It reminds me of my first date with my husband.'

'He took you to Paris on your first date? How the hell is anyone supposed to compete with that?'

Audrey laughs. 'Don't be ridiculous. I'm talking about solace. It's nice when your life is so hectic, to enjoy a moment when people aren't trying to get a piece of you.' She puts the lid back on her coffee and lies on her side, facing me. 'When we first met, I had just graduated from university and was travelling the world before I had to find the job I was going to be stuck in for the next forty years. I was waitressing and walking around with a tray of drinks, and he literally crashed right into me. Talk about a sign, right?' She smiles, and my stomach clenches.

'He sent the entire tray smashing to the ground. I was mad 'cause the owner was an asshole and made us pay for the things we dropped. It was an expensive place, so it was like my whole day's wage on the ground, slowly soaking into his designer shoes. When I looked up and saw who it was, it infuriated me even more.'

She finishes her coffee and my fingers brush hers as I take her empty cup.

'He must have known how mad I was because he looked so scared. Like he knew I would rip him to shreds.' She laughs. 'The look on his face made me feel bad for being so angry. He took the cloth out of my hands and started cleaning it up for me. He insisted it was his fault, and I should let him pay for it.'

She hesitates, and I think she is finally going to change the subject, but she keeps talking about him.

'I think that was when I fell for him. He went to so much trouble to make sure I knew he was sorry.'

'Hmph, apologising isn't that big of a deal.'

'I went to a lot of trouble to avoid him. He had his work cut out for him.' She pulls out some grass and plays with it.

I toss our empty cups into the bin bag. 'How does that remind you of this?' I scoff.

'When I eventually agreed to go out with him, he took me to this cafe that was right on the pathway to the beach. It was like a hut, with decking out the front and side, so that no matter where you sat, you felt like you were on the beach. It was completely empty apart from us, and we sat in the back, talking for hours. We clicked straight away, you know? I realised later he had paid the manager to close the place so we could have it to ourselves.'

'Well, in case you didn't notice'—I wave my hand around the empty tourist spot—'I paid France to close for the day.'

She beams. 'This is great. I only wanted you to know that I get it. I understand what it's like to have paparazzi and fans follow you and shout random things at the most inconvenient times. It's just—'

'You miss him.'

Her face falls. 'I do.'

My heart aches, knowing she loves someone else so much. But it hurts more that she's worried she might not make it back to him. 'You should talk about your family more often. You always look so happy when you speak of them. Finish your story.'

She hesitates. 'We ran onto the beach and took our shoes off to walk in the sand. He took my hand, and we ran down to the freezing water. I had no idea why this movie star wanted to take me on a date, and I was so self-conscious, I moved my hand away, but he grabbed hold of it again and wound his fingers through mine. I felt goose bumps all over me.'

My heart breaks as I watch her fall in love with the memory of him.

'We walked along the beach for a while, and he kept stroking my hand with his thumb. God, I thought I was going to die.' She giggles. 'We got back to his car, and he came around to open the door for me. He ran his hand around the side of my face and asked if he could kiss me.'

'He asked to kiss you? That's a bit lame.' I clear my throat. 'He should have just manned up and taken the plunge. I mean, that's what I would've done.' I can't look her in the eye. I've been wrestling with the idea of asking her to let me kiss her for years.

'He was being polite.' She kicks me playfully on the sole of my shoe. 'It was nice to have someone so breathtaking right in my space. Breathing the same air as me. Inhaling my scent and asking for more. It was kind of hypnotic.'

'So you kissed him and lived happily ever after?'

'No, I choked.'

'What?' I laugh. This is fuckin hysterical. He crashes.

'I had no idea what to say. I mean, you're right. No one's ever asked to kiss me before. It just sort of happens when you're on a date and the time is right.'

My laughter dies. Poor sod. 'What did he do?'

'Nothing. He opened the door and I got inside. God, I was so embarrassed. This was a guy who could get any woman he wanted. I had no idea what to say. But you know what?' She kicks my feet.

'What?'

'When he got in the car, it wasn't awkward. He kept chatting like we had been all morning, like . . .'

'Like?'

She tilts her head and smiles. 'Like we had been friends for a very long time.' She swallows. 'This was a little hiccup on the road that was going to be the rest of our lives.'

'Wow, that's pretty deep for a first date, Audrey.'

'Maybe, but when you've met the one, you just know.' She throws the grass she's been playing with on the ground. 'He drove me home and held my hand the whole way back. When he dropped me at home, I kissed him. I can still remember the way his lips felt, his hands on the back of my neck. God, it still gives me the tingles.'

'That's great.' I'm glad the first few tourists have shown up. It's almost eight and we've both been up most of the night.

'I wished there and then I could have known him more before he was so famous. It would have been nice to have more times like that to ourselves, like this.'

I've heard enough about Mr. Perfect. I tidy up our things, then remember why the hell I brought her here in the first place. 'I have something for you.' I pull out a small white leather box that I spent more than an adequate amount of time piking out; who knew there were so many colours? I chose the cathedral because in front of the Eiffel tower would have been far too romantic. Fuck it, just get it over with. Otherwise it will turn into a big deal.

'What's that?'

I want to watch her face when she sees the rings. I want to pretend to be the one who gave her these in the first place. I want to see if her face glows like when she speaks about her family.

I open the box and it works. Her smile fills her whole face and I grin along with her.

She jumps onto her knees and takes them out of the box, placing them on her finger. She twists the rings around her finger and strokes the diamonds. 'Thank you,' she chokes. 'It cost a lot of money to get these back,' she says, sitting on her heels.

'It did. It must have cost your husband a lot of money when he bought them. You're definitely worth it.'

Audrey clasps her hands over her face and sobs.

Fuck, please don't cry. The last thing I want is Audrey feeling this sad. I sit up and wrap her in a hug. 'I told you, we're going to get you home safe.'

CHAPTER
Seventeen

One year later.

Friday, March 1, 2002

11:07 (PST)

Los Angeles, California.

I am twenty-six today.

I'm sitting in my Saab in a driveway, waiting for Audrey's reassurance.

'Michael, one day you're going to have to grow up and make your own decisions. You wait around all year to ask my advice? Come on, what are you going to do when it stops? You need to trust you can make the right decision by yourself.'

'You said you didn't know when this will end.' I let go of the steering wheel and face her. 'Did David tell you something this morning?'

'I'm just assuming. This is going to end sometime. It has to, right?'

I sigh. 'It's just a house, Audrey. I wanted your opinion. Not your time travelling Mystic Meg opinion, just your friendly advice. Stella and David like it. Caitlyn likes it. Christ, I even showed Pamela the realtor photos. I want to know what you think too.'

'Why the hell are you so nervous about this?'

'Because we're sitting in the driveway of a fifteen-million dollar Beverly Hills home, and I'm contemplating spending most of what I have earned on a house. One house. One large house that has more rooms and space than I'll ever need.' But that's not why I'm sweating. I want Audrey to like it too. 'Don't think badly of me for wanting to live here. It's what Stella and I promised each other: Beverly Hills. I can afford to live here, and if I keep getting contracts like I have been lately, she'll be here soon.'

'Why would I think badly of you, Michael? It has everything you need. It's in a gated community, so you have security and privacy.'

'It feels selfish to spend all this money on myself.'

'It's your money, Michael. If you didn't want to spend it, you should have stayed poor.' She smirks.

'Very funny.'

'All your other obligations are taken care of. You've more than paid David back, and you're helping fund his research, which is something I'll never be able to repay you for.'

'Hey, you don't ever owe me anything, Audrey.'

She smiles. 'I have my rings back.' She wiggles her left hand in front of the dashboard.

'Hm. I gave Caitlyn money for whenever she wants to buy her own place.'

'I didn't know that. And your parents?'

'Mum kept the B&B, and Dad has his new country lodge in the tiny village of Singleton, a few miles from home.' I laugh, drumming the steering wheel with my fingers. 'I begged him to pick another location, but he said it was obviously meant to be. God, if he was looking for a sign, he should have picked Ladies Hill. At least that doesn't sound lonely.

'This is going to be the last big purchase I'll ever make. Honestly, I expected you to leap out of the car and get excited, looking around the house with me, not just sit there staring at the front door until we got into an argument about it.

'Do you want to go in or not? The realtor is letting me borrow the place for the day to make up my mind. I told her my family were coming to view it with me.'

'And not your girlfriend?' she pushes.

'I don't think Jessica and I are ever going to get to the moving-in stage. I live in hotels these days. We don't get to spend much time together anyway. I don't need her approval on what I buy. Things are moving pretty slow, but to be honest—'

'You don't need the distraction?' she says.

'I've been busy with work, and I don't want to have to justify my every move to a girlfriend.'

'Why are you still with her, then? If you want a relationship to work, Michael, you have to be in it one hundred percent. It doesn't matter how busy you are. You should be making the effort to be together. When my husband used to travel, I went everywhere with him. There wasn't a job or location when I wasn't with him.'

I tilt my head towards her, ready to make a sarcastic comment about her perfect husband.

'And before you go giving me that look, it wasn't because I was some crazy girlfriend. He asked me to come along. He booked my flights and helped me pack my bags and brought me with him. It wasn't a big deal. We wanted to be together every day, so we made sure we were. Home is about being with your family. Not some mansion in Beverly Hills.'

This always comes back to how she has her relationships all worked out. Not everyone is that lucky. 'God, Audrey, why the hell do you care so much anyway? What Jessica and I have works for us. So stay the hell out of my love life, okay?'

'Gladly,' she says, getting out of the car. 'But I've already seen this house, and I like it.'

I shoot her a questioning look.

Audrey strolls up the driveway. 'This has to be your decision.' She stops at the arched front doors. 'Why do you want to buy a family home anyway?'

'I hate moving. I want to look for a home big enough that I don't have to move if I ever get married.'

She laughs. 'That's confident of you. The young Michael Knight planning for a future wife and kids. What if you never get married? Then you're just this extravagant guy with a house too big for anything he could ever wish for.'

'Wow, that hurts. Just because I don't want to marry Jessica doesn't mean I want to be alone forever.' I open the door onto the marble-floored reception area. 'Besides, this place is a steal.'

'What happened to New York?' She crosses the threshold and perches at the bottom of the sweeping staircase.

'What about it?' I rest my foot on the step next to her.

'You always wanted to live there, didn't you? Why don't you move there now, while you're not tied down to your future wife and kids and a large family home,' she mocks.

I stare at the floor and kick imaginary dirt around. 'I never moved to New York? I love it when I get to work there. The city is incredible.'

'You still could. There's nothing stopping you.'

'Most of my work is in LA when I'm not on location. It would make no sense living on the other side of the country.'

'It's because you work on location so much that you can live anywhere.'

'But my friends are here, and you're—'

'I'm going to be wherever you are, Michael. We already know that.'

'In the future, we work together here. You live in LA.'

She nods.

'It'll be nice to be friends with you in the future. To not have you disappear at the end of the day.'

'I still clock out at five,' she teases.

My heart drops. She's going to be in my life but so out of reach. How am I going to be friends with her, knowing how I feel about her? Knowing that she loves someone else? David and I have already spoken and argued and agreed, when we meet Audrey in this timeline, we can't tell her anything. We don't need the future Audrey thinking we're crazy and avoiding us.

'We should make a date.'

'For what?'

'For us.' I gulp. I can't tell if she is sad or annoyed. 'I mean, for the future. We're going to know each other, but you won't remember any of this until you get back. It would be great to meet up once we both have all the same memories.'

'Let's worry about getting me back first.'

I sigh. 'Let me give you the tour.' I move down the hallway to the biggest kitchen I've ever been in. 'A small restaurant could open up in here, right?'

Audrey stops short in the kitchen and points at the back wall. 'Huh. That wall isn't there anymore.'

'Which part?'

'All of it.'

'It's the whole back of the house, Audrey.'

'Yeah, it's like this glass floating wall. You can push the whole thing open and run out to the pool quicker if that wall isn't there.' She looks lost in a memory, staring out the window. 'Pretty nifty for garden access for summer parties. Very *now*.' She smiles playfully.

'Well, I do like to keep up with future trends.'

Audrey walks over to the wall and looks out the window. Running her hand down the wall, staring out at the garden, she asks, 'Do you ever have the feeling you forgot something?'

'Like what?'

She turns to me and smirks. 'I don't know. I forget.'

I laugh. 'Like you forgot to lock your front door on the way to work?'

'Something bigger, something that makes your heart beat faster and your whole body buzz with anxiety.'

I gulp. 'Something important?'

'Yes,' she whispers.

'Maybe you really want to take a sledgehammer to that wall?' I try to make light of the situation. Only David can help her with this part.

'Maybe.' She laughs. 'It's kind of in the way.'

'How about *you* show me around the rest of the house then?' I ask and throw my arm over her shoulder.

We walk around the pool. Audrey takes off her shoes and dips her toes in the water, making small waves as she swings them back and forth. 'Don't these things need pool gates or something?' She rubs the side of her head.

I shrug. 'Don't the headaches usually get better as the day goes on?' I should have stopped and got her painkillers on the way over here.

Audrey nods.

I pull my vibrating cell phone from my pocket. 'Stella, can I call you back—WHAT?' I scream.

I drop to one of the patio loungers. Fuck, how the hell could this happen?

Audrey puts her shoes on and sits next to me.

'Okay,' I mutter into the phone. It's all I can manage. I can't believe this has happened, to me, of all people. Stella talks quickly to me, telling me what to do and what not to do. Who not to talk to and what not to say. All I can do is stare at Audrey. She's going to be so disappointed in me.

'Basically, hide out the rest of the day and let me and that shitty publicist deal with everything.' Stella takes a breath. 'This, Mike, is exactly where I'm going to earn that money you pay me.' She hangs up.

I keep the phone in my hand. I rest my arms on my knees and then go for full-blown drama of hanging my head in my hands.

'Everything okay?' Audrey asks.

I look up but keep my hands on my face, hopefully shielding some of the shame. 'Someone I used to work with sold a kiss-and-tell on me.'

'Oh.'

'Oh, indeed. We should get going.'

'Where are you going?' Her eyes are wide. 'If there is a tabloid exposé brewing, the paparazzi are going to be looking for you. You should lay low.'

'Well, we can't stay here.' I spread my arms.

'Why not? You have the keys, don't you? No one knows you're here.' She pulls me up and some of my worries dissolve away when she takes my hand.

Audrey drags me around the house, talking about each room in more detail than necessary. 'Do you like the colour of carpet in here?' and 'What do you think about making this room the office?' If we are going to hang out here all day, this is going to get old fast. I check the fridges and pantry when we are in the kitchen but there is no food, as expected in an empty property. 'We can order in,' Audrey says when I slam the fridge door.

'I thought we were hiding?'

'No one knows me. I'll pay the delivery guy.'

I nod. 'Want to look upstairs? I think the attic's been converted.'

'Oh, exciting. Definitely a selling point.'

'Shut up. We have a day to kill.' I head for the stairs to the second floor.

The master bedroom is left till last. It's a little weird taking Audrey in here when I'd rather pick her up and kiss her the entire way to the bed. The sheer size of the room is overwhelming. 'It is bigger than the downstairs of our old townhouse,' I tell her. There's an Alaskan king-sized bed made more impressive looking by the mahogany sleigh-style frame. 'Now that's a bed.'

Audrey turns slowly to me and smirks.

My face fills with heat, and I try to think of something to recover with, but I have nothing. I pretend there was no double entendre and walk over to the door that leads to the en suite bathroom. It's equally impressive, with a double shower housed behind a glass wall. Everything screams chic and expensive. Marble countertops and 'his and hers' sinks complete the look. The taps glisten, and I wonder how often you would need to clean it to keep it shiny. There are two carpeted steps leading to a huge freestanding bath with a view of the back of the property.

'Now that's a bath.' Audrey rests her chin on my shoulder and raises her eyebrows when I shoot a quick glance at her.

I wander back into the bedroom and check out the walk-in closet. My clothes aren't going to fill even half of this.

'The closet is bigger than the room I shared with my sister,' Audrey says. She settles crossed-legged on the foot of the bed. I throw myself down next to her and fall back, exasperated.

'It'll go away,' she says. 'The negative press. It will all go away tomorrow. Definitely the next day. No one will care. Unless they have pictures. Then they might get a week out of it, but after that, definitely over with.'

I glare at her. 'Gee, thanks for that pep talk.'

'This must happen a lot to you, because when I meet you, you don't care what people write about you. You don't even reply to articles. "No need to fuel the fire."' She imitates me, badly.

'Great, so in the future everyone I sleep with is going to sell a story.'

'That's not what I meant. The tabloids will write anything that will sell.'

'I know.' I rub my face and sit up. I point to the entertainment centre on the opposite wall. 'You think there are any movies in that thing?'

'I'll look. Find somewhere that will deliver food. I'm starving.'

We watch two movies and three episodes of a marathon, and my eyes are tired from sitting here doing nothing. It's amazing how you can get lethargic from being lazy. I've been on the go for months—years—I suppose. It's strange to stay still for so long. I think Audrey is fed up too. She won't sit still anymore.

She tosses the movie boxes and food wrappers to the floor and stretches out. She turns on her side to face me, tucking her hands under her cheek. 'You need help with anything?'

'Uh . . . my life.' I copy her and lie on my side.

'Things can't be all bad.'

'They're not,' I say, aware of how close we are.

She truly is the most beautiful woman I've ever seen. Her lips part and I feel her breath escape between them. I want to lean closer, taste her lips, and breathe the same air as her. Is it because I consider her my best friend that makes me want her more? Or that I already know I'll love her forever?

Now that my career is on another level, people swarm around me. It's claustrophobic. I run my hand over her hair and look into her bright hazel eyes, searching for a reaction, anything that tells me she doesn't mind me doing this. Maybe she wants it too. Maybe, if I kiss her, she'll kiss me back.

She opens her mouth and says, 'Michael.'

It's a warning. A little piece of my heart dies. It falls through my chest and hangs somewhere above my stomach. Her wedding rings catch the light. I swallow the moisture in my throat. I still have a hand on the side of her head, and she hasn't removed it. 'Why?'

She places her hand on top of mine and squeezes it. 'I just . . .'

'Are we close? In the future, are we good friends? I can't imagine living a life where we're mere work colleagues.'

'Yes, Michael. We are. It's why this is working so well and how I know so much about you.'

I need to kiss her. My mouth aches to touch her lips. I lean closer and softly brush my lips over hers.

'Please don't.' Her voice cracks.

I stop and trail my fingers down her cheek. 'Audrey, I—'

'No,' she shouts and sits up. 'Don't you dare finish that sentence. You're with Jessica. Don't be that guy. If you're not fully committed to your relationship, then you shouldn't be in it.' She shuffles off the bed and tears through the double doors. Her footsteps pound on the stairs as she runs away from me.

The next day I pace my trailer at lunch break, waiting for David. I called him to pick Audrey up yesterday, and I want to know everything that happened in her last few hours this year.

I bombard him with questions as soon as he shows up.

'You need to cut this emotional tie you have with Audrey.' He shovels half a burger into his mouth and chews. ''Cause this is coming to an end soon.'

'What do you mean? Audrey mentioned this too. What do you two know that I don't?'

David dips fries into ketchup. 'It's just an approximation. We've been working on it for a few years. We think your thirtieth birthday might be the last.'

I stop eating and look around for the trash can in case I throw up.

'There is a time-line basis for it. I went through a lot with Audrey yesterday, and the apparitions and disappearances are getting stronger and more violent. The crash that brought her here is getting stronger. It's having more of an impact on her physically. The headaches are getting worse. They might be from a head injury in the crash. Only it's manifesting itself more and more each year. I think on her last visit, the crash is going to steal her back for good.'

'What's going to happen to her? Is she going to survive?'

'I don't know,' he says and puts his food down in defeat.

CHAPTER
Eighteen

One year later.

Saturday, March 1, 2003

00:03 (ET)

New York City, New York.

I am twenty-seven today.

Leaning my forehead against the pane glass window of my apartment, I stare out at Central Park.

'Having any regrets?' David asks me from the dining table.

'No, but I hope I haven't messed anything up. I needed to take my life back in my own hands. Just because Audrey said I never moved to New York got me thinking. What if that's *why* I never moved here?'

'It's no big deal, Mike. You can always move back west.'

I nod, still staring out at the darkness.

'I'm going to turn in, get a few hours of sleep before she gets here.'

We both jump as the concierge desk rings the apartment intercom.

I look at my watch, groan, and walk to the door. 'Hello,' I say into the phone.

'Mr. Knight, apologies for the disturbance, but you have an unexpected guest this evening.'

I lean on the open doorframe, waiting for her to come up in the elevator. The doors ping open, and Jessica strides out, wheeling a small suitcase behind her.

She smiles when she sees me at the end of the hallway, and I take a deep breath. This is going to be difficult.

'Hey,' I say and kiss her cheek. I snake my arm around her waist. 'What are you doing here?'

'I'm on my way to visit the girls in Miami, so I thought I would stop here for the night. It is your birthday.'

I bring her suitcase inside and shut the door. 'I know. I'm working tomorrow and won't have much spare time.'

'That's okay. My flight is early. This is really just a quick—'

'Booty call?' I ask, slightly indignant.

'I was going to say birthday call.' She laughs. 'But whatever you'd rather me call it.'

'Come on.' I lead her to the kitchen. 'I could do with a drink.'

'Hi, Jess.' David smiles from the couch.

'Oh, hi, David. Didn't see you there.'

'You want a drink?' I ask him.

'No, thanks. I'm going to bed. Have to be up early in the morning.'

Five hours later.

Saturday, March 1, 2003

05:03 (ET)

New York City, New York.

'Mike, what the fuck?' David shouts from the living room doorway.

'Jeez, get out.' Jessica squirms for cover under me.

David shuts the living room door. There're two sets of footsteps. Fuck, this is not good.

Jessica finds her shirt, and I pull out of her and manoeuvre around the couch.

Why the hell didn't I check the time before I jumped her right here in the living room? I throw my jeans on. 'Stay here. I need to talk to him.' I find my shirt and run through the darkened hallway of my new apartment, out the front door, and down the hall to the elevator, where they are still waiting.

Audrey's auburn hair swings as she repeatedly stabs the call button.

'Where are you going?'

'You really are an asshole, Michael.' She spins round to face me. 'I mean, one minute you're trying to kiss me and making me feel guilty about it, and then you're fucking your girlfriend right in front of me.'

'Audrey, I lost track of time.'

The elevator doors open and she smacks the button as soon as she gets inside.

I look at David, but he averts his eyes as we follow her inside.

'Jessica showed up for my birthday. She's not staying long.'

'Obviously. You couldn't even make it to the bedroom?'

I ignore her comment. The couch really had been a stupid choice of location.

'You can't be mad at me for having a girlfriend, for fuck's sake. You have a husband. This is me, trying to move on. It's not like I've done anything wrong here.' But my heart sinks. I've just hurt Audrey.

She eyeballs me while I button my shirt.

The elevator doors open into the parking garage.

David is out first. 'Stay here. I'll get the car,' he tells Audrey.

Audrey holds on to the side of the wall, looking at the ground. She swallows hard. 'Where are we?' She rubs her head.

'My place. New York.'

Her head snaps up, and her face goes from pale to white with a tinge of green. 'You changed it.'

'I told you I always wanted to move to New York, and I was kind of gutted when you told me I never did. I thought I would take the plunge and make sure it happened. It's not like I have much waiting for me in LA, right?'

There's a beat of silence while my comment sinks in.

'I thought we couldn't change anything. I asked you to change her name in the movie and it never worked.'

'I did change it. Stella agreed to shorten it to Jess. That was the best I could do.'

'It was always Jess. I should have been more specific. Or if I hadn't tried to change something, it would have been different. Don't you see? We were never supposed to change *anything*. But if I managed to change something this big— moving states, what else can you change?' Tears roll down her cheeks.

'It doesn't need to be that big a deal. I'm still working. I'm still not really living here that much anyway.' My heart churns around in my chest. She's upset, and I can't be the one to comfort her.

The sound of David revving the engine in my new Audi approaches, and the tyres screech to a halt on the garage floor, echoing.

Audrey massages the side of her head and winces. She should be resting, not running off.

'You getting in?' David asks.

Audrey looks at my bare feet. 'I don't think that invitation extends to you.' She opens the passenger door and slides into the white leather seat. 'Things going well?' she asks David rhetorically while fastening her seatbelt. 'Just drive carefully.'

David grins as he rolls past me, both of them pretending I'm not even here.

It's 7 a.m. when I text David.

Jessica left for the airport. Bring Audrey back here, please.

I stare at the ceiling in my bedroom, waiting for a reply.

At nine, David and Audrey try their hardest to sneak back into the apartment, whispering loudly and sniggering.

I quietly pad across the bedroom in my bare feet and close the door behind me. The kitchen door is slightly ajar, and I glance through the crack to see what they're doing.

Audrey bangs her hip into the kitchen table as she tries to sit on one of the seats.

'Shh,' David whispers in a loud voice only a drunk person could manage.

Audrey laughs as she attempts to balance a pineapple on the edge of the table.

Great. David has got Audrey drunk, and they brought home a pineapple. Very fuckin funny.

'What the hell have you two been doing?' I ask.

'It's okay. We have a plan.' Audrey grins.

At least she's talking to me again. Maybe the pineapple broke the ice.

'Yep, Audrey is going to be my bit on the side.' David grins.

'Excuse me?' I slow the words to harden the impact, then walk faster than normal to the ten-seat table.

David crosses the room and throws an arm over her shoulder. His eyes twinkle as he tries to hide his smirk. 'For Jessica's sake,' he continues, 'Audrey can crash with me in my room, and if Jessica wonders who she is, we can tell her I picked her up on the street.'

Audrey thumps David in the ribs with an elbow, and he doubles over laughing. 'No need to make me sound like a hooker,' she squeaks.

'Jessica left for Miami.'

Audrey looks me in the eye, and her face falls.

'I sent you a text earlier to let you know.'

David pulls his phone out and squints at the screen.

'What the hell have you been drinking all night, or should I say morning?'

'Worry less about what we've been drinking and more about what we've been saying.' David drops his phone on the table and it bounces.

Audrey shoots him her no-nonsense look.

He holds his hands up in defence before turning to me. 'We've been bitching about you.'

Audrey laughs and gets up to pour herself a glass of water.

David continues, 'Turns out, even after your newfound fame, you still make quite a few stinkers.'

I roll my eyes. This is not what I need from my two best friends. 'Maybe you can fill me in after you get some sleep.'

'Don't worry about it. You get over it.' Audrey says, swaying slightly on her way back to the table.

'One day, you'll look back at this and laugh,' David tells me. 'Check this out: you're gonna get paid ten million dollars a movie, bro. You thought you had made it now, with five million.' He turns back to Audrey. 'Does he really get paid ten million a movie? 'Cause I gotta say, I've seen him act.' He laughs.

'Fuck off, David.' I toss a fabric table setting in his direction.

'He gets that for studio movies,' Audrey says. 'He still does small budget films if he likes the script or he's doing a favour. Oh, you have to do the kids' movie *Alarm Clock Runaway*. It's one of my favourites.' She yawns and rests her head and arms on the table.

'How do *you* know for sure that's what he earns?' David asks her. 'Maybe that's just a rumour he tells you to impress you at the office.'

'Shut up, David,' Audrey snaps.

'Weird, right?' David faces me. 'That there can be that much money in acting? People tell you what to say, how to say it, where to stand, and how to react. They dress you and make sure the lighting and makeup and everything is perfect. All you have to do is speak, and you're the one who gets all the money.'

'It's not speaking, it's acting. There's a difference,' I tell him.

He turns back to Audrey, ignoring me. 'Mike'll tell you how difficult that is, or you can always look at some of his early stuff and see how easy it is to fuck it up,' he teases. 'I mean, really.' He picks up the pineapple and offers it to me. 'How hard is it to say the word pineapple?'

'Don't you mean pine-*apple*?' Audrey snickers.

I thought I had finally lived down the mispronounced word from my first movie, but apparently drunk David and drunk Audrey have other ideas.

'Wouldn't you like some pine-apple for tea, my dear?' Audrey says in that god-awful English accent.

They're like school kids giggling in class, and I'm jealous. I want to be right there, drunk and happy and giggling along with her. I hide my feelings and go with the angry parent approach instead. 'You shouldn't have got her drunk.'

Audrey gets up and walks towards me, leaning over into my ear. 'I got myself drunk and do you know what? It was long overdue.' She stands up straight. 'Now I'm going to the bathroom to throw up, because that also is long overdue. And then I'm going to sleep all day. So you,' she says, poking my chest, 'and your crazy plan of spending all day extracting information from me on how to make yourself feel better, how to make yourself more successful, richer, and more desirable—can go fuck yourself.'

David leads her to the en suite in his guest bedroom, and I follow as she stumbles most of the way.

I wince when her knees smack the tiled floor before she vomits into the toilet.

Diving forward, I lift her hair out of the way.

She feebly tries to push me away.

'You done?' I ask her.

She nods.

I pick her up, carry her to bed, and tuck the blanket around her. She closes her eyes and relaxes.

I whisper into her ear, hoping she isn't asleep yet, 'Audrey, I really am sorry.'

I pass David at the door. 'Make sure you sleep on the couch.'

'Dude, what's with you? I'm not some fuckin asshole.'

It takes me a second to find a waste bin Audrey can throw up in, then I collect painkillers, fresh water, and crackers in case she's hungry when she wakes. When I reach the bedroom door, David is talking.

'Are you okay?' he asks Audrey.

She sobs quietly.

My stomach flips. I leave the things outside the door. My feet get heavier with each step as I walk away, when all I want to do is wrap my arms around her and let her sleep like she let me in Jasper.

At two O'clock I get restless. Audrey will be gone soon. I peek through David's door; they are both asleep, Audrey in bed, and David on the floor. I leave the door ajar and come up with an evil plan to wake them with the smell of bacon.

Fifteen minutes later, the sound of someone falling over the trashcan makes me grin.

'Fuck,' Audrey whispers in her sweet Irish accent.

I keep my back turned as I finish cooking.

'Morning.' Her voice is small and timid.

My heart flutters. I had no idea she might be embarrassed. I turn to give her a reassuring smile. 'Afternoon. Hungry?'

'God, yeah.' She scrambles to the kitchen island and sits on a bar stool.

I fill a plate with bacon and poached eggs, topped off with her favourite Irish sausages and white pudding.

She looks at the plate and smiles. 'You're getting used to spoiling me, aren't you?'

I keep quiet, present an overflowing pile of toast for buttering, and pour coffee.

'When David is up, we can work some more on the time travel. You were right. You've done enough for me. And I haven't made getting you home a priority. It should be. It needs to be.'

David joins us in the kitchen as we finish. 'Ah, Mike, dude. You're the best.' He slaps me on the back and picks up a plate.

'I need to call Stella,' I tell them. 'Talk through my schedule. You guys finish up here.'

'Why don't you just tell him?' David slams his cup on the re-marbled kitchen island.

I pause on the threshold, eavesdropping.

'I won't take the risk of messing this up,' Audrey replies. 'He's already made different choices, but this is so much more. Besides, he told me not to.'

'What do you need to tell me?' The words are out of my mouth before I can stop them.

They jump, eyes wide.

'I know you're hiding something from me.'

CHAPTER
Nineteen

One year later.

Sunday, 29, February, 2004

15:45 (GMT)

Dublin, Ireland.

I am twenty-eight today.

The butterflies tear through my stomach and into my lungs as I pace the hotel suite, waiting for Audrey. I switch on the TV for distraction, but the background noise irritates me, so I push the power button and slam the remote on the coffee table. Pouring myself a Jameson's from the mini-bar, I remember I need to drive later and abandon the drink.

Despite not knowing where in Dublin Audrey is from, I want her to be as close to home as she can get, and a central location is a good place to start. Caitlyn assures me Dublin's renaissance Shelbourne Hotel is *the* place to be.

My nervousness vanishes and the adrenaline kicks in as the spotlight appears at the other end of the room; she's on her way. The light intensifies and grows, I hear the ear-shattering screech, then it retreats.

Audrey screams and collapses to the floor. I run over and drop next to her, holding her as she thrashes around.

'Audrey,' I shout. 'I have you.'

She clings to my arm and focuses on my face, tears in her eyes. She looks around the room and takes short, hard gasps of air.

'Are you okay?' I search her face.

She nods and tries to stand, the colour returning to her cheeks already. 'I need some air.'

I help her to her feet and cross the room to open a window. Looking at the view of St. Stephen's Green below, I can't help but smile. I help her into the chaise lounge at the window and give her a bottle of water.

'Why are you grinning like a teenager?'

''Cause I hope you like it. Your trip home.'

'Home?'

I nod at the window. Will she recognise the view? The busy traffic and the blue and yellow double-decker buses navigating the tight roads will hopefully give it away.

'Oh, home.' She breathes an elated sigh and rests her forehead on the cold window. 'Michael, you don't have to keep doing this for me.'

'Yes, I do.' I shake a map of Ireland open and lay it flat on the breakfast table. 'We have a whole day here in Ireland. I know when you do get to come here, you're with your family, but today there are no kids, no responsibilities. Where do you want to go?'

'You look good when you smile.'

It makes me smile even more. 'Well, you know that old saying "I'm happy when you're happy"?'

She looks at the map. Sliding into the seat next to me, she traces Dublin city centre. Moving her fingers north, following the eastern coast, she taps her destination. 'Here.'

I lean over her and read, Lambay Island. 'Only you would want to go from one island to another.' I chuckle. 'Why there?'

She shrugs. 'Just always wanted to go, and it's expensive to actually get on the island, so I never had a chance when I was younger.'

'I'll get on it.' I pick up the phone and call the concierge.

'Turn right here.' **Audrey** throws an arm across the driver's side, nearly smacking me in the face.

'Where?'

'Here, for Loughshinny.'

'Loch what?'

'Right,' she screams at the turn.

After a quick check in the rearview mirror, I push hard on the brakes and make the turn. 'It's the wrong way.' I nod at the sat-nav.

'It's a detour. I want to see something. You need to slow down. This is a winding road.'

'And tight. How the hell do two cars pass each other here?'

She rolls her eyes. 'Silly city boy. What you should really ask is how do two tractors pass each other here.'

I glance at her and smile. I love it when she jokes with me.

'Tractor,' she says.

'I heard you.'

'No, tractor,' she yells, pointing. 'Slow the hell down!'

I slam on the brakes and move the car slowly to the left, scraping along the rough hedges.

We pass the tractor, and I raise my eyebrows. 'All under control.'

She laughs. 'Keep going about another mile.'

'You certainly know your way around.'

'Don't. You know you can't find me, even if you try.'

I stare at the road winding through green field after field, all the way to the coast on the horizon. The windows are open, and the sound of a traffic-free world is heavenly. 'It's like a different world out here.'

'You grew up in the middle of a tourist community and moved from one big city to another. Tractor.'

I follow the red tractor round the bends for a few hundred yards.

'We're going to stop on the right.' She points into the distance.

'Where?' I look around for a parking space.

'Here,' she yells. 'Quickly, pull in.'

I shift to the opposite side of the road. 'You can't stop here. It's a farm gate.'

She unbuckles her seatbelt. 'It's the same thing. Put your hazard lights on.'

I get out. The edge of the car is still hanging over the road.

'Don't worry about it. People around here are used to it. They'll get by.'

A tower in ruins sits in the middle of a field. 'What is this place?' I ask, beeping the doorlock.

'Baldongan. It used to be a church in the 1300s. The tower was added later to protect the priest.' She opens the pedestrian gate and holds it open for me.

'Protect the priest?'

'The churches were loyal to England in that time. It's a preserved landmark now.'

We saunter down the makeshift pathway through the field to the ruins.

'And now a graveyard?' I point to the modern, well-kept headstones.

She opens the cattle gate into the grounds. I wait for the gate to return and follow her through.

'The graveyard was here originally. There are a couple of priests buried on the east side, but they've started selling plots to the locals again.'

'You know an awful lot about this place.'

'There's a sign behind you.' She giggles, pointing over my shoulder.

A white sign is screwed into the wall, and I laugh with her. 'That's a nice mix of history with the graves.'

'That's exactly what I used to think. Mostly I love it because I used to play here when I was a kid.'

My mouth falls open. I can't believe she just told me that. 'You grew up here?' I turn a full three hundred and sixty degrees and count the houses I can see from here.

'I told you before you couldn't find me, even if you tried. Besides, we're not here anymore.' She zigzags around the graves, lifting some dead flowers and tossing them in the blue bins. 'I used to come here with my brothers. We would spend ages running around, hiding from each other. My mam didn't mind because she could see us from the kitchen.' She nods in the direction of the car, where a farmhouse sits on the opposite side of the road.

My heart thuds and tingles run through me. I parked my car outside Audrey's house. 'That's your house.' I gawk at her.

She smiles tightly. 'Not anymore.' She leads me to the entrance of the church ruins and pauses on the threshold. 'One day, I was playing around back.' She points straight through the empty building. 'And I broke the gate that surrounds the priest's grave. My brothers were mean and told me I would be haunted forever. I was too scared to tell my mam. I vowed I would pay my dues and keep the place clean and tidy, take care of the graves and water the flowers and pull up the weeds around the stones. I spent a lot of time here. My mother said she wanted to be buried here, because she would see more of me.'

'Kind of morbid,' I quip.

Audrey nods once. 'She's out back, next to the priest.' She pushes off the doorway.

I follow her through the broken down walls, glancing up at where the roof would have been. The sun shines down on the uneven grass. She leads me out the adjacent doorway to the graves at the back. The rusty gates around two graves are still there, the far side broken.

'I didn't realise your mother was dead,' I croak. My heart breaks for her. I don't want Audrey to ever have to suffer any kind of grief.

'Only recently for me, in this timeline. That's why you won't find me. I'm already gone. I couldn't stay, and it's why you shouldn't look for me. I'm not ready for any kind of life right now.'

I drop my eyes to the ground and notice the half-corpse of a crow that has wound up sharing a graveyard with two historical priests and the love of my life's mother.

'I know you want to find me, but you need to leave me be. In the future, I'm happy. My life is exactly the way I want it. Don't mess with it.'

My eyes dart to hers.

'You're in my life in the exact place you are supposed to be. At the exact time that it works. You might have wanted someone to show you the way, but I don't.'

She loops her arm through mine and leads me to a modern white headstone, which reads Joyce Kavanagh.

'It took years before I could come here again. My dad sold the house. My mam was sick for so long, his memories there were tainted. I get that now. This place was too sad for me to visit after she died. But now I see why she wanted to be here. All my good memories are in one place now.' She smiles at me.

'I would have liked to meet her.' I gulp.

'I know.'

We arrive in Skerries, an hour north of Dublin and ten minutes from Audrey's mother.

Eoin, the sailing captain, waits for us at the harbour. 'Afternoon.' He shakes both our hands. 'Need help with any equipment or anything?'

Audrey looks at me.

'No need. First trip is always just to get a feel for the place,' I lie. It was the only way to get onto the island. I had to convince the residents of small Lambay Island that we were considering using the location for David's new science TV show and we would pay inconvenience fees. It was the only way to get an invitation to dock. 'We just need free range to explore the island. Have a good look at the ruins and castles and manors.'

'Well, you're in luck. It's one of the few historical preservations that are untouched by the tourist trade,' Eoin tells us, and we climb on board. 'We usually circle round the island to point out the landmarks. Occasionally, we drop off local art groups for overnight visits.'

A resident guide waits for us to disembark. After a quick history lesson, I convince him to leave us alone as we wander down a rocky grass hill. I get my bearings at the most eastern side, before bringing Audrey to the edge of the rocks. She stumbles and I grab her waist to steady her. With all my strength and will, I release her when she gets her balance. Looking out in a north-eastern direction, I point. 'Follow that line of sight.'

'All the way out in the sea of nothing?' she asks.

'Yep,'

'What is it?'

'My home. Blackpool is about a hundred miles that way. I would love to be able to take you there one day. Show you where I grew up. Where I worked summers at the pier and eventually got fired.' I laugh. 'Meet my parents, show you what you've managed to do for all of us. But I figured I should bring you home first.'

'Maybe one day, I'll see it.'

I smile tightly, 'I have news.'

'What?' She stares at the ruins of a house.

'I'm getting married.'

Her jaw slacks in shock.

'What?' She wraps her arms around herself. 'Why?'

'What do you mean, why?' I'm indignant at her reaction. 'Why the hell do people get married? So they're not by themselves the rest of their lives.'

She narrows her eyes.

My heart drops. I already knew before she got here, I was making a mistake. 'Jess wanted to do it sooner, but I wanted to wait till after my birthday. To see what you think, to see . . . is she my wife?' I ask, not sure I want to hear the answer. 'I thought if I knew Jessica was my wife in the future, I could stop doubting myself and move on.'

'If you're asking me what I think, then you're making a mistake.' She brushes her hair behind her ear.

'A mistake? How can you say that?' I snap, feeding off her hostile energy. 'We've been together a long time, and it's the next step. She's nice, and she's not crazy like some of them have been. And let's face it, it's kind of ridiculous that I'm twenty-eight, and I haven't settled down yet.'

Audrey turns away and climbs the hill to the main street, the wind blowing her red hair. 'What happened to not wanting to be tied down? To not wanting any distraction? To having your career and being the best there is?'

'I've spent too much of my life wanting things to be perfect. With the mayhem and long hours in my life, I'm never going to get that perfect woman I've been waiting for.' I grab her by the arm and spin her around to face me. 'I want that love you keep talking about. I want . . . I want . . .' I let go of her. 'It's the right decision. I can't sit around and wait for something that's never going to happen.'

'The right one is out there for you, Michael.' Anger fuels her again. 'This is ridiculous. Every time I come through, things are getting more and more messed up. I'm making things worse.'

'What do you mean, worse?' I don't mean to yell. 'How is me getting married and settling down *worse*?'

I sit on the kerb at the top of the hill. 'Maybe this is what you were here for too?'

'I'm not here to get you a fucking wife. Especially not her.'

'What's with the sudden hostility towards Jessica?'

'Look what I did to David and Stella.' Her voice cracks and she wipes tears from her cheek. 'I have no idea if they were supposed to be together or if I ruined their lives.' She sinks down on the kerb next to me. 'They are going to rip each other apart when they finalise their divorce next year, and it might all be my fault.'

My gut churns.

'I've managed to stay out of your love life this long, but please, don't do this. You're happy in the future. You know what the right decision is.'

'How do you know I'm happy? I'm an actor, for god's sake, and a damn good one.' I jump up and pace. 'If I were miserable, no one would ever know. Why were you the one to come here, Audrey?' I goad. 'What's your motive?'

'Motive?' She leaps to her feet. 'You think I have a motive?'

'Yes, I do. Maybe you're trying to split Jessica and me up? Are you in love with me?' I snipe, when really I want to say, "I'm in love with you." 'Every time I try to tell you how I feel, you choke. You feel guilty because you married the wrong guy.'

For the second time in my life, a woman slaps me, and I deserve it.

'Don't you dare question the integrity of my marriage.' She struggles to keep her voice below a scream.

'I love her.' I'm talking about Jessica but when I say the words, my heart flutters for Audrey. This is as close as I'll ever get to tell her.

'You don't love her, and she doesn't love you.'

'You don't know that.'

'I do. The words are there, but like you said, you're a fucking actor and a damn good one, which basically makes you a man who gets paid to lie. Well, let me tell you this: I always know when you're lying.'

'Jessica wants to get married, and so do I. I'm going to do what she wants and make her happy. I'd do anything for her. I'd die for her.'

'Oh please, don't make me laugh. You'd die for her?'

'Sure.' I shrug.

'Why?'

'What the hell do you mean, why? Because that's what married people do.'

'That's not a good enough answer.' She marches back to the harbour, and I chase after her.

'Ah, for the love of god, what do you want me to say?'

'I want you to say that you would choose to die over *her*, because if she were to die, it would kill you anyway.' She stops. 'Your heart would crumple up inside, and you wouldn't be able to breathe.' She places her hands on her chest.

I swallow the lump in my throat.

'You would choke so hard without her, you couldn't bear to go on. That living without her would be worse than hell, and you couldn't survive it. That you would choose to die for her for the purely selfish reason that you don't want to be the one who's left behind.' She doesn't bother to wipe the tears away.

A stabbing pain attacks my heart like someone shoved a knife in there and has yet to pull it back out. To know that she loves someone that much is devastating. I'll never be able to compete with that. 'I'm sorry, Audrey.'

Audrey nods and wraps her arms around her waist, shivering.

I take off my jacket and hand it to her.

She slips her arms inside. 'Answer me this, Michael. It's the only question that will tell you what to do. Can you live without her?'

I don't have to think hard. 'Yes.'

'Don't marry her, Michael. She's not the one for you.'

'Be careful what you wish for, right? I got everything I asked for—no more, no less. I don't want to be alone, Audrey. Finding someone who fits into my crazy life is going to be a challenge.'

'That's the problem. You're too busy thinking about the wrong things. A relationship isn't built on whether it fits in your life. When you meet the person you love more than anything, you'll change your life so you can be together. You'll pack up and move to the other end of the world to be with them, and they would do the same for you. You'd quit your job. You'd leave your family and friends behind, and it wouldn't even be a hard decision, because you know the other person would do the same. You would do anything in the world if it meant you could be together every day, forever.'

'And what if they already married someone else?' I look away and don't give her time to answer. 'What the hell am I going to tell Jessica? The wedding is booked for next month. I can't do that to her. It would be awful.'

'You don't love her, Michael. You don't get married because you think it's time to grow up.'

'You were the one who told me I should start behaving like the man I want to be. Well, this is who I want to be. I want a normal life and a family to come home to.' *I want to marry my best friend, but I can't.*

273

Audrey exhales slowly. 'You break-up with Jessica after you find out she slept with some other guy on your twenty-eighth birthday. You were always working and out of town, and she was playing away.'

I feel sick. 'That's today. Are you sure?'

'You said you caught her red-handed. You flew to Miami to meet her the day after your birthday. She never knew you were coming. She was staying in her friend's apartment, and you arrived at midnight in the middle of a party. There were people in and out of the apartment, so the door was open, and you walked in. You didn't see her, so you checked the spare room where she always slept and saw her having sex with some model you worked with once.'

I don't say anything, and Audrey gives me the time I need.

'I've been a shitty boyfriend. What did I expect?'

'No one deserves to be cheated on, Michael.'

I nod. 'I could feel it with her. It was like both of us were with the wrong person.'

'At least you can get the ring back from her.' Audrey nudges me, trying to lighten the mood. 'Do something worthwhile with the money.'

'I had to cut back on that,' I admit as we circle the church. 'God, that's telling right there, isn't it? I just invested in some property for my family, the New York apartment, and your rings. And I'm thinking about buying that house we saw in LA. It's still for sale.'

'Do me a favour. Don't let Jessica stay there.'

'Why?'

'Trust me on this.'

'I'll deal with Jessica and the rest of my life tomorrow.' I hold out my arm. 'Let's see what else this island has.'

Dinner has been arranged for us at the only house that offers overnight accommodation. We have the place to ourselves and sit in cigar chairs next to the raised fireplace.

'I could go to Miami, stop her from ever doing this.'

'Michael. When you have time to absorb this properly, you're not going to marry her.'

'I'm engaged, for christ sake. The church is booked, the pre-nup is signed, the cake is ordered. All we have to do is show up.'

'You got her to sign a pre-nup?'

The thing nightmares are made of. 'It wasn't my idea in the beginning, but everyone told me I needed to protect my assets. It's not just me relying on my financial security.'

'You're going to marry someone with the thought that it just might not work out? With a plan of how to make your divorce a little bit easier? Didn't you learn anything from Stella's mum and dad?'

'It's not like that. It's business.' I defend myself. 'You married a rich guy. Don't you have a pre-nup?'

'No. I don't.' She scowls at me.

We sit in silence for what feels like an eternity. I keep my drink in my hand and watch the ice melt rather than meet her eyes.

'It came up,' she confesses, softening her tone. 'His family and lawyers said he should get one, but he always said no.' She hesitates a beat before continuing. 'They approached me privately and asked me to get one drafted. When his lawyer called to tell him, he did something else instead.'

'What?'

Audrey tries to hide her laughter. 'He gave me everything he owned.'

275

'He did what?' I sit forward.

Audrey stretches her legs out. 'When we started dating, I was still a student, and I didn't have, well, anything. He paid for everything: new clothes, new car, holidays. It took me ages to be comfortable with it. I was never with him for his money. We moved in together after a few weeks. We were only together, I think . . . five weeks before he asked me to marry him.'

'You moved in after a few weeks?' I scoff.

Audrey chuckles and crosses her ankles. She settles into a relaxed state when she talks about him. 'We knew we were going to be together forever.'

'You can't tell that quick. That's crazy.' I slump in my chair.

She smiles. 'Yes, you can. I know how it looks, marrying a rich guy so fast. He paid for everything all the time and when his family and friends kept bringing up the pre-nup, he wanted us to be on equal footing. He said, if he gave me everything he owned, I could walk away a millionaire. The only thing left to get married for would be each other. So he had his lawyer prepare everything and handed it all over, and then he asked me to marry him again.' She runs her fingertips over her top lip, staring into the fire.

'He must have been pretty confident you wouldn't do a runner,' I joke.

Her smile doesn't quite reach her eyes. 'He said he didn't ever want anyone doubting my integrity.'

So I'm just like everyone else who judged her marriage.

'And he never wanted me to feel he had a financial hold over me. That one day, fifty years down the line, if I ever wanted to leave, I wouldn't feel trapped. He wanted to know that every day we were together, it was because we chose to be there, not because anyone was scared of losing out financially.'

'That's pretty smart.'

'Is there anyone out there you're confident enough to give everything you own to?'

I smile to cover my heartache. Just you.

'Want to know the best thing?' Audrey nudges my arm. 'He gave me everything, so I had to pay for the wedding.' She laughs. 'He got so caught up in the grand gesture, he didn't even keep some cash. His next paycheck didn't come for, god, four months or something. He had to ask me for gas money one day. It was hilarious. Wouldn't take it back, though, no matter what I did to try and convince him. Once we married, it was ours again. Us facing the world together.'

'How did you know so quickly he was the one for you? I mean, what do you look for when you're dating someone?'

'It isn't anything to look for. It was this overwhelming feeling we were going to be best friends forever. Like a moment of peace and clarity. I'd met my soul mate.'

'You said Stella and David are going to be friends again in the future?'

She nods.

'They were good together, like best friends. Even now, when things are as bad as they are, Stella is still looking out for him. She manages him now too. Got him started on his own TV show like you said. They put all the money they earn from it back into his research on you. Just wanted you to know, you're still a priority. Even if another girl comes into my life.' I force a smile, knowing no one will ever take priority over her.

'I remember asking my husband when it was he knew he wanted to marry me. He said he knew before he even met me. He had been waiting forever for me to show up, and when he crashed into me in the restaurant, he knew I was going to be his wife. I didn't believe him at first, but I guess you just gotta have faith. There are people out there who believe in soul mates, and I never used to. You have a soul mate out there. Be patient. When you meet her, your life will just get easier.'

The next day.
Monday, 1st of March, 2004
17:45 (GMT)
Baldongan, Co. Dublin.

I toss the last of the dead flowers and weeds into the bin and wipe my muddy hands on my jeans. Jogging through the field, I check my watch. Still enough time to get to the airport. I grab the water bottle out of the car. I forgot how much bloody hard work it was doing gardening. The bouquet of lilies gives off a powerful scent as I return with them to the grave at the back of the church ruins. My heart feels lighter, knowing I've helped look after the place while Audrey couldn't.

'It was nice to meet you.' I lay the flowers on her mother's grave without a note and head to the airport.

I place my airline ticket, credit card, and passport on the counter at Dublin Airport. 'I need to change my flight destination to Miami.'

'Of course,' the assistant says, taking my documents.

'What's the arrival time?'

'Eleven p.m. local time. You travelling for business?'

I smile tightly. 'Surprising my girlfriend.'

CHAPTER

One year later.

Sunday, February 27, 2005

21:45 (PST)

Los Angeles, California.

I am twenty-nine tomorrow.

I can't hear well over the roar of the crowd.

'You need to go inside,' Stella shouts in my ear. 'They want to start the movie and they're waiting on you.'

'I need more time.' I sign someone's forearm halfway through the barrier and move onto the next, bumping into David, who is doing the same next to me. 'There must be thousands of people for this opening, and they don't even have tickets to get in.'

'You need to go inside now.' She leads me away.

Security opens the doors, and once I cross the threshold of the theatre, a feeling of calmness comes over me. My ears ring from the crowd. 'That was crazy out there.'

'Tell me about it.' She looks over my shoulder at David. 'Seems they like it when the two of you do your appearances together. The movie has started. We can sneak in the back. No one will see.'

'We need to talk,' David tells me.

'He needs to get inside,' Stella says.

Fuck, I hope this doesn't turn nasty between them.

'Can this wait?' I ask him. 'I'm already late.'

'It's about Audrey.'

My stomach flips. 'What's up?' I put my hands in my trouser pockets, pretending to be relaxed.

David hesitates. 'I need to show you something at the house. I know it's shitty timing, but some information has come together in the last couple hours.'

We both know I'm hopelessly in unrequited love with some supernatural time travelling chick, and he's always cautious when he has to deliver bad news.

'I'll see you tomorrow.' I kiss Stella on the cheek and follow David towards the back exit.

'I'm coming with you. If Audrey's in trouble, I want to help,' she says.

'Can you two put your differences aside for now?' I hold the door open for her. 'The last thing I want to do is play piggy in the middle.'

David's car is waiting out back, and the three of us climb in. As he pulls out, exhaustion overtakes me and I yawn.

'Tired?' he asks.

'You have no idea.'

'You need better time-management,' he says.

'Hey, I manage his time pretty efficiently,' Stella snaps from the back seat.

'That's not what I meant,' David says, staring in the rear-view mirror.

'It's only fair to give people what they want.' I interrupt their bickering before it escalates. 'They spend a fair chunk of their money going to these events, and movie theatres can be expensive.'

'Yeah, Mike. But three hours? No one spends that long at a premier signing autographs and posing for pictures.'

'Some of those people travelled all day to get there. I couldn't just wave and head inside. That'd be pretty shitty.'

'Don't take your foul mood out on me.' He pulls to a stop at a set of traffic lights. 'You're working way more than anyone expects you to.'

I heave a long, exaggerated breath. 'I've been thinking about the charity Audrey told us about. To do it right and make it work well, I'm going to have to invest a lot of time in it. I'm scared I'll screw it up.'

'I thought that's what Audrey was going to help with, when we meet her in this timeline,' Stella says. 'She obviously does a good job. Just wait until she and her husband set it up and approach you. I'm sure she'll have it all worked out.'

I quickly look out the window.

'What?' David asks sternly.

Shit. 'I got the ball rolling early and started investing in some of the capital assets we'll need to get started. It's just taking up more time that I thought it would.'

'Why the hell would you start something like that without talking to me first?'

'I've only paid for some things upfront. I know you told me to wait, but I thought this was a good way to change things. See if we can actually make a difference in the timeline.'

David's jaw sets tight, and he grips the steering wheel.

'It's expensive to start something this big. At least it won't be a huge financial hit all at once. Audrey always spoke with such pride about our charity work and the difference it makes for people that I couldn't sit here and wait. Other people's welfare is on the line.'

David glances at me from the corner of his eye. 'I was trying to change things. To see if it could be done.'

'Audrey's husband had a lot of things set up before I got on board. Me doing this has changed things too.'

'That's what she told you. But she let me know you came in with some of the capital assets. We didn't tell you, with the hopes of changing things. It's not your fault. I guess Audrey's right. We can't change things for her either.'

The third floor attic of David and Stella's house was originally converted into storage, but David has been using it as an office/lab, even after he moved out. It's set up like a serial killer investigation, the walls lined with photos and location maps, highlighted sections and crossed paths. The room runs the length of the five-bedroom home and so do his notes. Every piece of the wall is used and the entire investigation is connected with different coloured pieces of string tacked to pieces of information before leading you on to the next. Some colours cross over repeatedly and others don't touch until the end of the line. There is a lot of information at the far end, which is headed up with next year's date. A yellow string runs the entire way from start to finish, darting in different directions along the way, returning in full circle. There is a small section headed 2016, but most of the papers have been removed, leaving behind pin holes and blue tack stains.

'No wonder you didn't want to pack this room up when you left,' Stella says.

David looks at her but doesn't answer.

Part of the room is a high-tech lab, with multiple computer screens, lab equipment, and a hospital bed, with monitors and a glass cabinet filled with medicine bottles.

'What's that for?' I ask, terrified of the answer.

'You said she was in pain more often now, and since she left in bad shape last year, I'm expecting her return this year to be the same. You should be here for her arrival, so we don't need to worry about moving her.'

'If it's that bad, shouldn't we be at a hospital?'

'We probably should,' David says, but we both know that's not an option.

'Where did you get all this?'

'I manage my own budget and team at the university. As long as I do the projects they ask, I get my funding and an entire floor where no one bothers us.' He shrugs.

'What's going on, David?'

'Remember when I told you this might end when you turn thirty? Well, you might not actually get your thirtieth birthday with her.'

'So this year could be her last visit?' The strength in my legs is about to give out. I sit on a lab stool. I'd known this conversation was coming one day, like I know people around me are eventually going to die, but when it happened, my peace and tranquillity were thrown off their axis. The very idea of time travel has infinite possibilities and never-ending loops, but my worst fear was coming. Audrey's travels would stop in my timeline, and our friendship would be suspended in some black hole, waiting for us to meet in real time. Even then, her time would be numbered.

'How do you know for sure?' Stella asks.

'I've been piecing things together from what Audrey has told me over the years, the things she knows and her experiences. The timeline always comes to an end.' David hasn't looked at me the entire time he's spoken.

'When?' It's the hardest thing I have ever had to ask.

'There is a near positive chance this is going to end when you're thirty, so I've been working from that conclusion, although I'm not sure if you'll even get that day.'

This conversation went better in my head, when infinite possibilities kept me going. Looking at the floor, the carpet sways under me. I feel like I am standing on the ledge of a high-rise building, staring down into a vast forever. My eardrums close, and I feel sick in the back of my throat. I can't breathe. The tension builds into a huge lump in my throat, and it's choking me. Breathe, damn it. Swallow and keep breathing. 'Why didn't you tell me sooner?'

'She asked me not to.' He avoids my eyes.

'Why the hell would she keep this from me?'

'She'll be here in a few hours. You can ask her then.'

Three hours later.
Monday, February 28, 2005
01:55 (PST)
Los Angeles, California.
I am twenty-nine today.

David and I sit on lab stools on either side of the hospital bed, waiting for Audrey. I bounce one foot off the other, trying to keep myself occupied.

A small speckle of light shines, suspended in mid-air. Here goes.

After the light and sound vanish, there's Audrey. She's okay, thank god.

I smile and open my mouth to greet her.

She grabs her head and screams.

I dart over to catch her. Her eyes are closed, and her head is low. She continues to scream, and I pull her into my arms. 'Audrey,' I yell. She needs to know I'm here, that I'll help her. 'Audrey.'

She thrashes and pushes me off her.

'Get her on the bed.' David pulls things from the medicine cabinet.

I drag her to the bed, squeezing her close so she doesn't fall.

She grabs my jacket and holds on as I lead her to the bed, her frantic screams subsiding to cries of pain.

'My head,' she whimpers. 'It feels like it's going to explode.' Her eyes are full of tears. When she blinks, they run down her cheeks. She places a hand on my face. 'You're still here?'

'No, you came back again.'

She leans on the side of the bed, sobbing. 'I thought it was over. I thought I was home.' Her knuckles turn white as she digs into the pillow. Holding her life raft, she cries her heart out.

David circles the bed and attaches wires to her chest to monitor her heart and wires to her head to monitor brain activity. He pushes a switch and the machines produce printouts of their readings.

I sit on the lab stool and slide over to the head of the bed. I wrap my arm over the pillow and stroke Audrey's hair.

Consumed with grief, she looks past me and continues to cry.

An hour passes. David prints off readings from the machines and takes notes on the other side of the bed.

Audrey's silent tears still flow as I play with her hair.

'Audrey, your head is better now?' David asks.

'Yes,' she croaks, throat raw from crying. 'But I don't remember it ever being this intense before. Mostly, when I travel, I feel it right before I leave and then when I come back.'

David manoeuvres the bed into a sitting position. 'I think it's an injury from the crash that brought her here.'

'How can you know that?' I ask.

'We've been working on this for a while.' David eyes me cautiously. 'People's perception of time slows in extreme circumstances. I think this facilitated everything else that was falling into place.'

I stare at her. 'Why didn't you tell me? This is important if you want to get home. Damn it, Audrey. Is this what you've been keeping from me?'

She scrunches her eyes and holds a hand to her forehead. 'I didn't want you to feel guilty over this. It wasn't your fault, and you would be distracted if I told you about it.'

'Of course I feel guilty. I caused this to happen to you.'

'Not that.' She takes a deep breath. 'The car accident.' She turns to me. 'We were arguing before I got in the car. I'm still not sure exactly what happened before, but I've been putting pieces of information together. I was crying and driving faster than I should have been. I remember being upset the whole day and crying a lot like I was devastated over something. I think you were driving behind me or looking for me. You kept calling. I might have been on the phone to you. You were trying to get me to pull over.'

My mouth goes dry. I couldn't stop it.

'I was hit from the side—a truck, I think, or something big. I heard the horn first, then the screeching of the tyres as they braked. There were blinding white lights—headlights?'

'I think, when you leap from year to year, although it seems instantaneous for you, you do actually return home for a split second,' David explains.

'Or a leap second?' she asks.

'Maybe. I think you go back to your own time. The light and noise that bring you here are all part of the car accident. It's like a suspension in time. The truck or whatever hit, and the impact, and the time of the accident, are enough to facilitate what Michael's wish needed to materialise.'

'What does the time of the accident have to do with anything?' I ask.

'Audrey told me the accident was the morning of your birthday. The crash must have occurred at your birth time that year,' David tells us.

'My fortieth.' I take her hand. I did this to her.

'And the fact that it was a leap year—' David says.

'Makes it stronger. My grandad always said leap years are stronger for me.'

'It's the most accurate your birthday will ever be.'

Audrey finally speaks. 'I go back into the car every time I leave?'

'Only for a second. Those truck lights come back and claim you. Jerking you back into the accident before you get released into our next year.'

'But why?'

'I don't have an answer for you.'

'Why are the headaches getting worse?' she asks.

'Each time you go back, you're there a little longer. The impact is building. Nine years, or nine split seconds worth of experiencing the impact.'

'And this year it'll be ten,' Audrey whispers.

'But now we know this.' I lean into Audrey. 'We can fix it.'

Audrey swallows. 'What about the year I don't come back? What if I don't return because I die?'

I squeeze her hand. 'I'm not going to let that happen to you. We're in your future. We know this is going to happen to you. And we can stop it.'

'I don't think this is something you can stop. I chose to be there. You were trying to stop me, but I decided to keep driving. Something is going to happen, and all I know is this was the better choice.'

David has left us in his serial killer-decorated attic and gone downstairs to make lunch.

Audrey has regained her strength and humour in the last few hours. Breakfast gave her energy, and she is out of the bed and spinning on a lab stool as we read the wall of our tangled lives.

'You're going to make it home, Audrey, if it's the last thing I ever do. And maybe we could finally get that date. I would love to talk to you about all this in the future.' I point at the notes on the wall.

'Do you think your wife would appreciate you taking someone else on a date?' She cocks her eyebrow.

So I'm married. She always gives me the information I ask for eventually. A shame. It's not my priority anymore. 'Not a date, just a meeting between friends. I'd very much like us to still be friends.'

Audrey grimaces as she turns to the wall. She tries to assure me she's fine. 'That would be nice. Where would we go?'

'How about the Beverly Wilshire Hotel on Rodeo Drive? I generally get left alone there.'

'Mr. Knight, you're taking me to a hotel?' She acts offended.

I wish. 'Just for coffee. We'll have a chance to talk with no one bothering us. Some solace, you know.' I look her in the eye. She knows all about being left alone. 'And then, if we both realise we're in unhappy marriages, we're already in a hotel.' I nudge her, hoping to make her laugh.

She takes it more seriously than I'd like. 'Do me a favour, Michael. In the future, if you feel you're in an unhappy marriage, don't have an affair, like a sleazeball who doesn't have the guts to face his wife and go through a divorce. Get the divorce and then you can sleep with whomever you want.'

'Jeez, I'm kidding. You know I'm not that guy. I just . . .' *Love you.* 'It doesn't matter.'

'Okay, coffee. When?'

'Well, you're from 2016, so how about then? My fortieth birthday.' If she is with me, maybe she won't be in a car driving somewhere. 'Let's keep the tradition going? Midday, in the hotel lobby.'

'Oh, god.' Audrey grips the side of the stool. I nearly fall off mine, trying to get to her and place a hand on her arm, ready to help her, whatever is happening.

She chokes. 'It was me.'

'What?' I give her a quick look. She doesn't seem to be in any pain. I relax but still hold onto her arm. 'What was you?'

'It was me you were going to meet.' She relaxes her grip on the side of the stool.

'In the future? Audrey, do you know what this means? I tried to stop this from happening, and I can make sure you don't get in the car and you don't crash. I can keep you safe. You don't have to worry about whether you're going to make it home alive or not. I can make sure this never happens at all.'

'You can't change things, Michael. It just keeps happening. I just have this feeling, that you were trying so hard to protect me, something worse happened. I'm scared. I've been scared for a while.' She looks at me.

I sit down, pulling my chair closer to her.

'I told David about it. There's something to do with water. I don't know if I crash into water or a lake or something, but something scares the shit out of me. Like my life depends on it. David is trying to figure it out for me, but I can't stop thinking about it.'

We sit in silence for a moment, staring at the wall of evidence, not really seeing anything.

Audrey runs a hand up and down her arm. 'Even if you stop me from getting in the car, Michael, none of this will ever happen for you. What if you stay in England? Are you going to be content being a teacher the rest of your life?'

'Maybe.' I don't care. You'll be safe. 'The rest of my life might fall into place anyway.'

'What do you mean?'

'I have everything money can buy. The career I dreamed of, except the most important thing.'

'Someone to share it all with?'

'Someone to share my life with,' I correct.

'You're going to get that, Michael.'

I nod and look at my feet. *But it won't be you.*

The next day.
Tuesday, March 1, 2005
01:47 (PST)
Los Angeles, California.

'You're making her worse,' I hiss at David. 'Stop.' I pull the wires off Audrey and push him out of the way. Leaning over her, I stroke her cheek and wait for her to open her eyes. After a few seconds of silence, she still has her eyes scrunched shut in pain. 'Audrey, are you okay?'

'I feel sick,' she gasps.

Audrey bends over the side of the bed, and I jump back as she throws up on the lab floor.

David holds up a needle, syringe, and vial bottle. 'Since your headaches are getting worse each time, you might want some pain medication? It will help you relax as well, through the next travel, and we can monitor you more precisely.'

'You want to send her off drugged?' I demand. 'What if she needs help on the other side? We still don't know what's pulling her through. She needs to have her wits about her.'

'She's in too much pain to have her wits about her,' David argues.

'Give it to me, please. I can't take this anymore.' Audrey sobs.

David takes her arm. 'Her travel from this year to next is nearly instantaneous. She'll come back to us in a second. We can look after her then.'

'You don't even know if she is returning next year. What if you just drug her up and send her off to survive a car crash? How the hell is she going to get out of the car?'

'Just give it to me, David,' Audrey screams. 'I'm coming back.'

I lean closer to her, running my hand over her hair. 'How do you know?'

'Because'—she grabs my shirt and pulls me close, knuckles turning white—'I'm not finished with you yet.'

CHAPTER
Twenty-One

One year later.

Wednesday, March 1, 2006

06:50 (PST)

Los Angeles, California.

I am thirty today.

I slam my coffee mug down on Stella's kitchen island. 'I told you to push it back, Stella.'

'And I told you I did, Mike. This is as long as I could get them to wait.'

'Tomorrow would be pushing it back. Four o'clock is a delay. You know I don't work the days Audrey is here.'

'This is Oprah, Mike. She's recording on the West Coast, and she asked for you. No one says no to Oprah, even if it is your birthday. I have to go. If Audrey comes, tell her I said hi.' She turns to David. 'And I'll see you at the parent-teacher conference tonight?'

'I'll be there,' David says from the breakfast stool.

'Lock my house up when you leave.' Stella gathers her keys and coffee cup and heads out the door.

'How bad do you think it might be?' he asks me, running his hands over his chin and dropping them between his knees.

'I'm usually the one asking those questions.' But I don't want the answer from him this year. 'What if she doesn't come back?'

'Then we concentrate on how to save her in the future.' He slaps his palm on the countertop and stands from the breakfast stool.

Five hours after her arrival, Audrey is still lying in the lab bed, attached to David's monitoring equipment. 'Why do you keep looking at your watch?' she asks. 'Think I'll disappear on you early this year?'

I chuckle. 'No. I might have to disappear for a while.'

She raises her eyebrow at me.

'Oprah.'

'Ah, the Oprah interview. I remember it. A lot of people fell in love with you after that.'

'Why? What'd I do?'

'You were just your honest self. No bullshit, very humbling.' She winks, and I laugh.

'You sound like you're feeling better.'

'I'm okay.' Her eyes shift from me to David. 'I can't believe how bad it's become. It's getting really scary.'

'I'm working on it,' David tells her.

'Hey, I was going to get you to come along with me today if you want.'

Her eyes widen. 'No, Mike. I can't have people see me.' She sits up on the bed.

'Calm down.' I help her off the bed as David detaches the wires.

'They're recording in a hotel. I'll have Caitlyn book me a suite. We can go there now, and David can stay with you when I have to leave, go over anything he needs. I'll be close by.'

She nods.

'Why are you so concerned about people seeing you all of a sudden?'

'Because our real timelines are going to meet soon. Someone might recognise me. Can't have them wondering what I was doing following Mike Knight around, can I?'

Audrey rolls her window up as we drive down Rodeo Drive.

I pull into the driveway of the Beverly Wilshire Hotel.

'You have got to be kidding.' She laughs.

'What? I don't control where Oprah records her show. Plus, we can have that coffee in peace and quiet.'

Out of the elevator on the top floor, a door takes us outside to the terrace. A cast iron staircase wound with ivy leads us to a hidden doorway. Once inside the veranda suite, even Audrey is impressed.

'Wow, I've never been here before. A suite at the Beverly Wilshire. You must be looking for something from me,' she jokes, and I blush.

She smirks and bites her lip. She tours around the room, stopping at the open balcony doors. 'Oh my god, it's huge.'

'I thought you might want some fresh air. Up here no one will bother you. And I've ordered some things for you to make it more comfortable.' I point to the pile of blankets and magazines, DVDs, chocolates, and of course a set of fleece pyjamas. 'No offence, but we should launder your clothes again.'

She punches me in the arm. 'Well, if you were a half decent host, you would have gotten me out of these clothes a long time ago.'

I cock my head. 'Now there's an offer.'

The knock at the door breaks our eye contact. 'That'll be the coffee.'

When I tip the waiter and show him where to set the coffee tray, David and Audrey are talking.

'What's going on?'

'I have to go speak to Liam about a few things.' David takes his phone out. 'I'll meet you over at Venice beach tomorrow after Audrey leaves.'

'Why don't you come here? We might need you, for when she leaves.'

He shakes his head. 'Meet me at The Moon restaurant, just off the beach. I'll buy you breakfast.' He pats me on the arm and is halfway towards the bedroom to make his call before I can answer him.

'You hungry?' Audrey asks.

I turn my attention back to her and pour her coffee. 'Yes, but I need to find something to wear for this interview. I'm going to run down to Cici's and pick out clothes. Can you order for me? I need to get back to eating healthy. These past four months have been great eating whatever the hell I want, but filming is over, and the next movie Stella has lined up is an action movie.'

'You've got to love you in the action movie.' She smiles. 'Fine, I'll just order a bacon cheese burger and fries for myself. You can have the girly chicken salad.'

'Hold on here.' I clatter the coffee pot on the tray. 'You said nothing about bacon and cheese. I totally want in on that.'

She smirks. 'Since this is my last day, I'm ordering wine for tonight for when you get back, and chocolate fudge cake and probably a cheese board for dinner.'

I chuckle. 'Count me in then.'

'I'll get them to set it up on the veranda. At least out there I can breathe.'

I nod. 'Ask them for heaters. We can lie out there all night, watch the sun come up.'

She smiles at me, and I hand her coffee and kiss her on the forehead. 'I'll be back soon.'

Thursday, March 2, 2006
07:59 (PST)
Beverly Hills, California.

The screech that accompanies the light retreating rings in my ears. The nightmare noise seeps so far inside, I can feel my brain shake. The light changes from bright yellow to blinding white. Time is running out. 'I'll change this,' I tell her.

The light engulfs her, imploding into nothing and taking her with it.

A deafening silence left behind.

I drop my arms that held her a second ago. I sigh and pinch the bridge of my nose and finally let myself cry.

All the time and energy and waiting we'd done, trying to find a way to control time—or at least our perception of it—has been useless. I couldn't stop it. I couldn't control it. I couldn't keep her.

I let her go.

I inhale sharply to recover my equilibrium. Rubbing my face, I stare at the empty space where Audrey had disappeared. Her fate now lay in my ability to change her future.

The white cashmere blankets are on the loungers where we left them. I pull one to me and catch her scent as I throw it over myself. My heart crushes. God, I hope I'm not having a heart attack. Surely Audrey would have told me. I recognise the feeling. It's the same heartbreaking grief I felt when Grandad died. Like a machete has snuck inside my chest and is hacking away.

Pressing the blanket to my face, I close my eyes and will her back to me.

I imagine being hers, being this close to her and feeling her snuggle into my embrace.

Christ, what if I never manage to change things? What if she's already dead in the future? Fear runs through me and I throw the blanket off. When will David and I find out? Pacing the balcony, I retrieve my jacket on the second lap. Surely we don't need to wait till our timeline catches up with hers? Questions about her safety and whereabouts overflow in my mind.

Going to the door, my stomach rolls with disappointment. I should have bought the house. We could have spent our last day together somewhere I could keep memories of her. This hotel suite is the extent of what I've achieved in life: success and loneliness. It's luxurious and convenient, and there are people on stand-by to do everything I need. But like my life, it feels empty, like no one really lives here. Maybe that's why I prefer hotels. There's nothing worse than being lonely in your own home.

The restaurant at Venice Beach where David arranged for us to meet isn't as busy as I thought it would be. Only a few tables are occupied, but there is a small crowd of about ten people at the bar, and I know damn well David is in the middle of them.

I hang around inside the doorway and ring his phone. There's no hostess, but I spot a partition separating some of the restaurant tables from the rest of the room. I bet it's the least popular area in the whole place. If you're dining at the beach, you want a view. The phone continues to ring as I head to the last table. Hopefully this buys us some privacy. My feet drag with exhaustion. I've not slept in . . . a day-and-a-half? The idea of bunking down in the hotel for a week, shutting out the world and wallowing in my self-pity sounds nice.

I collapse into a seat and David answers the phone. 'I've got a table around the corner,' I tell him.

'Michael, shit. Sorry, I lost track of time.'

Chatter and laughter echo through the phone.

'I'll be around in a few minutes. Order breakfast. I'm in the middle of something here.'

My grip tightens around the phone. If I could crawl through it and grab him by the neck, I would.

'David, Audrey's in trouble.'

'Is she gone?' he asks.

'You know she's gone,' I snap. 'But I have no idea if she'll be back or if she made it home.'

'If she's coming back, it will be another year before we see her again. You can hang on five minutes till I'm finished here.' It sounds like he's smiling. It angers me he can be happy. I try to think of a smartass comment, but he hangs up.

I sit and wait. David's right, but I want him to treat this with urgency. The waitress is taking an order a few tables away. My chest tightens as I attempt to get her attention. Her red hair is similar to Audrey's. Well, Audrey's hair is nicer, smoother looking. God, it's going to be like this forever. Always seeing a piece of Audrey everywhere I go. I sigh, trying to lock those precious memories away.

Is she the only waitress working? I should have stayed in the hotel and had David come to me. At least they are on the ball with their service.

I sit and stew, turn my phone over in my hand, and tap it on the table. Over, tap. Over, tap. My head hurts as I gauge the things we may have changed. How can we ever know what is meant to be? What did we ever achieve on our own? Over, tap. What was Audrey's influence? Or was influencing Audrey influencing us? Over, tap.

I need coffee.

David approaches me, passing the waitress as she finishes with her customer. I motion for him to get her, but he ignores my request. I sigh and shake my head as he slides into his seat.

'I promised her I would fix this.'

'Of course you did. Hi, by the way.' He picks up the menu from the table.

'Please take this seriously.' I bang my phone down on the table.

He laughs. 'I have been taking this seriously. She's my friend too. I care whether she lives or dies as well.' He leans over the table. 'And I'm doing everything I can to figure this out.'

'I just need to know if she's safe.'

'In all honesty, I don't think we'll know for sure until 2016.'

'I can't wait that long.'

'You're going to have to.' He tosses the menu on the table. 'Unless, you know, you figure out how to time travel before then?' He grins.

I stare at him defiantly. 'All I want to know is can we make sure this set of circumstances never comes about? We have a ten-year head start. We could save her by making sure she never starts time travelling in the first place.'

'And change her fate?' He raises an eyebrow.

'She changed ours, didn't she?'

'If we do, what else in her life do you think you can change?'

I hesitate. 'Nothing. I just want to make sure she stays alive.'

'No, you don't. You love her. You want your chance with her. Why wouldn't you? It's not a bad thing, Mike. I only want to know where your head is at.'

'The woman I love is probably going to die. Best case, we figure out how to save her so she goes home to another man. So yeah, my head is all over the place.'

'But you've thought about it? What could have been if you had met her first?'

'Would she love me if she never met her husband? Yeah, I've thought about it.'

I can't wait another ten years for my friendship with Audrey to happen. A carefree, twenty-something version of Audrey is out there. A grin tugs at my mouth at the thought. For the first time in my life, I'll be older and possibly wiser than Audrey. She's alive and well and—unmarried. Dating him, yes, but married? Not yet.

If I find her, she might think I'm perfect for her, like she is for me. I like who I've become since she's been in my life. She forces me to be the best version of myself, and she won't accept anything less. How different could she be, just a few years younger? I can make her happy. *I* can be her Mr. Everything.

'Ugh.' I sigh. 'She loves him. I would be stealing her from her family, derailing her from her life's course, without her ever knowing. Regardless of what I want, I need to save her.' My heart skips a beat with a new grief. 'Set them free and all that bullshit.' I clench my jaw. I look up in annoyance as the waitress rushes past in the opposite direction. 'Excuse me,' I shout and raise my hand to get her attention. Christ, what's a guy got to do? As she turns, I yell my order for two coffees.

'Coffee? Thought you would be drinking something stronger.' David sniggers, keeping his attention on whatever he's reading on his phone.

'Oh my god.' I gasp.

'You never told me, did you have a good birthday?' David asks, ignoring me.

I glare at him. I try to speak, but I choke.

He knew.

Of course he knew.

CHAPTER
Twenty-Two

'**What's wrong with you**?' David asks.

'It's Audrey.'

'I know it's Audrey. That's why we arranged to meet. I mean, what's wrong with you now? You turned a little pale.'

'*That's* Audrey.' I point.

'You said she already left.' He turns awkwardly to look behind him. 'Didn't she disappear?'

The waitress comes back with two cups and pours the coffee in front of us. 'Sorry for the delay.'

Audrey's familiar Irish accent catches David's attention, and he raises his head.

'Do you need anything else?' she asks.

David smiles at her, then stares at his coffee, grinning, leaving me to answer.

'N-No,' I stutter.

Her look is stoic. She must be as mad as hell at me for being an asshole.

'Not just now. Thank you. I know you're busy, and I, well, thank you.'

She looks at me like I'm a lunatic. 'You're welcome,' she says and leaves.

'Wow, that's Audrey. She said it wouldn't be long. What is she, twenty?'

'Twenty-five,' I answer, staring at her across the room. I can't believe I didn't recognise her hair tied back like that. 'What wouldn't be long?'

'A totally hot twenty-five. Way to go, man.'

'Stop it. She's always gorgeous. What won't be long?'

'Sorry, dude. Just saying, if she weren't attached, I would totally make a move on her.' He laughs at his inappropriate comment.

'What are you apologising to me for? Go find her husband or boyfriend or whatever the hell he is right now and apologise to him for drooling all over her. And what wouldn't be long?'

He looks at me for a beat.

'Spit it out, David.'

'I know some stuff.'

'Tell me.'

'She told me it was right after your thirtieth birthday that she would come into our lives. That's how we knew her travelling would end here, and it's the only reason I agreed not to tell you.'

'Tell me what?' I plead.

'You know how she is about messing with the future.'

I stab the table with my finger. 'It was you who started all the worry over the butterfly effect and shit. She's already messed with the future. I mean, look at us. When we first moved here, I couldn't even afford a can of Coke from a vending machine. We never would've had this life if it wasn't for her. And don't forget what she did for Stella and Max.'

'That's the thing. Don't get me wrong—I loved Stella, and Max will always be my son, but, why would I put myself through all that again? If we really were sitting here with the ability to change all the shitty things that've happened, why wouldn't I have done that? Despite everything, Stella is our friend, and she needed that help for a while. And despite what happened to me, I'm a damn good dad, and I'll never give that up.

'We think we should change things that go wrong in our lives, but what if things are still exactly as they're supposed to be. If we change the bad things that happen to us, we might be making things a hell of a lot worse for someone else. Not just a stranger, but someone close to us. Liam and I have been trying to affect little things, but it always stays the same.'

'Audrey thinks you and Stella were never destined to be together?'

'We were. That's why I have to spend the next ten years proving to the Audrey we just met why marrying my ex-wife is the best thing I ever did.' David's eyes stay on me.

'What else aren't you telling me?'

'That's why she was so sketchy with her own details. She was scared they might influence your decision.'

'What decision?' I slam an arm on the table. 'What on earth could she tell you that she couldn't tell me? I mean, she put a million ideas in my head over the years.'

'Some of them didn't work out the way they were supposed to, did they?'

'This is ridiculous. I'm going to speak to her.' I get out of my chair and lean over David. 'I came here to ask you to help me find her and here she is. If that's not a sign from the universe, then I don't know what is.'

'Wait.' He catches my arm. 'Why did you want to find her?'

'You know why.'

'Be specific.'

'I love her, and I want to be with her.' The thought of stealing her away is deflating. I sit back down. 'I know she belongs with someone else. That he is her destiny. But I promised her I would save her.' I close my eyes and the tears escape before I know they are there. I quickly brush them away. 'I'll save her, but I won't take away her happiness.'

David taps his phone on the table. 'Do you remember the day we were in New York, Audrey and I got drunk?'

'Of course I do.'

'I left her crying at a table while I ordered drinks. She was upset after seeing you with Jessica. I'd a feeling for a while and that just confirmed it, so I asked her.'

'Asked her what?'

'I dropped a tequila shot in front of her and asked if she loved you.'

My mouth drops open. 'You asked her that? Why?' I rub my eyes and hope the embarrassment will go away. I hesitate. 'What did she say?'

'The tears kept running down her cheeks, so it was pretty obvious what the answer was. I was worried this was going to get complicated between you two. She kept distracting me with questions about revolving circles of time travel loops. Wondering if she was going to die and be stuck in this same loop, over and over again. Never dying, never moving on, just coming back to the past and making the same decisions, over and over.'

I panic at the thought. 'Will she?'

'I don't know. And I didn't want to be that blunt with her, so I tried to cushion the blow by saying I didn't have an answer for her. I tried to make it sound more appealing.'

'Appealing how?'

'I told her that maybe, when this was done, she would go back to her life, to her family. She took a swig of beer and told me.'

'Told you what?'

'She said, "Michael's my husband." She downed another tequila shot and wiped away her tears. She knows she had no right to be angry at seeing you with Jessica. That you and she weren't together, but it hurt like hell to see you with someone else.'

My eardrums are ringing. 'She told you I was her husband?'

David nods.

'Are . . . are you sure?' My voice cracks.

'I'm sure.'

I hold my head in my hands while the rest of me falls apart. 'Why didn't she tell me?' I look up at him. 'She knew how I felt about her all this time. I would have waited for her. She knows I would have been faithful to her.'

'She wasn't worried about Jessica. She knew it was all over before you two met in this timeline. That wasn't what she was worried about influencing.'

'Then what was it? What the hell did she need to be worried about with us?'

'She was concerned about what came first.' David finishes his coffee and slides the cup aside. 'She wasn't sure if she was travelling through time because she was your wife and could help us, or if you married her because you knew she would eventually be a time traveller and help us.'

The blood drains from my face, and I have to clench my teeth to stop myself from throwing up. 'She thinks I only married her to use her?'

'I told her you love her. Even then, I knew you did. She was just scared. Apparently, this Audrey'—David nods to the front of the restaurant—'is a little insecure. That and the fact you made a big deal over her picking out a specific set of wedding rings.' He shrugs. 'Oh, and she loses the diamond out of her engagement ring one time.' He grins. 'It's in the pipes to the washing machine.'

'How can she think I don't love her?'

'I don't think it was a question of whether you loved her. She was only worried there was never a first time you loved her, without knowing what she was going to do for you.'

'Every time I met her I fell in love. How can she not know that?'

'She knew, Michael. You just need to make sure, no matter what happens, she doesn't forget it. You're her husband, Mike. You always were.'

My heart is breaking. 'I sent her off to die, and she isn't even sure I love her in the future for the right reasons.' What kind of a shit do I turn into? 'She couldn't even tell me I was her husband. She told me to look after our kids if she dies. Why the hell didn't you tell me?'

'She wanted to make sure you fell in love with her of your own accord, and not because you were supposed to. But despite her fears, she loves you and wants to be with you. Guess that's why she told me to meet you here for breakfast.'

'That's why you weren't at the hotel with us.'

He nods.

'I thought you had given up hope for her.'

'We're making real progress at the lab, despite Liam shooting down most of my theories with arguments about artificial science and rationalisation. But we have another ten years to research this. 'Go get her.' He points behind him. 'Now don't freak out, but . . .'

'There's more? What the hell more can you tell me?'

'She told me when she first met you, she thought you were a dick. And you pretty much have to fight tooth and nail to get her to go on a date with you. Must have been the whole coffee incident, eh?' He chuckles.

Great, just fuckin great.

My legs shake and feel like they might buckle as I walk to the server's station to find Audrey. She has her back to me. I thought I knew every inch of her. I can't believe I didn't recognise her. I'd stopped trying to see her in every redhead on the street, but this is ridiculous. I dry my sweaty palms on my trousers.

'Hi, there,' I say as I approach.

She gasps and turns quickly. I've startled her. And I'm standing too close, and fuck, she bangs into me with the tray of drinks she's holding. I manage to catch the tray, but the drinks still crash to the floor.

She stares at the spillage, seeping through my designer shoes like she said it would.

The poor guy I once pitied is me. I smile from ear to ear. She's going to be my wife. I glance back up and her jaw is set tight.

Fuck. Please don't hate me. I pull a cloth from the station behind her and clean up the mess. 'I'm so sorry. That was my fault.'

Audrey takes a brush and pan from the bottom shelf and sweeps up the broken glass. 'What can I get you?' she asks through gritted teeth.

'Nothing. Thank you.'

She glares at me. Oh shit, yeah, what the hell do I want from her? 'Just the check. And I'll pay for the drinks.'

She purses her lips. It must be killing her not to yell at me.

I take a pile of cash from my pocket. Fuuuuuck, how much do you tip someone you want to ask on a date? Too much, and it looks like I'm trying to buy her.

She rings up my bill, and I throw in an extra twenty and hope for the best.

When she hands me my change, I take a step back. 'Keep it.'

'You look like you need it more than me,' she says.

I stare at her, waiting for an explanation.

'For the new shoes.' She nods to my soaked feet, still holding the bills out to me.

'Fair enough,' I say as I take them. 'Can I have your number?'

'Excuse me? No. You cannot.'

'Why? Are you not allowed to date customers?' Shit, that makes me sound like an arrogant asshole. Sweat runs down my back. She hates me. My future wife and love of my life hates me.

'I can date whomever the hell I choose to.' She picks up the empty tray and goes to the bar, ignoring me.

I want to stomp my feet and scream at the universe.

David walks up behind me. 'Don't worry, dude.' He smacks me on the shoulder. 'She told me you didn't give up. And you know full well, she's totally worth it.'

The next day I'm back at Audrey's restaurant for opening.

'She's not working today,' the hostess says. 'Can I get you a table, Mr. Knight?'

I crack the biggest smile.

'I need Audrey Kavanagh's phone number.'

Her eyes grow wide, but she keeps her smile in place.

'I was here yesterday. I spilt some drinks on her and never got to apologise.' I take a theatrical deep breath. 'I was a bit of an asshole too. I wanted to clear the air. Do you think you could help a guy out?'

'We aren't allowed to give out employee numbers, but she's on the early shift tomorrow. Six till two.'

'Thank you.' I put my sunglasses on and leave.

See you tomorrow at two, Audrey.

I stalk the restaurant at 1:00 p.m., determined not to miss her. I can't believe this is when I meet Audrey for real. I can honestly say, in the past ten years I don't think I've been as out of shape as I am now. It's not that I have let myself go, but I just finished filming a movie that required me to gain fifteen pounds. When you're trying to impress someone, it helps if you feel good about yourself. I pull at the bottom of my shirt and hope it looks okay.

At two-fifteen, she glides out the front door with her jacket hooked over her handbag. I take a step towards her, and she stops.

'Audrey.'

She checks behind her, like I might be talking to someone else. 'What are you doing here?'

'I wanted to apologise for yesterday. The truth is I was a little nervous. Then I made you drop your tray. Then you were mad at me. And then I thought I would look like an asshole if I tipped you too much for two coffees and asked you out on a date. Or if I tipped you too little and asked you on a date, well, I ended up blurting it out. Not my smoothest moment.'

'Really wasn't.'

My grin stretches across my face. She sounds good when she's mad. I try to keep things light. 'I've upgraded from asshole to stalker, but I thought we could go for lunch?'

'I already ate.'

'Coffee then? There is a cafe around the corner. I've booked a table,' I lie. I've booked the whole place, like she told me I did. It's a great idea. I'd be mortified if any fans approach us while I'm trying to impress the unimpressed.

'Em, okay.' She looks at her watch. 'But it needs to be quick. I have plans later.'

I nod. I hope she doesn't.

We sit in the middle of the beach-hut café and the manager closes the door behind us, discretely placing the closed sign in the window. The walls are lined with bamboo shoots on the bottom half, and accordion windows on the top half, which are pushed back, giving the feeling you're sitting right out on the beach. We're surrounded by empty tables and it's total bliss.

I ask her questions about her travel plans. She's hoping to see most of the east coast of the US. I ask where she has been before and about her parents and siblings at home in Ireland.

Turns out, we have travelled to quite a few of the same countries: France and Germany, as well as Australia and New Zealand.

I'm surprised. I always thought Audrey had seen the world with her husband, travelling on a first-class ticket. She spends her year at university, saving to travel through the summer months.

She's keen to get my perspective on the cities we've visited. It seems like our experiences are completely different. Compare one person on a budget with a backpack to someone on the company dime, and they'll get different things from it.

'Why did you move to LA? Did you always want to be an actor?'

What can I tell her? My guardian angel turned up and showed me the way?

'A friend believed in me. Told me I could do it, so I took the plunge. Scariest thing I ever did.'

I steer the conversation to relationships. 'Are you going out with your boyfriend later?'

'If I had a boyfriend I wouldn't be having coffee with you right now. Why did you ask so subtly?'

I grin. 'Just checking I'm not stepping on any toes.'

'How about you? Surely it goes with the territory to always have a model girlfriend hanging off your arm?'

'No girlfriend. Nothing.'

'Weren't you engaged recently?'

I'm a little taken aback. I had no idea she knew anything about me.

She puts down her coffee cup. 'Look, I don't want to get in the middle of anything. I don't invite drama into my life.'

Her choice of words amuses me, and I laugh heartily. 'If you don't like drama, then you shouldn't have moved to LA.'

'I came for the sun.'

'I came for the fame and riches.'

'Well, at least you're honest about it.' She laughs.

'Seriously, though, that's all behind me. There's nothing to get in the middle of. I don't date that often. It's the part of the job I hate, having your personal life up for grabs.'

She stares into her half finished coffee cup.

'What's with the coffee anyway? Thought the Irish love tea even more than us Brits.'

'Just trying to fit in with the LA lifestyle. I normally drink tea. I can only handle one cup of coffee, then I get a little cross-eyed, like I've had too much alcohol.'

'Shut up.' I laugh.

'I'm serious. Get a little head spinny too. This one's kind of strong.'

I slide her cup to the centre of the table. 'We need some water over here,' I call to the manager, laughing. 'You don't strike me as someone who needs to fit in.'

'Everyone wants to fit in.'

I would've never have thought I'd still have so much to learn about Audrey. She's ten years younger and almost a different person. 'You're going back to university next year?'

'Yeah, I needed to take a break. Everyone was telling me to get a job, but I honestly hated the idea of being a lawyer. I want to go back and do my PhD, so I decided I would do all the irresponsible travelling and partying before I go back and start the rest of my life.'

My jaw literally drops. 'You're a lawyer?'

'Oh, no. I have a law degree, but I never applied for the traineeship. I did my masters last year instead.'

'Wow, that's pretty impressive. How old are you, twenty-five?'

'That's exactly how old I am.' She chuckles. 'How did you know that?'

'Lucky guess, I think. Mental note, though, probably shouldn't tell women how old they look, right? So, PhD? That's impressive.'

'And pricey. One of the reasons I wanted to take a break and travel. There is so much freedom living out of a backpack and moving from city to city. It gave me time to think if academia is something I wanted to invest the next four years in. Hopefully, once it's all done, it will be a great career move.'

A knife twists in my gut. Audrey never had that career. She married me instead. My crazy work schedule and flying from location to location meant that for us to be together, she had to give up her dream job. She spends her time raising our kids, so I can have the career I wanted. Did we argue over it? Did I assume my career was more worthwhile? Did I argue that I could earn more money? Did I convince her to give up on her dreams? Part of me dies when I think about it.

'What? What did I say?' she asks.

'Nothing. I was just thinking, how people's lives can take such drastic directions for no apparent reason.' I lean over the table and whisper, 'Can I have your number now?'

'Why?'

'So I can call you.'

'But why would you want to call me?'

'To ask you out again.'

'I'm here. Ask me now. I don't play games. I'm not going to sit by the phone and wonder what it means if you haven't called by a certain time. If you want to ask me out again, ask. It's going to be more difficult for me to say no to your face.'

'You said no last time,' I remind her.

'And yet here I am.'

'Okay. Will you go out with me again?'

She hesitates. 'I don't know.'

'Come on.' I grin. 'You just said you couldn't say no to my face.'

'Look, Mike—'

'Michael. Please call me Michael. Mike is my work name.'

'Okay, Michael.'

My heart flutters, hearing her say my name.

'I don't think being in the middle of your life, even for a brief time, is going to be something I'm comfortable with.'

'It's a job. Please don't judge me on that basis. Get to know me, and if you don't like me, tell me. I promise to keep the drama to a minimum.'

'Fine.' She smiles. 'But this is going to be a casual get-to-know-you date. Like the Americans do. Not like a serious, on a date British thing.'

'Don't worry. I'll do my best to be the least English I can be. And since it's not a serious date, you can pay for your own dinner and call yourself a taxi when it's over.'

'Fine, but I better choose the restaurant. I can only afford certain places in LA. Service wages here are pretty much criminal, and some people skip out on the tip.' She raises her eyebrow.

'Well then, how about to make up for not tipping you, I will pay. Because I don't want you remembering our first date as the worst date of your life.'

'If it were that bad, you wouldn't get another.'

'Tonight then.'

'Isn't that a bit keen?'

'I don't want to wait. You're finished for the day, and I'm on a filming break for the next few weeks, so there really couldn't be a better time.'

'Okay, half six. I still eat on the GMT clock.'

'Okay.' I look at my watch. 'I'll run you home and pick you up later.'

I pay for the coffees and the cafe and walk her out the door. I take her hand outside. She stares at our hands but doesn't pull away. This nervousness in her is strange. Bringing the confidence out in her is going to be something new. On the way to my Mercedes, I remember what's next. I tighten my grip on her hand. 'Come on. There's something I want to do first.' I pull her across the pavement and run straight to the sand.

I move into the left lane at the traffic lights when Audrey points out where she's staying.

I tap my foot, waiting for the lights to turn green. When I park, she's going to kiss me, and my stomach is jumping with nerves. I reach over and take her hand, running my thumb over her knuckles.

I make the turn and park the SUV, killing the engine. I turn to her, thinking of something to say, but she places her hand on the side of my face. It sends shivers through me.

Her eyes drop to my lips and I wait.

She kisses my bottom lip slowly. She catches my lip between her teeth and gently tugs, forcing my mouth open.

I think I just died. I kiss her back, sliding my tongue past her lips. I wind a hand through her hair, finally, and my heart beats faster. I let her kiss my lips again. She places small kisses on the top one, then the bottom. Taking turns nibbling and caressing and kissing.

I want to groan and pull her on top of me, to never let her go, but she's only just met me.

I kiss her back slowly and nudge her lips open again.

She smiles against my mouth and my tongue caresses hers. She tastes better than I ever imagined. There's a thudding constriction from my heart at the top of my throat and I groan to shift it.

'Michael,' she whispers.

I stop kissing her but don't move away. 'Yes?' I trail a hand through her hair.

'We've not even had a date yet. I don't think I should be kissing you at the side of the road.'

I slide my hand down her arm, and take her hand in mine. 'I'm counting this afternoon as our first date. Tonight can be our second.'

Audrey smiles. 'See you in a couple hours.' She shuts the door and jogs up the steps to her front door.

I wait until Audrey is inside, then dial Stella's number before manoeuvring back on the road.

'Hey, Mike, what's up?'

'Remember the house I nearly bought in Beverly Hills a couple of years ago?'

'Yeah. It was still on the market the last time you had me check.'

'Buy it. I want to move in straight away.'

'You do know I'm not your assistant, right?' she asks. The scribble of pen on paper comes through the speaker.

'But you do such a good job.' I laugh. 'And find me a contractor. I want to knock down the back kitchen wall. And I need to sell the New York apartment.'

Almost two weeks later.

Thursday, March 16, 2006

20:10 (PDT)

Beverly Hills, California.

'**Are you saying you're** not enjoying our dates?' I ask Audrey with mock horror. 'I'm just glad I have a break in filming and get to monopolise every minute you're not working.'

She grabs my hand and holds it tight. 'It's all a bit extravagant, and in such a short space of time. Rock climbing lessons; track driving; swimming with dolphins. When you do such amazing things, of course you're going to have a good time.'

I snort. 'Audrey, I've done lots of amazing things on dates with girls and not had a good time.'

She raises an eyebrow at me.

'That's not what I meant.' I hold up my hands. 'It's the person who makes the difference. Plus, we do lots of regular date things. We're having dinner.' I gesture at the table.

'We're having dinner in a Beverly Hills restaurant, Michael.'

'Where is the conversation going?'

'Sometimes I wish I had met you before all this. Seen what you're really like.'

'I'm the same guy, Audrey.'

'How about we spend time together doing something for free?'

It's my turn to raise my eyebrows.

'Not that.' She laughs but stops, cheeks flushed. 'How about you arrange a fabulous date tomorrow that doesn't cost a thing? Show me what it would be like to date Michael Knight if you'd never moved to LA.'

'Hmm, interesting. I can totally do that.' I lean back on the floral cushion of the wooden bench. 'Tomorrow was supposed to be Vegas,' I tease, knowing she missed an opportunity for a trip there.

She smirks at me.

'I need to have some allowances, like even a picnic on the beach is going to cost something for the food.' I run my fingers over her knuckles, then dip a fork into my apple crumble.

'You can have twenty dollars.'

'Come on.' I laugh. 'I need to buy a picnic basket.'

'Twenty is your limit. That includes gas.'

'I'm going to have to impress you with ham sandwiches and crisps from a plastic carrier bag?'

'I'm sure you can think of other ways to impress me.'

I turn her hand over in mine, stroking her wrist and the inside of her arm. I lean over and kiss her softly on the lips. 'Your ice cream tastes great, by the way.' I grin and stab my fork into her sundae, stealing as much as I can before she hits me on the chest.

Once outside I wrap my arm around Audrey's side, running my fingers across her waistband as I go. I plant a kiss on the corner of her mouth.

A girl calls my name and rushes towards us, followed by a guy. 'Mike Knight, can we get a picture?'

Audrey moves out of my embrace and steps to the side.

I grab her hand and wind my fingers in hers to keep her from moving too far away.

'Sure,' I tell the couple. 'You want one under the street sign?'

The girl grins. 'That would be awesome, thank you.'

'Thanks, man,' the guy says. 'I loved you in *Four Holes*. No one else can shoot and drive and kick ass like that.'

I let go of Audrey's hand as the couple arranges the camera to get a snap. The three of us shake hands. 'Have a good day,' I tell them.

I swiftly lead Audrey to the valet to collect our car before a crowd forms.

'That must become exhausting,' she says.

'It's the bread and butter of the business.' I open her door. 'If you don't look after your customers, they're going to spend their money on a different movie.'

'Hm, never thought of it like that before.'

'Plus, it's kinda cool.' I wink at her, and she bursts out laughing.

The next day.
Friday, March 17, 2006
17:02 (PDT)
Los Angeles, California.

Our twenty-dollar picnic on Santa Monica beach is quiet and perfect. We choose a spot well away from the pier and spend the day sunbathing and talking. Lying next to Audrey all day with minimal clothes on is challenging.

'You've a very nice body,' she tells me between kisses. 'I always thought they did special effects on abs in the movies, but you're just as impressive up close.' She caresses my shoulders and the top of my arms.

'If you're impressed now, I wish you could have seen me a couple of months back, when I really was in shape.'

She tries to bite back a grin.

'It's getting chilly, and I'd love to lie here all day and have you compliment my whole body but—'

'Can't compliment it all. Haven't seen it all, yet.' Her fingers tease the back of my waistband.

I practically lie on top of her, gripping the side of her hip, and kiss her neck.

'I was thinking about dinner at my house tonight,' I blurt out. 'I just bought it a couple of weeks ago and I haven't had a chance to cook there yet. Since we're on a no-spend day, I thought we could finish our date there.' I keep stroking her naked stomach through the moment of silence. 'You don't have to, obviously. We can eat out, but you're going to have to up my spend limit, unless you want to survive the rest of the evening on'—I look through the leftovers—'warm water and soggy strawberries.'

She laughs. 'Dinner at your house sounds nice but—'

'Just dinner. I'll drive you home straight after.'

'No,' she says quickly.

My heart sinks. 'Okay, another time then,' I say roughly. I didn't expect her to shoot me down. I thought she was right there with me.

'No, I mean, I don't want you to drive me home.'

I raise my eyebrow at her.

She sits up and touches my arm. 'Is that all you're asking me for? Dinner?'

Go with honesty, Michael. 'I was asking you to spend the night with me. Only if you want to. If not, it's okay. I don't want to ruin what we have here.'

'Like spend the night, *with* you?' She grins as she waits for my answer.

I stammer with my answer and laugh at my inability to form a sentence.

She snakes her arms around my neck and pulls me down, so I'm lying on top of her. Her fingernails tease my neck. 'I think it might be about time.'

I pick Audrey up at seven and drive across town. I push the button on the key fob as we approach the gates to my new Beverly Hills home that she'll one day help me pick out.

Audrey sucks in a breath. 'Wow, this is impressive,' she says as I park.

We get out of the car, and I take her bag. I unlock the front door and run my hand down her back as we cross the threshold. 'It's pretty overwhelming for me too, sometimes.'

'How did you get moved in so quickly?'

'Stella's mom, Pamela, did most of the work. Think she felt she owed me for setting the last place we lived on fire.' I chuckle.

Audrey's face falls.

'Just the kitchen. She's been great this last year. She's really come back to her old self, or so Stella says. She nearly flipped with excitement when I asked her to decorate this place and manage the move. I think she's found her calling in life.'

'Helping people?'

I tilt my head. 'Decorating on someone else's budget.'

Audrey gives the reception area a three hundred and sixty-degree survey. 'She did a good job.'

'I'll give you a tour later. Let's get dinner started first.'

In the kitchen, I explain my parents' financial struggles when I was in university. I need her to know that this is new to me as well. I pull pans from the cupboard and tell her how I sponged off David, and then Stella, for the first couple of years. I pour Audrey a glass of wine at the kitchen island. As I prepare dinner she listens to me explain how I paid everyone back before saving enough money to finally buy my own place. I season the pork in a casserole dish, pour over the barbeque sauce that Pamela taught me how to make, and slide the dish into the Aga and set the timer.

'You could have bought somewhere smaller, sooner?'

'I liked this house. I've been debating whether to buy it for a few years. I just never felt settled in LA. I actually wanted to move to New York, and that kept me from buying here.'

'Why aren't you in New York then?'

I smile tightly. 'Never worked out. Grab the wine, let's wait outside.' I open my arm, let her slide into me, and lead her out back.

My first order of business was to make the outdoor space an astonishing place to spend time. The apple trees are covered in twinkling fairy lights, and there are multi-wick church candles housed in oversized glass holders around the pool.

'Oh my god, this is gorgeous. Pamela?'

'Me. I love it out here and wanted to make sure it was exactly what I needed.'

'What's that?'

'Enough space to throw my head back and breathe.'

I follow her to the edge of the pool, where she takes off a flip-flop and sticks her toes in the pool, just like she did when we viewed this a few years ago. When I wanted to kiss her and couldn't. An animal instinct takes over me. I want to touch her, kiss her, have my mouth on her body and finally explore every inch of her.

I pull her flush against me. I kiss her hard and fast, knotting her hair in my fingers.

Her hands tug on the lapels of my jacket, securing me against her. I twirl her around and walk her towards the wall of the house. I lift her leg up, wrapping it around mine, getting closer to her heat.

She pushes her hips hard against me. Her breathing becomes harsh and her hands demanding.

I devour her scent with each kiss, moving our mouths and hands around each other.

Audrey runs her hands down my chest to the bottom of my shirt. She slips her fingers under the fabric and makes her way back up my naked skin.

'Dinner or bed?' I ask, gasping for breath.

'Bed,' she says without missing a beat.

I smile against her lips and sweep her up into my arms. 'Your wish is my command.'

She giggles as I carry her through the kitchen and pause at the cooker to turn down the temperature. Once upstairs and in the bedroom, I set her on her feet.

'Now that's a bed.' She surveys the Alaskan-king bed.

'You should see the bath,' I mutter, nibbling at her neck. I run my hands around her legs across the hem of her black dress.

I want to draw out each and every moment with her. Relish in the feel of her skin, the taste of her mouth, the pure sight of her.

I tug her dress over her thighs, trailing her skin as I go. Dropping to my knees I kiss her stomach, knowing that one day this perfect body will carry my children. I stand and take her dress with me, leaving her in her mismatched lace underwear. Trailing my mouth over the fabric of her bra, I kiss the soft exposed skin, delighted with the goosebumps I've created.

Gripping my hair, she takes a deep breath.

I slide my nose along the swell of her breasts and undo her bra clasp. When she falls free, I clasp her breasts in my hands and run my tongue over her nipples, taking turns to suck on each, making them pucker. I grin at the sight of her. This woman was made for me. Placing a kiss over her heart, I grip her ass and pull her sharply to me, those perfect breasts bouncing before she's flush against me. Excitement pumps through me and I kiss her deeply, keeping my eyes open to relish in the sight of her.

She shares my urgency. Her hands are rough when she rips my shirt off. 'I want to feel you next to me.' She yanks the shirt over my shoulders and runs her nails over the line of my bicep and across my abs. After undoing my belt, she pauses to stroke the hair under my navel. I gasp when she yanks my jeans open and slides a hand inside the rim of my boxers. Desperate for her to touch me, I hold my breath. She kisses me before catching my bottom lip in her teeth. Tugging on my lip, she dives her hand into my underwear and takes hold of my erection.

'Audrey.' I catch her hand, stopping her strokes, and rest my forehead against hers. 'I need to get you in bed before I explode.'

I gasp as she rolls a hand around me, smiling.

Kicking off the rest of my clothes, I playfully toss her on the bed. Climbing over her, I clutch the top of her panties with my teeth. She holds her breath as I slide my fingers under the fabric, twist my fingers around the lace, and pull them down, kissing every inch of skin I expose on the way. She lets out a gasp when my lips kiss the centre of her legs. Calmness comes over me. We're going to get to do this forever. Taking her moans of approval, I lavish attention here. I lick and suck her clit over and over until it hardens. I reluctantly pull away to follow the trail of her underwear, kissing down her smooth legs, inhaling her vanilla scent as I slide the lace off. 'I've been waiting so long for you to show up in my life.' I want to worship her whole body, to let her know how much I care for her. I run my tongue over her instep and nibble on her toes.

She giggles, and I grin against the base of her foot. She's beautifully naked in a pile of sheets and pillows in my bed, a bed I thought I might have to sleep in alone, forever. There's an ache inside me, running the length of my body, knowing that for the first time in my life, I'm about to make love to someone.

I slide up and claim her mouth with mine, leaning my body against hers. She opens her legs, and I settle between the cradle of her hips, finding my place of solace with her. I squeeze her thigh and wrap her leg around mine, allowing me to rub against her heat, and she groans.

Unsure of her noises, I ask, 'Is this all okay?'

'Yes.' She pushes her hips against mine. 'I just need you. Right now.'

I take a condom from the bedside cabinet and kneel over her.

'That's quite something you have there.' She giggles when I roll the condom on.

My cheeks fill with heat. I have no idea why, but Audrey Kavanagh paying a compliment to my junk is something I never thought I would hear. I guess there is a time for everything.

'What?' She nudges my leg with her foot. 'Don't you normally give girls enough time to check you out?' She sits up and runs her hands over my abs, dropping a hand to my cock, and trails her fingers over the condom.

I nearly whimper when she turns her head towards it, feeling her breath, through the thin sheath of the condom. 'Audrey. You're killing me here.'

She darts her tongue over the tip, and I let out a pained gasp. Not being inside her right now actually hurts. My dick twitches, trying to find its own way to her tongue, pulsing, knowing it would be soothed inside her.

She lies back and circles her legs around me. Knocking her feet against my ass, she pulls me over her.

Gripping her hands in each of mine, I hold them above her head. My body heats when I lie flush with hers. 'Tell me how you like it,' I whisper in her ear and ease inside her. Her warmth sucks me in, the feeling of her tightness around me keeps me in place, and I take my time, relishing in the feeling as I move back and forth. Rearing the whole way out, I use the slick of her arousal to tease around her clit.

'Harder,' she tells me.

With more certainty, I slam into her.

She groans and pushes her hips up, grinding her clit on me.

'Fuck, Audrey.' I pick up the pace and pound into her, feeling more at home with each groan she makes. I lift her ankles into the air and tilt her hips up, kneeling on the bed next in front of her, I keep the pace fast. She tightens around my cock, and I let my head fall back and close my eyes.

Her walls start to flutter around me, and she chokes out my name, 'Michael.'

I take the nub of her clit between my fingers and tease it back and forth, pulling her over the edge with me. 'Come, Audrey.'

She cries out and lets herself go.

I keep up the pace until I feel her relaxing and then I pound into her, finding my own release inside her. Despite the sensitivity, I can't stop from moving inside of her. I pull her hand to my mouth and kiss the back of her hand, letting my breathing calm.

She stares up at me, and I swear, my heart misses a beat.

Still moving inside her, I'm getting hard again.

'Michael.' She grins. 'You're going to have to stop a second and give me a minute.'

I chuckle, and she gasps when I pull out of her. I can see the same loss in her expression as I feel at the break in contact. Instead of going to the bathroom, a colossal ten feet away, I tie a knot in the condom and ditch it on the floor, not wanting to move away from her. I gather her in my arms and pull her flush against me. I kiss her head as she buries herself in the crook of my arm and wraps a leg over me.

She laughs. 'I can't believe you're hard again, Michael.'

'That's because you're goddamn amazing.' I breathe heavily. 'Do you believe in soul mates?'

She leans up on my chest and looks at me. 'I never used to.'

I grin and tuck a strand of hair behind her ear. 'Let me know whenever you're ready to go again, and I'm all yours.'

Audrey is asleep in my arms. I stroke her hair, shorter now than I'm used to. I slide a hand up and down her naked spine, tickling her with my fingertips, as I pass her waist. She shivers and the hairs on her arms stand up, so I pull the sheets up to cover us and give her a tight squeeze. Audrey's future takes over my thoughts. Did she make it home, to me, to our kids? A lump forms in my throat as the fear of the situation hits home. Sometime in the future, my wife might die.

One week later.
Sunday, March 26, 2006
20:07 (PDT)
Los Angeles, California.

'You got a second to talk?' David asks from the doorway.

'Sure.' I toss the script I was reading onto the pile on my desk. 'But better make it quick. I have to pick Audrey up from work at nine.'

'It's about Audrey. We want to meet her, Stella and me.'

'Like a double date with your ex-wife?'

'Take this seriously, Michael. We're friends, all of us. I kind of miss her.'

I nod.

'You've been together a few weeks now. It's a normal amount of time to start meeting each other's friends.'

'You and Stella are going to have to swear you're not going to say anything that is going to freak her out.'

'You have my word. Besides, there's no point in questioning her about her son when you don't even have kids yet.'

'What do you mean, question her about her son?'

'Michael, when she was scared, she said she couldn't stop seeing her son when she closed her eyes. You don't think

330

those two things are related? I need you over at Stella's attic. We have work to do.'

'What work?'

'Everything that happened over the last ten years is all there. It's going to be the longest script you've ever memorised, everything you ever told Audrey about our lives. You're going to have to make sure she knows it all.'

Four days later.
Thursday, March 30, 2006
08:42 (PST)
Los Angeles, California.

Audrey is finishing off her PhD proposal in my office when I check to see if she needs anything. She stands and stretches, and I steal her seat in my office chair, grabbing hold of her hands. She perches on the edge of the desk, raising her bare feet to the chair between my legs. I put my hands on them to heat them up. Why she won't wear socks or real shoes is beyond me. She hasn't looked me in the eye.

'Everything okay?'

'My visa is up next month, Michael. I don't want to leave, but I have to go home eventually, and I was thinking this might be a good time.'

I straighten and my office chair snaps to full upright position.

'University is starting in a few weeks. I need to get sorted. I'm nervous about going back, actually. A PhD course is going to be on a whole other level.'

'We spoke about this before. Neither of us wants a long-distance relationship, do we?'

'It wouldn't be ideal.'

'Audrey, do you still want me? After all this? Now you know exactly what you're getting into with me. I could come with you.'

She relaxes. 'What about work?'

'I can ask Stella to only schedule movies on European shoots for the next few years while you finish. I could take time off and write. There are a few projects I need to work on.'

Her face falls. Oh shit.

'Michael, I want you to come, I do. But I don't want you to give anything up for me. This is your career, a very successful career. I don't want us fighting a year or two down the line, and you throwing this in my face.'

'I wouldn't do that. You know I love you. I don't care about a career.' But I should. Audrey will sacrifice everything in the future to make sure my life plays out this way. I want to fight for her, rather than a job. 'I want to share my life with you, and if that means moving to Ireland, then that's okay by me. We can move back here when you're finished. We'll work it out. We can travel on your holidays. We can be together. The only question is, do you want me to come with you?'

'Yes, of course I do.'

'Good. Then I'll come. I'll never regret giving anything up for you, Audrey.' I lean forward to kiss her, but she tenses.

'What if I stayed?'

'What about uni? It's important to you.'

'It is, but you just admitted you would be giving something up to come with me.' She drops her gaze. 'I could look into staying here. Perhaps I could qualify for a student visa and work my PhD out of UCLA. But . . . I don't want this to sound like I'm asking you for anything . . .'

'What?'

'I can't afford the fees here.' She doesn't look me in the eye when she says this. 'I'm not asking, Michael. I won't mind if you would prefer not to. I have a grant sorted to cover the fees at home, so it's not like I won't be able to do it. It's something to think about if we want to stay here.'

I smile and try to keep myself from giggling with relief. 'I'll pay for school, Audrey. It's not even an issue. It would be easier for my work if we stayed here.'

This is the moment I steal her future career. My heart drops. It was easier than I thought it would be.

'Don't worry about money. I have enough to take care of us forever. And since you bring it up, maybe you won't feel so weird about it if it was yours too.'

'You're not giving me money, Michael. The last thing I'm—'

'Marry me, Audrey.'

Her mouth drops open.

'I know this is soon, but I'm serious. You're my best friend. I love you, and I want us to spend the rest of our lives together. I want to have children with you. I feel like in this crazy world my life is a little bit easier knowing I have you with me. I never realised that's what a relationship was all about—supporting each other. It works, it really, really works, and I want you to be my wife.'

'Michael.' She slides off the table and sits on my lap. 'Since our first coffee date, I knew I was going to marry you.'

'You did?' I kiss the tip of her nose.

'I can't explain it. I just knew this was it. You were the person for me, like a moment of clarity or an epiphany.'

'I feel like there's a but coming.'

'You're right, this is crazy. It's too soon. People will say I'm a gold digger. That I'm pregnant. Anything to make out our relationship isn't real. I can't handle that kind of judgement,' she whispers.

I wipe her tears away with my thumbs. 'So you want to wait. How long?'

'I don't know. A couple of years?'

'Years?' I sigh and kiss her. 'Audrey, if I was a regular guy with a regular income, would you say yes and get married now?'

'Yes. 'Cause no one would care.'

'Then let's get married. One thing I have learned over the years is some people are going to judge you no matter what. True friends support you. So if it's now, or later, it doesn't matter.'

A giggle escapes her, and she quickly covers her mouth with her hand. 'We haven't even met each other's family.'

'We'll fly out this week, then we'll get married wherever, whenever you want. Just don't make me wait because of the job I have.'

'Okay.'

'Are you saying yes?'

'Yes, I'll marry you.'

Three weeks later.
Sunday, 23 April, 2006
15:07 (GMT)
Blackpool, England.

'She's not signing a pre-nup, Mum. Don't be ridiculous.' It's exhausting having this same conversation day after day. I sit on the back steps to the B&B I grew up in. My mum now runs it with another man. I feel like I'm a guest here rather than on a visit home. George tried his best to welcome us in, but all I could think of when I looked at him was how much my dad disliked him over the years.

'You don't even know the girl, Michael,' Mum says, hanging another sheet on the line. 'Of course she's behaving like the perfect match. She stands to make a fortune off you.'

'Is that how much you think of me?' I ask.

'What do you mean? This has nothing to do with you,' she tells me, shaking the towels rougher than necessary.

I grab one from her. 'Do you think no one could ever love me? That they only want my money?'

'That's not what I meant.' Her expression softens.

'She's not a gold digger, and I do know her. I know her better than anyone, and we're getting married. I take that vow seriously. I'm not anticipating my marriage coming to an end.'

Her face crumples, but she almost immediately regains her composure. 'Even your dad thinks I'm right on this one.' She snaps the towel out of my hand and clips it on top of the line.

Footsteps thud down the steps behind me. 'Everything okay out here?'

'Fine, honey,' Mum answers and smiles over my shoulder.

Like hell it is. I turn on my heel and nod at him on the way inside. 'George.'

'Michael,' he replies.

'Audrey, I need you to do this.'

'This is crazy. I'm not taking all your money,' she whispers in the small en suite attached to the B&B room we've been in all week.

I went to see Luca Vargas before we left the States. My assets will be gifted to Audrey. My cash and stock shares have already been transferred. This last part only needs her signature. Once it's done, I'll be worth the two hundred pounds in my wallet. Audrey will have everything I own: my houses, my cars, my investment properties, and bank accounts. All in all, around twenty million dollars. I don't care if I ever get it back. If I get to spend the rest of my life with her, it'll be a bargain.

I smile and pass her the toothpaste. 'Just think, you'll no longer look like you want to curl up into a ball and die of embarrassment at spending our money. Don't feel bad. If the shoe was on the other foot, I'd totally be happy spending everything you had.'

She looks at me in the mirror but doesn't laugh, like I expected her to.

My stomach churns with nerves. 'When you walk down that aisle, everyone will know you're doing it because you want to marry me.'

Ten months later.

Wednesday, February 14, 2007

11:22 (PST)

Los Angeles, California.

My thirty-first birthday is approaching, and I have no idea what to do. David and I have met with Stella in her office so we won't be disturbed.

'I'm telling you, Audrey won't show up this year. She told me you spent the weekend of your thirty-first birthday at a beach house you rented in Malibu. That's how we figured she had stopped travelling by then,' David tells me.

'But you're not positive?' I ask.

'She did say you were inseparable for three days, if you know what I mean.'

'I bloody well know what you mean, David,' I snap and feel bad straight away. He wasn't being crude on purpose. 'We've hidden Audrey from people before. God, remember the time she showed up when I was with Jessica in New York? We managed to hide that. What if Audrey did show up this year, and we hid it?'

'Why would we do that?' Stella asks.

'Because she might freak out at meeting her future self? She's not ready to deal with that.'

'When would you ever be ready to deal with that?' David asks.

'I don't know. When you're twenty years old and think the universe is out to give you a helping hand?'

'Why did you lie to her?' Stella asks.

'I never lied to her.'

337

'You told her you were in a movie in college, an un-released one.'

I shift in my seat. 'I didn't want to feel complacent when Audrey visited me in the beginning. I needed to feel like I'd already fucked up. Otherwise, I might have never taken that plunge and moved to LA.'

'*The Cat's Hat*? You couldn't come up with a better fake title?' David crosses his ankles on the coffee table.

'Hey, I wasn't the one who made it up.' I pause. 'I think.'

'And New York?' Stella inquires. 'You told her you always wanted to live there.'

'That's not lying. I was being careful with my words. At that stage in my life, I had to feel I was the one in control of things, not some greater universal power.'

'And now?' Stella tosses her empty water bottle in the waste bin.

'Now, all I need is her.'

'Then it's decided. If time travelling Audrey shows up, I'll take her away, like I did the year you were with Jessica, and the Audrey here will never know,' David says.

'How can you be so confident?' Stella leans back on the sofa.

'Because Audrey already told me she never saw anything to do with time travel until it happened to her. So one of two things is going to happen. She doesn't show up, and we're in the clear, or she does, and I take her off for the day, and our Audrey here is none the wiser.'

Audrey might visit, and I won't get to see her. I won't get to tell her I love her, that I know she loves me. Should I be more worried if she doesn't show? That could mean she didn't make it home safely. We've been so occupied with helping Audrey in 2016, thinking we had ten years—nine now—I never realised, whatever happens then, has already happened for her. She could be dead.

'Anything you want me to say to her if she shows?' David asks tenderly.

'Tell her I love her. And that I'm keeping my promise.'

Two weeks later.
Wednesday, February 28, 2007
06:22 (PST)
I am thirty-one today.
Los Angeles, California.

There are no blinds in the Malibu beach house. The sun hasn't risen yet: it's not even 7:00 a.m. Audrey is wrapped in my arms in a deep sleep, and I daren't move at the risk of disturbing her. The other Audrey never showed last night. I waited up well past three, pretending I had some writing to finish before I dragged myself off to bed.

I lie here for the few hours, thinking about whether I should be grieving or not. Audrey's right here. I haven't lost her. But somewhere out there, her future fate is hanging in the balance. I held her all night, grateful we managed to find each other, even if there was something bigger at work to send her to me.

I'm just selfish because I want to keep her longer than ten years.

Audrey wakes and grins. 'Happy birthday, boyo,' she whispers then kisses me.

Her lips linger, and my heart beats faster, not wanting it to end.

'Stay here.' She jumps out of bed and runs down the hallway.

She returns in a few minutes, pushing the door open. Her hand protects a soft yellow fire on top of a small homemade, chocolate cake. She pulls her hand away when fully inside the room, revealing two candles. 'Happy birthday, Michael.' She climbs into bed and presents the cake to me. 'Make a wish.'

CHAPTER
Twenty-Three

Friday, February 29, 2008
I am thirty-two today.

'Happy birthday, Michael. Make a wish.'

CHAPTER
Twenty-Four

Saturday, February 28, 2009
I am thirty-three today.

'Happy birthday, Michael. Make a wish.'

CHAPTER
Twenty-Five

Sunday, February 28, 2010
I am thirty-four today.

'Happy birthday, Michael. Make a wish.'

CHAPTER
Twenty-Six

Monday, February 28, 2011

I am thirty-five today.

'Happy birthday, Michael. Make a wish.'

CHAPTER
Twenty-Seven

Wednesday, February 29, 2012
I am thirty-six today.

'Happy birthday, Michael. Make a wish.'

CHAPTER
Twenty-Eight

Thursday, February 28, 2013

I am thirty-seven today.

'Happy birthday, Michael. Make a wish.'

CHAPTER

Twenty-Nine

Friday, February 28, 2014
I am thirty-eight today.

'Happy birthday, Michael. Make a wish.'

CHAPTER
Thirty

Saturday, February 28, 2015

I am thirty-nine today.

'Happy birthday, Michael. Make a wish.'

CHAPTER
Thirty-One

Sunday, February 28, 2016

11:22 (PST)

I am forty tomorrow.

Beverly Hills, California.

The gate bell rings, followed by David letting himself into the house. He finds me in the kitchen with the kids. The glass wall is pushed back, and I am gathering the BBQ tools for our impromptu summer afternoon in February.

'Morning,' he says, sitting with Andrew at the table. 'Where's Audrey?'

'Getting dressed. Was a long morning. Woke up screaming again.'

'It's only normal your nightmares are going to get worse the closer we get to your birthday. Your mind's trying to anticipate what's going to happen.'

'Might happen.' I slam the cutlery drawer shut and join David and Andrew at the table.

'Is that why you had her Merc converted into an armoured car? Way to freak the wife out, Mike. You made her think someone was sending you death threats.'

'Who wants maple syrup?' I call to the kids, ignoring him.

Siobhán, Sinéad and Mná bounce to their feet from playing on the floor and scramble into their seats.

'No way,' David tells the kids. 'I'm having some of those cinnamon bun things.' He jumps from his seat to the kitchen counter, closely followed by four screaming children.

'We're having a bar-be-coo for Daddy's birthday,' Andrew says.

David rips off a piece of bun and pops it in his mouth. 'You know your dad's birthday isn't until tomorrow, right?'

Andrew looks at me in confusion.

Audrey enters the kitchen, and I drop the butter knife straight into my coffee cup.

The kids laugh and scream as David tears the kitchen roll and cleans up the table while I continue to stare at my wife.

Audrey crosses the room and ruffles Andrew's hair. 'Yes, but Daddy is the biggest kid in the house and makes us have a two-day birthday.'

'I want lots of birthdays,' Andrew says.

Noticing my pointed look, Audrey asks, 'What?'

'What are you wearing?'

'Clothes.' She elongates the word to make her answer sarcastic.

She's wearing the clothes I've seen her travel to me for ten years of my life. I've never seen them here before. I would have noticed her wearing the black Capri pants around the house, or that short blue cardigan with the white trim hanging in the wardrobe, or her putting the exact outfit together, ballet pumps and all. 'Where did you get them from?' I demand as my heart beats faster and my mouth goes dry.

'I went shopping at Cici's yesterday. Stella picked them out. What's the problem?'

I can't control myself. I walk to the other side of the table and pull David by the back of his shirt. 'Get up,' I yell as I half drag him.

'Michael.' Audrey gasps.

'Stay here,' I tell her.

'Mike, don't be ridiculous,' David says. 'If this is going to happen, we can't stop it.'

I push him from the kitchen out to the hallway. 'You told me you had this fixed. That you had worked it out.'

'I lied.'

My hands clench into fists. 'You lied?' I scream. 'Why did you fuckin lie to me?'

Audrey appears and grabs my arm. 'What the hell is going on?'

I'm still gripping the front of David's shirt.

'I tried, Mike. I really did. For years, but I couldn't figure out how to control it, or even if we should. The consequences might be bigger than we can imagine.'

'Why are you doing this to us?' I ask as tears run down my cheeks.

Audrey moves to my side. 'Michael, what's happened?'

David tears free of my grasp and sits on the bottom step, head bowed.

Audrey ignores him, her undivided attention on me. 'Tell me.' She places her hand on my cheek and wipes the tear that's fallen.

'He thinks you're going to die tomorrow,' David answers.

'What?' she snaps, not quite looking at him. 'Why would you say something like that? It's not funny.' Her demeanour towards him is accusatory and loyal towards me. I can't help but love her a little more.

David stands. 'Audrey, what do you remember about my work on time travel?'

'Don't do this,' I warn.

'She needs to be prepared. She can't be scared. She needs to know what's happening to her.'

'What the hell are you talking about?'

'Ever wondered why Michael asked you out that morning you met him?'

I move fast and I'm lying on the ground with David under me. I punch him and my arm is raised to hit him again. I scream instead. 'Don't you dare! Don't you dare have her doubt me. You know that's not the reason.'

'What's not the reason?' Audrey's voice shakes.

I drop my shoulders in defeat and climb off David, who sits up and leans against the wall. Wiping the blood from his nose, he stays down.

'There is a reason why I came to LA,' I tell her. 'And managed to succeed here.' It sounds so vain now, but when I was twenty and first met Audrey, it was an aspiring notion. 'I had some help—from you.'

'What do you mean, from me?'

'On my twentieth birthday, you visited us from the future and told me what I was to become and how to get there.'

'What the hell are you talking about?'

'David's theories on time travel are all based on our experiences with you.'

'Why the hell are you saying this?'

'Audrey, think about it. If I'd never moved to LA we might have never met. And that's pretty damn important.'

'But it comes at a price,' David tells her.

'Don't listen to him. I'm going to make sure you're okay. I'm going to stop it.'

'What price?' she asks.

'Audrey, listen to me. Stay home tomorrow. Stay in the house and this will never happen and you'll be okay.'

'Michael, this isn't funny. You're freaking me out.'

'David and I will deal with this. Go back to the kids. I have to talk to David.'

She nods, tight-lipped, and returns to the kitchen.

I call as she is leaving, 'And change your clothes.'

She ignores me and closes the door behind her.

The commotion of the kids being ushered outside to play in the back yard travels through the hallway.

'Mike, we need to let her go.' David touches me lightly on the arm. 'The changes could be cataclysmic if something this big is altered.'

I shrug him off. 'There has to be another way. I won't risk losing her.'

'If you don't let her go, you risk everything.'

'I don't care about the money or the job.'

'I mean your life. You're right. If you never moved to LA, do you think you ever would have met her in the first place? Had your children?'

'We might have met eventually. I wanted to be an actor when I was younger, you know. Maybe, this will all still play out without her help?' I walk the few steps to my office and hope David follows.

'It won't. You tried to bail out so many times when things got tough. You would have never made it without her.'

I sit behind my desk, which is cluttered with notes and scenes from a new script I'm working on. 'I don't care about my job. All I need is my family.'

'And you might lose them too.'

He stops near my display cabinet of awards that lines the side wall. The top shelf holds my two Oscars, and I sigh at how naive I once was, working towards that goal as if it was the most prominent thing I could achieve.

I gulp.

'And don't forget, even if you do manage to meet and have your family. There's something about Andrew.'

I nod and the anger and fight in me deflates.

'What do you know, Mike?'

'As soon as he was born, I knew. Remember the year, Audrey told me she had a feeling something worse had happened? At the time, all I could think was, what could possibly happen to you that would be worse than the threat of dying in the middle of a time-travel loop.' I drop my gaze. 'Then we had kids. The girls first, and I knew. The only thing worse than dying would be one of them dying.'

'Mike.' David's voice trembles.

I hold my hand up to let him know I'm not finished. 'I thought, when we had the girls, one after the other, maybe things had changed. And then Andrew was born, and I knew Audrey's timeline was all still progressing like it always did. So I'm going to ask you again. Can you stop this from happening?'

David looks me in the eye. 'We can try. We can make sure she doesn't get in a car. Liam and Caitlyn are due back from their honeymoon today. We can do all the things we planned, but I want you prepared for the fact that sometimes the universe is much stronger than us. And if you try and change too much, it might bite you in the ass.'

My office door is pushed open. Audrey is standing at the threshold.

'How long have you been there?'

'The kids want to swim. I need you to watch them while I get their stuff.' Her voice is flat, but she's pale and looks at me in a way that makes my blood chill. She's heard too much.

'Audrey . . .'

She runs up the stairs. Runs away from me.

I storm out of my office and stride towards the kitchen with David calling after me.

'We don't have all day to think about this,' he shouts.

He veers off to follow Audrey, taking the stairs two at a time. I chase after him.

'David, stop,' I yell. My momentary delay has me at a disadvantage and when I catch up to him, he is already inundating Audrey with information on his theories and the things we tried to help her get home. She strides around the girls' room, gathering towels and bathing suits, ignoring him the best she can.

'David, stop it. You're scaring her.'

'She needs to know what's going to happen,' he hisses.

'Are you having an affair?' Audrey asks.

'No.' My voice catches in my throat. My heart tightens. 'Why would you ask that?'

A tear slides down her face, but her face is filled with rage. 'I couldn't work up the courage to ask before but something big is going on with you two, and you don't want David telling me. You booked a hotel suite for tomorrow. A hotel near our house. For a noon check-in. The booking was sent to your personal email. You're still getting notifications on my phone. You don't use your personal e-mail for work things. We have plans with the kids all day. You're telling me not to leave the house. There's no reason for you to book a hotel in the middle of the day, in the town you live in, unless you're going there to meet another woman.'

How do I tell her it was for a coffee date I've yet to make with her? 'Audrey, it's not what you think.'

'What is it then?'

'I can't tell you right now because you wouldn't understand it fully. But you need to know it's not what you think. I'm not having an affair. I never have, and I never will. I love you too much to ever do that. You're going to have to trust me on this.'

The three of us hear the screams at the same time, silencing our argument. Audrey runs to the window, and I go straight to the stairs.

Audrey howls behind me in the manner only a mother could. 'Andrew's in the pool.'

Hurried footsteps are right behind me.

I dash across the landing and down the spiral staircase. I curse the staircase for being so long, for the kitchen and back door for being so far away, for our argument taking over what was important, here, now.

Through the opening in the glass wall that separates the kitchen and patio, I get outside quicker. I see the three girls at the pool edge, crying and pointing at the pile of clothes floating in the centre. It's not only clothing, it's my son.

David and I reach the pool at the same time, and I jump in. I reach Andrew in seconds and turn him face up. I swim to the edge and pass Andrew to David. I haul myself out and bend over him, checking for a pulse. My world collapses when I can't find it. 'Andrew,' I scream at him, then sob. 'Please no. Just please, wake up.'

Audrey strokes Andrew's wet hair, the girls clinging to her side.

I lay Andrew on his back and tilt his head. I place my fingers over his chest and pump his chest, stopping to breathe air into his lungs through his nose.

'Call an ambulance,' I shout.

David's already on his phone, giving our address.

The paramedics revive him on site, and I sink on the ground, sobbing. Seeing your child breathe is the only thing that matters in the world. It's hard to think straight when he's strapped to a gurney and wheeled through the house, Audrey running at his side. There are things that need to be taken care of before we rush off into the ambulance, but I can't get the words out.

'The girls,' I tell David. 'Stay with them. Put on a movie or something. The one with the bear—they like that one. They need to have lunch. Call Stella to babysit if you need to leave. Or Max if he's free. Make sure the girls stay inside and give them ice cream if they want and—'

I've forgotten something, but I'll call from the hospital once everything is okay. 'Call Caitlyn and Liam.'

'Just go,' David says.

My son sleeps on a hospital bed under heated blankets. Audrey and I sit in silence, staring at him and the machines that help him breathe. Hypoxemia lung damage, hypothermia, lack of oxygen to the brain, abnormal heart rhythms, acidosis, and substantial decrease in circulating blood are all words and phrases that have been spoken to us. Spoken around us. I don't understand what it means, or whether he even has them all or if the doctors are worried they might develop.

All I can do is hope and pray and wish that my son will be okay. Every hour or so, the vitals monitor bleeps, and Audrey gets up to silence it like the nurse showed us. This is not a price I'm willing to pay. The universe can have all its fuckin money back.

Audrey's tears fall continuously, occasionally turning into sobs and then into slight hysteria. I rise from my chair and take her in my arms, squeezing her tight. I'm stuck in my own mental agony and can't offer her any words of comfort. Sometimes she calms quickly. Sometimes I cry with her, but we always return to our seats and wait.

David has called, as have our parents, friends, and work colleagues. I send most calls to voicemail, with the exception of David and Stella, who are still looking after the girls.

Night comes, and the darkness and rain that fall outside the window bring feelings of despair.

CHAPTER
Thirty-Two

Monday, February 28, 2016
00:30 (PST)
Los Angeles, California.
I am forty today.

Andrew's vitals are re-checked early in the morning and we're told we need to wait for him to wake up before they can be sure of any recovery.

Audrey climbs onto the bed and touches his cheek. 'Please wake up, baby. Come back to us.'

My phone vibrates in my pocket, and I let it go to voicemail. 'I'm going to get coffee and call everyone back. You want anything?'

Audrey shakes her head.

I take the stairs instead of the lift. The muscles in my legs come back to life. After ordering two coffees and muffins in the hospital coffee shop, I scroll through the missed calls and text messages.

Falling into a chair, I let myself relax as I return the calls to my parents, then Audrey's dad. It takes me twenty minutes to talk to everyone and promise to keep them updated. I call Caitlyn and Liam, but both their phones go to voicemail. It's still early. My phone buzzes. It's David returning my missed call.

'Hi,' I say.

'Mike, I'm so sorry. I want you to know that.' His voice is shaky.

'I know. I shouldn't have gone off on you earlier. It's just. . .' I sigh and pinch the bridge of my nose.

'No, Mike. I mean I'm sorry for today. It's done. Stella and I have told Audrey everything she needs to know.'

Who knew anger could rise so quickly. I check my watch. It's seven forty-five. 'Why?'

'There has to be a reason for all of this, Mike. We need to play our part.'

I swipe the phone to hang up, and run through the lobby and up the stairs to Andrew's room.

Stella and David are sitting on either side of our son's bed.

'Audrey's gone,' Stella says. 'She took my car.'

I slam my fist into the doorframe. 'You drive a fuckin Mini.' I turn to David. 'If you wanted to give her a chance of surviving this, you could have given her your bloody Jeep.'

'We can't change anything. Remember when I told you not to set anything up with the charity? I was trying to see if I could change the timeline. I already knew you were her husband and thought if I could delay the charity setup until after you met Audrey, we would have a chance at changing other things in the timeline. You wanted to change it too. But because you didn't have all the information, you ended up doing the exact same thing you always did. Liam's been trying to change things ever since he got here, and he can't do it. Even the fake info you gave Audrey about not moving to New York, or that fake first movie you shot in college, it was always misinformation. We *can't* change anything.' He sighs. 'You are one of the important people, Mike. You can't change your life or the effects on everyone else will be too great.'

'Audrey wanted to try and save him. If she goes back, she can warn you about this,' Stella answers. 'She had to do whatever it takes to protect her son.'

'Stay with Andrew,' I tell Stella.

'Mike, wait.' David follows me out. 'I tried to help her. I wrote Andrew's name on the inside of her arm, so she'll know to be more specific. That when she feels like there's something wrong, she'll have his name right there. I didn't have time to put more information, but with this extra insight, we'll work harder to figure it out.'

I pull my phone out and scroll for Audrey while dashing to the stairs. I can catch her. I can stop her.

She answers on the first ring. The sound of the road hums in the background.

'Get out of the car, Audrey. We don't even know if this is safe.' I take the stairs two at a time. 'You don't even remember to warn us what happens to him,' I scream in the phone.

Audrey sobs and hangs up.

'It's not just about Andrew,' David says behind me. 'It's your whole relationship and family she is trying to facilitate. Every scientific advance I've made on this was because of Audrey.' He gasps for breath at the bottom of the stairs. 'We never would have pursued half our theories if it wasn't for her. Don't even get me started on the catastrophic changes it could make to the world if she doesn't travel back in time.

361

Think about it, Mike. What would have happened if we never came to LA?' He spins me round at the main door. 'Think about all the people you've helped; Stella and Max and the people at FEED US. That's not something to dismiss lightly. Some of those people were starving to death or worse. We used to worry about the ripple effect of having Audrey in our lives once a year, and the things she was influencing. Well, now I'm worried about the ripple effects of not having her.'

'It fades,' I tell him. 'By the time Audrey sees the writing on her arm, it's faded, and she has no idea what it means. I saw it one year but thought it was her husband's name, so I didn't push it.' I grab him by the collar. 'You fucked this up. You didn't change anything. You're talking about possibly killing my wife.' I should have known someone like Audrey wouldn't be mine forever. 'We have to go after her. If we're too late, we need to be there for her. Where's your car?'

'It's out front.' He pulls his keys from his pocket and runs with me across the parking lot.

In the Jeep, I call Audrey again, but it goes to voicemail.

'What do we know about the accident?' I ask him and call Audrey again. 'Can she survive it?'

'We don't know much.' David weaves into traffic. 'Liam's been the one working on the theoretical side of car crashes and what could be facilitated with them in relation to time travel theories. There's no precise location but I think it must be on the freeway, for a vehicle to have worked up enough speed to cause the force of impact Liam thinks is needed.' He looks at me out of the corner of his eye.

I flinch. 'You sent her to the freeway?'

He nods, and his eyes fill with tears. 'I understand the ramifications of what might happen, Mike. Don't think I'm the bad guy here.'

Saliva catches in the bottom of my throat as I think of a truck slamming into the side of my wife's car and eventually her head.

'The car acts as a base for her return to. Liam's back and he's following her. He'll help her as soon as she's back. He'll call for an ambulance, a few minutes before the accident is due to happen. We have the time worked out.' He glances at his watch.

I dial Audrey's number again. I keep dialling when it continues to go to voicemail. On the seventh attempt, she picks up.

'Audrey, don't do this. Pull over.' I look at my watch. 'It's almost time.' I clear my throat.

When she doesn't answer I know I have to let her go. 'You have to be clearer, about Andrew. We never knew what happened to try and stop him from nearly drowning. Make sure you tell us.'

'Okay,' she whispers.

'And, Audrey?'

'Yes?'

'Don't tell me you're my wife. I'm too young to know,' I whisper. 'I want to fall in love with you all by myself.'

'Put me on speaker phone,' David says.

I do it and turn the handset towards David. 'I think there is a reason you didn't remember that Andrew was in danger.'

'What?' Audrey asks.

'You may be suffering from PTSD when you get through. When you were with us in the past, you only gave us snippets of information. You were scared, and you mentioned water to me once, but we always thought it was due to the crash. You are about to experience the third recent trauma in your life, and your brain might not be able to cope.'

'What three things?' I ask.

'Andrew's accident, a serious head injury, and being sent through time multiple times. It's enough to mush up anyone's memory. You can do it, Audrey. Now that you know to concentrate, you can remember.'

I look at David, and he sets his jaw straight. He has no idea if that's true.

'Michael?' she whispers through the phone.

'You're going to be okay, Audrey. I'll be there. I'll look after you.'

'Wait,' she says. 'I need to find a pen. I'll write this down so I remember.'

'You don't have to do this, there's still time. If you pull over we can stop this,' I tell her.

There's a screeching sound of tyres and metal grinding on the road and echoing through the phone. The same piercing noise I've become familiar with over the years. It's coming in all directions, through the speakerphone and from outside. David brakes and presses hard on the Jeep horn, and I realise we are the ones who got Audrey in trouble.

Time slows as we crash full speed into the driver's side of Audrey's car.

I brace for impact seconds before the car ricochets off the Mini then barrels into the crash barrier. The seatbelt jams over my legs, pulling me down and forcing my chest back into the seat.

The Jeep comes to a standstill, and I unbuckle my belt. I pull on the door handle, but it's jammed. I swivel and kick the door. After a few blows, it gives way. 'This isn't a price I'm willing to pay, David,' I shout over my shoulder, ready to run out.

CHAPTER
Thirty-Three

Monday, 28, February, 2016
15:12 (GMT)
Blackpool, England.
I am forty today.

'You have got to be kidding me,' Caitlyn shrieks next to me.

'I'm serious.' David picks up his beer, laughing. 'Jessica agreed to go out with Mike one time.'

I look at Jessica, seated opposite me, and roll my eyes.

Jessica pulls the beer bottle away from David's mouth. 'Only because you dated everyone on campus and wouldn't give me the time of day.' She glances at me guiltily. 'Oh god, Mike. I didn't mean it like that.'

I wave away her apology.

'In my defence, we were young. We were like twenty,' Jessica continues.

'Twenty-one,' I tell them. 'It was my birthday.'

'That's right.' Jessica laughs. 'Well'—she leans across the table, speaking to Caitlyn—'I showed up at his party, and

David practically pounced on me in the kitchen. I ended up talking to him all night. I never even saw Mike.'

'I ended up getting dumped by my current psycho girlfriend and had beer thrown all over me.' David chuckles. 'How do you like running your own store?' he asks. 'Working two full-time jobs must be tough.'

I shrug. 'It's not as bad as it sounds. I can't exactly stop helping at the B&B. Things are bad enough, and the store pays enough to make up any shortages at the end of the month.'

Caitlyn rolls her eyes. 'Mum and Dad really need to sell up. It's not fair to have us all work in a doomed business.'

'Don't be so spoiled, Caitlyn,' I tell her. 'They're going through a bad patch, is all.'

'Their whole life together is a bad patch.'

David waves over at the door. 'Liam, over here.'

All eyes turn to David's friend, who has just moved here from America.

'Who's the hottie?' Caitlyn asks, giggling.

Liam approaches, and David introduces us all.

'Hope you don't mind me crashing your birthday, man.' He shakes my hand. 'Dave is the only person I know here, and he was kind enough to invite me along.'

'Not at all.'

Caitlyn nudges me out of the way as she leans over and shakes Liam's hand. 'Nice to meet you. David tells us you're from LA?'

'Yes,' Jessica answers. 'We met Liam a few days after we moved there right after graduation.'

'Oh, you worked at the hospital with Jessica?' Caitlyn asks him.

'No, I was working in the lab with David.' He skirts his eyes at David.

'Speaking of LA,' Caitlyn says to Jessica, 'did you see that article on E! News about the director's daughter and grandson who were murdered by the ex-husband?'

'I saw that,' I tell them. 'Simon Lewis. He was a director in the '80s. We got some of his old movies in the store a while back. *Blue Sky* was one of them.'

'What happened?' Jessica asks.

'A domestic that got out of hand. She was only a few years older than us. Her name was Stella, you know, like *How Stella Got Her Groove Back*. I loved that movie,' Caitlyn says.

David interrupts us. 'Where's the damn cake?'

'You didn't bring a cake?'

'Of course we did,' Caitlyn says. 'I picked up a homemade one from Mum and Dad's today.'

'Okay, I'm going to the bathroom,' I tell them.

When I return from the bathroom, David and Liam are talking animatedly across the table. 'Everything okay?' I slide back into my seat.

'Fine,' David says. 'Just difference of opinion.'

'More like differences of what the reasonable, sane person might think is acceptable,' Liam says. 'Mr. Hotshot TV Scientist thinks he has all the kinks in some mad philosophical time travel theory all worked out.'

'All I said was, if you had the chance to go back in time and change one thing about your past, would you do it? Would you change it? And more importantly'—he turns to me—'would you let someone change *your* life?'

'What about the ripple effect in people's lives? Who gets to decide what is *meant to be*?' Liam taps on the table to underscore his point. 'The experiences and mistakes you have in life shape who you are. You have no idea what might change by making sure your spouse made better choices in life,' Liam argues.

The waitress appears with my birthday cake and sets it on the table.

'What things in life would you change?' David asks me.

'There's nothing wrong with my life. It's fine the way it is.'

'You're completely and utterly happy?' he asks.

'I'm not unhappy,' I tell him, staring at the candles.

The end.

Epilogue

'Make your wish, Mike,' David says, looking me in the eye.

'Fine, if I could have anything right now, I'd wish for an amazing career. That earned millions, and none of us would have to worry about money.' I wink at Caitlyn.

Time slows. There's ringing in my ears that turns into a harsh piercing screech as I blow out the candles.

Monday, February 28, 2016

08:03 (PST)

Loa Angeles, California.

I am forty today.

By the time I get to Audrey, the ringing in my ears has stopped, and there's a small crowd of motorists around the crushed car. They are shouting at each other and trying to get her out.

'Call nine-one-one,' someone shouts.

I push them out of the way and have to jump on the hood of the Jeep to get to her door. The window is smashed from the impact and I lean through it, touching her face. Ambulance sirens drone in the distance. 'Audrey,' I scream.

Her eyes are closed, and it looks like she might be sleeping, only her hair is covered in shards of glass and blood flows down the side of her head.

I pull off my T-shirt and apply pressure to the wound.

Fire trucks show up with the police and ambulance crew.

I'm forced out of the way while someone places a neck brace on her. Someone hands my shirt back. It's covered in blood. The paramedics hold Audrey's head straight and the fire crew prepare to cut the door off the car.

The sound of the saw starting makes me jump and a cop puts his hand on my shoulder to steady me.

I place my hands on the back of my head and pace, saying a silent prayer. Please, let my family be safe.

The saw stops abruptly and I hear Audrey screaming.

I bolt for the side of the car as the cop grabs me round the waist.

'Wait,' he tells me. 'We can't move the other car, and the doors are jammed. They're trying to get her out.'

The paramedics try to keep a now conscious Audrey still while they cut her out.

'Let me go,' I tell the police officer. 'I can keep her calm.'

He looks at another officer behind him and nods. They lead me over, and I crawl in the back window and over the backseats. I bend over the driver's seat and take her hand.

'I'm here, Audrey. You just have to stay still while they get you out.'

Tears fall down her face.

'You need to stay calm when they turn the saw back on, okay?'

'Michael?'

'Yes?'

'I've missed you so much,' she sobs.

I squeeze her hand tight. 'I know, baby, I remember.' I nod at the fire crew, and they power up the equipment.

In the ambulance ride to the hospital, I stroke Audrey's hair as she slips in and out of consciousness. 'I knew you'd come back,' I whisper in her ear. 'The universe doesn't create that one perfect person for you and then never let you meet.'

The automatic doors to the ER hiss as Audrey is wheeled through and taken down the hallway. I hold her hand and we're ushered into a semi-private room.

Stella, Pamela and Liam are waiting for us.

Doctors and nurses surround Audrey, and she moans as they manoeuvre her to the bed and check her over. Someone attends to her head wound, while another shouts orders to the team that are attending to her. I'm pushed out of the way and find myself standing next to Stella and the others at the edge of the curtain.

'How did you know where we would be?' I ask. 'Who's with Andrew?'

Stella gawks at me. 'Max is with him. But there's a problem,' she says.

I spin to face her. 'Is he okay?'

She pulls the curtain to the neighbouring bed open. 'The problem is David.'

David is lying in the bed, unconscious, covered in cuts from the crash and hooked up to machines.

'He got here ten minutes ago. They can't wake him up.'

A NOTE FROM
The Author

Did you know the best way you can support an author is to leave a review? If you enjoyed this novel, please take a few minutes to click on the AMAZON link to leave your rating. I appreciate the support!

Enjoy this story? Want FREE deleted scenes from the novel? Want Giveaways? Advanced Reader Copies? Exclusive sneak peeks of future chapters?

Visit the the link (http://dl.bookfunnel.com/uo2624h93p) to sign up to my mailing list (I promise not to spam you) and keep up to date on future releases and claim your first FREEBIE!

I use a service called BookFunnel to deliver my books. It may take a few steps depending on your reading device. If you have trouble, just tap the Help Me link at the top of the book download page.

The amount of social media platforms out there kind of scare me, but you can find me on Facebook where I know how to work it (ha, kind of!)

https://www.facebook.com/bronamillsauthor